STRAIGHT RIVER

CHRIS NORBURY

BookLocker

Published by BookLocker.com, Inc., St. Petersburg, Florida.

Printed on acid-free paper.

BookLocker.com, Inc.
2019

First Edition

Library of Congress Cataloging in Publication Data
Norbury, Chris
Straight River by Chris Norbury
FICTION / Thrillers / Suspense | FICTION / Thrillers / Domestic |
FICTION / Mystery & Detective / Amateur Sleuth
Library of Congress Control Number: 2018914866

DEDICATION

To Sandra, who makes this all possible.

ACKNOWLEDGMENTS

First, a huge thank you to Lynette Labelle of Labelle's Writing on the Wall Editorial Services and D.J. Schuette of Critical Eye Editorial and Publishing Services for their combined tough-love editing insights. If not for their work, this book would not have seen print. It goes without saying that I'm responsible for any faults that remain in the manuscript. Carl Graves of Extended Imagery created the excellent book cover.

My double-duty beta readers—Polly Rodriguez, Val Rudy, and Betsy Wade—read both the old *Straight River* and the new and improved *Straight River*. Their positive comments on the updated version confirmed that I had indeed made the story much better than where it was two years ago. I affectionately refer to them as my "Colorado Springs Beta Queens."

Thanks also to first-wave beta readers Jody Brown, Chris Dibble, Deb Early, Sonja Sigler Harris, Tim Jones, Paula Matsumoto, and Daniel Williams. Additionally, John Kriesel provided useful information on the farming situation and terminology in southern Minnesota.

Finally, I've met dozens of writing experts and authors either in person or online. Each has added to my knowledge and skill in bits and pieces over the years and helped me become a better writer and storyteller. Thank you all for your contributions.

CHAPTER 1

For the third time in the past two weeks, a loud noise jolted Ray Lanier awake from a sound sleep. The metallic, creaking squeal followed by a percussive thump cut through the dead silence around his farm. Jack, his old black Labrador, growled softly at the foot of the bed.

"Now what?" Ray said, groggy and annoyed.

He slid from the bed, groped for his eyeglasses on the nightstand, and shuffled to the window to peer through the lace curtain. Starlit blackness was surrendering to the hints of blue in the east. He pulled his .38 caliber Smith & Wesson revolver from the nightstand drawer, crept downstairs, and moved to the backdoor window. Seconds later, an engine turned over in the distance, but Ray saw no headlights or tail lights. The sound of tires on gravel faded as the vehicle drove away.

"Damnation." Ray said, then flipped on the kitchen light and dialed 911 for the third time in the past two weeks. He'd initially reported that someone had thrown a rock through a barn window. The second call was to report a fire that torched an old shed. Now this rude awakening. After one ring, the dispatcher answered and made her standard inquiry.

"This is Ray Lanier again, out west of town," he said. "No emergency. Just heard a strange noise, then a vehicle driving away. I'm startin' to think it's not punk kid vandals who are responsible."

The dispatcher promised to send a patrol car. *Like that'll stop all this mischief,* he thought. Still, he'd gotten each incident on the record in case something worse happened later.

Because it was close to his regular wakeup time, Ray started a pot of coffee and walked upstairs to dress while he waited for the police.

Returning downstairs, he strode to the back door with his gun poised at waist height. He flipped on the porch light and stared out the west window toward the barn, feed pen, and distant cropland, still fallow in March. Outside the north-facing kitchen window were the dark outlines of the grain silo, two-car garage, and charred remains of the old storage shed. Nothing looked amiss.

For weeks, he'd harbored a mounting worry that all the strange recent events were related to his repeated refusals to sell his farm. Even though it had officially ended a few years ago, the damned Great Recession had left a legacy of still-depressed crop *and* land prices that brought all sorts of land speculators and other vultures into farm country.

One of those vultures was Wayne Hibbert, a local real estate agent who had signed on with some faceless corporation and brokered the purchases of a few farms in the area in the past several months. Ray had resisted, but Hibbert was also trying to scare Ray's friends and neighbors to sell their farms. High-pressure, unsubtle sales tactics too. The lummox seemed too dense to understand that "no" meant "*No!*"

Ray was suspicious of Hibbert because he never referred to his new associates by name, claiming the principals of the company had sworn him to secrecy regarding their identities. But what had troubled Ray most over the past month was the unnerving sensation of being watched. Another reason to be wary of a bumbler like Hibbert. *Maybe he's resorting to vandalism as a tactic to worry me into selling.*

Within ten minutes, a black-and-white pulled into the driveway. Ray met the officer at the door and explained the situation. The officer circled the entire house and adjacent structures with a flashlight but found nothing unusual, broken, or on fire. Not surprising, since it was too dark to see much. Also, Ray couldn't describe the sound in detail because he'd been asleep when it started. He thanked the officer and returned inside to make another call.

"I don't care if the boy works crazy night hours and travels all the time," he muttered as he dialed. "Gonna keep callin' until he calls back."

After the recorded greeting and the beep, he said, "Matt, it's your father. I know this is the fourth time I've called this week. I promise it ain't about you takin' over the farm. Somethin's goin' on around here. Makin' me nervous. Smells like grade A pig manure."

He gritted his teeth and sighed to relieve the tension born of asking his son for a favor after so many years of estrangement. "Please call me as soon as you can."

With nothing to do but wait until sunrise so he could check things in daylight, Ray fixed breakfast: bacon, eggs over easy, and the coffee he'd made earlier. After cleaning up the kitchen, he entered the dining room, hit the light switch, and scanned the mess of papers and file folders spread across the dark walnut table. Based on Hibbert's nervous behavior around him, along with the vandalism of his farm, Ray suspected these piles of research into this real estate business might lead to something much bigger than a few farms in pissant little Straight County, Minnesota. He sorted and filed the papers into the three-drawer metal filing cabinet.

With the sun now well above the horizon, Ray returned his revolver to the bedroom nightstand, donned his Carhartt jacket and gloves, and stepped outside onto the back porch. Jack remained curled up in his bed next to the wood stove, preferring real heat over the weak rays of an early morning March sun.

Inhaling the cold, clean air bolstered Ray's mood. This might be the day that the first aromas of thawing earth reached the area. Temperatures were forecast to hit the forties. Decent for a March day in southern Minnesota. That whiff of dark, rich loam always sparked excitement for the new growing season. He'd once again do his small part to feed the livestock of the nation with his corn and soybeans and, by extension, feed the people of the world.

Gazing around his property, Ray spotted the source of the morning's odd sound. The top hatch of the grain silo was open. Why had the vandal targeted that? He wanted to believe the open hatch was a product of one of his more frequent senior moments. But he would've remembered that activity due to the fear factor of climbing so high. Nevertheless, he needed to investigate immediately for two reasons: to close the hatch and keep the stored corn dry, and to make sure whoever opened the hatch hadn't fallen in or tampered with the crop.

Ray spat onto the remnants of snow in the yard and crossed the barnyard. Unfortunately, spring's promise of rebirth couldn't extend to his old body. His failing eyesight, hearing, joints, and overall vigor were long past rejuvenation. Anxiety radiated from his chest, growing with each step. At the base of the silo, he stared up the ladder to the top. His heart pounded faster. Sweat chilled his gloved hands. His mouth dried up. Here, the distance seemed twice as high as it had from the house.

Just go up fast, check inside for any sign of vandalism, close the hatch, and come down. Five minutes and you'll be done. Heaving a deep sigh of resignation, he grabbed a rung and began to climb.

~

Matt Lanier had never been so grateful to return home after a tour. The music had been triumphant, but the traveling had been a nightmare. His trio earned rave reviews and enthusiastic ovations at every venue on the nine-day, eight-performance circuit of some of the best jazz clubs outside of New York or Los Angeles.

Starting with the Dakota Jazz Club in Minneapolis, the group's whirlwind route took them to Kansas City, St. Louis, Columbus, Cleveland, Chicago, and Detroit. In Chicago, a record producer had been so impressed with the group's tightness and musicality that he met them backstage after the show and said he might be interested in signing them. No guarantees, the producer warned, but his people would contact their people next week. That possible deal and the group's inspired playing had made the hellacious trip worth every white-knuckle mile of driving.

The problem had been the unpredictable and often treacherous weather in the Midwest in March—snow, ice, rain, thunder, lightning. They even saw a tornado between Kansas City and St. Louis. The slower-than-expected travel each day cut into precious downtime and two planned rehearsals midtrip. The lowlight was the drive home from Detroit.

Thanks to freezing rain across southern Michigan and Indiana combined with horrendous traffic through Chicagoland, the expected twelve-hour drive back to Minneapolis stretched to sixteen hours. Fortunately, the weather cleared soon after they left Chicago, and the last leg went smoothly. But the accumulated stress of nightly performances, long drives, living out of a suitcase, and less sleep than usual had Matt feeling like a zombie as he dragged himself the final distance from the elevator to the door of his downtown condominium.

Once inside, Matt checked his answering machine—four messages from his father. "Aww, damnation. Not Dad. Not now."

He exhaled upward through his extended lower lip as his insides sagged. *I don't talk to the guy for years, and now he pesters me daily with phone calls.* The overwhelming urge to go back out on a music tour, any tour, hit him.

Even though his father was usually asleep at eleven o'clock at night, Matt considered calling back immediately. Except his old man hadn't said the problem was life or death. Something that "smells like grade A pig manure" registered about midway up Ray Lanier's paranoia scale. Whatever his father wanted to discuss could wait until morning. Matt reluctantly set his alarm clock for seven a.m. because sleeping until noon would be selfish considering the repeated requests for help. He'd tell a white lie when he called and say he'd just walked in the door from a tour. Hell, after eight days, what was another eight hours?

CHAPTER 2

The next morning, Matt called his father immediately after waking. The old man didn't answer then or after a second call twenty minutes later. Annoyed, Matt showered and dressed, then went out for breakfast at his favorite breakfast joint. He returned home an hour later and was shrugging off his coat when the phone rang.

"Hello?" he said after picking up, expecting to hear his father's voice.

"Mr. Lanier, this is Sergeant Gebhardt of the Straight County Police Department."

A spark of recognition flickered in Matt's brain. "Are you the *Clay* Gebhardt who grew up in Straight River?"

"Yes, I am. Sorry about the formality. I wasn't sure you'd remember me."

Matt hadn't connected the name to his brother's childhood best friend until Gebhardt's diction, speech patterns, and rhythms recalled old memories. And his voice was a lot deeper, a *basso profundo* now, Matt thought.

"How could I forget?" he said. "What can I do for you, Clay?"

"I have some news about your father. Are you able to drive down to the Straight River Hospital now?"

A tight knot of dread clogged Matt's throat. "What happened?"

"I'm sorry, but I'm not at liberty to say."

"Come on, Clay, we go back to grade school. I think I know what the news is. I'd rather have you tell me now."

After a pause, Gebhardt said, "Okay. He fell into his grain silo yesterday and died from suffocation."

Matt recoiled as if he'd been gut-punched and stared uncomprehendingly at the wall. He'd sensed the worst, but the cause

6

of death caught him off guard. As did the fact Ray had called him for the first time in years yesterday, and with an urgent message no less.

"I'm sorry for your loss," Gebhardt said. "A neighbor became concerned when he couldn't get ahold of Ray yesterday afternoon. He checked all over the farm and finally found him early this morning. The coroner needs you to identify his body."

Vague numbness flowed downward from Matt's brain. If he'd arrived home a day sooner and called back right away, events might have changed enough to have kept the old man from climbing a silo. *No. Dad's a stubborn old cuss. He'd have gone up there no matter what I said.*

Gebhardt broke the long silence. "You okay, Matt?"

"Oh, uh, yeah. Sorry. I'll come right down."

~

Matt drove south to Straight River in a daze. He had long expected his dad would die from natural causes, so a farm accident shocked him. Silo deaths weren't uncommon among farmers, nor were deaths caused by overturned tractors or machinery dismemberments. But something didn't make sense. His father had always been a stickler for safety. He would've either harnessed up and had someone spot him or enlisted a younger neighbor like Dave Swanson to do the chore.

At the hospital, Matt identified the body, filled out the necessary forms, and wandered out of the small basement morgue up to the hospital lobby.

Gebhardt was waiting for him and stood when he approached. He reached into his pocket and removed a business card and a piece of paper. "Here's my card and the contact names and numbers for your dad's church and the funeral home. Call me anytime if I can help in any way."

Matt muttered a toneless, "I will."

He took the information and stared at it, seeing nothing but a vision of his father half buried in a pile of yellow corn. Numbness lingered under his skin. He struggled to maintain his composure.

"I still can't believe Dad climbed up there without someone to spot him."

"The safety harness was untouched," Gebhardt said. "It's possible he slipped before he was able to hook up. Hard to say. Might've been senility or vertigo. Pretty common in old folks."

Ray was seventy years old, but Matt had assumed the old guy would live well past ninety. He'd rarely gotten more than a head cold, quit smoking when Matt was a kid, and didn't drink much. Farm work had kept his body lean. He'd always been the picture of health, at least up until the last time they'd seen each other. Maybe his mind *had* faltered.

"If there's nothing else you need," Gebhardt said, "I'll get back to work." He patted Matt's shoulder. "My condolences again."

"Thanks, Clay. I appreciate that *you* called me. Means a lot."

After Gebhardt left, a sudden weariness overcame Matt. He ran his hand through his hair, then headed for his car and back to Minneapolis. He was in less of a daze now, but his mind whirled with thoughts of how to handle the funeral, the estate, and adjust his teaching and performing schedule to allow enough time to manage the responsibilities. Getting organized couldn't happen until he was sitting in his recliner listening to Keith Jarrett's *The Koln Concert*—on vinyl—and making a to-do list.

At home, Matt closed the door and leaned against it for a moment before walking to the sliding glass door to his deck. Swirling snow partially obscured the Minneapolis skyline. In the distance, the Mississippi River resembled a faint brownish-gray stripe of emptiness.

He turned on his sound system and cued up Jarrett's album, then went to the liquor cabinet, poured two fingers of Jim Beam Black—his dad's favorite—and silently toasted his memory. At that moment, the full impact, the finality, of his father's passing hit him like he'd been blocked by a football tackle clearing a path for his running back. He slumped into a chair, dog-tired. Jarrett's music resonated with him, helped to focus his thoughts, relaxed him with its effortless, meditative flow. He let the sublime piano music wash over him for a few minutes before readying a notepad and pen.

Reality number one took precedence—funeral arrangements. Mild panic flared Matt's nerves. He was the sole surviving family member.

His mother, Arlene, had died of cancer when he was twelve. When his brother, Mark, a corporal in the Marines, was killed overseas fifteen years earlier, his father, also a veteran, had handled the arrangements. Was there a will or final instructions that stated his father's last wishes? First thing Monday he'd call his father's long-time attorney, John "Max" Maxwell, and ask for some initial guidance if not major assistance in how to proceed.

Reality number two—deal with the farm. Planting season was imminent. Ray more than likely carried some debt, so Matt didn't think he could afford to let the acreage lie fallow for a year. He jotted a note to check his dad's business ledger. He expected to sell the farm eventually, but that might take years. More headaches. A throbbing knot of anxiety had already formed behind his forehead.

Working the farm himself was out of the question. Matt had less interest in farming than he did when he was a kid. Most importantly, he had his own full-time music career to maintain—rehearsals and performances with the Minnesota Orchestra, giving private lessons to ten double bass students at the University of Minnesota, and sporadic club dates around town for the next several weeks. And now, a possible recording contract might consume any remaining free time.

Reality number three—settle Dad's other financial affairs. Was there a business succession plan? A mortgage? Corn or soybean futures contracts that were in place to hedge against the farm's expected production? He jotted down another note to remember to check with his father's financial advisors if any existed. More time, more cost, more phone tag. Dealing with lawyers, accountants, government officials, red tape, searching for records. Those thoughts soured his stomach. He contemplated the bottle of Beam he'd placed on the kitchen counter. *What the hell. A man's father only dies once.* Matt poured another shot, walked to the living room window, and sipped the booze as the sun struggled to pierce the March gloom.

CHAPTER 3

Wayne Hibbert pulled a plastic flask from his coat pocket and took a swig of the contents. With closed eyes, he savored the familiar, rough burn of vodka in his throat. Shivering, he flipped the heater switch to *high* in his idling, eleven-year-old Lincoln Town Car.

"Global warming, my ass. Anyone who believes that crock oughta come to Minnesota in March." The dashboard clock read *9:45.* "Come on, old man, finish your damn beer. Time to go home."

After wiping the condensation from his window, Wayne focused again on the entrance to the Straight River Eagles Club, one of the fraternal organizations in town. None of the few patrons going into or coming out of the club seemed to notice him. A quick swirl of the flask indicated it was almost empty. He gulped the rest in one swallow, shuddered, and tossed the flask onto the back seat. *That'll steady my hands.*

The club door opened, spilling light and noise into the dreary night. A little old man limped into the parking lot, bent forward against the wind-driven snow flurries. Wayne got out of his car and hunched his own shoulders against the icy chill. As the man approached, Wayne tensed. "Well, well, fancy meeting you here, Helmer."

Helmer Myrick glanced up without breaking stride and said in his thick Swedish accent, "What da hell do you want? I told ya this afternoon I ain't interested."

Wayne stepped into Myrick's path. "Not so fast. We made a deal."

Myrick stopped and peered down his bulbous, hooked nose at Wayne. "I didn't sign nothin.' I thought you was gonna make a serious offer. My lawyer said it was da same deal as last time, only with different words."

Despite the cold, blustery wind, Wayne's forehead was damp with sweat. That annoying pain in his temples was back. The door to the club opened again. Wayne struck a pose of nonchalance until the old man who came out crossed the lot, got in his car, and drove away. Then he threw up his hands and spoke in an angry stage whisper. "Damn it, Helmer, why'd you back out?"

"I want enough money for my wife to live on when I'm gone. With this deal, once I pay off my bank loan, there's hardly anything left."

"But you're forgetting the—"

Myrick burst into an unintelligible rant in Swedish, then switched back to English. "You God damn vultures. All you want is to rob us farmers blind, take our land, pave it over, make yer precious money, and da rest of da world be damned."

Shaking with frustration, Wayne took a step forward and rose to his full height. "Do you know what my boss is gonna say when he finds out you screwed him over?"

"I don't care what yer boss says." Myrick snorted and thrust a gloved finger at Wayne. "Dat's your business."

Wayne's boss had issued an ultimatum a few days ago: "Produce another sale by next week or you're history." The only sales he'd closed in the past six months were one here in Straight County and two in an adjacent county. Myrick, a second-generation immigrant, was his last hope. Should've been a slam dunk. Eighth-grade education, poor health, married, no living children. The lone possible successor was a nephew who showed little interest in taking over his uncle's farm. A textbook motivated seller.

Wayne leaned forward and poked his finger into Myrick's chest. "You're damn right it's my business. Big business. Big players. Big money." He resisted the urge to grab the old man's throat and squeeze until he agreed to the deal. "We don't give a shit about penny ante dirt farmers like you."

Myrick sniffed the air, wrinkled his nose, and leaned back. "Yer drunk. Git da hell outta my way."

He started to leave, but Wayne grabbed his arm and spun him around. "I'm not through with you, asshole. We. Had. A deal."

The old man wrenched free, ashen-faced. "If'n ya don't leave me alone, I'm callin' da police." His voice trembled as he tried to retreat to the Eagles Club.

"Call anyone you want after I kick your ass." Wayne caught Myrick by the collar, intent on connecting his fist with the man's nose. He swung but lost his balance and grazed Myrick's temple. The old farmer tried to back away but stumbled and fell. Wayne hauled him to his feet and delivered a solid blow to his midsection.

Myrick doubled over in pain and squeaked out, "Help."

The gusty wind swallowed his cry.

Wayne shoved him to the iced-over asphalt and gritted his teeth, trying to contain his anger. "You have any idea how much you're costing me? Commission's one thing, but I'll get canned if I don't make my quota. You were that quota."

"Please," Myrick said, groaning. "Leave me alone." He attempted to stand but only made it onto one knee before he clutched his chest and stared upward with a contorted expression on his face. Gasping for air, he collapsed onto the ground.

"Jesus, Helmer, you okay?" *Is he faking? I barely touched him.* Small wisps of breath escaped from Myrick's lips. Wayne gaped at the stricken man, then knelt beside him.

Myrick groaned louder, tried to raise himself up, then made a frantic, choking sound before collapsing again with a soft thud.

"Helmer!" Wayne shook Myrick's shoulder, then took off a glove and felt Myrick's neck. His trembling hand couldn't find a pulse.

Wayne shook his head and tried to clear his mind. That last slug of vodka must've put him over the edge because fog now shrouded his brain. His breath came in rapid-fire huffs. *Is he dying? I've never seen anyone die.* Wayne stood and gripped the side of a car while he waited for the earth to stop spinning. His heartbeat thundered in his ears.

From behind, a deep, raspy voice said, "What's the problem?"

Wayne gasped and froze, startled that the stranger had gotten so close without him noticing. His first urge was to flee. Then again, running might cause the stranger to call the cops on him. Or maybe this guy *was* a cop. Risking a slow turn to face the man, he mentally scrambled for a way to explain the situation. *Think, damn it.*

A huge silhouette loomed between Wayne and the streetlight. Squinting to get a glimpse of his face, Wayne could only discern the man's shiny bald head. He wore dark trousers and a dark jacket that appeared to be leather. *At least he's not a* uniformed *cop.*

"Ah, my friend here, he's drunk," Wayne said, trying to sound matter-of-fact. "Had a little too much and passed out."

The bald man jerked his thumb to the side. "Outta my way."

Wayne stepped aside as the stranger crouched next to Myrick and pulled out a small flashlight. He shone the beam on Myrick's body for a few seconds, felt for a pulse, then stood and reached into his pocket.

Damn! This yutz is an undercover cop, and I'm busted. The sinking sensation that gripped Wayne's core was intensified by an image of the man cuffing him and throwing him into the back of an unmarked police car.

The man pulled out a cell phone, tapped the screen a few times, and put the phone to his ear. "Sorry to bother you this late, sir, but we have a situation. Hibbert confronted Myrick."

The man glared at Wayne as if he'd tracked dog shit all over his new carpet, then backed away out of earshot.

Wayne's body spasmed as he fought the urge to flee, but he didn't dare run because the man's intimidating stare had paralyzed him. Despite the thirty-degree temperature and gusty wind, sweat ran down Wayne's back, chest, and face. He glanced at Myrick, the club door, Myrick, the bald man.

A blown sale had spiraled out of control into a major fuck up. *Even though it wasn't my fault.* Lost commission. Lost job. Lost hope for the future of his business. The business his father had built for thirty years. The business Wayne had driven to the brink of bankruptcy in less than ten years. He turned away and took a quick hit from a flask of peppermint schnapps he'd stashed in his coat pocket.

The stranger returned and pocketed his phone. "He got a car here?"

Wayne peered at the man in the dim streetlight and shivered. The yellow tint of the light gave the man's white skin a waxy appearance, like that of a beige candle. Sloped forehead. Cold, cruel eyes. Screw-the-world expression cemented to his lips and chin.

"I don't know," Wayne said. "I—"

"Think fast before someone else walks by. Let's assume he does. Find his keys."

Wayne searched Myrick's pockets until he found a set of keys. He held them up to the man. "Who are you? Why are you here?"

The man thrust himself into Wayne's personal space. "I'm Witt. Think of me as your supervisor."

Wayne recoiled from Witt's hot, sour breath and swallowed the few drops of saliva left in his mouth.

"Sure, sure. Supervisor." He pawed at the sweat trickling down his face.

"Just in case you're stupider than you look," Witt said, "give me your cell phone."

Wayne did so, and Witt shoved it into his coat pocket. "If you want to live to see tomorrow, do exactly as I say."

CHAPTER 4

The shrill ring of the phone broke the early morning calm of the Straight County Law Enforcement Center, or LEC, in downtown Straight River. Clay Gebhardt was walking past the dispatch room with his first coffee of the day and stopped in the doorway to eavesdrop.

Courtney Johnson, the operator on duty, frowned at the interruption and put down her knitting. She punched a button on the console and intoned in her well-trained voice, "Nine one one. What's your emergency?"

Seconds later, she sat up, fully alert, and gave Clay a glance indicating this was serious. Maintaining a professional demeanor, she softened her tone. "Are you certain your husband is dead, ma'am?"

Clay tensed as a small rush of adrenaline told him to prepare for action. His expectation of a typically dull Saturday morning vanished, replaced by thoughts of personnel, procedures, and protocol for handling a reported death.

After hearing the response, Johnson winced. Sorrow showed on her face. "I'll send an officer, ma'am. Will you verify your name and address for me, please?"

While Johnson contacted a squad on duty, Clay checked the name she had jotted down. *Betty Myrick.* He didn't need the address. The Myricks owned the farm adjacent to the Lanier farm. His mind flashed back to his youth as his insides swelled with sorrow. Betty had often provided treats for Clay, his best friend Mark Lanier, and sometimes Matt Lanier and Dave Swanson when they stopped by the Myrick farm for a refreshing drink of water from their well after long hikes or bike rides through the countryside.

Ten minutes later the dispatch radio crackled. "We've got us a body, Courtney." The voice belonged to Officer Scott Sandvik, Clay's newest mentee. "Send reinforcements."

Clay collected his coat and cap and shuffled to his car. By the time he arrived at the Myrick farm, two squad cars and an ambulance were on scene. He entered the barn and stood in the doorway to let his eyes adjust from the bright sun of the morning to the dim barn light. The smell of hay and manure stung his nose. He'd never grown accustomed to farm odors despite having lived in Straight River his entire life.

A group of officers and Emergency Medical Technicians stood ready to remove the body as soon as the coroner arrived and gave the go ahead.

Clay stepped forward to view the bluish-white face of the corpse. He'd seen several dead bodies in his career but never got used to the sight. The rope around Helmer Myrick's neck was a generic, braided natural fiber. The shadow of a stain marked his crotch and upper thigh. *Poor old guy pissed himself.* Clay swallowed hard and silently prayed he'd be in bed when the Lord came for him, not in public with police and emergency personnel gawking at his body.

He looked at Meg Lysne, the nearest EMT. "Any other visible trauma?"

"Nope. All signs point to hanging." Lysne pointed at a stepladder lying on its side. "That's how he got up high enough to jump."

At the sound of an approaching vehicle, Clay stepped outside. Dr. Anne Vincent, the Straight County Coroner, stepped out of her familiar red Audi sedan. She wore a black down jacket covering gray sweatpants. A lace nightgown collar showed at her neck. Ankle-high hiking boots completed her outfit. Vincent had been quite pretty when Clay first met her years ago. Still attractive, her facial lines signified the wear and tear from decades of stressful work as a physician, and flecks of gray lightened her brown hair.

"Hope I didn't keep you kids waiting too long." Her tone exuded the clinical efficiency she employed at death scenes. "Just finished a twelve-hour night shift at the hospital and was getting ready for bed."

Although Clay had seen her compassionate bedside manner around live patients firsthand, as a coroner she was casual when possible but still all business if the situation required propriety.

"This'll be quick, Vince." He gestured to the barn door. "An obvious suicide."

Vincent narrowed her eyes and cocked her head. "You finally got that mail order medical degree, eh, Sarge?"

Clay grinned. "You're pulling down your shingle at the end of the year. Someone's got to take your place when you retire."

If any superior officers had been present, Clay would've been all business too. But the Vincents and the Gebhardts attended the same church and had known each other for years. Anne and Clay's wife, Margaret, were friends. Vincent's husband, Martin, sang bass with Clay in the church choir.

Vincent walked over to Myrick's body and studied the rope around his neck. "Hmm."

"Weird he pulled his collar up," Clay said. "You ever see that?"

"Not often." Vincent sounded concerned. "But people who commit suicide don't all follow the same step-by-step instructions." She nodded at the paramedics. "Take him down, please."

Clay shivered and turned away when the EMTs began the task, not wanting to see the corpse manhandled. Once the small commotion of untying the body from the rafter was completed, Clay turned around. The EMTs placed Myrick into a black unzipped body bag.

After the officer with the camera had taken the necessary closeup pictures of Myrick, Vincent untied the rope around Myrick's neck, unzipped his coat, and inspected his throat. Then she lifted one of Myrick's eyelids.

"That's odd."

"Something wrong?" Clay asked.

"I'm not sure. There's no evidence of bruising."

Clay was about to step in for a closer look when Sandvik entered.

"Sarge," he said from the doorway, "I tried talking to Mrs. Myrick, but she's pretty shell-shocked."

Clay glanced from Sandvik's defeated expression to Vincent's puzzled countenance.

She glanced up. "I'm good here."

"Okay." Clay clapped his hand on his protégé's shoulder. "Come on. Let's talk to the widow together."

They walked to the farmhouse. Clay was glad the young officer was getting a lesson in both crime scene investigation and interviewing a grieving woman shortly after her husband's unnatural death. Nearing the end of his probationary period, Sandvik would soon be taking the lead in more investigations.

Clay tapped on the front door as he let himself in. Sandvik followed.

Betty Myrick sat staring at a framed picture on the living room wall of a young couple in wedding attire. The diminutive woman—petite and white-haired but farm-tough—appeared lost and forlorn on the large sofa. Her eyes had a faraway, nostalgic look.

Clay cleared his throat.

Momentarily startled, Betty caught a small breath. When she focused on the two uniformed men in her house, she returned to the present.

"Mrs. Myrick, I'm Sergeant Gebhardt. You've met Officer Sandvik. May we sit down?"

"Yes, of course." She gestured for them to sit, then raised her hand to pat her hair as if she was ensuring it was presentable.

Clay sat on the edge of the La-Z-Boy recliner near her. Sandvik sat at the opposite end of the sofa.

"Gebhardt." Her voice sounded high and soft but a little shaky. "I remember that name. You used to come over with the Lanier boys, way back when you weren't much taller than the watering trough."

"Yes, ma'am, I did." He was pleasantly surprised she remembered him after more than twenty years. "You made the tastiest oatmeal raisin cookies in the county."

She gave him a weary, distant smile. "Thank you, dear. I loved to have all you kids come around after . . ."

The Myrick's two children had died young. The boy, Loren, who'd been Clay's age, perished in a tractor accident at age eight. They'd lost baby Agatha to crib death at nine months.

18

Clay motioned for Sandvik to take notes. "Mrs. Myrick, what time did you discover your husband's body?"

"Around seven. I got up and knocked on his door but noticed he wasn't in bed. He snores, so we have separate bedrooms. I assumed he must have gotten up early to do some chores. He wasn't in the house, and his car was in the driveway instead of its usual place in the garage. I thought he was in the barn, so I called to him, but he didn't answer. I walked out there to make sure he was all right. And . . ."

"That's when you found him," Clay said, then patted her hand.

Her eyes glistened as she nodded without looking up.

"When did you last see him alive?"

She sniffled and dabbed her nose with a lace-edged hanky. "He always goes to the Eagles Club on Friday night for a bump and a beer. He left about eight. I usually wait for him to come home before going to bed, but he was late, so I turned in around ten fifteen."

"I see." Clay glanced at Sandvik to confirm he was taking notes, then refocused on Betty. "Did your husband have any health issues?"

"Helmer's had two heart attacks in the last five years. He hates vegetables and insists on dessert most every night." She made a tiny surrender gesture with her hands and sighed. "I'm sorry. I meant to say that last sentence in the past tense."

"No need to apologize." Clay gave her a wan smile and shifted on the recliner as he fiddled with his notebook. Interviewing next of kin was one of his least-favorite duties. "I'm sorry if these questions are difficult, but I have to ask. Had you noticed any unusual behavior from your husband lately? Stress? Money problems? Marital issues? Depression?"

Betty took a deep breath, which seemed to stabilize her posture and expression. "Helmer's not senile, not depressed, not mentally ill. He's a good husband and a good farmer. He wants to farm for a few more years, but he's heard from some of the other farmers it might be better to sell now. He's been talking to real estate people. Other than that, he's been his usual grumpy old self."

"Can you give me the names of the real estate people he'd spoken to?" Clay asked, sadly noting that Betty had slipped back into referring to her deceased husband in the present tense.

"There was only one lately. Hubbard—no—Hibbert, I believe. I just can't keep that man's name in my head. He came over yesterday afternoon."

Clay recognized the name. Hibbert Realty had been around for decades. Wayne Hibbert had taken over the family business when his father retired. "What did they discuss?"

"Helmer didn't say. He was mad that I'd let Hibbert into the house, but it was so cold yesterday. I couldn't make him wait outside, could I?" She looked at Sandvik for confirmation.

Sandvik gave her a tight smile. "No, ma'am."

"They went into the parlor," she said. "I was ironing in the laundry room downstairs, so I couldn't hear much. They did raise their voices at one point. Then Hibbert left, and Helmer was grumpy the rest of the day. He wouldn't talk about it though."

Clay shook his head. Typical Scandinavian stoicism. No one talks to anyone or shares their feelings. Instead, they suffer in silence and mystery. An old man hangs himself, and his wife doesn't have a clue as to why.

"Thanks, Mrs. Myrick. Those are all the questions I have for now. I'll look around outside for a while, then we'll leave." He stood and gestured for Sandvik to follow him out.

"Sergeant," Betty dabbed at her eyes with her hanky, "Helmer didn't kill himself. We're God-fearing people. Suicide's a sin, and Helmer's not a sinner."

Reluctant to point out the obvious, he hedged. "Yes, ma'am."

Once outside, Clay and Sandvik walked toward Myrick's Chevy. The ambulance crew had left with the body. Officers Noble and Hansen spoke in hushed tones near the barn, comparing notes. At that moment, a white sedan turned into the Myrick's driveway and parked.

A tall, lean man emerged wearing street clothes and sporting closely cropped hair—Chief of Police Michael Flannery. His eyes radiated their usual coldness, and his square jaw and stiff demeanor reinforced that impression. He intercepted Anne Vincent on the way to her car. They exchanged words but were too far away for Clay to hear. Vincent spoke animatedly for a moment. Flannery responded.

Vincent's expression hardened with anger. She hung her head, spoke again, and trudged to her car.

Flannery glanced over his shoulder at Clay. "Heard about this on my home police scanner," he said. "Came over to make sure things are under control. Carry on."

Before Clay could respond, Flannery got back into his car and drove off.

Up until now, Clay had gotten along passably well with his new boss but hadn't yet adjusted to his leadership style and administrative skills. One thing he'd learned from the mistakes of a few of the patrol officers was Flannery's lack of tolerance for questioning his orders or actions. Asking Flannery why he'd shown up at the scene might earn Clay a place on his shit list for the next three months.

However, unless a case was high-profile, police chiefs rarely appeared at a crime or accident scene. Even Clay's presence as the investigative sergeant on duty hadn't been required. He'd only come because he recognized the Myrick name and was also worried about Sandvik handling his first death scene alone. *Don't rock the boat* had served him well during his career. No sense changing his philosophy after so many years.

Clay turned back to Sandvik. "Notice anything unusual in what Betty Myrick said or how she said it?"

Sandvik contemplated the question. "No. She seemed calm but still sad. Not sure if that's her way or if she's hiding something. Plus, the religion thing, suicide's a sin. People sin all the time, including suicide."

"Not bad, but not what I was hinting at. She mentioned he parked his car in the driveway, not in its usual place, the garage. Old folks become set in their ways. A weekly ritual to the Eagles Club. A bump and a beer every time. Home by ten, rarely late. This week he was late and didn't park his car in the garage. My guess is, he had more than one bump or beer and was drunk when he came home. Maybe too drunk to drive the car into the garage without hitting something."

Sandvik nodded. "Nice catch, Sarge."

Clay shrugged. "The big question is, what might've upset him so much that he got drunk and hung himself? Something to do with selling the farm? Hard to say. Last time I said more than hello to him, I was a kid."

When they reached the car, Clay opened the driver's door with a latex-gloved hand and peered inside. "Anyone examined this yet?"

"Not entirely," Sandvik said. "We inspected the outside and looked through the windows. Didn't want to compromise any possible evidence until you got here."

Clay leaned in and examined the interior. Nothing in the back seat. A slip of paper and some coins in the center console. He pulled a small magnifying glass from his pocket and inspected the driver's seat from top to bottom. A few gray hairs showed up, and the few fibers he found were all the color of Myrick's coat. He inhaled deeply, then gestured for Sandvik to stick his head inside the car's cabin.

"What do you smell?"

Sandvik leaned into the interior and exaggerated a sniff. "Peppermint. Real faint. Alcohol too. Schnapps maybe?"

"Yep." Clay stood and Sandvik followed suit.

"Who gets drunk on schnapps and kills himself?" Sandvik said. "My farewell booze will be single malt Scotch."

Refocusing on the car, Clay studied the relationship between the driver's seat and front passenger seat. Something didn't look right. He pulled out his flashlight and searched under the driver's seat but found only a few candy wrappers and a small, dusty box of tissues. A check of the backseat driver-side floor revealed nothing unusual or noteworthy.

"What was that all about?" Sandvik asked.

"For some reason, Helmer pushed the seat back when he got home last night."

Sandvik furrowed his brow. "How do you know?"

"Both Myricks are relatively short. Helmer was about five feet five or six. Yet the driver's seat is in the maximum-legroom position. There's no way Helmer could've reached the pedals."

"Maybe he dropped something on the floor and pushed the seat back to retrieve it."

"Probably. I found nothing significant under the driver's seat."

Clay checked the right-side back seat, trunk, and windows, then circled the car looking for fresh dents or scrapes. He signaled Noble and Hansen to come over and report. They'd also come up empty regarding suspicious evidence. The logical conclusion? Myrick had indeed committed suicide.

"Need us to do anything else, Sarge?" Sandvik asked.

"No. File your reports and get back out on the street."

Clay drove back to the LEC, drumming his fingers on the steering wheel, working his jaw back and forth. Unnatural death calls were rare in Straight County, especially suicides. On the surface, Myrick's cause of death seemed obvious, yet something was amiss. He wanted to put the case out of his mind, but Betty's adamance that her husband had not committed suicide wouldn't let him.

CHAPTER 5

Matt parked his Toyota Sienna in the open space between the farmhouse and the outbuildings that comprised the Lanier farmstead. His father's funeral had been a week earlier. Since then, he'd been able to get caught up with his students' double bass lessons and his own Minnesota Orchestra rehearsals. Unfortunately, his restored energy from teaching and performing waned when he exited the interstate at Straight River. It was time to refocus on the tedious, unpleasant chore of settling his father's affairs. Staying at the farm would save him multiple hours of driving to and from Minneapolis.

He took a dozen leaden steps across the gravel driveway to the farmhouse, then stopped and scanned his boyhood home. Everything looked the same but different. The ambient noise from the interstate bordering the farm to the east was louder than he remembered. More semis for sure. SUVs also, both in town and on the country roads. He'd noticed one parked on the shoulder before he'd turned off into the long driveway to the farm. Pickup trucks hadn't waned in popularity either. They'd only gotten bigger and louder.

The house and other structures showed their age. Matt and Mark had painted most of the barns and sheds as kids and helped Dad paint the farmhouse. The barn-red outbuildings were tinged with gray from decades of weathering. The white farmhouse with navy shutters was scarred by peeling paint. The same but different.

A black Labrador Retriever appeared from inside the main barn and ambled over to greet him.

"Hiya, Jack. Miss me?"

Jack replied with a tail wag and a sniff of Matt's hand.

Matt set down his luggage to pet the old dog. Despite having only met Jack once before, some ten years earlier when he was a puppy, the two had bonded quickly after getting reacquainted. Whenever Matt was present, Jack stayed close to his new master.

According to the neighbors, Jack never strayed from the property, rarely barked, and was as gentle as any dog they'd met. Independent for a Labrador, he seemed content to roam the acreage and entertain himself. The Myricks had agreed to feed and water Jack until Matt could resume that responsibility, but he didn't want to impose too much, so taking care of the dog was the other reason Matt had decided to live at the farm temporarily.

~

By midafternoon, man and dog were in the storage barn, a structure dating from Grandpa Lanier's day. After Ray built a new, larger barn, the original barn had been repurposed as a garage for the old farm vehicles and other equipment. Chilled to the bone by the damp March air, Matt cut lengths of one-by-ten boards with a table saw to replace a section of rotted siding on the barn. The body heat generated by his exertions barely offset the frigid wind whistling through the gaps between the weathered gray boards.

The creak of the door startled him. He turned to see a large silhouette step inside. A denim-clad figure strode forward into the light cast by the bulb hanging from a rafter. The omnipresent Jack stood and ambled over to nuzzle the visitor's hand.

The man put his hands on his hips. "Matt Lanier doing manual labor? Now I've seen it all."

Matt grinned broadly. "Swanny! I wondered if you'd ever show your face, you old fart."

"Look who's calling who an old fart, you fossilized piece o' manure," Dave Swanson said as he knelt and ruffled Jack's fur.

A bear of a man—with the strength, agility, and body hair to match—Swanson had been Matt's best friend growing up. Along with physical maturation—thicker body, full beard—Swanson had, by all accounts, matured from a party animal in his high school days to a respected farmer and landowner who had difficulty accepting any native son leaving for "the big city life." They hadn't stayed in touch primarily because of that difference of opinion. The emotional wedge was still between them as they shook hands and embraced in an awkward man hug.

"Sorry we missed Ray's funeral," Swanson said. "Amy and I took our first vacation in five years. Florida. Nonrefundable tickets." Over the years, his voice had gotten tighter, but in the spectrum of musical instruments, it was still a baritone horn.

"I understand," Matt said. "Thanks for the flowers. They got a lot of compliments."

Swanson waved him off. "The least we could do."

"Which reminds me," Matt said. "Thanks for keeping an eye on Dad all these years. Gebhardt told me you were checking up on him when you found him in the silo."

"Yeah, I get kind of protective with my neighbors. Farmers need to stick together, watch each other's backs. That so-called Great Recession is only a few years in the past. Lotsa farmers still in a fuckin' Great *Depression* as far as I'm concerned. Housing prices being down is one thing. Throw in crop prices that are falling faster than shit in a deep outhouse, rising property taxes on our land, and a lot of us are on the brink of disaster." Swanson spat a stream of tobacco juice at the floor, then scuffed the dirt and straw with the toe of his boot to cover the puddle.

Matt stifled the urge to chastise him for such a disgusting habit. Rural and urban had different standards of acceptable behavior. Better out here than in the house.

"We got some more depressing news yesterday," Swanson said. "I wanted to tell you in person if you ain't already heard."

"What news?"

"Helmer's dead."

"Oh my God. What happened?"

"Cops said he hung himself in his barn. Happened Friday night."

Matt gaped at Swanson, speechless. He shook his head in disbelief. Everything he knew about his old neighbor, or thought he knew, clashed with the idea of Helmer Myrick killing himself.

"I can't believe it."

"Betty found his body yesterday morning."

Matt groaned. "Oh no. What a lousy way to wake up. How's she doing?"

Swanson shrugged. "Ain't been over to see her yet. Bunch of relatives and friends getting together at Betty's tonight. Me 'n' Amy'll go over later, bring some lasagna or seven-layer bars, pay our respects."

"I wish I could've been here for her yesterday. But I played a two-night gig in Minneapolis over the weekend. Stayed at my condo and drove back here a few hours ago."

"Well, sure, you're always busy. Your music keeps you in the city most of the time. Hard to stay current on hometown news." Swanson's tone exuded condescension.

"Yeah." Matt stared at the straw long enough to manufacture a sigh and initiate a topic change. He looked up. "How're things with you?"

Swanson scratched his beard. "Real busy this winter. We bought more land and are gonna try dairy farming in addition to the crops. I hired a guy to work the cows, but he's new to dairy. Keeps me hopping. Lotsa little fires to put out."

"Wow. You'll be a land baron soon at the rate you're going. How long until you own the entire county?"

Swanson grinned. "Lemme think." He glanced at his watch. "Sometime around the year 2199." He turned serious again. "I wasn't planning to expand again so soon after I added the Laughlin acreage five years ago, but old man Schultz was selling a parcel to raise some cash. It's in a prime location not far from the freeway. If the developers had found out it was available, they'd have swooped in like a flock of turkey vultures."

"Good for you, I guess," Matt said, although he believed that any farmer who bought more land and piled on more debt was half nuts no matter the reason. Nevertheless, his friend's ostensible prosperity impressed Matt because Swanny hadn't been much of a go-getter in school.

Swanson hooked his thumbs into his front pockets. "Schultz offered it to several of us farmers. His price was fair, so I took the plunge. I'd rather keep it a farm for now. We've lost so much cropland around here lately; I got tired of watching them developers pave over the county. How you doing with the farm?"

"Hectic to say the least." Matt frowned and kicked a piece of scrap wood across the floor. "Dad didn't keep up with maintenance as much as I thought he would. Cosmetically, things are okay, except for this siding." He gestured at the stack of lumber he'd been cutting. "Internally, things are falling apart. I doubt I'll be able to sell fast enough for someone to take over this season. I've got almost no time to find someone to rent the land. On top of that, I've forgotten most of what I learned about farming."

"Yeah, Ray was slowing down the past year or two. I did some emergency repairs for him during harvest a couple times."

"If he was slowing down so much, what the hell was he doing up in the silo *alone*?"

"Don't know. He never should've been up there in the first place. If he'd called me, I would've helped him out."

The subtle putdown stung Matt. Heat crept into his cheeks. Swanson had shown him up again, the caring surrogate son. "I appreciate that, Swanny. You're a good neighbor."

"I try."

"You ever consider buying this place?"

Swanson eyed him apprehensively but shook his head. "If I'd known Ray was gonna die, I would've saved my cash. But I'm tapped out after the Schultz deal."

Resigned to the fact that dealing with Dad's estate would probably take months, Matt frowned and nodded. "I suppose I can at least spread the word I'm selling."

"Gotta be careful though." Swanson tilted his head and raised his eyebrows. "Some buyers want to turn all this land into Asphalt Acres. They prey on the older farmers, especially the ones whose kids have moved away. They know some are in trouble. Try to get them to panic sell. Only one agent around who seems legit."

"Who's that?"

"Wayne Hibbert." Swanson punctuated his words with another gob of tobacco juice fired into the straw.

"Vern Hibbert's kid?"

Swanson nodded.

"Didn't know he went into the family business." Matt absently kicked a small clump of straw toward the tobacco spit.

"Hibbert's been telling his prospects if they sell to his buyers, they'll keep their farms intact. Said they'll let the sellers stay in the farmhouse and pay rent on the acreage. Even so, some of the old farts have been listening to the fear mongers in the past few months. That's the main reason I bought Schultz's parcel. I wanted to show 'em not everyone wants to bail."

"That's good, I guess."

"Ray said he's made several lowball offers for this place since last fall. Of course, I couldn't imagine *Ray* ever selling." A sly grin formed on Swanson's face. The implication was *Matt* would sell the farm the first chance he could.

Matt ignored the gibe. "My biggest problem right now is finding a renter. Any ideas?"

"Try the Farm Advocates program at the Ag department up in St. Paul if you're into red tape and have six months to kill."

"Thanks, but I'm not interested in going through the bureaucracy. Call me cynical, but I don't trust the government." He contemplated the pile of boards waiting to be sawn and nailed and abruptly wearied of playing farmhouse carpenter. "Come on, let's get some coffee."

Swanson pantomimed wiping sweat from his brow. "Thought you'd never ask."

Jack trotted ahead of the men, leading them toward the house. The old dog seemed eager to get inside and settle down on his bed next to the wood stove.

When the coffee was ready, Matt poured two cups, joined Swanson at the kitchen table, and handed him a cup. "Any other ways to find a renter?"

"Right now, I guess word-o'-mouth, talking to the locals same as if you were trying to sell. Someone might know a young couple or a nephew or a friend of a friend who'd like to get into the biz." He pulled a cell phone from his shirt pocket. "Got your phone handy? I can give you a few numbers to call."

"You might not believe this." Matt reached for a notepad and pen. "But I'm both old school and a technophobe." He waggled the writing tools. "No cell phone."

Swanson regarded him with an expression combining shock and bemusement, then he laughed. "Why am I not surprised?"

"Tried one years ago," Matt said. "Hated it. I've never liked talking on the phone. Having one with me all day increased the odds I'd get overly dependent on the darn thing like so many people seem to be these days. My old answering machine filters the calls down to the ones I need to function for business."

"Suit yourself. But they come in handy for a farmer. A lot of us bought these newfangled smartphones that are like tiny lil' computers. I got one a while back. Kept my old one just in case. Hell, even agriculture is getting computerized. GPS guidance for planting and all that other high-tech shit. I'm learning, but it comes slow for me."

"Getting back to farming, where do the old-timers hang out in the off-season these days?"

"Most of the fellas around here go to Hy-Vee."

"Mornings?"

"Around nine. Gotta get home for lunch, or the wives'll slap 'em silly."

Both men grinned at the knowledge that as tough as the old farmers were, their wives were the ones in control.

"Nice to know some things never change," Matt said. "I'll drop in tomorrow."

CHAPTER 6

The next morning, Matt hurried across the Hy-Vee supermarket parking lot, pelted by a freezing rain blown sideways by gusty northeast winds. There was little chance any reasonable farmer would be outside today getting the jump on spring planting. He hoped the lousy weather would boost attendance at the farmers' coffee klatch—a Straight River custom for decades.

The warm, yeasty aromas of the bakery mingled with those of Chinese cuisine and pizza featured at the nearby takeout counters. Matt stopped at the coffee bar and ordered a cup of dark roast as he brushed the rain off his anorak. His non-planting theory was confirmed when he walked into the dining area. Six men, none of whom appeared younger than seventy, sat around two pushed-together tables, sipping coffee, and chatting. A few nibbled at pastries. Each head sported a billed cap bearing a logo from one of the agricultural businesses in the region. Most wore blue jeans, heavy work jackets, and boots.

As Matt approached the group, six wizened, weather-beaten faces turned toward him. One pair of eyes belonging to a short, stout man at the end of the table showed vague recognition.

"Sweet Jesus, Mary, and Joseph," the man said in a raspy voice. "You ain't Matt Lanier, are you?"

Matt strained to place the voice and face. "Uh, yeah, I'm Matt."

"Well, I'll be damned," exclaimed the man. "Don't know if you remember me. George Schultz. Just west of your place."

"Of course I do, George," Matt said, relieved to know one of the farmers in the group.

"Good to see you again." Schultz extended his right arm.

"Same here," Matt said and shook Schultz's gnarled hand. "It's been a lotta years."

"Yeah, time sure flies. You know the others? Probably not. I'll introduce you."

The surnames sounded familiar. All were at least acquaintances of his father's if not close friends. A few had expressed their condolences to him at Ray's funeral, but he'd been in such a fog, their faces didn't fully register. Other than that, he hadn't spoken with any of them since he was a teenager.

"Heard you were back in town," Schultz said. "Shame about Ray. He was a damn good farmer. You gonna run the place now?"

With that question, the atmosphere changed as if a light had been turned off. The wizened stares became judgmental glares. Matt's skin prickled from the sudden dampness generated by a rush of warm blood to his face. Expecting that to be their opening question, he'd worked on his response the night before. These men wouldn't help him if they didn't trust his motives. Any answer he gave other than, "Yes," might erect an invisible wall between him and the farmers. Still, lying always made him uncomfortable. He coughed to clear his throat.

"Hard to say. I know Dad wanted to keep the farm in the family. However, I haven't lived here for a long time. I'm not up on the business side of farming, and the technology you gentlemen use today is way over my head. I might do more harm than good."

The assembled faces remained stony and cold. Getting help from any of them might be impossible. Despite the frosty reception, Matt took a nearby chair and sat next to Schultz, the man he thought he'd have the best chance of connecting with.

"Dave Swanson mentioned he bought a piece of land from you, George."

"He did." Schultz sounded like a judge announcing a solemn verdict.

"I hope you took him for an outrageous price," Matt said with a mischievous tone, hoping to lighten the mood.

Tony Czarnowski took the bait. "Heh-heh. You got that right. Schultzy's a Kraut to the bone. You'd think he was a Jew for Christ's sake. Got a fair price and then some is what I heard."

"Look who's talking, you big, dumb Pollack." Schultz jerked a thumb in Czarnowski's direction and winked at Matt. "He sells his kid a couple acres, then goes out and buys himself a goldurn Cadillac."

Matt chuckled and heaved an inner sigh of relief. The ice hadn't broken, but he'd engineered a small crack.

When the laughter died down, Matt spoke. "I do want to keep the farm producing, no matter what. Do you fellas know anyone who wants to rent six hundred acres for the season? Planting starts soon, and I'm desperate. Not sure I can handle it."

"Can't help you," Czarnowski said before anyone else could respond. "We'll all be too busy in a few weeks to worry about other folks' farms."

The atmosphere returned to frosty. Matt forced his expression to remain neutral. These damned stubborn-yet-proud farmers wanted to rake him over the coals because he'd chosen what they considered a cowardly path—run for the city and get as far away from farm life as possible.

"I seen you at the hardware store the other day," said Harold Thorson, the oldest-looking member of the bunch. He glanced Matt's way but didn't make eye contact. "Buyin' paint, were ya?"

Matt didn't remember seeing Thorson, but he'd been concentrating on his shopping list. "Putting on some new barn siding," he said. "Gotta paint it as soon as the weather allows."

"Oh," Thorson said as he examined his cupcake.

Schultz frowned and gave a small shake of his head. "Harold's gettin' a little senile," he said softly. "He sorta floats in and out of the conversation."

Matt nodded. "Getting back to my farm, I hear real estate agents have been buzzing around trying to make a deal with my dad, Helmer Myrick, and some others."

The way the men shifted in their seats suggested he had touched on a sensitive subject.

"There's a few shysters pokin' around," Czarnowski said.

"Swanny told me some farmers in the area are considering the offers," Matt said. "He mentioned an agent named Hibbert who'd talked to my old man for the past few months."

"Ray was suspicious of Hibbert from the get-go," Schultz said. "Of course, Ray suspected everyone."

Matt nodded, reminded that his father had serious trust issues, especially concerning people with wealth or power. To Ray, trust fought a zero-sum game against money and power. If one side gained, the other side lost an equal amount.

"Him and his conspiracies," Schultz continued. "Last fall, he mentioned somethin' about this area bein' prime real estate because of NAFTA. That's when I thought he'd gone off the deep end. There ain't nothin' special about Straight County. Just good farmland is all."

Matt squinted quizzically at Schultz. "NAFTA as in the North American Free Trade Agreement?"

"Yessirree," Schultz said. "Ray had all sorts of documents about them and some other organizations."

Was this the topic Dad had wanted to talk to me about when he'd called? Matt made a mental note to check for these documents at the farm.

"I sure ain't sellin' to no one, conspiracy or not," Warren Longley said in slow, terse tones. "Especially a damn real estate speculator. Hibbert tried to lowball me, for Christ's sake. Thinks he can take advantage of us 'cause we're old. I ain't stupid. He can turn around and sell to a homebuilder tomorrow for ten times that amount." He folded his arms across his chest and nodded decisively. "Besides, why would I want to sell? I got a boy who'll take over from me when I can't get up on a tractor no more."

"Are we talking about the same Hibbert?" Matt said. "Swanny told me he's legit."

Either he'd missed something, or this discrepancy was some kind of generational distrust. After all, Hibbert had taken over from his father, who had started the family business more than forty years ago.

"We don't like any of them real estate sharks," Longley said. "But Hibbert's the one who's been hangin' around the most, scavenging for carcasses."

The others murmured their assent except for Ken Trask, who waited until the other voices had subsided.

"I guess I'm one of those carcasses Hibbert preyed on. Might as well spill my guts now. I was . . ." He glanced at the others, shame in his expression, hesitancy in his voice. ". . . forced to sell."

All eyes widened as heads turned toward Trask.

"When was this, Kenny?" Czarnowski asked.

"About six months ago." Trask stared at his coffee cup. "I got a little too deep into debt a few years back. The flood last year wiped out my soybeans while you guys up on higher ground harvested a bumper crop. Didn't plant much corn. What I got wasn't near enough to pay my loans."

Several of the men shifted in their seats and avoided Trask's gaze.

"Sorry to hear that, Ken," Schultz said. "I didn't know you was havin' trouble."

Trask's shoulders drooped, and he kept his eyes focused on a spot on the table in front of him. "The bank got real strict because of the housing crisis. Told me they couldn't bend their terms any. It was either sell or get kicked off my land. Hibbert's buyer gave me a decent deal. I get to stay as long as I want to keep farming. Just gotta pay him enough rent to cover taxes and a little extra."

"Ain't it kind of strange he's lettin' you stay on the farm?" Longley asked. "Who's Hibbert's client?"

"Said the buyer was Saxony Partners somethin'-or-other," Trask said. "He was authorized to sign all the papers. Probably some local who don't want me to know he's making money off my misery."

Matt said, "What's so strange about Hibbert's buyer allowing Ken—"

"I saw Helmer over to the Eagles Club Friday night talking to Hibbert," Thorson blurted. "We was both walkin' out, I was behind him a ways. Hibbert starts lip-jacking Myrick in the parking lot." He resumed the study of his half-eaten cupcake. A tiny smear of chocolate frosting highlighted his upper lip.

The others seemed annoyed at Thorson's outbursts, but Matt's jaw dropped. "That was the night Helmer died. Did you tell the police?"

Thorson's expression turned foggy and confused. "Why tell the police I went to the Eagles? Ain't none of their damn business."

"Because Hibbert might've noticed something unusual about Helmer's behavior that could explain why he hung himself," Matt said. "When I talked to Betty last night, she refused to believe Helmer committed suicide. She was so stunned she forgot to insist the police look for another cause of death."

"Oh," Thorson said.

Matt persisted. "Did you talk to Helmer?"

Thorson waved his hand dismissively. "Nah, we don't get along. He sits at the bar by himself. Never talks to no one, not even the bartender. He comes in, plops down, and they give him his usual shot and a beer."

Matt turned to the others. "You mean to say the police haven't interviewed everyone who was at the Eagles on Friday?"

"Police never called me." Thorson said. He looked at his sticky fingers, then reached for a napkin.

"Unfortunately, that's common around here," Schultz said. "When it comes to detective work, the police have lots of style but not much substance. I say it all started when the county got permission from the state to experiment with consolidating the sheriff and police into one county-wide department run by the police chief. The population has dropped so much in the past twenty years that the commissioners figured it would reduce administrative costs.

"Then they hire this new guy, Flannery, as chief. All he likes to do is talk and spend tons of money. Fancy new computers. High-tech squad cars. Some cost savings, huh? Like we're some big city that needs all that technology to catch speeders and throw drunks in jail for beatin' their wives."

Matt looked at the old farmers. "Then I'll pay Hibbert a visit and see what he remembers about Helmer's state of mind. Is Hibbert Realty still downtown on First Street?"

"Yup," Schultz said, "just west of Town Square Park."

"I also know a guy on the force," Matt said. "I'll give him a call, tell him what Harold told us, see what he can do."

"Mighty nice of you," Schultz said.

Matt glanced at his watch. He stood and gave them a shoulder-high wave. "Thanks, fellas. I appreciate your time."

Halfway to the exit door, he stopped and reversed back to the tables.

"Forget something?" Schultz asked.

"Yeah. Did any of you notice if Ray or Helmer were getting senile, having memory problems, not acting normal?" Matt hadn't entertained the possibility that his father might have had cognitive issues until Thorson's behavior reminded him that dementia and Alzheimer's Disease were a growing problem for his parents' generation.

"Hell no," Czarnowski said. "Ray was the sharpest razor in our little ten pack. Helmer wasn't far behind."

"Ray's body was going downhill a bit," Schultz said, "But he always kept up on current events, told us about books he'd read, newspaper articles, that sort of stuff. Why you asking?"

"I still wonder why my dad climbed to the top of the silo alone and didn't ask someone to spot him. And Betty said there's no way Helmer would kill himself."

Schultz rubbed his chin stubble. "Maybe Ray had a dizzy spell before he could connect the harness. He never much liked heights, you know. As for Helmer, maybe your theory about him not hanging himself has some legs. That son of a buck was too damned ornery to get depressed. I think he got his jollies being the gruff old goat of our group."

The others chuckled. Matt studied their collective expressions. No hint of guile. No nervous glances. "Thanks, gentlemen. I appreciate your help."

He turned and walked out, spurred by a sudden nervous energy gnawing at his gut. *Why does this whole real estate situation sound off-key?*

CHAPTER 7

In the years since Matt's childhood, First Street North had deteriorated into the low-rent area of downtown Straight River. He parked his Sienna at the end of the block and pulled the hood of his anorak over his head as he stepped out into the rain. A few people scurried along the sidewalks, dodging puddles as they went about their business. Walking down the street searching for Hibbert's office, Matt recognized familiar buildings but not the business names.

Atkinson's Dry Cleaners, Deetz Hardware, and Bloomenrader's Appliances were now, respectively, a tattoo parlor, a computer repair shop, and a rent-to-own furniture store. Flo's Bunch-a-Lunch Diner—revered by a young Matt as having the best chocolate malts anywhere—was now a Mexican taqueria. Huntington's Five & Dime used to stock the best assortment of comic books and baseball cards a boy could imagine. In its place stood a therapeutic massage parlor, its interior shielded by red curtains over the windows.

Even Town Square Park, Straight River's focal point for more than 150 years, appeared different. In addition to a new band shell, the park looked smaller because the trees had grown so much. The only structures he recognized were the old fire hall, the county courthouse, and the century-old bank building. After almost twenty years of living in the Twin Cities and performing with bands and orchestras around the world, Matt felt like a stranger in his hometown.

Near the end of the block, he spotted the words *HIBBERT REALTY* painted on a glass door, the letters faded and chipped. He struggled to open the sticking door and walked into a large, square office. The soft *ding* of a bell announced his presence. The scent of floral perfume mingled with faint smells of mold and pine-scented air freshener. A weak stream of warm air from a small electric heater in the corner blew across the entryway. To his right, a young woman with long blonde hair sat behind an L-shaped desk and a computer workstation. She spun her chair to face him.

"Hi. May I help you?"

Her voice possessed that perky, valley-girl quality he could tolerate for a few minutes before his ears started to protest. But her dazzling smile and perfect, bright-white teeth made him forget her annoying voice. Immediately self-conscious of his own unremarkable teeth, he gave her a tight-lipped smile.

"I'd like to see Wayne Hibbert, please."

She glanced toward the back hallway. "He, uh, stepped out for a minute." She pointed to a threadbare chair to the left of the door. "You can wait there."

"Thanks." He'd sat for mere seconds when a door opened in the back hallway. He heard the end stages of a toilet flushing, and a tall, thick man walked out wiping his hands on his khaki slacks.

"Someone's here to see you, Wayne," the woman said.

Hibbert wore a sheepish expression as he approached Matt. "I wasn't expecting anyone, Bridget. Did you forget to schedule him?"

"No." Her long blond hair shimmered as she shook her head. "He just walked in."

Hibbert straightened the yellow-stained navy tie losing the battle to confine his neck flab within the collar of his light-blue shirt. He smiled and extended his right hand.

"Hi. I'm Wayne Hibbert."

Matt eyed the hand warily.

"Oh, sorry." Hibbert chuckled and nodded toward the bathroom. "Out of paper towels." He held up his hands as if surrendering. "They're clean."

Matt shook Hibbert's damp hand, introduced himself, then discreetly wiped his hand on his thigh as he sight-read the balding, round-headed man.

Hibbert's ruddy complexion resembled that of the many jazz musicians and listeners Matt had encountered who were alcoholics. A long, thin swoosh of oily hair arced from one temple to the other. His clothes needed ironing, and his shirt collar was frayed. His tie bulged over a sizeable paunch. Beady brown eyes under bushy eyebrows, and thin lips outlining stained, crooked teeth, completed the picture.

Hibbert's smile widened. "Looking to buy? I'm your guy."

"Uh, no—"

"Looking to sell? I'll serve you well."

Matt gave him a puzzled look. "No, I—"

"Looking for land? I'll give you a hand." Hibbert's voice reminded Matt of a trombone played by a beginner: bloated, brassy, wobbly pitch. His smile—more of a smirk, actually—had frozen into a mask.

Behind Hibbert's back, Bridget's gaze rolled upward. She gave Matt a flirty grin.

He suppressed his own grin. "No. I'm here to ask you about Helmer Myrick."

For two seconds, Hibbert's eyes ricocheted back and forth as if he were watching a professional table tennis match. The smirk dropped off his face. "What about him?"

"He was my neighbor. His widow told me you tried to buy their farm."

Hibbert glanced at Bridget and motioned Matt toward his desk. "Let's talk in private."

The office measured about twenty-five feet square, with no rooms other than the bathroom and what Matt assumed was a closet or storage room in the short hallway to the back door. It was unlikely the twenty or so feet between desks would prevent Bridget from eavesdropping.

Hibbert gestured for him to sit in a wood-and-vinyl armchair facing the desk as he sat in an overstuffed, well-worn executive chair behind his desk. "It's a shame about Helmer, huh?"

"Yes, Betty's quite upset," Matt said. "That's why I'm here. I heard you talked to Helmer on Friday night at the Eagles Club. I—"

"Lotta people there that night. Why do you want to talk to me?" Hibbert's voice had become tense and defensive.

"Helmer was old, perhaps a bit senile. He could've had a ministroke. Betty can't imagine him committing suicide. It's breaking her heart that she doesn't know why. Did you notice any unusual behavior when you talked to him? Anything that might explain how he ended up hanging from a rafter in his barn?"

Hibbert glanced around and drummed his fingers on the desk. "I talked to him for barely a minute. Come to think of it, he did sound a little different. For starters, he didn't recognize me right away. Had a weird expression, like he wasn't all there, you know? Couldn't find his car. I had to point it out to him."

"Really?"

"Oh, yeah. I didn't make much of it at the time, not knowing how much Helmer had tossed back, you know?" Hibbert winked and made a drinking motion with one hand.

"Right," Matt said. According to Betty, Helmer's weekly trip to the Eagles Club had been a ritual, not a binge.

The term *born loser* crept into Matt's perception of Hibbert, which raised questions concerning Swanson's favorable judgment of the man. By all appearances, Hibbert was the antithesis of a competent, successful real estate broker. Maybe that's what his father had called to warn him about—avoid hiring Hibbert to sell the farm after he died.

"So, uh, Matt is it?"

Matt nodded.

"I don't know if that helps." Hibbert shrugged. "I barely knew the guy. Hard for me to tell what normal was for him, right?"

"Betty also said you stopped by Friday afternoon and things got a little heated."

The façade of pleasantness vanished from Hibbert's face, replaced by redness. "We'd come to an arrangement, but Helmer backed out. I'll admit I was disappointed. I've got deadlines and quotas to meet. The Myrick deal would've made my month. I guess I let off a little steam. Shouldn't have but did. You understand."

"No. I don't," Matt said. The more Hibbert spoke, the less believable he sounded.

Sweat beaded on Hibbert's forehead and his Adam's apple shot up and down. He pushed back from his desk and glanced at the door, looking ready to make his escape. "Is there anything else?"

"Yes. I understand you talked to my father a few months ago about buying our farm. What kind of a deal did you offer him?"

The table tennis match in Hibbert's eyes resumed. "Uh, what was your last name again?"

"Lanier."

"Lanier. Hmmm . . . I'm not sure I wrote up a purchase offer. I'd have to check my files. Probably buried under six months' worth of paper. We've been swamped lately. If you give me some time, I'll call you later with the details."

Swamped? Bridget had been filing her nails and fiddling with her cell phone a few minutes earlier. Despite his doubt, Matt played along. "Sure."

"Oh, okay." Hibbert's plastic smirk reappeared. "I'll call as soon as I find that file."

"Have you stopped by our place in the past month to ask if my father had reconsidered selling his farm?"

The smirk disappeared. "Uh, no. He lives next to the Myrick place, right?"

"*Lived*," Matt corrected. "He died recently."

"Oh, sorry. I forgot. My condolences." Hibbert tugged at his collar with a trembling hand.

"One more thing," Matt said. "What can you tell me about Saxony Partners?"

Hibbert stiffened. "Ah, well, they've asked me not to reveal their identities. Client-realtor privilege, you know."

Matt furrowed his brow. "Client-*realtor?*"

"Not like lawyers or doctors. Just in my contract. I say anything, I'm out."

"Are you working on any other deals for them?"

"Can't say."

"Can't or won't?"

Hibbert shrugged. "Can't. How'd you hear about Saxony, anyway?"

"Ken Trask."

"Oh . . . right . . . Trask." Hibbert resumed his finger tapping.

Matt stared him down, waiting to see if he would volunteer any more information.

Hibbert's eyeballs ricocheted back and forth for the third time. "Well, I need to get to an appointment." He stood, appearing eager to push his visitor out the door. "Sorry I couldn't help you with Myrick."

Matt stood.

Hibbert held out a business card. The phony smile made its third appearance. "If you're ever in the market . . ."

Giving the card a cursory glance, Matt said, "No thanks," and left.

CHAPTER 8

After Helmer's funeral the next morning, Matt changed into work clothes and resumed his siding replacement project. He distracted himself by composing melodies and jazz riffs in his head. In his mind, he saw and heard treble and bass clefs, musical notes, and chord progressions written under each bar of music. He wasn't a talented composer, but this mental exercise occupied his mind and transported him into another world. Deep in thought, he almost jumped off the ground when a tap on his shoulder startled him out of his reverie.

He whirled to see Betty Myrick standing before him, a tear on her cheek and a thick manila envelope in her hands. She still wore her black funeral dress under her unbuttoned coat. In the harsh glare of the fluorescent lighting in the barn, the wrinkles on her face seemed more pronounced, and her hair looked whiter than fresh snow.

"Forgive me, Matthew. I didn't mean to startle you. I called your name twice, but you were humming and singing."

"Sorry, Betty." Matt waved a dismissive hand. "My brain's locked into a music thing. What's wrong?"

Her lips quivered as she handed him the folder. "This."

He removed his work gloves, pulled out the documents, and scanned them.

She pointed to the thickest document. "This is Helmer's life insurance policy. Five hundred thousand dollars. The policy won't pay the benefit because of the suicide clause."

More tears streamed down her cheeks, but she held back sobs. "I'll lose the farm."

He paged through the policy. "When did Helmer buy this?"

"Last spring. The suicide exclusion clause lasts two years."

Matt found the suicide clause in the policy and read. Sure enough, death by suicide within two years of issue voids the payment of proceeds to the beneficiary. "Why did Helmer buy a life insurance policy at his age?"

Betty took a deep breath and regained her composure. "He bought new machinery last year—a combine and tractor. We borrowed against the land and bought the insurance in case he died before he could harvest this year's crop. Because of the Great Recession, interest rates dropped so low he figured borrowing now was a smart business move. He planned to use the crop proceeds to pay off the loan in full after harvest and then cancel the policy. Helmer always talked about how important it was for him to provide for me if he died first. That's why I can't believe he'd kill himself and leave me in this pickle."

She covered her face with her hands and sobbed openly.

One of his mother's favorite expressions came to mind: *Family takes care of family. End of discussion.* Betty had stepped in after his mother died and been an equally strong parent—better than his father had been during Matt's stressful teenage years. Now it was time for him to step up and be a good son to the woman who'd been like a mother to him for all those years. Matt put one hand on Betty's shoulder and waggled the policy in his other hand.

"If you say Helmer didn't commit suicide, I believe you. I'll do whatever I can to make this right."

"Thank you, dear. I appreciate your help."

"Let's go inside. I need to think." He offered his elbow to Betty, who struggled to walk across the frozen, rutted dirt of the barnyard.

Matt lacked insurance expertise, but because the official cause of Helmer's death was suicide, he knew the burden fell upon Betty to prove otherwise. But she was old, probably hadn't dealt with a life insurance claim until now, and, because of her gentle, trusting nature, might be reluctant to challenge the insurance company.

As they walked, Matt noticed a black SUV parked on the intersecting county road at the end of the driveway. City dwellers sometimes drove out to the country and parked to spend some time enjoying the landscape and quiet, but it didn't happen regularly. He dismissed the sighting as a coincidence and returned his attention to guiding Betty to the house.

After fixing a cup of tea for her, Matt decided to start with the police. He went to the phone, dialed the Straight County police, and was connected to Gebhardt within seconds.

"Sorry to bother you, Clay, but Betty Myrick came to see me, and she's distraught."

"She just buried her husband," Gebhardt said. "That's a damn good reason to be upset."

"That's not the reason. There's been a new development." Matt related what Betty had told him about Helmer's life insurance policy.

"I feel bad for her," Gebhardt said. "But the police department can't do anything about a legitimate insurance policy."

"Are you sure the cause of death is accurate?"

"That's the coroner's responsibility. She sounded fairly certain—"

"*Fairly?*" Matt interrupted. "Didn't she perform an autopsy to be one hundred percent sure of the cause of death."

"Doing an autopsy is also the coroner's call. You'll have to ask her why. If Dr. Vincent didn't do one, Betty can order an independent autopsy from another forensic pathologist. But I hear that costs big bucks—three thousand or more."

Matt glanced at Betty. Could she afford it? The fact that Helmer was over seventy and hadn't retired yet suggested the Myrick's hadn't saved much of a nest egg. "I'll pass that information on to her."

"I'll give you Dr. Vincent's number," Gebhardt said. "You can ask her about the cause of death and who she'd recommend outside her jurisdiction."

Matt jotted down Vincent's number and waved the paper hopefully at Betty, who smiled weakly.

"Listen, Clay," Matt said. "I know you have protocol and procedures and all, but I found out that Wayne Hibbert of Hibbert Realty talked to Myrick at the Eagles Club hours before he died. According to Betty, the two men argued earlier in the day. I went to see Hibbert the other day to ask him about his dealings with Helmer and my dad. He acted evasive and nervous. The local farmers say the deals he's offering aren't typical. Not to mention he works for a secretive corporation called Saxony Partners. Can you at least talk to the guy?"

"I already phoned Hibbert twice to ask him about last Friday," Gebhardt said. "He hasn't returned my calls."

"Then go to his office and talk to him. He's hiding information. If you squeeze him a little, he might confess to something."

"What? Like murder?" Gebhardt scoffed.

Matt drummed on his thigh with his free hand. "I doubt it. But maybe he saw something or someone else on Friday night."

As Betty sipped her tea, she seemed older and frailer than she had at Helmer's funeral.

"I'm trying to be a good friend," Matt said to Gebhardt. "Betty might lose everything. End up on the street. I owe her big time. If not for her, I would've ended up in jail or dead."

"Right. Sorry. I'd forgotten about the trouble you got into after your mom died." Gebhardt's tone changed from businesslike to one of consolation. He exhaled an audible sigh over the line. "I suppose I can stop by his office tomorrow morning before my shift starts. See if he triggers my b.s. meter."

"Thanks, Clay. I appreciate it." Matt hung up and sat at the kitchen table. He met Betty's expectant gaze and forced as much conviction into his voice as he could muster. "Two things. First, the coroner wasn't required to do an autopsy on Helmer, which is the only way to confirm he didn't hang himself. I'll call her and ask her to perform one. If she can't or won't, I'll ask her to refer us to someone else."

Betty clutched her hands together prayerfully. "That's wonderful news."

"Second," Matt said. "The police are ninety-nine percent sure Helmer committed suicide, but Sergeant Gebhardt will ask Wayne Hibbert about his encounters with Helmer on Friday."

"That's also good news," she said. "I know in my heart the Good Lord will make sure this gets straightened out."

He called Dr. Vincent and explained Betty's dilemma. Vincent said she hadn't performed an autopsy because Helmer's cause of death was clear-cut and the police didn't find any evidence to suggest

47

foul play. She stressed that doing an autopsy now would be less accurate and comprehensive after embalming had taken place because testing blood and other bodily fluids and examining stomach contents couldn't be done. There was also the added expense of exhumation, transportation to a morgue, and re-interment after the autopsy. During the conversation, Vincent's tone was curt and aloof, as if she felt insulted that anyone would question her ability. Matt asked for a total estimate of those expenses plus the typical fee for an independent medical examiner.

When he repeated the total cost to Betty, she immediately agreed. "After all," she said, "If we don't prove his death wasn't a suicide, I'll go bankrupt. It's worth it to tighten my belt for a while."

Matt relayed Betty's approval to Vincent, who responded with a long silence.

"I tell you what," Vincent said, suddenly sounding conciliatory and apologetic. "I'll make an exception and perform the autopsy myself. No charge."

Matt pulled the phone from his ear and stared at the receiver, wondering about the abrupt change of attitude.

"Have Mrs. Myrick come to hospital administration at her convenience and sign the authorization form," Vincent said. "I'll have the form ready for her within the hour."

He thanked her and hung up, then relayed the good news to Betty. He half smiled and reached out to touch her hand.

"Bless you, Matthew." Her smile seemed as real as Matt's smile felt forced. She raised her teacup and sipped.

Matt drank a bottle of water from the fridge as he tried to pay attention to Betty's small talk about how supportive everyone had been at Helmer's funeral. He managed a few nods and noncommittal words of acknowledgment. His father's death had been accidental. Now he wondered if anything about that case had given Gebhardt the slightest reason to question his father's cause of death. Two elderly next-door neighbors dying days apart from causes other than illness might be more than a coincidence.

CHAPTER 9

"Like I told you before, I tried to reason with him, but all of a sudden he keeled over." Wayne Hibbert struggled to suppress the trepidation in his voice. "One minute he was cussing me out, calling me a crook; the next, he was clutching his chest. What was I supposed to do?"

"You were supposed to close the deal," Leland Smythe said in an annoyed tone.

"I had everything but the signatures. His damn lawyer didn't like the way an *i* was dotted on the purchase offer."

Wayne struggled to hold the phone steady with his trembling hand. Helping Witt deal with Myrick back in Straight River had seemed smart, a convenient excuse to deflect attention from his lost sale. Now, after Lanier had given him the third degree and a cop had subsequently appeared at his office, Wayne wondered if Witt had set him up as a patsy who would take the fall for Myrick's death.

Hoping to sound confident and assured, he said, "I didn't kill him, Mr. Smythe. I—"

"Protocol, Mr. Hibbert. Use our code words please."

"Screw your protocol. I'm in a jam here, and I want to know what to do." Smythe was such an anal-retentive jerk about his damn rules. *My ass is on the line, not yours.*

After a pause, Smythe said, "We discussed this three days ago. I assured you then, and I'm assuring you now. We have things under control. A bereaved son asking questions about his father and a neighbor is hardly grounds for concern—as long as you keep your mouth shut and don't panic."

"I didn't skip town because of Lanier. It was the cop who came by my office this morning who spooked me."

"Which cop?"

"The fat one. Gebhardt."

A door slammed outside. Wayne flinched. His nerves were pinpricks inside his body. He opened his pocket flask and took a swallow of peppermint schnapps.

"When I got near my office this morning, I saw him walk in. I assumed he wanted to ask about Myrick and me on Friday, so I figured I'd get out of town for a while. Let things cool off, you know."

"I see," Smythe said. "Why did you presume he wanted to discuss either Myrick or the elder Lanier?"

"I . . . I just—"

"I'm disappointed, Mr. Hibbert. I expected more backbone from you. What's more disappointing is the fact you have *zero* deals in your pipeline."

Wayne's stomach lurched. He thought he'd camouflaged his lack of results by sending Smythe a list of a few dozen marginal prospects he hoped would fool the man into giving him some slack about not closing the Myrick deal. "How did you know?"

"Two reasons. One, you're neither talented nor clever. Two, my business is predicated on knowing more than my competitors and enemies. Tell me about your meeting with Lanier."

Wayne described their conversation in his office. As he talked, he walked to the window and peered between the curtains into the dark night. Dim lights illuminated the handful of cars in the lot. No one appeared to be surveilling his room.

"Is he a farmer too?" Smythe asked.

"No. He's a fancy-ass musician up in the Cities. Plays jazz and classical. Smart too. Went to college on a full-ride scholarship. I'm several years older, but I've heard of him. I played dumb and pretended I didn't know him."

"I see."

The silence that followed made Wayne nervous. He drummed his fingernails on the metal flask, pounding out a frenetic, tinny *ping*. He checked his cell phone to make sure the battery hadn't died. Expecting a tirade, and apprehensive that anything he said might spark a verbal barrage from his employer, he ventured a timid "Hello?"

"Where are you now?" Smythe eventually said. His tone was calm and businesslike.

"At the Super 8 motel in Rapid City, South Dakota." Wayne paced back and forth across the claustrophobic room. "Seemed far enough away to be safe and big enough that no one will notice me."

"How long have you been there?"

"A few minutes. Figured I should call you right away."

"Did you tell anyone you were leaving?"

"No."

"Who else knows your location?"

"Nobody."

"Good. Stay there for now. Eat dinner at a decent restaurant. Buy some souvenirs. Go out to breakfast in the morning. Use your credit card for all transactions."

"Oh, yeah. Pretend I'm on a planned vacation."

"Correct. I'll get back to you with further instructions in an hour."

"Yes, sir." Wayne hung up and took a slug of vodka from a different flask, hoping *this* shot would calm his trembling hands.

CHAPTER 10

At the Dakota Jazz Club in downtown Minneapolis, Matt tuned his double bass one last time before going onstage. A fellow bassist had called earlier and asked him to take his place backing one of the hottest acts in music, Justine Daigneault. She was a rising star in the vocal jazz world and had embarked on a nationwide tour after winning a Best New Artist Grammy. Despite his troubles in Straight River, Matt couldn't afford to pass up this gig. Not only was the pay more than double what he'd earn backing a local performer, but he also needed a break and some musical challenge and stimulation. He'd driven up for a five o'clock rehearsal to prepare for the show, then grabbed dinner at a much cheaper restaurant down the street, since the Dakota's prices were as *haute* as its *cuisine*.

At nine o'clock, Justine announced the first-set playlist. Matt and the other band members shuffled charts into the correct order, made last-minute adjustments to clothes and hair, and filled water bottles. The emcee finished his announcement of upcoming performances as the quartet filed onstage to enthusiastic applause. Justine waited backstage for her introduction. Compared with most of the gigs he'd played at the Dakota, this crowd eagerly anticipated tonight's performance.

Once Matt's eyes adjusted to the spotlights, he saw a packed house abuzz with excitement. Adrenaline surged through his veins and gave him nervous energy so intense his fingers tingled. This was what he lived for—to create great music with supremely talented musicians for an eager audience of enthusiastic jazz lovers. The high compared to no other, drug-induced or otherwise.

The pianist, Roberta Valero, counted off "It Don't Mean a Thing if it Ain't Got That Swing," and the musicians dove in. The tempo was faster than in rehearsal. Matt guessed she was excited about the performance too. He was glad to get a bit of sweat worked up right away. Dan Kerr, the sax player, ripped off a two-bar break at the start of his tenor solo that raised the eyebrows of the musicians and elicited some *Yeahs!* from the audience. Matt, Valero, and drummer Eric Larose caught his energy and kicked into high gear.

The quartet finished the tune with a finger-busting unison riff followed by a crashing final chord. Larose's drumsticks flew around his drum kit as if he possessed four hands. Kerr shrieked and squealed strident runs in the highest register of his sax. Before Valero could nod her head for the cutoff, the crowd began cheering and clapping. To Matt, the energy level equated to the end of a great final set, not the beginning of the first.

The audience was still applauding as the emcee spoke over the P.A. system. "Ladies and gentlemen, please give a warm Dakota Jazz Club welcome to *Justine Daigneault!*"

~

Seated at the bar after the second set, Matt sipped on a screwdriver as he cooled off. As he chatted with Sam, the bartender, someone settled onto the stool to his right. He glanced down and noticed a pair of slender legs flowing out from under the hem of a short black dress. Then he got a whiff of Beautiful perfume. That mild erotic rush paled in comparison to the emotional surge he experienced when a familiar voice said, "Hello, Jazzman."

"*Diane?*" He whirled on his bar stool to face his ex-wife. She smiled coyly. His heart thumped against his ribs as desire and hostility grappled for dominance in his mind.

Diane Blake wore a tailored, sleeveless cocktail dress cut low enough to draw attention to her cleavage. Her blonde hair was swept back in a French braid. A few delicate strands floated down around her ears. Her oval face framed high cheekbones, straight white teeth, and deep-blue eyes that could melt any man's heart—or freeze it. Tall and lithe, she'd maintained her sensual, not voluptuous, figure. Well into her thirties and fully matured, she possessed a combination of Lauren Bacall's sultriness and Ingrid Bergman's elegance—a near-perfect package.

Matt ran a hand through his tousled hair. Remnants of sweat on his forehead helped slick back his wispy locks. *I must smell worse than the inside of my gym locker.* His jazz musician's uniform—khaki slacks and a black, long-sleeved, collared shirt—paled in comparison to her *haute couture* attire. As always, her mere presence made him feel vaguely inadequate.

"Imagine my surprise when they pulled the curtain back and I saw your handsome mug grinding away on the bass." Her smile seduced. Her voice teased.

Reminiscent of a jazz saxophonist, Diane could manipulate her alto voice all the way from breathy and sensuous to sharp and commanding. But mostly, her voice sounded like a flute played in its lower range. Of all the voices Matt—ever the musician—had analyzed over his career, hers intrigued and beguiled him the most.

"I was a last-minute sub."

"You're the best they could do on short notice?"

She still enjoys toying with my insecurities all these years after our divorce. "Gee, Diane, I'd forgotten how supportive you were of my career."

A corner of her mouth slid upward, bringing her chin along for the ride. She narrowed her eyes. "The Blake family has always patronized the arts. How else would we keep all you jazz musicians off our street corners?"

He matched her smug smile with one of his own. "Do you miss having me around as the butt of your jokes?"

"It's difficult, but I manage."

Matt took a gulp of his screwdriver and tapped his fingers on the bar. He decided against a full out verbal war. Keeping focused for the next set was more important. "So, how've you been? Still working for the Attorney General?"

She nodded. "The governor has us policy wonks working twelve-hour days. If I hadn't taken a catnap after work, I wouldn't be here. Dinner at nine is a bit late for me."

"So why *are* you here? You never were a big jazz fan." He injected enough disdain into his voice to subtly remind her she'd never supported his career as much as he'd supported hers.

"To hear Justine Daigneault, silly. She's the hottest ticket in town."

"Of course. Anyone who's anybody must be here tonight. Should I quake in my boots in the presence of all this royalty?" He gestured to the tables with an outstretched arm.

She turned on her bar stool and made a show of crossing her long legs as she surveyed the room. Her eyes narrowed, and her lips widened into a confident smile. "If you must."

His gaze lingered on her legs. *God, she's still gorgeous.* A hint of lust welled up from deep inside his memory. "So you're not here to gloat about our divorce?"

"I've moved on. I'm sure you have too. I merely thought I'd be polite and say hello."

"How big of you."

Despite the apparent sincerity of her remarks, her talk of moving on still stung. Their divorce had hurt more than any physical pain he'd ever experienced, but he'd come to realize over time that their split wasn't as much her idea as it was her father's and his powerful cronies. They had coerced her into putting her career before her personal life with the false promise of achieving great things for society as a high-powered attorney.

He swirled his screwdriver and took another sip. Then a recollection clicked in his brain. It had taken him a while to recall all her vocal nuances, her pitch, her timbre, how she sounded when tense, nervous, masking anger … or keeping a secret.

He gave her a conspiratorial grin. "You must be running for office, Counselor. Working the crowd for votes?"

Her face tightened, and she averted her eyes. "What an absurd idea, Jazzman."

Busted. The nearly imperceptible tremolo of extra energy when she was holding back gave it away, along with a slight rise in her baseline pitch from G above middle C to G-sharp. He stared at her profile, waiting for her to look at him. "Are you?"

"What difference does it make?"

"*Are* you?"

She gave him a petulant frown. "Matt."

"I read the news. I follow politics. I've heard rumors. I'll bet you don't want your adoring public to find out too soon, right?"

"No comment."

He tossed down the rest of his drink, then chewed on the ice cubes in his glass, fully aware that the crunching annoyed her like nails on a chalkboard. She cringed and gave an exasperated sigh but continued to scan the room. Matt was pleased to score at least one little dig at her expense.

"I'd offer to buy you a drink, but since you want to do some politicking, you're probably planning your exit any second now."

"I'd love a drink." She turned to Sam, who been hovering close by, polishing the same three feet of bar top and stealing surreptitious leers at her ever since she sat down.

"Dom Perignon, *sil vous plais*." Her French accent, like much of her life, was perfect.

Looking heavenward, Matt groaned inwardly but maintained his composure. "There goes most of tonight's paycheck."

"Just kidding," she said playfully. "The house sparkling wine will do."

He covered his annoyance at her zinger with a weak grin. "Put it on my tab, Sam, and you might as well give me one."

"Comin' right up," Sam said.

Diane raised her eyebrows. "Wow. Two drinks between sets. Twice your usual. Have you become an alcoholic?"

Matt clenched his teeth. "You certainly came prepared with snide remarks tonight. I'm celebrating the fact I've grown a new heart after you broke mine."

Sam placed two Champagne flutes on the counter, popped the cork on the bottle, and poured.

"I'll let that remark slide," she said. "Truce?"

He raised his glass. "Truce."

Smiling with her eyes, she raised her glass and touched its rim to his. She stared into his eyes as she took a sip. Her full, ruby lips lightly puckered on the edge of the crystal.

He held her gaze, remembering the taste of those sensuous lips. *Was* there some desire still smoldering deep inside her? She'd always been a calculator, not quick to show her emotions, always hiding behind decorum and self-control.

A tap on his shoulder broke his concentration and caused him to turn.

Roberta Valero leaned close and whispered, "Five minutes, Casanova."

"Thanks, I'll be ready," he said and turned back to Diane as Valero departed.

Diane regarded Valero with a disapproving expression. "Really, Matt, it's impolite to make a date in front of your ex-wife."

"Ahhh, jealous, are we?"

The slight flush on her face indicated he'd struck a nerve. "Why be jealous? Your sex life is none of my business now."

Game on again. He stared haughtily at her. "What about all those women you claimed threw themselves at me after gigs while we were married? You certainly were jealous then. But I turned them all down for you."

She twirled the stem of her glass between her fingers. "I'd forgotten."

"If I recall, we met at a bar in college, similar to this situation. You threw yourself at me. Not unlike all the other women."

"*Threw* is such a desperate word. Let's just say you intrigued me." She gave him a knowing grin. "As I recall, *you* threw yourself at *me*."

"I'll bet revisionist history skills come in handy for a politician." But she was right. He recalled the night they met. Her initial infatuation with him, the cute bass player, soon morphed into him falling head-over-heels for her—a brilliant, ambitious, charming, sexy law student.

As they sipped their drinks, he studied her in the mirror behind the bar. "Let's call it mutual attraction, okay?" he said. "We don't need to argue semantics."

She relaxed her tight half-smile and touched his arm. "I'm sorry we didn't work out, especially after so many years. However, people, most people, change over time. I did. You didn't."

That glimmer of desire returned to her eyes. She didn't pull her hand away from his forearm. He suspected she hadn't completely moved on from their failed relationship. Matt softened his tone. "I knew you might lose some of your idealism. I loved you so much it didn't matter. I was ready to help you save the world—or at least support you."

"I still possess those ideals. Public defense is a noble occupation, but it has its limits. I can help people so much more from the Attorney General's office. That's where the substantial changes happen."

"Uh-huh." He decided against pursuing that fight topic—the noble lawyer helping the masses merely to pad the resume. The ultimate goal for most trial lawyers was the cushy corporate or government job and its concordant money and power.

She stood. "I'd better get back to my seat. Steven might actually notice I'm gone."

"Steven?"

"My escort."

"What *does* a good escort charge these days?"

Diane shot him an annoyed glance. "Steven Crossley."

Matt raised his eyebrows, simultaneously jealous and impressed. "The governor's chief of staff?"

According to the political news, insiders considered Crossley the real power in the Governor's office. Dating Crossley was a brilliant career move, yet he was surprised she had time for a relationship. "Is he the best you can do on short notice?"

She ignored his retaliatory gibe. "You know him?"

He snorted. "Oh yah, sure, you betcha." He exaggerated the stereotypical Minnesota accent. "We hang out all the time at the St. Paul Grill. I give him advice whenever he asks."

"Do you now?" She tilted her head back enough to suggest she was looking down her nose at him.

Matt shrugged at his unfunny wisecrack, then checked his watch. "Gotta get back to work. Earn a couple more days of gas money. I'd say it was nice to see you, but I'm not sure."

As they stood, she said, "It was good to see you. Really."

He watched her hips sway as she glided across the floor toward her table, an intimate, half-round banquette against the back wall. Crossley was talking on his cell phone and didn't react to her arrival.

Had Diane thrown herself at Crossley, or vice versa? Matt decided he didn't want to know. Suppressing his desire for her, Matt gulped the rest of his sparkling wine and trudged back on stage.

The Dakota was still three-quarters full for the final set at 11:30—a tribute to Justine Daigneault's ascendancy in the jazz world. Matt glanced at Diane's table while he tuned his bass. She and Crossley sipped coffee and conversed. She appeared disinterested and glanced at Matt several times.

He forced lustful thoughts of her out of his mind and focused on his performance. Justine had saved some of her best material for last: a few ballads and love songs that gave understated thrills to the crowd, followed by a mini-set of hard-swinging tunes intended to generate high emotional and energetic impact at the end of the performance.

As the final number ended—a vocal arrangement of "Anthropology" written by local singing legend Connie Evingson and performed at a breakneck tempo—the crowd stood as one and put all their remaining energy into resounding cheers and applause. They clamored to hear more, but an encore would be anticlimactic. Still, they gave the musicians a standing ovation that lasted until long after they'd left the stage.

In the green room, Matt floated on a post-gig high. Tonight was as good as it got for making music with consummate professionals who poured their hearts and souls into each performance. Justine Daigneault was indeed on a fast track to stardom. He hadn't heard a voice as powerful, versatile, and capable of a complete range of emotion and style since he'd seen the late, great Eva Cassidy years ago in a small club in Washington, D.C. Best of all, he hadn't thought about his father's death, the Myricks, or the farm for twelve glorious hours.

CHAPTER 11

Matt packed up his gear, toweled off, thanked Justine and the band for the opportunity to play with them, left the green room, and took a seat at a table near the stage. It was his way of winding down after a great show—soaking up the residual ambiance of an exceptional performance. He turned back toward the bar.

"Hey, Sam, anything left in the bottle you opened for me?"

Sam glanced at Matt, then checked the bar fridge. "Yep."

"Bring the bottle and a glass, please."

Sam waved his hand in acknowledgment. "You got it."

Matt scanned the Dakota. Most of the patrons had left. Two couples sitting on either end of the bar flanked a lone woman in the middle. All were silhouettes in the low light illuminating the bottles against the back mirror. A foursome sipped coffees at one table. A would-be Lothario was putting the moves on an unimpressed young woman in another of the intimate banquettes. Soft jazz saxophone played over the sound system. The air smelled of gourmet food, stale booze, warm bodies, and a faint potpourri of colognes and perfumes.

A moment after Matt had turned toward the stage and focused on listening to the music, a woman's hands appeared from behind him and placed a bottle of Dom Perignon and two glasses on the table.

"This one's on me, Jazzman." Diane touched his shoulder. "In appreciation of tonight's musical excellence."

He did a double take but quickly covered his surprise with a tight grin. "Thanks. That's very generous. But I thought you'd have gone home by now. Where's Crossley?"

She sat at his table. "The Governor called him in to work during the last set. I swear Steven's more in love with him than he'll ever be with me."

"Too much information," Matt said, wincing playfully. He removed the foil from the bottle, eased the cork out, and poured two glasses of bubbly.

They raised their glasses, clinked them together, and sipped. After swallowing, he said, "Why'd you stay?"

She put an elbow on the table and rested her chin on her upraised hand. "I loved the music. Justine Daigneault was spectacular. Even a novice like me could tell. I've always harbored a secret fantasy I could sing half as well as someone like her, except I'd perform show tunes and love songs like Barbra Streisand or Celine Dion."

He appraised her with raised eyebrows, wondering what other secrets she'd concealed during their marriage.

"Also," she said, "I was rude for not asking how your life is going. I wanted to apologize."

With the performance over, his nerves had mellowed, and he didn't see the need to spar with her anymore. "Apology accepted."

He took a large swig of his drink, then remembered what he was drinking. He rolled the effervescent nectar around in his mouth, let it coat every taste bud, then swallowed. *Damn. I'd love to drink this every day—with her.*

"So, how *is* your life going?" she asked in an earnest tone.

He stared at her, still doubting her sincerity. "To tell you the truth, horribly."

"Oh. Really?" She seemed taken aback by his bluntness. "What's wrong?"

His musical high vaporized and he was back to real life again. "Well, let's see … two farmers died under suspicious circumstances a week apart, a sweet old lady is facing bankruptcy, and a shady real estate broker seems to be the eye of a local hurricane."

Her eyebrows went up as her jaw went down. "What the heck happened?"

For the first time that night, she sounded genuinely concerned. This was the real Diane. No animosity. No verbal barbs.

He recited an abridged version of the recent events in Straight River. Her features softened, and her expression of concern and sorrow grew at his suspicions about Helmer and Ray's deaths and

Betty's financial crisis. She touched his arm. "I'm so sorry for your loss and all this trouble. I know you weren't close with your father, but it still must hurt to lose him."

"Thanks." He gave her an appreciative glance, then bit his lower lip. He was unsure about asking his ex-wife for help. "You *could* do me a small favor, Counselor." He presented his most convincing sad-puppy expression. "Payback for your earlier rudeness."

She frowned. "I'll try."

He explained his suspicions about Wayne Hibbert's mystery bosses, Saxony Partners. "If I weren't a technological Luddite, I'd discover the identity of Hibbert's puppet master myself. But a legal eagle like you could do it about ten times faster."

"It's possible to find out the organizational structure in a situation such as this," Diane said, "but you're right, it takes time. These corporations are often set up to simplify their tax situations. A large company will set up smaller subsidiaries to keep the accounting and taxes separate for each entity. That way, they can more easily monitor the success or failure of each business within the corporation."

Matt nodded. "Makes sense."

She rested her forearms on the table and spun the stem of her glass with her fingers. "On rare occasions, the corporation is a shell used to hide assets, identities, launder money, or engage in other shady or illegal activities to evade taxes. We deal with that a lot in the AG's office."

"Considering the way Hibbert reacted when I asked him about Helmer's death, his connection to Saxony Partners is suspicious. Perhaps someone at the corporate office can explain things."

"I'm sure I can get you a contact name. Beyond that, I don't know what I can find."

He picked up his glass and leaned back in his chair. "That's all I'm asking. Betty is literally betting her farm Helmer didn't kill himself. If the police say there's a one-percent chance he didn't commit suicide, I can't give up until that chance is zero. Also, if something's not kosher about Helmer's death, then my father's death becomes more suspicious. We didn't get along since Mom died, but I still get royally pissed off at the thought someone might've killed him. If that's true, I want to nail the bastard who did it."

She nodded, but it didn't appear to be a nod of agreement.

"Then again," he said, "I may have somehow turned into a paranoid nut job and blown this mess out of proportion."

"Maybe. But remember you're still grieving. Take things one step at a time."

They sat in silence and listened to the music. Everyone else had left.

After stifling a yawn, he drained his glass and rose from the table. "I'd better go. I've had one hell of a long day, and I know I'll crash sooner than usual."

Diane stood. "I should go too."

"Can I give you a ride home? I'm parked nearby."

She gave him a disdainful glance. "Not a chance, lover boy. I'll take a cab."

He furrowed his brow. "What's with the attitude?"

"You were always horniest after a good performance. I didn't mind too much on weekends, but I got a bit tired of your lustful advances at two a.m. on weeknights." Her eyes sparkled above her frown. "If I let you within a mile of my bedroom, I'm pretty sure I'll hate myself in the morning."

"Ohhh, right. I'd forgotten. I'll have Sam call a cab for you."

"I'll contact you with whatever I find out about Saxony Partners," she said. Stepping forward, she put her hands on his shoulders and placed a tender kiss on his cheek. "Good night."

When she stepped back, the light in her eyes was more than fond remembrances of good times from a failed marriage. Her ice-cold blues glowed with warmth. He inhaled slowly so she wouldn't notice. The citrus-tinged, rose-and-jasmine scent of her perfume lingered in his nostrils.

He exhaled a shaky, "Good night."

CHAPTER 12

Inventorying the farmhouse was a necessary pain in the ass because Matt had no idea what sort of assets his father had accumulated. He doubted he'd find much of serious value, but he knew he should check before he dared to allow an estate sale organizer or real estate agent to snoop around and perhaps steal a valuable item or keepsake.

With a notebook and pen in hand, he walked from room to room, digging in drawers, searching closets, peering under beds, opening dust-covered boxes. He smiled when he entered the bedroom he and Mark had shared as children. The bed linens, paint job, and wall decorations—sports posters for Mark, music posters for Matt, and PG-13-rated posters of female actors, musicians, and models for both boys—were still in place. For whatever reason, his father hadn't removed any of the memorabilia.

Matt stared out the window and reminisced about his early childhood when his mother was alive. She was intelligent, pretty, modest, and caring. He loved her as much as any boy had ever loved his mother. His father was content to work hard and support the family. Mark had been a good brother—a partner in mischief, adventures, and sports, and a shoulder to cry on when the abuse started.

Back then, Matt's career ambition was to take over the farm with Mark when Ray decided to retire. His mother's death had changed everything. After the years of beatings that followed, Matt vowed to never willingly help his father, let alone choose farming as his profession. His one-eighty had as much to do with honoring his mother as it did with spiting his father.

She'd possessed a beautiful voice and was often the featured soloist in the church choir. Whenever she was in a good mood, she'd hum and sing as she went about her daily routine. When he woke panicked and crying from bad dreams, she soothed his fears and tears with a sweet lullaby, and his nightmare faded into a distant memory as he fell into a dreamless sleep.

Motivated by that magic ability of music to entertain, heal, and inspire, Matt decided to make the best use of whatever musical talent he'd inherited. He poured himself into playing bass, practicing for hours at a time, often until he was forced to stop because of bloodied or blistered fingers on his left hand. The blood, sweat, and tears had paid off. Matt Lanier could proudly state he was one of the small percentage of musicians who earned a respectable salary solely through music. During the past twenty years, he'd visited numerous countries and performed with world-class musicians. He'd made good friends in the music business, been part of many great performances, and created a respectable musical legacy through his jazz trio recordings and his work with the Minnesota Orchestra. Pretty impressive for a farm kid.

His failed marriage notwithstanding, Matt never regretted his decision to abandon Straight River for the big city, the farm for his condo, and his father for a chance to blaze his own trail. Knowing his biography still had many more chapters to be written, he exhaled a long, wistful sigh and refocused on the household inventory.

Ray had also left the master bedroom intact, and he'd cleaned and dusted recently. Arlene Lanier's taste had run less feminine than most women's when it came to colors, decorations, and knickknacks. Given that Ray had never redecorated, he'd obviously been comfortable with the taupe wall paint, lace curtains, and tasteful, understated art and photos on the wall.

Downstairs, Ray had converted the dining room into an office. Consequently, the dining table had become a desk, and a three-drawer filing cabinet stood against one wall. Ray had been congenitally neat, so the table top was clear of any papers. On it sat a desk lamp, an old electric typewriter, a rectangular blotter trimmed with leather, and two stacked plastic trays for incoming and outgoing mail.

The comments from the farmers at the Hy-Vee rose to Matt's consciousness. He went to the filing cabinet and rifled through the drawers. The headings on each manila folder suspended in the larger hanging files were printed in neat block letters. Most were mundane items: insurance policies, bills, tax records, and investment statements. However, the contents of the bottom drawer gave him a start. Just as Schultz had mentioned, Ray possessed files with headings such as *NAFTA, NASHCO,* and *OTHER CONSPIRACIES.*

The title of the last file in the drawer chilled Matt's blood: *HIBBERT.*

With nervous excitement running through his body, he extracted the contents of the drawer and spread them on the table. The top page of the Hibbert file contained a list of properties plus real estate deals Hibbert had closed. Each entry consisted of a name, property location, tax identification number, and date of sale. All were within the past few years. The remaining document in that file was a folded map of Straight County marked up in yellow highlighter ink with a handful of rectangles. The salient features of the highlighted properties were their location. All at least partially abutted Interstate 35.

He gazed out the window as he digested this information. Why was dimwitted Hibbert buying up plots of farmland along a major north-south interstate highway? Was there a connection between Hibbert, Saxony Partners, and NAFTA? What was NASHCO? He set aside the Hibbert file and opened the much thicker NASHCO file. Starting with the top page, he read. And read. And read some more.

~

Hours later, after short breaks to eat lunch, use the bathroom, and stretch his limbs, Matt sat back in his chair, ran his fingers through his hair, and exhaled. He now knew far more about NASHCO—the North American Super Highway Coalition—than he ever wanted to. That knowledge gnawed on his nerves like the scraping noises produced when a beginning student applied too much pressure on the bass strings with the bow.

While appearing to be the musings—or rantings, depending on whom one asked—of a man mistrustful of all forms of government, his father's theory contained enough basis in logic and facts that Matt thought it was reasonable. One of the items he'd discovered was a small notebook used by Ray to log three recent phone calls to the police regarding vandalism at the farm: a broken barn window, a shed fire, and the strange noise the night before he died. If the vandalism was somehow related to Ray's suspicions about local sales, then the coincidence of his death shortly before Myrick's might not be so coincidental. Preposterous as it seemed, his father might have unearthed something worth investigating.

Matt checked the time. The Swansons had invited him to dinner, but he still had an hour to kill. He donned his shoes and coat and hurried to the grain silo, dodging mud puddles and patches of iced-over snow.

As he climbed the steel ladder to the top, he wished it were dark so he wouldn't be as aware of the lethal drop if he should lose his grip. His insides bubbled with nervous tension as he imagined exploding into a messy pile of blood and guts after a fifty-foot fall. He hooked one arm around the top rung and opened the hatch with his free hand. After flipping on the interior light, he strapped on the safety harness, primarily for his own safety but also to ensure it functioned properly. Next, he checked that the air vents were open to allow the escape of toxic gasses formed by fermenting crops. He then began to circle the catwalk on the off chance he'd discover some sort of clue as to why his father had climbed up alone.

When he reached the far side, facing west, an engine started up in the calm air. A dark vehicle drove away from the farm on the county road. The glare of the sun and the distance prevented him from getting a good look, but the vehicle was larger than a sedan and smaller than a pickup truck. The SUV again? Across the road from the Lanier farm lay the far eastern section of Schultz's farm, but Schultz's house and buildings weren't visible from that road. Sighting the same vehicle three times in a week or so was no longer a coincidence. Was the driver watching the farm for some reason? Uneasiness took root, but he wanted to finish his examination of the silo before sunset.

He descended and inspected the doors from where the grain flowed out. All the latches were locked. He circled the silo, examining a ten-foot swath of earth next to the base. Halfway around, he realized the footprints left by the first responders who'd retrieved his father's body had obliterated any evidence that might connect another person to his father's death. He trudged back to the house, frustrated because he hadn't magically discovered evidence the police had missed.

Twenty minutes later, after he'd fed Jack and stoked the wood stove, Matt sat in the recliner in the living room analyzing what he'd learned that day. Was the lurking SUV significant? If so, was the driver Hibbert or someone else connected to Saxony Partners? Did his father's speculations about suspicious farm sales adjacent to the interstate have any validity? He was stumped but not ready to give up. He wanted one hundred percent confirmation that both his father's and Helmer's cause of death were indisputable.

He called Gebhardt at the LEC. "I'd like you to investigate my father's death as a possible homicide."

"What?" Gebhardt said in a surprised tone.

"I'm serious, Clay." He relayed his suspicion about the lurking SUV, his discovery of his father's detailed research on local farm sales, his gut feeling that his father wouldn't have taken the risk of ignoring the harness in the silo, Myrick's death, Hibbert's connection to both men, and how all the unrelated facts taken together couldn't be ignored.

"Don't you think that's all a bit farfetched?" Gebhardt said, now sounding annoyed.

"Does Hibbert own an SUV? Maybe he's trying to spook me out of town. If my father stumbled onto something about farm sales around here that Hibbert or his boss wants to keep quiet, that would be a reason to harass him or worse. Buying and selling farms involves serious money—millions in many cases."

Gebhardt's silence was long. Right then, Matt decided not to mention his father's NAFTA-NASHCO theories. Better to confine his concern to local matters until Gebhardt agreed to investigate his father's death.

"Look," Gebhardt said, "we can't send out a forensics team from CSI or the FBI and solve this case in an hour like on TV. We're a small county with a budget tighter than my Uncle Frank after one of his weekend benders. All you have is a suspicion, some flimsy circumstantial evidence, and hearsay from a bunch of old, disgruntled farmers. I can't help you unless you bring me something rock solid. The probable cause of your father's death, and what our investigation found, was an accidental fall resulting in asphyxiation. Chief Flannery himself called this one. Case closed."

Matt got a powerful urge to rip into Gebhardt and deride him for lacking initiative. But nothing good would come from alienating a friend and potential ally. Matt forced down his frustration and politely ended the call.

He slid the recliner to the *recline* position and stared at the water stains on the living room ceiling. He'd already used the left side of his musician's brain to analyze the facts he'd taken in since arriving in Straight River. Now he turned on his right brain to synthesize his interpretation of the combined body of knowledge. Taken all together, these facts again recalled Ray's initial suspicions: *Something's goin' on around here. Smells like grade A pig manure.*

As if he'd sensed his master's state of mind, Jack appeared from his bed in the kitchen, laid his head across Matt's lap, and stared sideways at him with huge brown eyes.

When Matt had first heard his father's message, he dreaded returning the call. Now Ray's death and its aftermath had changed his dread to regret, then to frustration, to worry, to anger. His nerves were frazzled from dealing with funerals, estates, repairs, finding someone to rent his fields for the season, and investigating mysterious deaths and shady real estate transactions. He slammed his palm onto the leather arm of the chair, wincing from the sting but satisfied with the loud *smack* of flesh on cowhide.

The old Labrador sat back, startled, but didn't bolt.

The chance for Matt to help his father when he was alive had vanished. The least he could do now was stay at the farm and find out if his father and Myrick had been victims of Saxony Partners. If they had, he'd do everything possible to make sure they received justice.

His pity party ended when he realized he was due at the Swanson's for dinner. He washed up and changed into clean clothes before heading out for what he hoped would be a cordial, relaxing evening with an old friend and his wife.

CHAPTER 13

Two hours after arriving at the Swanson's, Matt, Dave, and Amy sat in the living room savoring the last of the chardonnay Matt had contributed to the meal. Amy had delivered on Dave's promise and prepared a delicious roasted pork tenderloin with apples and onions, baked potatoes, and steamed green beans topped with a locally made blue cheese.

The Swansons occupied their Colonial-style sofa. Matt relaxed on the matching love seat that faced the sofa across the walnut coffee table. Matt's latest CD, a collection of jazz standards recorded with his trio, played in the background. His gift to Amy—an enthusiastic fan of his music—for cooking dinner. Dave merely tolerated any sort of jazz. As "My Funny Valentine" played, Matt vividly remembered the great vibe the trio had generated for that session.

It felt good to get reacquainted with his boyhood best friend and get better acquainted with Amy. He'd met her at Myrick's funeral and liked her immediately. If Dave resembled a bear, Amy resembled a deer: petite, graceful, ever alert. An elementary teacher at the local school, she possessed bright, intelligent eyes and a natural beauty gently sanded down by the rigors of farm life.

Intent on enjoying the evening, Matt kept his silo suspicions and research findings to himself during dinner. But he couldn't help tapping his toes and drumming his fingers on his legs, two nervous traits that manifested themselves whenever his subconscious shifted into high gear thinking about a problem or situation.

"Swanny," he said, then hesitated.

"Yeah?" Dave said as he idly caressed Amy's thigh.

Matt huffed a deep breath in and out. Best to just put it on the table. "I'm not sure my father's death was accidental."

Dave arched his eyebrows skyward as if to balance his dropping jaw. He glanced at Amy, who seemed equally startled, then back at Matt. His face reddened. "You're kidding."

Matt shook his head and stared at the floor. "Two old farmers, neighbors, dying so close together, both having recently dealt with Hibbert, keeps eating at my brain. Betty says there's no way Helmer killed himself. I say there's no way Dad forgot to use his harness."

Dave nodded but didn't make eye contact. "Hey, old folks have senior moments all the time."

"What also bothers me is all the old farmers don't trust Hibbert and think he's some sort of crook, yet you say he's legit. Who's right?"

Dave rubbed his still-red face with a meaty hand.

Amy sat back, searching her husband's expression for a response.

"It's complicated," Dave said. "Hibbert's got some issues, and nobody likes him much. The bottom line is, his purchase contracts give the sellers the option to stay in their houses and farm the land they've sold. I'm in favor of keeping farms producing and farmers working, that's all. So far, he seems to have been straight about that."

Thanks to decades of training himself to detect the minutest differences in pitch, tone, and timbre, Matt had developed the ability to quickly analyze verbal cues. Either Dave was hiding something, or he had changed significantly since he and Matt were kids.

"You called nine one one about Dad, right?" Matt tried to keep the accusatory tone out of his voice.

"Yeah," Dave said. "Ray talked for weeks about needing to check his grain storage, so when I didn't see him anywhere around the property or the house, I climbed the silo and found him inside. I called the police from there with my cell phone."

"Did you happen to see a black SUV in the area that day? Or before or since?"

"Who's got time to monitor neighborhood traffic? I work all day. Don't have time to stand sentry next to the road."

Swanson had deployed his defenses. His tone sounded irritated and edgy. Higher pitch, more tension. The same way a high note played by pressing a finger on the lowest string of a violin has more tension and less resonance than the same note played on a higher open string.

"I know it's a stretch." Matt tempered his suspicious tone. "I'm just trying to put a tricky puzzle piece into place. I've seen a black SUV more often than I consider coincidental. Does Hibbert or someone he works with own one?"

Dave shrugged and eyed Matt as if daring him to push farther. Stress showed in his tensed eye muscles. "I dunno."

Amy shifted her position on the sofa, glanced back and forth between the two men, sipped her wine.

Matt hid his expression behind his wine glass as he took a large gulp. A song ended. The room fell silent, which amplified the tension. When Cole Porter's "Just One of Those Things" began, Matt reluctantly took the hint and dropped the matter.

"How do you guys like the wine?"

Dave's eyes lit up with relief to be given a new topic. Not known as an oenophile by any means, he swirled his wine glass, spilling a few drops, and inhaled a long, slow sniff of the aromas. Doing an exaggerated imitation of an effete British wine snob, he proclaimed, "Ahhh yes, the nose resembles Durante's." He raised his glass to the light. "The legs are definitely Betty Grable." He sipped, swished his wine like mouthwash, and swallowed. "Lean body. Hints of Kate Moss." He smacked his lips. "And the finish is . . ." He switched to a racetrack announcer's voice. ". . . Richard Petty by a car length."

Amy grinned and shook her head with the patient tolerance only a wife can possess for her husband's unique sense of humor. Dave beamed as if he'd made the most intelligent pronouncement in the history of wine commentary.

Matt suppressed a bemused grin. "Swanny, I wonder how my life would've turned out if our farms were on opposite sides of the world and I hadn't grown up with you and your bizarre wit and humor."

"I would've enriched some poor Chinese farm kid's life immeasurably, of course."

"Right. You keep on believing that, farm boy."

"Diss me all you want, but don't forget if it weren't for my heroics, you wouldn't have lived to regret knowin' me."

Amy said, "What do you mean?"

Dave inhaled in preparation for a long-winded explanation, but Matt interjected. "He's under the delusion he saved my life up in the Boundary Waters when we were in high school."

"*Think?*" Dave feigned indignation. "I *know* I saved your scrawny ass."

"Oh, *that* old story?" Amy rolled her gaze upward in mock annoyance. "The *epic* three-week canoe trip?"

Both men agreed in unison, but Dave dismissed her protest with a wave of his hand.

Amy gazed admiringly at her husband. "I know you're brave in real-life situations. You don't need to tell the story a dozen times to prove your manhood."

"A dozen times? Nah. Nine, ten tops. None in the last year." Dave kissed her forehead and patted the hand resting on his belly. She curled her feet under her body and rested an elbow on the back of the sofa as she hugged his gut with her other arm. "And I don't *need* to tell it, but you *let* me, which is why you're an absolute queen."

Matt cracked a cynical smile. "Actually, I'd like to hear it to find out how much you've altered the facts to suit your own inflated ego."

"It was all Matt's idea," Dave said, ignoring Matt's barb. "He wanted me along as his personal pack mule. But I proved to be more than a dumb grunt. He was the expert since he worked for an outfitter up there a bunch of summers." He looked at Matt. "Olson's, right?"

"Ferdie Olson," Matt said. "Owned Olson's Wilderness Canoe Outfitters up on Snowfall Lake. Still does, last I heard."

"Yeah, Snowfall," Dave said. "Old man Olson sure was a piece of work. Orneriest bastard I ever met."

Matt refrained from defending his sometimes tyrannical but goodhearted former boss. Working for Olson had been tough but rewarding. He turned many boys into strong, confident young men by teaching them survival skills along with a solid work ethic.

Dave got a reminiscent look in his eyes. "The summer after we graduated from high school, we wanted to go on a monster trip, sort of a last hurrah. Start from Snowfall in the west, paddle across the northern edge of the Boundary Waters to the northeast corner, then loop down to the south and paddle west back to Snowfall. Three weeks to circumnavigate the eastern two-thirds of the Wilderness."

Matt flashed back to the glorious freedom he'd felt at the start of that trip as if it were yesterday, not twenty years earlier.

"Four days into the trip," Dave continued, "we got to Seagull Lake after conquering the narrow little eastern arm of Saganaga, straight into a thirty-mile-an-hour south wind. I tell ya, it was like paddling through a God damned wind tunnel. Then we paddled to the far end of Seagull, still into the wind, and found this spectacular campsite. Up high on a flat, rocky ledge at the end of this long peninsula with plenty of tent space. Must've been a hundred twenty in the shade, and we're exhausted, so we decide to go for a swim. We were drenched in sweat and couldn't wait to jump into that icy water."

"Yeah, yeah," Matt interjected. Swanny loved to go into graphic detail about the next part of the story. He claimed Matt was unconscious and might've drowned. Matt knew he'd only been momentarily stunned by the impact and was in no danger of drowning.

"I jumped in," Matt said, "banged my head on a submerged boulder, and you saved me." He formed air quotes around *saved*.

Dave frowned but took the hint. Smiling again, he shook his head. "Man, we survived everything on that trip. Remember the thunderstorm that almost blew us off Pine, followed by the near-miss lightning strike?"

"What about the portage from hell between Grace and Beth? Knee-high mud the entire way."

"And the bear on Tuscarora who wanted our food in the worst way."

"Don't be too hard on your hubby for overtelling the story, Amy," Matt said. "We had one hell of an adventure despite my broken nose and the gash on my forehead, which your husband patched up nicely after he, ahem, saved my scrawny ass." He grinned and turned to Amy. "I can't believe I'm going to say this." Letting out a small groan, he thrust a thumb in Swanny's direction. "But I'd do it again anytime with this moolyak."

"And I'll admit city boy here knows his wilderness shit," Dave said. "You could've gotten your own TV show, like that Bear Grylls dude."

They all laughed when Matt explained he was definitely not in that class of adventurer. After a few more minutes of conversation, Amy yawned and glanced at the grandmother clock on the fireplace mantle.

Matt took that as his cue to leave, so he thanked them for an excellent dinner and a pleasant evening, which was mostly true. He stood and began the traditional Minnesota Goodbye—a departure that invariably required a minimum of ten minutes of further chitchat before guests worked their way out the door.

He'd walked the quarter mile from his farmhouse to the Swanson's, so Matt used the return trip to synthesize what he'd discovered in recent days. The bitter wind and spatters of snowflakes sharpened his thinking but only enough to emphasize the struggle between his sense of duty and his desire to return his life to normal.

At home, he poured a shot of Jim Beam Black and sat in the recliner to mull and mope. How the hell was he going to squeeze part-time investigating of Straight River issues into his full-time musician's schedule? He stared at Jack, curled up on the floor next to him.

"Got any suggestions?" Matt raised his eyebrows.

Jack looked up, yawned, and laid his head back down.

"Thought so." Matt gulped the last of his bourbon and poured another shot.

CHAPTER 14

Helmer Myrick's autopsy report lay on Clay's desk. He read the last line: *Cause of Death: Self-Inflicted Asphyxiation. Other significant conditions: Simultaneous Myocardial Infarction.* Suicide with a side order of heart attack. Talk about ironic.

Clay should've been pleased, or at least relieved, because further investigation wasn't required. Less work for him. However, two facts buzzed around in his mind like pesky mosquitos on a steamy summer night: the pushed-back driver's seat and the smell of peppermint in the car. Then Lanier had called about his father's death and insisted he reopen the investigation. More suspicion. Enough to gnaw at his gut like heartburn.

Nevertheless, Clay was reluctant to challenge both the medical evidence and his by-the-book chief. Dr. Vincent's reputation was above reproach. For their first hire in the state-sanctioned experiment to allow Straight County to consolidate the sheriff's office and police department into one unit, the county commissioners had hired the highly regarded Flannery. He'd replaced the previous police chief, Peter "Pistol Pete" Ostlund, who retired for health reasons. Ostlund had represented the folksy, low-key approach of Sheriff Taylor in the 1960s sitcom, *The Andy Griffith Show*. Flannery was the antithesis of the long-time former chief: young, ambitious, high-tech, paramilitary approach to policing, ruled like a dictator.

Those few officers who dared to question Flannery on a case had been disciplined for insubordination. Clay had no desire to join that group. He intended to retire from the SCPD when he was eligible for his pension. Risking his job security for an old friend based on coincidence and wild speculation put him way out of his comfort zone. Still, this particular heartburn wouldn't go away by popping a Zantac. He called Dr. Vincent.

"You're calling about Myrick's autopsy, right?" Her defensive tone caught him off guard. How had she guessed the reason for his call?

"Yeah. What gives with the suicide?"

"What don't you understand?"

"What about the simultaneous heart attack?"

"Myrick had a history of heart disease. He probably got so agitated and stressed that his heart gave out seconds before asphyxiation occurred."

"How often does that happen? Once in a million suicide attempts?"

"Are you questioning my credibility, Sergeant?" Vincent used formal titles in conversation when she became either angry or defensive. "I'm telling you it's medically possible."

"I'm simply trying to reconcile my questions about the evidence I compiled at the scene and the widow's insistence that suicide was not the cause of death."

"Keep in mind I performed this autopsy post-embalming. It's not as comprehensive as a pre-embalming procedure."

"Right. It's just that I can't get the driver's seat position and the peppermint odor out of my mind. Betty swears Helmer *never* drank schnapps and never *ever* had more than a shot and a beer. Then a crazy idea popped into my head. What if Myrick was drunk and someone at the Eagles Club who is tall and was drunk on schnapps drove him home? What if Myrick had his heart attack on the way. What if the guy panicked because he thinks he'll get either blamed for the death or cited for a DWI? What if *he* strung Myrick up in the barn to cover his ass?"

Silence.

He pressed harder. "Did you find any evidence of drunkenness?"

"People do crazy things, especially old people." The tension in her voice increased.

"Vince—*Anne*, you sound upset. What's the deal here?"

More silence.

He sat forward in his chair. "If Myrick's death isn't a clear-cut suicide, I need to—"

"Heart attacks can happen in stressful situations." Vincent's tone seemed almost pleading. "This is one of those rare cases—"

"Rarer than someone stringing up a dead man to make it look like a suicide?"

"I can't talk anymore," she said and hung up.

~

Clay tapped on the closed door to Flannery's office, heard a muffled "Enter," and walked in. He held Myrick's autopsy report in one hand and wiped the sweat from the palm of his other hand on his pant leg.

Flannery was at his desk. He nodded at the report.

"What's this?" His tone was cheery, for him.

"I'm not quite sure, sir." Clay tossed the paper onto the desk.

Flannery picked up the report and read the cover page. His eyes radiated their usual coldness, and his square jaw and military bearing reinforced that impression. He glared at Clay as if he was deciding whether to fire him.

"Exactly what don't you understand about a simple cause of death?" The cheer in his tone switched to suspicious annoyance.

With armpits already damp, Clay struggled to steady his voice. "Myrick purchased a half-million-dollar life insurance policy last spring to cover a loan he took out against this year's crop. Why would an old man kill himself knowing the insurance was the only way to guarantee his wife wouldn't lose their farm?"

"How did you learn about this life insurance business?"

Clay didn't want to get a friend into hot water, but he also didn't want to lie. "From Matt Lanier. He's a friend of Betty Myrick's."

"Not our problem, Sergeant." Flannery's face tightened. "Let the widow deal with the insurance company. As far as the SCPD is concerned, this case is closed."

"But sir, what about the driver's seat and the peppermint schnapps aroma in his car?"

Flannery paused as if to let his sour expression sink into Clay's visual memory. "If we had unlimited resources, manpower, and time, we'd solve every case and be one hundred percent sure of all the causes of suspicious deaths. Because we don't, and we're ninety-nine-point-nine percent sure Myrick committed suicide, I made a judgment call."

Clay fought the urge to give up and retreat. He tried to steady his nerves with a deep breath. "I'd like permission to investigate further. On my own time, if necessary."

Flannery glanced away for several seconds, then leveled a steely gaze at Clay. "You're worried about the heart attack."

Clay nodded.

"I had the same doubts," Flannery said, "so I talked to Dr. Vincent. She's been the county coroner for decades. She's willing to swear in court that, in her expert opinion, Myrick committed suicide despite the fact he suffered a simultaneous heart attack." He stressed the phrase *expert opinion* as if he was telling an upstart subordinate to stop playing forensic pathologist. He flattened his palms on top of his desk and focused his laser-like stare on his subordinate. "Is there anything else, Sergeant?"

"No, sir." As Clay walked back to his cubicle, Betty Myrick's words echoed between his ears. *Suicide's a sin. Helmer's not a sinner.*

CHAPTER 15

An icy west wind blew across the parking lot of the Rushmore Mall in Rapid City, South Dakota. The sun made a feeble attempt to warm the landscape, but according to a nearby bank sign, the noon temperature was only thirty degrees.

Charlie Witt parked his black Mercedes-Benz SUV in a space near the main entrance, then stepped inside the entry doors and turned to monitor the cars arriving in the lot. When pedestrians approaching the doors saw his massive bulk, shaved head, scars, and perpetual scowl, they veered to the other sets of entrance doors. He smiled. *Intimidation is such a useful tactic.*

Within minutes, a dirty, slightly rusted Lincoln Town Car stopped in front of the mall entrance. When the driver got out, Witt stepped outside and approached him.

"Mr. Witt?" Hibbert said, gawking. "What are you doing here?"

Witt nodded at Hibbert's car. "Get in and drive."

"Where's Smythe?" Hibbert glanced from side to side as if expecting to see Smythe waving cordially at him. "He said he'd be here."

Witt gave him a nasty look as he circled to the passenger side of Hibbert's Lincoln.

As if he understood that Witt wouldn't answer *any* questions, Hibbert got into the driver's seat.

Witt got in and said, "Drive west on Highway 16."

"West? What's out there?"

Witt's glare cowed Hibbert into shutting up and starting the engine.

Minutes later, the Lincoln was on Highway 16 rising steadily into the Black Hills. Each time Hibbert attempted to make small talk, Witt replied by staring straight ahead. He enjoyed keeping this pea-brained loser in the dark about his immediate future.

Hibbert reached into his coat pocket and pulled out a flask. "You mind if I have a sip or two?"

Witt glanced at the flask in Hibbert's trembling hand. A little alcohol would enhance his planned scenario. "Knock yourself out."

Hibbert took two quick gulps and offered the flask to him.

"I don't drink on the job."

Hibbert took several more pulls off the flask as he drove.

When they reached the junction with Highway 16-A, Witt said, "Turn here."

Hibbert complied, and Witt directed him south through the old mining town of Keystone. A short time later, they were driving higher into the Black Hills on a winding mountain road where tourists enjoyed the majestic views. Witt pointed to a turnout a few hundred yards ahead. "Pull over there."

"A scenic overlook?" Hibbert expelled a nervous giggle that sounded like a Woody Woodpecker impression.

Witt didn't care much for Woody Woodpecker either.

Hibbert parked the car. "If you want scenery, Mount Rushmore is a few miles away. I've been there. Got a nice visitor center. We could stay warm while we enjoy the views."

Witt turned off the ignition and removed the keys. *Now for some real fun.* "Get out."

A bewildered expression formed on Hibbert's face.

Witt pulled a .45 caliber Colt 1911 from his jacket pocket and jammed the barrel against Hibbert's forehead. "I said, *get out.*"

Eyes crossed and gaping at the gun barrel, Hibbert fumbled for the door handle, opened the door, and sprang from his seat. "Okay, okay! I'm getting out. What the hell's going on?"

Witt checked the highway in both directions. No cars were approaching. He got out, keeping his pistol pointed at Hibbert as he tossed the keys to him. "Don't want you to lose those now, do we?"

Hibbert crammed them into his coat pocket. His expression was a combination of relief and bewilderment. He pulled out his flask and took another long pull.

Witt walked around the car until he stood next to Hibbert, then holstered his Colt and gestured over the guardrail to the canyon below—a drop of several hundred feet. "Nice view, huh?"

After glancing over the precipice, Hibbert gripped the railing and closed his eyes. Steam rose from his damp forehead. He gulped and shot a sidelong glance at Witt. "Yeah. Nice."

Witt cocked his head to the side and allowed himself a fake smile to further confuse Hibbert. He got off on jerking this stupid asshole around. "How much cash you got? Mr. Smythe says cash solves lots of problems."

"Cash?" Hibbert's eyes darted back and forth. "Um, ah, let's see now . . . I know I've got several hundred, at least." He groped for his wallet, opened it, and pulled out the bills. "Here, take it all. Is that enough?"

"Not even close. I'm just screwing with you."

Witt widened his grin as Hibbert's expression grew more confused.

"I'm gonna use this for some special entertainment tonight," he said as he plucked three Benjamins from Hibbert's sweaty hand and slid the bills into his hip pocket. "I don't charge personal expenses to Mr. Smythe. He's got scruples."

Hibbert gaped at him. "You're robbing me?"

"What do you think, dumb shit?" He tossed the wallet to Hibbert, who nearly fumbled it over the guardrail before securing it in his pocket.

"Hey, if he wants money, I can get plenty more. I've got properties back home I can sell. Worth a half mill, easy." Hibbert glanced back and forth, at Witt, over his shoulder, up and down the highway, like an animal sensing imminent danger. "Can't we call him, set up some sort of payment plan? I'll do whatever he wants."

"Wayne, Wayne, Wayne." Witt shook his head. "Money don't feed the bulldog this time. Mr. Smythe was quite upset that you screwed up. In this business, there ain't no room for error. Those who screw up gotta be punished as a lesson to the rest of us."

"I never had a prospect die on me before." Hibbert's voice rose in pitch and volume. "What was I supposed to do?"

"Boss says it wasn't because Myrick died. It's that you never closed the sale, then made the situation worse by assaulting the guy. We were forced into damage control."

Hibbert's expression sagged along with his shoulders. His eyes glazed over, uncomprehending. "Give me another chance, please. I'll make up for this and then some. I'll double my sales. Work for half the commission. Anything."

Witt almost felt sorry for the poor sap. He shrugged. "Not my call. I'm just following orders."

Hibbert's face glistened with sweat in the subfreezing temperatures. "What orders?"

"Wayne, ol' buddy, here's the deal." Witt forced his voice to stay calm as an erotic surge of bloodlust ran through his body. Damn, he was going to have one hell of a good time with some lucky hooker tonight. He clamped his hands onto Hibbert's shoulders and stared into his nervous, beady eyes.

"You got two choices: jump off this cliff or get thrown off."

CHAPTER 16

Matt returned to the farm after a long day of rehearsals and making calls from his campus office. Over the past few days, he'd been gradually getting his father's estate in order. He requested death certificates and investment statements, inquired about how to file his father's tax return, and called the local lending agencies to ask about possible outstanding loans.

When Matt pulled into the long driveway, Jack sat up in the back seat and yawned. Matt had dropped him off at the veterinarian that morning for his annual round of shots and to have a worrisome lump examined. The lump turned out to be a sebaceous cyst, and the vet removed it using a simple, painless procedure called fine needle aspiration. Matt stopped the car, got out, and opened the back door.

Jack sprang out, quickly did his business, then checked the barn to make sure his little kingdom hadn't been disturbed. After that, he hurried inside to keep his new master company. Over the previous weeks, Matt had learned it was his normal post-car-trip routine.

Once both were inside, Matt gave Jack a few doggie chews. He prepared a peanut-butter-and-jelly sandwich—one of his comfort foods—for himself and poured a glass of pinot noir. Tonight's project was to study his father's conspiracy theory documents again. He intended to poke holes in them to the point of discrediting Ray's speculations so he could refocus on helping Betty Myrick resolve her problem. Expansive conspiracies only happened in world capitals, masterminded by powerful world leaders, not in Minnesota farm country by twitchy real estate agents and shadow organizations. *Didn't they?*

He swallowed a bite of sandwich, took a sip of wine, then carried both to the dining room. After setting his meal on the table, he opened the top drawer of the three-drawer steel filing cabinet. Empty. *Hmm, I don't remember moving anything.*

He opened the middle drawer. Inside were some other files of Ray's, but not his NAFTA/NASHCO research. A sinking feeling spread across his stomach.

He opened the bottom drawer. No NAFTA/NASHCO files. The sinking feeling morphed into panic. He was certain he'd returned all the documents to one of those three drawers.

With his pulse racing and his muscles tensed against an unknown dread, Matt's panic grew enough to spark a surge of adrenaline. Intuition told him a burglar might still be in the house, so he raced to the kitchen and armed himself with the closest weapon he could find—the chef's knife from the knife block.

Jack rose from his cushion next to the wood stove and sauntered to Matt's side, sniffing the air and rotating his ears back and forth. Matt crept upstairs, gripping and regripping the knife, unsure of the proper way to hold it. Jack followed him. Matt checked all the rooms—first to make sure they were empty, then to search for the documents.

In Ray's bedroom, he opened the small safe in the closet to see if the burglar had stolen anything of value. Remembering the combination was easy. It was the two-digit numerical representations of each family member's birth month: Dad's first, then Mom's, Matt's, and Mark's. He rotated the dial back and forth in the proper sequence and opened the door. The contents were untouched. Matt released the breath he'd been holding since entering the bedroom.

Downstairs, still holding the knife in a death grip, he checked the possible places where he might've absent-mindedly put the documents to be sure they were indeed missing. As Matt searched, an animated Jack sniffed the perimeter of each room. The documents were not in any logical locations inside the house.

Matt stepped outside into the late-afternoon hazy sunshine to check the locks on both front and back doors. Neither door showed signs of pry marks or other forced entry. He walked from end to end of the wraparound porch and checked each window. None had been disturbed. Unless another method of entry had been utilized, he concluded he'd either left a door unlocked or a lock had been picked. Hibbert came to mind as a burglary suspect because he'd merited an individual file in Ray's collection, but the information in that file didn't appear to incriminate him in any wrongdoing unless it turned out Saxony Partners was up to something illegal.

If someone *had* killed Matt's father, he might've done so to both stop him from digging further, but also to get the information he'd already compiled. Why not at the same time? Had Ray's killer intended to take the documents right after killing Ray, but was interrupted by an approaching car or visitor? He scrutinized Jack, wishing the dog could tell him what had transpired in the days leading up to his father's death.

Jack gave him a blank, attentive stare.

Matt had told no one about Ray's conspiracy theory and his own research into Hibbert and Saxony Partners. The logical explanation for the burglary was . . . well, there was no logical explanation other than one of the local farmers who knew about Ray's theories had unwittingly mentioned them to the apparent burglar. Queasy, tense, irritable, and now worried about his safety, he called Gebhardt.

"Should've called nine one one first." Gebhardt's dry tone implied impatience as if Matt were seeking preferential treatment because of their childhood friendship. "But I'll come out anyway because we've got three squads at a multi-car accident on the east end of town."

When Gebhardt arrived minutes later, he checked the premises with Matt, then took out his notepad. "What's the value of the stolen items?"

"No monetary value," Matt said. "They're papers. Although, the information may be valuable in solving Myrick and my father's deaths." He explained the core of the research—NAFTA, NASHCO, Ray's suspicions about Hibbert and his work for Saxony Partners—as concisely as possible.

Gebhardt glanced away, scratched his belly, and returned his gaze to Matt. "You want some free advice?"

"About what?"

"Get a grip on yourself. Take a vacation. Recharge. Your imagination has shifted into overdrive. Losing a parent is stressful enough. Don't make your dad's death more complicated. No matter what the truth is about what's going on around here, solving this burglary won't change a damn thing."

"Why not?"

"Unless you can prove those documents exist or find an eyewitness who saw the crime and can identify the suspect, stealing a stack of worthless papers only you know about is a classic your-word-against-the-crook's situation. The county attorney won't file a burglary charge in that case.

"But let's assume we somehow catch the thief and prosecute for Breaking and Entering," Gebhardt continued. "That's a misdemeanor. If the suspect is convicted on the B and E, he'll get a slap on the wrist. That'll get plea bargained down to a love tap unless he has prior convictions. I doubt he'd spend one night in jail. In the end, a bunch of people will have wasted their time and taxpayer money, and you're no closer to solving the deaths of Myrick and your old man."

Matt massaged his aching forehead.

Gebhardt said, "Suppose you're right about this being some sort of big conspiracy. Hibbert's not bright enough to be the ringleader of a flea circus, which means he works for someone. That means your burglar is either Hibbert or some other hired muscle because brainiacs rarely do fieldwork. And no burglar will rat out his boss if there's no upside for him, like getting paid or, hell, staying alive. Unless Hibbert, or whoever stole your papers, confesses and fingers some individual or group of masterminds, the conspirators keep conspiring. Even if you get justice for this theft, you won't be any safer."

Matt's spirits sunk in tandem with the logic of Gebhardt's advice sinking in. "Yeah, yeah, I get it. But if I don't resolve this mess, Betty Myrick loses her farm. I won't leave her hanging. And if this involves my father, I sure as hell want justice for him. Every day my intuition is stronger that he didn't die accidentally. If Dad died because he knew too much or indeed stumbled upon a conspiracy, then all the recent weird occurrences in Straight River make sense."

"Look," Gebhardt said, sounding exasperated, "I'll admit Myrick's death raised some questions, but I can't haul Hibbert down to the LEC and charge him with anything unless I have real, tangible evidence. I want to help the folks in this town too. But I'm not very hopeful. I'll dust for prints, check on other recent break-ins, and treat this like any other crime. Just remember that a significant number of crimes never get solved."

Resigned to the fact that the SCPD required more than some stolen paper and a nagging suspicion to devote some serious manpower to his case, Matt nodded. "Sorry to have wasted your time, but if you find anything—"

"You'll be the first to know," Gebhardt interjected.

CHAPTER 17

"You are fucking kidding me!" Clay's deep, resonant voice echoed off the squad room walls. The expletive went public before he realized how loud he'd spoken. He glanced over his shoulder. No one had noticed. He refocused on the computer screen. *Did I misread the message? No. Is this an April Fool's joke? No.* He massaged his jaw as he studied the bulletin from the Pennington County, South Dakota, sheriff's office confirming Wayne Hibbert's death near Rapid City.

Clay had gone to Hibbert's office several days ago to question him about his confrontations with Myrick at the Eagles Club. Not only was the man absent from his office, he'd also left town without informing his assistant or any family members. Clay had issued a BOLO on Hibbert simply for questioning, not because he suspected him of committing any crime. Now that Hibbert was dead, his connection to Myrick and Ray Lanier required rethinking. Clay had to give credit to Matt for suspecting Hibbert of something underhanded, especially considering Matt's burglary report earlier in the day.

His sense of duty clashed with unease about pressing Flannery for permission to re-examine both deaths. He also fought the urge to bend the rules where Lanier was concerned and inform him of Hibbert's death before the family was notified. But he owed a lot to his childhood friendship with the Lanier brothers. Could he repay some of their kindness with this small gesture? Would it matter if he did?

As kids, the Lanier boys hadn't cared that he was pudgy, shy, and uncoordinated. They accepted him when acceptance was hard to come by at school and at home. They stood up for him when the older kids bullied him. Endless days spent playing backyard sports, riding bikes, swimming in the Straight River, and adventuring with the Lanier brothers had strengthened his body and bolstered his self-confidence.

However, his strongest urge was not to warn Lanier, not to mention this news to Flannery, and not to pursue any sort of investigation of Hibbert. *Don't rock the boat.* His fingers and toes tingled with tension as he fidgeted, spun side to side in his chair, and repeatedly glanced at the bulletin from Rapid City.

He reread the highlights. *Jumped or fell from a scenic overlook. Suitcase full of clothes and toiletries in the trunk. A paper bag containing a plaster-cast miniature of Mt. Rushmore. Credit card receipts in his wallet from a motel, gas station, restaurants, and a souvenir shop.*

Hibbert had apparently taken an impromptu vacation to Rapid City. But in *March*? Nowhere close to prime tourist season. Why would someone who intended to kill himself perpetrate the ruse of making the trip look like a vacation? That raised the odds of his death being accidental. Conversely, Hibbert's abrupt departure and the fact he'd met with Myrick so soon before his death added doubt to the accident theory. Clay grimaced. His head throbbed from the tension of indecision. The accumulating circumstantial evidence felt like wave after wave rocking his boat.

The hour was late. He was tired. His stomach gurgled with hunger, maybe heartburn. He wasn't sure. Flannery wouldn't be in until the following morning, so he had some time. He'd come up with an action plan after a decent night's sleep.

~

When morning roll call was completed the next day, Clay headed for the chief's office but hesitated outside the door. He wiped his damp hands on his trousers and knocked.

"Enter," Flannery said.

Clay walked in. Flannery appeared to be engrossed in paperwork.

"Chief, I've got an FYI for you."

"What is it, Sergeant?"

Clay took a deep breath. "I put out a BOLO on Wayne Hibbert a few days ago and got a hit from the Pennington County sheriff's office in Rapid City, South Dakota. They found him dead at the bottom of a ravine below a scenic turnout in the Black Hills. The two likeliest causes are suicide or accident."

Flannery glanced up from his desk. The muscles around his eyes tensed. "Hibbert, you say?"

"Yes, sir."

"Why did you put out a BOLO?"

"I wanted to talk with him about his last meetings with Myrick. I couldn't reach him by phone, so I checked his house and business. His secretary hadn't heard from him and was worried something might've happened."

Flannery's jaw muscles tightened. He leveled a glare at Clay. "Rapid City?"

"Yes, sir."

"You thought he could enlighten us about Myrick's state of mind?"

"Hibbert's death coming so soon after Myrick's, coupled with Hibbert talking to Myrick on the night of Myrick's death, makes the coincidence too suspicious to ignore." Clay drew himself up to his full height, and discreetly sucked in his gut. "I didn't waste the department's time, and the only resources I used were two minutes of computer time to post the BOLO. *Sir*."

He held Flannery's gaze and braced for the response. The subtle fury in the Chief's face made Clay worry that the man might explode. He was now convinced Flannery knew more than he was letting on.

"I see." Flannery took a deep breath and refocused his attention on the stack of papers on his desk. "That'll be all, Sergeant."

"Yes, sir." Clay pivoted to leave.

"Oh, one more thing," Flannery said, almost too quickly for it to be an afterthought.

Clay did an about-face. "Sir?"

Flannery brusquely said, "I'll take charge of any investigation into Hibbert's death and his possible connection to Mr. Myrick's death. I know the Pennington County Sheriff. I'll work with him to cut through the red tape, get our answers faster."

"Yes, sir." Clay walked out. A tight smile formed on his lips. Suspicion gnawed at his thoughts. There was no sensible reason for a chief of police to take over a death investigation of such minuscule importance, unless Hibbert's death *was* important.

CHAPTER 18

Diane Blake paid little attention when Governor Bob Cameron rose to leave, ending the mind-numbingly long Monday morning staff meeting with a directive to "show a united front to the media" about some issue or another. For most of the meeting, she'd focused a laser-eyed glare on Steven Crossley, who sat across the large conference table. Abandoning her at the Dakota Jazz Club Friday night was the latest in a string of slights and brush-offs. When he noticed the hostility in her expression, he avoided eye contact for the rest of the meeting.

After Cameron dismissed the group, Crossley gathered his belongings and headed for the door, obviously hiding behind other staffers as they filed out.

Diane intercepted him in the hallway. "Thanks ever so much for leaving me at the Dakota," she said in a sharp, barely audible voice.

He stared straight ahead and kept walking. "Hey, I offered to take you home. You chose to stay."

"Friday at midnight? What was so urgent it couldn't wait until morning?"

"I warned you this is a twenty-four seven job. You chose to join the team. Cameron comes first. A social life doesn't even make the top ten."

"How romantic."

"Besides, hadn't you heard enough of the French babe? I got my fill of her music within twenty minutes."

"Gee, what a surprise." She exaggerated her sarcasm, then waited until they'd crossed the threshold to his office and he'd closed the door. "I wondered why your hands were all over me the entire second set."

"Hey, just because her singing didn't turn me on doesn't mean her body didn't." His breath smelled of coffee and cigarettes. He gave her a suggestive leer and slid his hands around her waist, then thrust his pelvis against hers. "We could've had a smokin' three-way."

She shoved him away and crossed her arms.

He extended his palms out and up. "What? It's a *fantasy*. Don't be so fucking serious all the time."

"Steven . . ."

"Yeah?" The lust in his voice and the fire in his eyes meant he was ready to toss her onto his desk and screw her like a ten-dollar whore.

"Forget it." She moved toward the door. *Men are pigs. Why did I think he was different?*

"Okay." He shrugged. "Is there anything work-related you wanted to discuss?"

She stopped, remembering she'd entered his office for a specific reason. "Sorry. You didn't exactly give me a chance to ask when you were drooling all over me."

His lip twitched as he struggled to subdue a scowl. He raised his hands in surrender, sighed, and relaxed his face into a vacuous smile. "What can I do for you?"

"Ever heard of Saxony Partners, LLC?"

The muscles around his eyes tensed briefly. "Why do you ask?"

Given his non-answer, she knew he'd heard of them but wouldn't admit it. "A friend asked me for Saxony's contact information. I only asked because you've been dealing with real estate companies working on that downtown revitalization project."

"Who's the friend?"

"A friend." She would've preferred to say, "None of your damn business."

"Real estate?" He rubbed his chin with his hand. "Hmm, I might've seen their name on a list of companies who submitted bids to get into that program."

"Can I see that list? Then I won't have to waste time searching. My friend says they might be an umbrella corporation for lots of small companies."

"The list? It's been months since I've been in on any discussions. Try the EDO."

She sagged in frustration. Economic Development Office personnel were notorious for stonewalling anyone who asked too many questions. They behaved as if they possessed top-secret information and one needed clearance to obtain it. Steven had performed a classic buck pass, which meant he wasn't eager for her to investigate Saxony Partners. Again, why?

"I see," she said, drawing out the last word, letting it drip with suspicion. "Thanks for the classic bureaucrat's response."

She spun and stormed out as Steven repeated, "Who's the friend?"

Back in her office, Diane speed-read some documents as she dug into the salad and mini-baguette her ever-efficient assistant, Leah Peterson, had brought her for lunch. Finished with one memo, she saw a sticky note at the top of the pile with *ML* scrawled on it, her cryptic reminder to check on Saxony Partners for Matt. A political truism was to do everything in secret until it no longer benefitted from secrecy. She had no idea where this search might lead since it involved a corporation and shady dealings, so she'd decided discretion was best.

Her thoughts drifted back to Friday night at the Dakota. She'd been surprised to run into Matt, having been careful since their divorce to avoid his usual music venues and prevent any awkward meetings. More surprising were her rekindled emotions when she realized he was the one plunking away at his bass on stage. That's how she'd fallen for him back in college—watching him perform. Matt always poured his heart and soul into his playing, immersing himself in the experience. There was a natural elegance to the way he held his instrument, how his fingers caressed the strings, his expression when he closed his eyes while playing. Pure passion for the music. She'd sensed he would be passionate in other ways, and she'd been right. A shudder of sexual excitement ran down her spine when she recalled their first night together. They made slow, sensuous love for hours in his small off-campus apartment, with mellow jazz playing on the stereo and a cool summer breeze caressing their sweaty bodies. *Quit daydreaming and get back to work.*

She checked her schedule, which showed nothing until 1:00. She could at least get started on this favor for Matt. On the public State of Minnesota website, all she discovered was Saxony Partners had incorporated within the past year, and the principals were two local lawyers she knew only by name.

Next came the State's internal website and database. She checked her watch while waiting for the search results to download. *I'm late again.* As she stood to leave, the screen flashed to life. She scanned the information. A name jumped out at her. *Leland Smythe.* She slumped back in her chair and exhaled slowly while staring at the ceiling. *What on Earth is Jazzman getting into?*

The buzzing intercom startled her. "Yes?"

"They're waiting for you in conference room C," Leah said.

"Tell them I'm on my way."

"Already did."

"Thanks. You get another brownie point." Diane clicked her computer into sleep mode, grabbed her briefcase and purse, and hurried out of her office.

CHAPTER 19

When news of Hibbert's death hit the *Straight River Press*, Matt read the brief "Word Received" entry on the obituary page twice to make sure it was *the* Wayne Hibbert. Since no details were included, he called Gebhardt at the LEC.

"What the hell happened, Clay?" Matt was barely able to contain his agitation. "Hibbert might've had information about both my dad's and Helmer's deaths, and now *he's* dead? What about that *doesn't* smell fishy?"

"I'm not at liberty to give any details until Flannery says okay."

"The Chief? Why does *he* care?"

"He's taken a greater interest in the Myrick case. Not sure why, but I think he wants to filter information before it goes public."

"A cover-up?"

"I didn't say that."

"What's there to hide? Can you at least tell me how he died?"

"No."

"A hint?"

"Well . . . if you guessed and were wrong, I could tell you that."

"Like twenty questions?"

"Yeah."

"Fair enough. Accident or suicide?"

"Why did you guess those two causes?"

"Simple," Matt said. "Statistically speaking, diseases kill the majority of people in this country. Hibbert appeared to be in reasonable health when I saw him last week, although his ruddy complexion implied a drinking problem. After disease, the next two most common ways to die are suicide and all sorts of accidents."

"Son of a—"

"Which was it, accident or suicide?"

Another uncomfortable silence ensued.

The light clicked on for Matt. "Ambiguous, like Helmer and my father's deaths."

"Damn. You always were the smartest one in school."

"Details, Clay. Give me the details."

"That's all you get. I shouldn't have bent the rules that far."

Matt kept forgetting Gebhardt's job was strictly defined and loaded with chain of command, orders, directives, discipline, rules, and regulations. Distinctly different from a musician's life—freewheeling, improvisational, and much more democratic—except for the occasional tyrannical guest conductor with the Minnesota Orchestra.

"You're right. Thanks for this at least."

"I will admit this has gotten me more concerned about Myrick's death," Gebhardt said. "Your dad's death still seems cut and dried. But I can't investigate further without Flannery's okay. I let you push me a little bit, but Flannery doesn't tolerate civilians poking around in police business. So we never had this conversation. And please don't go snooping around anymore."

"Snooping? Hell, I'm simply a concerned citizen," Matt said. "I've got a right to ask questions and dig for information."

"Leave the police work to—"

Matt hung up, frustrated but mindful of Gebhardt's job restrictions. Hibbert's death meant one less source of answers for Betty. One less connection to his father's death. Impatient because he felt like he'd been spinning his wheels so far, he called Diane.

"I couldn't wait," he said when she answered her cell phone. "Did you find a name to connect with Saxony Partners?"

"I did, but you might not like what I found."

"After all the crap that's happened, any information is welcome." Matt heard the unfamiliar ring of hope in his own voice. "Plus, I've got some news that'll make this interesting. Why the warning?"

"This guy plays in the big leagues. Money, power, influence, he has it all. For starters, he's on a first-name basis with Governor Cameron." She sounded winded, as if she'd been jogging.

"Are you okay? You're breathing hard."

"I'm fine. Just walking fast between meetings. Short on time."

"I understand. What's this big shot's name?"

"Leland Smythe."

"Never heard of him."

"He's Minnesota's version of Donald Trump without the hair or celebrity. Worth millions and extremely secretive. What's your news?"

"Remember the guy I told you about at the Dakota? Hibbert?"

"The realtor?"

"He's dead."

"Oh my God. What happened?"

He related what he'd pried out of Gebhardt, then said, "Don't tell anyone until after the obituary is published in tomorrow's paper."

"This is *not* good," she said. "Really not good."

"Why?"

"If Hibbert worked for Smythe, his death might not be a coincidence."

"You think Smythe killed him?"

"Or had him killed. He can afford to hire anyone to do anything. Unless we can prove Hibbert's death wasn't a suicide or accident, we can't even suspect Smythe, let alone accuse him of anything."

"Okay," Matt agreed. "Let's change course here. Is it logical for a real estate mogul of Smythe's stature to buy a bunch of farmland adjacent to the highway?"

"No. Most of his holdings are commercial property, shopping malls, and luxury condominiums in the Twin Cities. At least as far as I know from a legal perspective. He's tried to soak the state for every cent he can get in tax breaks and special considerations. So far, he's stayed on the proper side of the law, but he pushes the envelope."

Matt digested that information, then said, "Any other theories?"

"Nothing leaps to mind, but I'll think about it later. I'm three hours behind on my day, which means I'm now a week and three hours behind on my work. I've got an endless list of projects to do, and all of them needed to be done yesterday."

"Sorry I wasted your time. I forgot your job is so high-pressure."

"It's okay. I just feel overwhelmed sometimes. I have a meeting in my office in a few minutes. Got a pen and paper? I'll give you the phone number and address for Smythe's company."

Matt scrounged up a pencil and notepad. "Go ahead."

She gave him the information. "Please remember that men with his power and money usually get what they want. I don't want you to lose your farm, or worse, because you got in over your head. Whatever he's up to, be careful."

"I will." He softened his tone. "I'm grateful for your help."

"You're welcome."

After an awkward moment, he said, "I just realized this is the second mostly civil conversation we've had in the past week. You weren't condescending at all."

"Hmmm, I must be slipping. I'll take some extra bitches brew before bedtime."

He laughed. She'd reminded him of one of his favorite jazz fusion albums, Miles Davis's *Bitches Brew*. "Oh good, I'm glad it was temporary. I have enough to worry about without you turning all nice on me."

"Goodbye, Matt."

"Goodbye, Diane."

Thirty seconds later, she called back. "Someone's been snooping in my office." She sounded distraught. "I noticed that a notepad and pen on my desk had been moved. Whoever it was might've noticed I was researching Smythe on my computer."

"So what?" he asked. "You folks research all sorts of people and businesses, don't you?"

"Of course, but I didn't want anyone to know what I was doing. Unfortunately, I forgot to log off and left my computer screen on a page with Smythe's information. It's against policy not to log off when you leave. My assistant had a doctor's appointment this afternoon, so it's possible someone came in here while I was gone. They might've seen that page."

"Don't computers have passwords you have to type in before you can access them?"

"Yes, and I don't *think* anyone knows mine, but—"

"So there's little chance you were hacked."

"But it's still possible."

The way she trailed off, along with the doubt he heard—like a singer's voice cracking on a long note—concerned him. "What's wrong?"

"Probably nothing, but Steven might have my password."

"Crossley? Your boyfriend?"

"I change my password every few weeks like we're required to do. They're supposed to be complicated, so I write each one on a piece of paper and keep it in my purse in case I forget. He might've inadvertently seen it or snooped at my place when I was in another room."

"Is that a problem?"

"He knows Smythe pretty well."

"How well?"

"Well enough for you to be extra careful now. Steven's charming and talented, but he's also an ambitious pit bull and a power player in state and regional politics."

"Duly noted, but I can't get into trouble for poking around, can I?"

"You can if you ask the wrong people or dig in the wrong places."

The conversation had somehow morphed into cloak-and-dagger stuff. Secrets and intrigue. Still, whenever politicians and wealthy men were involved, anything was possible.

"Okay," he said, "I'll watch my ass. Let me know if Crossley starts acting weird around you. I got a bad vibe from him at the Dakota."

Matt said goodbye and hung up. Despite Diane's warnings and genuine concern, he wasn't about to stop digging for answers. Over the past few days, he'd left repeated messages on voicemail to Saxony Partners but had received no call backs. So he decided to phone Smythe at his Smythe Properties number. To his chagrin, he was firmly but politely rebuffed by Smythe's assistant; a woman with a cold, dry tone. Matt flopped onto the living room couch, frustrated by his lack of progress. The time for passivity and patience had ended.

CHAPTER 20

A pre-sunrise glow backlit the distant Minneapolis skyline the next day as Matt walked into the lobby of the west-suburban skyscraper that housed Smythe Properties. He hoped Smythe, like many high achievers, would arrive early and without a secretary or staff to insulate him from anyone without an appointment.

Matt located the proper floor number on the building directory and punched the elevator button. He checked his appearance in the mirrored door. The suit and tie were so other employees would assume he was there on business and not question his presence. After a quick elevator ride, he entered the reception area of Smythe Properties. *No one in sight. So far, so good.*

He walked purposefully around the perimeter of the large, cubicle-filled floor, until he reached a corner of the building and came to a plate-glass door. The nameplate next to it read *Leland Smythe.* Unfortunately, a woman occupied the desk in the outer office. Probably the ice queen who'd stonewalled him over the phone. She'd be hard to get through if he told her his real purpose, so Matt opted for improvisation mode as he walked through the door.

"Good morning," he said in a confident, business-like tone. "I'm Mr. Smythe's eight o'clock. Early, I know, but I've got a plane to catch and wanted to meet with him ASAP."

The woman scrutinized Matt as if trying to remember if she'd seen him before, then consulted her computer screen, presumably to check Smythe's online calendar.

"Ah yes, Mr. Hager." She looked up and smiled curtly. "Mr. Smythe is finishing up a regular breakfast meeting with his staff. He usually gets back before eight. Please take a seat."

Matt quietly exhaled the breath he'd been holding since he'd spoken. *Score one for improv.* "Thank you."

The success of his impersonation had depended on five presumptions: One, Smythe *had* an eight o'clock appointment. Two, the appointment was with a man. Three, his assistant wouldn't ask for Matt's name before matching it with the appointment time. Four, she wouldn't recognize the man from a previous visit. And five, the name wasn't a name common to a different racial group such as African, East Asian, or Indian. He was relieved and shocked that he'd been five-times lucky.

He sat in a leather chair in the waiting area, picked up a magazine, and paged through it. For the first time ever, he wished he owned a cell phone so he could pretend to check emails or make a call, the way a modern businessman would work between appointments.

Five minutes later, a middle-aged, medium-sized man with steel-gray eyes and a square jaw strode into the room, ramrod straight, minimal paunch. He wore a gray power suit, white shirt, red tie, and polished black shoes. Two points of a red handkerchief poked above the breast pocket. If the jacket had been adorned with epaulets and insignia, the man could've passed for a military officer. Matt instinctively knew this was Leland Smythe.

The man gave him a cursory glance and then turned to his assistant. "Good morning, Mary."

"Good morning, Mr. Smythe."

Without looking around, Smythe half nodded toward Matt. "Who is this?"

Matt's face flushed hotly. Time for chorus number two of his improvisation. He shrugged apologetically toward Mary.

She glared at him, tight-lipped.

Smythe turned to face him.

Matt stood and introduced himself. "I apologize for the deception. I called you here and through Saxony Partners several times yesterday with no luck. I'm desperate for some information, and I hoped you could spare a few minutes."

Smythe studied him with sharp, alert eyes, then tightened his lips into a hint of a smile. "What sort of information?"

From a musical perspective, Smythe's tenor voice reminded Matt of a lifeless saxophone: reedy, metallic, passionless, mechanical. Its prominent features were cold-hearted restraint and calculation. All business.

Matt's flimsy new improvisation switched to talk fast and ask all his questions before Smythe ejected him from the office. "I need to ask you about Saxony Partners and one of your realtors, Wayne Hibbert."

He recited a capsulized version of what had gone on in Straight River since his father's death, Betty's plea for help with her husband's life insurance policy, and Hibbert's possible involvement in both cases and his subsequent suspicious death.

Smythe listened with a bemused expression.

Matt finished with, "I'm hoping you can provide the answers I couldn't get from Hibbert about what's going on in Straight County."

Smythe's expression iced over. "I'm sorry. I have no idea what you're talking about. I'm quite busy, and the *real* Mr. Hager will arrive momentarily. Good day."

The terse brush off stung Matt like a slap across the face. He tensed, trying to come up with a question or statement that would force the man to reconsider. *All business. No emotions.* In desperation he said, "I also have a ton of questions about NASHCO, the North American Super Highway Coalition."

Smythe's eyes widened briefly, then narrowed and darkened. The hint of a smile faded to a tight-lipped stare. He stiffened and gestured over his shoulder to a doorway. "Step into my conference room."

They entered, Matt first, and Smythe closed the door behind them. Matt sat in one of the six chairs at the large conference table and swiveled to face his host, eager to finally get some answers. Smythe remained standing and folded his arms across his chest.

"You're operating under some serious misconceptions, Mr. Lanier. The realtors I hire through Saxony Partners are independent contractors. I neither know, nor do I care, about their personal lives. If you believe your father and your friend died suspiciously, take it up with the police. I do not build any sort of highways, so I know nothing about NASHCO. For you to barge into my office, impersonate one of my business colleagues, and then brazenly demand answers to your accusatory questions raises concerns about your mental state. Implying I am somehow involved in this supposed crime spree borders on slander."

Matt withstood the verbal barrage with a stony face but boiled inside with anger and frustration. He assumed Smythe was trying to sound offended yet sincere, but he couldn't help thinking his categorical denial was the vocal equivalent of a poker face. After letting Smythe stare him down for a moment, Matt said, "You sound rather defensive for someone who claims ignorance *and* innocence."

"Ignorance? Be realistic, please. I utilize hundreds of temporary contractors. Dozens of full-time, highly trained employees work for me on myriad projects. CEOs delegate, then we trust our people to do their jobs. My only goal is for everyone to perform their job well enough for Smythe Properties to realize a profit. I don't become personally or emotionally involved with any business associates. I don't even host company picnics or holiday parties."

Smythe hadn't moved other than to lower his head and narrow his eyes as if he were focusing a laser beam on the center of Matt's forehead. Matt held his stare, searching for a crack in the man's façade of calm superiority.

"Profit motives tend to overshadow legal and ethical behavior," Matt said. "Hibbert had a lot to gain in commissions. If Saxony Partners is buying numerous farms in Straight County, you obviously believe in the profit potential of either developing the land or reselling those farms."

"Mr. Lanier, you try my patience with your prattling and repeated slanderous suggestions. Unless you have a business and real estate management background, I'm afraid you're out of your element. I can't help you because I have no answers for you." Smythe glanced at his watch. "Now if you'll excuse me, I have an appointment."

The calm intensity of Smythe's denials triggered an alarm with Matt. It also drove home the point that he was at a disadvantage. All his suspicions were merely that—essentially baseless. If Smythe refused to offer answers, Matt doubted he could say anything to force them from the man. Unless . . . He tried one final gambit.

"I guess I can find a sympathetic newspaper reporter looking for a scandalous story about Minnesota farmers getting trampled by a millionaire real estate mogul. The public loves reading that stuff. Maybe that will jog your memory."

Smythe opened the door. "Mary, please call security."

Matt smiled at this weak attempt to get rid of him. Some feeble old retiree who worked a cushy part-time security job in a swanky office building wouldn't be able to force him to leave before he pressed Smythe for some answers.

Smythe remained stoic until his attention was diverted to Mary's voice saying, "He's in the conference room."

One of the largest humans Matt had seen outside of a professional football game filled the doorway. The man stood a full six feet six inches tall and displayed the physique of an NFL defensive tackle. He wore all black—shoes, pants, blazer, T-shirt. The dark clothes offset the permanent scowl and his shiny bald head, which sat on a neck barely discernable under the muscles sloping upward from his shoulders.

Panic clutched Matt's throat so tightly he had trouble swallowing. He assessed the situation and concluded that the logical option was flight. Putting up any sort of resistance against this behemoth might result in a trip to jail or the hospital.

"Is there a problem, Mr. Smythe?" The goon's voice was the aural embodiment of the man's physical stature: deep, powerful, menacing.

"Only if this man is still inside this building in thirty seconds," Smythe said. He strode into his office and closed the door.

Improv had lost out to advanced planning and preparation. Matt had no riffs to soothe this savage beast. He raised his hands in mock surrender and left, feeling the goon's piercing stare on the back of his head as he walked Matt to the building entrance.

As Matt crossed the parking lot to his car, his breath caught in his throat. A black Mercedes-Benz SUV occupied a space in the front row of spaces reserved for employees of Smythe Properties. He desperately wanted to wait for the owner to come out, but he had his own job to do and couldn't wait until the end of the workday to see if the owner might be Smythe. He did, however, write down the license plate number in case he ever got a close look at an SUV lurking around the farm in the future. It was a longshot, but deep down, he thought the information might come in handy someday. He noticed that the letters in the plate were three of the open strings of the bass: *G*, *A*, and *D*. Easy to remember. The numbers were easy to remember too: *388*, which happened to correspond to Rod Carew's batting average in the 1977 baseball season when he made his historic attempt to finish the season with a .400 batting average. Any serious Twins fan had that number etched into their memories.

~

Back at the University of Minnesota campus later that morning, Matt listlessly sat through lessons with two of his double bass students. He made few comments or critiques, content to have them run through their jury pieces in a dress-rehearsal atmosphere. That way he could contemplate his next move regarding Saxony Partners during long stretches of music playing.

As soon as his second lesson was finished, Matt hustled over to the University's Wilson Library. He queried the reference librarian about researching NAFTA and looking up information on business moguls. The librarian described the various search engines and told him to use his faculty ID number and password to access the computers.

He frowned. "What's available in hard copy?"

The librarian raised her eyebrows and directed him to periodicals and reference books she thought might be useful.

After paging through magazines for a few minutes, he realized that method of research might take days. Possibly weeks. Too slow. The time had come to join the computer revolution. But how to begin? Possessing near-zero computer experience, he expected to encounter a steep learning curve. He gazed at the bank of computer terminals and the people seated at them. Most appeared to be college students—the generation of children born into the Internet Age and computer literate before they could read. The people for whom an online search was as second nature as playing bass was to Matt.

He walked past the long rows of terminals, scanned the faces, noticed typing speeds, and gauged demeanors, hoping for some clue as to each individual's competence. The process was similar to sizing up new musicians who were auditioning for either his jazz group or one of his classical lesson slots. He'd found he could discern a great deal about any musician's character by their general demeanor, the way they handled their instruments, the air of confidence they exuded or failed to exude.

One student caught his eye as he turned the corner on the back-to-back terminal table. A bespectacled student stared at him from the far end of the tables. Scraggly, long black hair topped an oval face with light-brown skin, offset by brown eyes and a day's worth of whiskers. He wore a hooded sweatshirt and baggy jeans. He looked like a slacker frat boy who'd slept in his clothes after an all-night party and was now at the library cramming for an exam. The tell was that his fingers were poised and fluid at the computer keyboard, similar to how skilled pianists worked their magic on music keyboards. Matt noticed how fast the kid had been typing compared to several of the other computer operators. His eyes exuded intelligence, and his body radiated an aura of relaxed confidence.

The kid looked away as Matt approached, then glanced up again as if he knew Matt wanted to talk to him. Matt circled to the end of the tables so he could speak with the student face-to-face and as privately as possible. Crouching, he made eye contact. The kid's expression was placid.

"Hi," Matt said, unsure how to proceed.

"Something wrong?" the student said.

"I have a slight problem. I need some information, but I'm pressed for time and have limited computer skills. You're the best person in this room to help me, if you're willing."

"Me?" The kid snorted and cracked a wry smile. "Why do you say that?"

His voice was monotonic with a hint of a Spanish accent; reminiscent of a bass clarinet played in its middle register—reedy but full and rich.

"Intuition," Matt said. "I need someone who's better than great with a computer. You look like a natural."

"Not sure about a natural, but I've been doing this for about ten years," the kid said.

"Seriously? Are you as good as I think you are?" He peered into the student's eyes for some sort of indication. He wanted an expert, but he didn't want a prima donna or an egotist who only talked a good game.

"Probably. I'm majoring in Computer Science *and* Computer Engineering." He spoke calmly, without boasting.

"*Quelle surprise,*" Matt deadpanned. As a technology neophyte, he was certainly impressed by that statement.

Any computer major was close enough, but a double major made this college student a home run. Now it was time for the pitch that could qualify him as a grand slam. Matt glanced around to make sure no one was within earshot, then leaned toward the student and whispered, "Do you know anything about hacking?"

Caution sparked in the young man's eyes. "Who wants to know?"

"Just me."

"Who the hell are you?" His monotone didn't waver.

"Oh, sorry. Matt Lanier." He extended his right hand.

The student ignored Matt's hand. "No. I mean who *are* you?"

Huh? Matt managed to form a quizzical expression.

"Like, are you an undercover cop? A crook? The most naïve dude I ever met?"

Matt bristled at the veiled insult but forced calm into his tone. "I teach here, but I'm not representing the University in any way."

The student considered the explanation while he appraised Matt's appearance and demeanor. Then he extended his right hand. "Zach Perez."

They shook hands.

"Why you wanna know about hacking?"

"Because I'm stumped. The guy I'm looking for is very secretive. He might've committed a crime that affects my friends and me. I'm trying to find out what happened."

"He a crook?"

"I don't know. He's got a ton of money, and people are dead from suspicious causes, including my father."

Zach started. "Oh, sorry to hear that."

"He also tried to buy my father's farm and wants to get his hands on my neighbor's farm."

"What's wrong with that?"

"It's complicated. Things are going on that might be unethical or illegal. But I don't have any evidence a crime was committed."

"That sucks."

"Yeah, well. I may be delusional too. This whole mess is driving me crazy because I'm trying to help my old neighbor keep her farm and avoid bankruptcy."

Zach searched Matt's face as if he was trying to gauge his honesty and sincerity. "I dunno, man."

Matt frowned. "Look, I've got to get to rehearsal with my trio. I've been straight with you. Can you help me or not?"

Zach glanced around the library and shifted in his chair.

"I'll pay," Matt said.

Zach widened his eyes for an instant but narrowed them just as quickly. "How much?"

"Whatever's reasonable. I need to see what kind of information a hacker can dig up."

Alternating between glances at Matt and the nearby patrons, Zach said, "I *might* know a guy who knows a guy."

Matt was reluctant to involve a second person, but desperation overruled reluctance. "Good enough. How soon?"

"Tell you what." Zach held Matt's gaze. "You know the Java Joint over on Riverside?"

"Yes."

"Meet me there tomorrow at noon."

"Thanks."

"Not so fast. If your story doesn't check out, we won't show."

Matt opened his mouth to protest, then hesitated. Zach and his hacker friend would be taking a considerable risk for a stranger. "Understood."

CHAPTER 21

A few minutes before noon the next day, Matt arrived at the Java Joint, an off-campus coffee shop on the West Bank of the Mississippi River that featured the lowest latte and cappuccino prices in the area. The place catered to hip, college-aged caffeine addicts, so a loud stream of urban-contemporary-techno-hip-hop-computerized noise assailed his ears when he walked in. He sighed, and for the thousandth time bemoaned the fate of pop music since the advent of the music video. The aroma of fresh coffee, laced with hints of industrial-strength cleaning products, filled the spacious room.

Matt didn't see Zach Perez among the clientele, so he ordered a skinny latte from a barista with an ostentatious display of tattoos and body piercings and a shock of fluorescent purple hair. The Java Joint clientele was internationally diverse, and he heard bits of conversations in Spanish, Somali, and Chinese, as well as English. He hummed "Java Jive" and tapped its rhythmic accompaniment on his thighs while he resisted gawking at the most exotic-looking customers. The neighborhood—Cedar-Riverside, named for the major intersection in the area—was an eclectic old assortment of small businesses, classroom buildings for the University of Minnesota's West Bank campus and nearby Augsburg College, and inexpensive housing for students, recent immigrants, and low-income individuals and families.

Before Matt could sit down with his coffee, Zach walked in and came over. He wore the same hooded sweatshirt and baggy jeans he'd worn the day before.

Matt glanced over Zach's shoulder. "Where's the guy-who-knows-a-guy-who-knows-you?"

"Follow me." Zach walked outside into the early April mist and around the corner to a rickety old building whose back wall stood adjacent to the Java Joint. He opened the dented aluminum storm door and led Matt up a creaky flight of stairs to a metal door. Zach unlocked two locks, stepped into the room, and motioned him inside. "I got lucky. Found an apartment with a steel door. I installed the extra deadbolt to protect my computers. The original lock is crap."

The stale smell and shabby décor reminded Matt of the rooming house he'd lived in for a time during college. Arranged against two walls were computer towers, monitors, laptops, printers, electronic equipment, and tools stacked on two long, narrow tables, several shelves, and one large desk. Cords and cables dangled under the tables like thick black spaghetti interspersed with a few strands of red, yellow, white, and blue. Crammed into one corner stood an unmade twin bed and a dresser. Another doorway led to a tiny bathroom. Clear insulating plastic covered the two double-hung windows. In front of one of the windows stood a mini-refrigerator with a microwave perched on top.

"Nice place," Matt said, trying not to sound sarcastic.

"It's all I need. Have a seat." Zach rolled a threadbare office chair across the hardwood floor. He flopped into a second, more comfortable-looking office chair and leaned back.

"I rented a place like this when I was a student here," Matt said as he sat. "Over on University Avenue. Except I filled my floor space with instruments, sheet music, albums, and stereo equipment."

Zach nodded. "It's cheap, close to school, and I can get Java Joint's Wi-Fi for free. I do most of my school work at the computer labs in the department, my social stuff at the library, and the fun stuff here."

Matt's stomach growled with nervousness. He was about to break the law with the help of an innocent college student. "When does our hacker show up?"

Zach thrust a thumb at his chest.

Matt leaned back and raised his eyebrows. "You?"

The corners of Zach's lips curled upward. "Yeah."

"Why didn't you tell me yesterday?"

"Figured you might be a cop. I googled you. You're harmless."

A small flash of panic rushed through Matt. "Really?" One reason he'd avoided computers was to protect his anonymity from prying strangers. "How did you find any information on me? The last time I used a computer was in college when the Internet was just getting noticed. Hell, AOL wasn't even a household name back then."

Zach snorted. "Man, you're kind of dumb for a professor. Everyone's online these days. You're listed in the credits of a couple of music CDs and in an online catalog with photos of the Music School's faculty. I didn't find any other Matt Laniers out there who resemble you unless you're actually a professional rugby player from Australia."

"Nope. I'm just the bass-playing professor." He was relieved to learn Zach had found nothing incriminating about him, such as his juvenile arrest record. "Have you been hacking for long?"

"Long enough, but I don't do it often. Once you get the basics, it's a matter of adjusting to whatever website you're trying to hack. You'd be amazed at how outdated the security is on most sites. A lot still use twenty-year-old technology. Governments are the worst."

"You've hacked government sites?"

"The city website once, to see if I could erase a couple of parking tickets from my record."

"And?"

"Took about thirty minutes. So, what do you want me to hack?"

"The state of Minnesota's internal website." Matt expected a shocked reaction, but Zach's eyes were emotionless voids.

Zach scrunched his face. "Never tried, but I don't expect the firewall to be much stronger than the one on the city's website."

"My ex-wife works for the Attorney General. She made an offhand comment about finding Smythe's name on their private site. If we dig there, we might get something on him."

"Why don't you ask *her* to find more info on this guy?"

"I said *ex*. Our divorce wasn't amicable. I was lucky to get this favor."

"Oh, right." Zach turned to the keyboard in the middle of his impressive collection of electronic toys and began typing and clicking.

Matt stood and hovered over him, watching the screen change every few seconds. He soon got bored and walked around the room. When he noticed threatening clouds outside, he whistled "Stormy Weather." Moments later, Zach clicked on a radio to a Spanish music station and turned up the volume enough to end Matt's performance.

One hour later, Zach cracked the website security. An hour after that, all he'd found was the same data Diane had found on Smythe. Jumping off from that point, they discovered nothing that linked him to the North American Super Highway.

"For a millionaire, this dude hides pretty well," Zach said. "I can't even find a private phone number."

"What if we're looking at the wrong end of things?" Matt said. "If he's buying in one area, maybe he's buying in other areas too. Expanding his empire into other counties."

Matt jotted down the southern Minnesota counties fronting I-35. "Start with this list." He gave it to Zach, then pulled two maps from his jacket pocket. "I'll check the paper maps I brought for the Iowa and Missouri counties that I-35 runs through."

Zach's knee bounced up and down. "I guess."

He hesitated and looked as if he might say more.

"What's wrong?" Matt asked.

"This might take hours, if not days, and we haven't discussed money."

"Oh, right. I have no idea what's fair and reasonable."

"I monitor one of the computer labs for the other electro-geeks in school. I get quiet study time and the use of the lab's computers if there's an open slot. Not bad for ten bucks an hour."

"I'll double that," Matt said, hoping to reach a quick bargain.

"Deal."

"Can you keep working now?"

"For twenty an hour, I'll work all night, but I don't want to rob you blind." He pointed to a laptop computer. "Why don't you help?

You'll save some money, and you might get more comfortable with computer research."

"Good idea." Matt pulled five twenties from his wallet and handed them to Zach. "Here's one hundred for today so far, to show I'm good for the rest."

The kid snatched the bills and jammed them into his pocket. "Let's rock 'n' roll." He pushed over to his keyboard. "Tell me again what you're looking for."

"Find corporations that recently bought, or currently own, land abutting I-35. Keep an eye out for the name Saxony Partners no matter where the property is located. Print out any data that meets those criteria—names, phone numbers, addresses, et cetera. We want to see if there is any sort of pattern of buying along the interstate that indicates a large-scale acquisition by one entity."

"Large-scale as in the North American Super Highway?"

"Yep."

Zach nodded. "Okay."

"If you see the name Leland Smythe anywhere, holler."

Zach taught Matt how to navigate search windows and websites, often pausing to guide him back on track. A five-year-old probably still had him beat, but Matt gradually caught on to the basics.

After they'd worked in silence for a while, Zach leaned back in his chair and pumped his fist. "Found something."

"What?" Matt hadn't expected to find anything of substance, but the prospect of a breakthrough recharged his waning hopes.

"Two purchases by Saxony Partners in Straight County. Two in Rice County. Each adjacent to the interstate. Each lists Wayne Hibbert as the authorized buyer for Saxony."

Matt's pulse raced, and he let out a low whistle. Were they actually on to some sort of scheme?

"Wow, dude." Zach pushed his eyeglasses up the bridge of his nose. "I thought this was gonna be a waste of my time and your money. Who's Wayne Hibbert?"

"Oh, sorry. He was a realtor who worked for Smythe. He was trying to buy my dad's farm and my neighbor's farm."

Zach's eyebrows arched. "Was?"

"Yeah, Hibbert died a few days ago."

"Whoa. He died too? You sure you wanna be messin' with this shit?"

"No, but I'll keep digging. What concerns me most is the cops saying my father's death was accidental when he may have been murdered. If so, I damn well want justice for him. I can't walk away until I know the truth. Blame it on the German stubbornness I inherited from my mother."

"Okay." Zach shrugged and turned back to his desk. His fingers danced across his keyboard, and he finished up with some fifteen counties in two states before Matt had slogged through four. They took a bathroom break, and Matt bought coffee and muffins for them from the Java Joint before they sat down to compare findings.

As he scanned Zach's data, Matt noticed most of the counties showed one or two corporate buyers who owned more than one property adjacent to the interstate, but none were Saxony Partners. His spirits sagged as he considered that his quest had reached a dead end. "This doesn't look promising. You got any ideas?"

"Dude, if there's some sorta scheme, you gotta dig deeper. Look for some clues, connections, whatever. Let me see those lists."

Matt handed both sets of data to Zach. "Okay, Sherlock, tell me what you see."

Zach examined the lists. After a few minutes, he frowned. "Damn, I got nothing."

"Let's try a different approach," Matt said. "Read them out loud. Start with the companies in the Minnesota counties. Then Iowa and Missouri."

"What good's that gonna do?"

"I'm a musician. My best sense is hearing. Maybe I'll *hear* a clue."

Zach began reciting the company names.

Matt leaned back in his chair and stared at the water stains on the grimy ceiling. After hearing several names, he held up his hand. "Stop. They're cluttering my ears with noise. Reread them without the Corps, Incs, Partners, or LLCs."

Zach started again. "Flint, Celadon, North Iowa Land, Jadeski, Verde Valley, Numedahl, Kelly, Plimetrics, Luy, Tealander, Nelson, Oliver, Grunewald, Hanna, Tri-County, Emerald—"

"I've got it." Matt sat bolt upright, tingling with anticipation.

"So fast?"

"Give me those lists." He snatched them out of Zach's hand, reached for a pen, and circled several names. When he finished, he handed them back. "Now do you see the link?"

Zach studied the circled names, then shook his head. "Sorry, man. Not a clue."

"The key is the color *green*." Matt struggled to subdue his excitement as he waited for Zach to make the connection.

"Outside of *verde*," Zach said, "which is Spanish for *green*, none of these contains the word *green*."

Matt tapped the pages with his forefinger. "Not all, but some do. Not just plain green; *shades* of green. See?"

Zach peered at the page as if staring would reveal a clue.

Matt pointed to each circled name. "Celadon is a shade of green. Kelly—green. Grunewald—German for *green woods*. Plimetrics contains the word *lime*. Emerald green. Tealander—teal. Jadeski—jade. Smythe named his shell companies with variations of the color *green*."

Zach pondered the explanation, then gaped with realization. "The color of money!"

Then the final connection hit home in Matt's brain, causing his stomach to drop as if he'd crested the highest peak of a roller coaster and begun the exhilarating freefall. "If I remember my Western European history class from college, the flag of the German state of Saxony contains green."

"Get outta town," Zach blurted. "You remember bits of information like that from way back then?"

"Some days it's a curse. Today it's a gift."

Zach's eyes seemed to glaze over. He shook his head repeatedly in small motions. "I dunno, amigo, you really think *green's* the connection?"

"Do you have a better explanation?"

Zach rolled his lips inward over his teeth and gazed upward. "No."

Matt rubbed his tired eyes, frustrated he'd solved only part of the puzzle with no clue how to proceed. "The real question is still *why* Smythe wants to buy up every piece of land he can along the interstate. If a North American Superhighway comes into existence, how does he benefit?"

"He puts up businesses along the road and gets loads of traffic."

"From what I've read, it'll be a limited access corridor, thirty miles or more between junctions. Not every piece of property will be as accessible as our current freeway system allows. There's no way all those properties fit that profile."

The light from the windows had faded. Matt checked his watch. Almost 7:00. "I need to let things incubate and get some ideas from my ex-wife."

Standing, he pulled out his wallet and paid Zach for the extra two hours. "You did well. Thanks."

Zach grinned as he pocketed the money. "I had fun playing spy."

"I might need you in the future if you've got the time. Same pay rate."

"You're on. Beats the hell out of babysitting the computer lab."

"The next time you have an hour or two, check for websites of Smythe's companies—the ones we found today. If you find any, call the listed phone numbers during business hours."

"Me? Call these businesses?" His monotone veneer cracked, and his tone became apprehensive. "I'm not so good at talking to strangers on the phone. What should I say?"

"*If* someone answers, say you called the wrong number and hang up."

"I can do that."

"I'll bet my condo you get a recorded message every time. Probably the same message for each company."

Zach shook his head. "Dude, you're crazy, but I won't bet against you. You deciphered that green shit damn fast."

As Matt turned to leave, Zach said, "By the way, ninety-five percent of what I did today wasn't hacking."

Matt stopped and glanced over his shoulder, eyebrows raised. "Really?"

Zach cracked a conspiratorial smile. "If it was, I'd have charged you ten times as much."

CHAPTER 22

Back in his condo later that day, Matt called Gebhardt and shared his newly discovered sales information about Saxony Partners. After another contentious verbal exchange, Gebhardt explained that since no crimes had been committed, the SCPD couldn't offer any increased investigative assistance into the deaths of Matt's father and Myrick.

Exasperated, Matt called Diane. A fresh pair of eyes might help him figure out his next step. It took some cajoling, but when he offered to whip up a late dinner for her, she agreed to look over his research.

En route to Diane's condo, Matt stopped for ingredients and gifts. Laden with a bag of groceries, a bottle of wine, a small bouquet of flowers, and a manila envelope containing the research he and Zach had compiled, he walked into the lobby of her building shortly before 9:00 p.m. The security guard behind the massive mahogany desk eyed him suspiciously. Matt flashed an I-mean-no-harm smile, and the guard turned his focus back to his video monitors.

Plush carpet cushioned his steps as he crossed the lobby to a chair and sat. A Picasso print he couldn't identify hung on one wall. A copy of Van Gogh's *Café Terrace on the Place du Forum, Arles, at Night* graced the opposite wall. Two marble busts on pedestals flanked the elevators—those of Hubert Humphrey and Harold Stassen, both famous Minnesota politicians who'd run unsuccessfully for President of the United States. How Minnesotan—competent but ultimately overlooked by the nation.

Diane arrived within minutes lugging her briefcase, purse, and two bags of merchandise from Target. Even at the end of a long workday, she appeared more beautiful than she had at the Dakota.

Matt stood and gestured toward the elegant lobby with the hand holding her flowers. "Good to know my tax dollars allow state employees to live in such luxury."

When she lowered her chin, he immediately regretted his gibe. "Do you want this favor or not?" she said with a hint of annoyance.

"Sorry. Nervous idiocy. Old habits die hard." He handed her the bouquet. "Truce?"

She buried her nose in the flowers and regarded him with barely raised eyebrows. Was that her coquettish smile hidden behind the blooms?

As they rode the elevator, Matt's nerves jangled like they had during his last blind date. Neither spoke until she opened her condo door and stepped inside.

"Steven! What the hell are you doing here?" The sharp edge in her voice sliced through the silent entryway.

Matt tensed when he heard *Steven* and made an involuntary fist when he saw Crossley reclined on the sofa, paging through a magazine. His dark-blue tie hung loosely around his light blue shirt collar, and his charcoal-gray suit jacket lay draped over a chair.

Crossley stood and walked toward Diane, holding out his arms as if he expected a hug. "I thought I'd surprise you, baby."

Then he noticed Matt. "And whom do we have here? Oh, right, Diane's ex. The musician from the nightclub."

Matt stood tall and nodded slightly.

"Mack, isn't it?" Crossley smirked as if he were a Cheshire cat who'd eaten a sour rat.

"Matt . . . Lanier." Asking this favor had instantly become his worst idea in a long time.

Crossley nodded toward the grocery bag in Matt's hand, then gave Diane a sidelong glance. "Is this some sort of delivery service you signed up for?"

She blew past Crossley and placed her bags and the bouquet on her kitchen counter. "I told you to call before coming over."

"Sorry. I thought you needed some of my unique brand of relaxation after all the long hours you've clocked."

"Not tonight. I've got a meeting to prepare for in the morning. Go home and watch some porn."

Matt stifled a laugh.

Crossley's rat-eating sneer remained stuck to his face, but the anger in his eyes looked venomous. He jerked a thumb toward Matt. "So why's he here?"

Diane removed her black coat to reveal a charcoal-gray business suit and white blouse. "Matt's going to make dinner in exchange for a favor."

"A favor?" Crossley snorted. "That's what you call it these days?"

"For God's sake, get your mind out of the gutter." Diane's eyes glowed with irritation. "It's strictly business."

Matt had learned early in their marriage to get as far away as possible when she got *the look* in her eyes. Did Crossley know he was courting a full-blown outburst? "I'd leave if I were you, pal."

Crossley shot him a sideways glance, then refocused on Diane. "What kind of business?"

"She's going to give me some legal advice on—"

"Matt," Diane interjected with a raised hand, "he doesn't need to know." She crossed her arms. "Go home, Steven."

How far would Crossley push? The comprehension that eventually registered in his eyes disappointed Matt. The pompous bastard might survive the night with his testicles intact.

Crossley shot him a glower of recognition and warning that went beyond the glare of a jealous boyfriend. Did Crossley know about his failed interrogation of Smythe that morning? If so, Diane had been right about the two men being close associates. Matt worried that his inquiries might place his ex-wife in danger. He struggled to maintain a poker face.

Softening his expression to a self-satisfied smile, Crossley turned toward Diane. "Okay, okay. I see this is an inconvenient time."

He picked up his suit coat from the chair, brushed past her, and walked toward the door. But he paused as if he expected Matt to move out of his way, then drew himself up to his full height to look Matt straight in the eye.

"It was nice meeting you, Mack."

Glancing at the two feet of space next to him that Crossley could have used to pass, Matt fumed inside. He wanted nothing more than to cold-cock the prick. But for Diane's sake, he silently counted to ten and attempted to stare a hole through his adversary.

Crossley turned to look at Diane, expelled a low hum of disapproval and inconvenience, stepped around Matt, and exited the condo.

Diane walked to the door after it had clicked shut, engaged both locks—doorknob and deadbolt—then returned to the kitchen.

Matt followed and placed the groceries on the counter. "Well, *that* sure was fun."

She sighed and massaged the back of her neck. "I'm sorry. He pulls shit like that all the time."

"No need to explain. Unfortunately, he suspects I've confided in you about this." He held up his manila envelope.

Her eyes widened with concern. "You think so?"

He nodded. "The look he just gave me couldn't have meant anything else. I don't want you to get in trouble over this stuff, so maybe we should stop now. You can tell him my idea's insane, we had a big argument, I stormed out, and you never want to see me or talk to me again."

"Once Steven gets suspicious, he never lets up until he's sure the problem is resolved to his satisfaction."

"But—"

"Don't worry about me. I'm a big girl. I'll handle him."

"Are you sure?" He doubted he could persuade her to change her mind, but he felt obligated to try.

She nodded at his grocery bag. "How about that omelet?"

He brightened, glad for the topic change. "Coming right up. Just show me where the equipment is."

She gave him a thirty-second tour of her kitchen, then said, "I'm going to change. Holler if you can't find something."

"Okay," he said as she walked down the hallway.

He evaluated the condo's décor as he removed his jacket, tossed it onto a dining room chair, and rolled up his sleeves. The stainless-steel appliances were spotless; he doubted they got much use. Cherry wood cabinets supplied the only warmth in her beautiful, sterile, state-of-the-art kitchen. The living area featured off-white walls, gray carpet, a sparse collection of expensive-looking knick-knacks, and ultra-modern furniture. Perched on a china cabinet, a photograph of Diane with her parents seemed to be the lone object of any sentimental value. Was she happier now, alone with her all-consuming career, than she'd been with him during their marriage when they'd enjoyed a reasonable balance between careers and personal life? His heart ached when he concluded she was probably happier now without him.

Matt washed his hands, ignited one of the burners on the five-burner Viking stove, and placed an omelet pan over a low flame. He chopped and sliced green peppers and mushrooms on the butcher block cutting board. Opening the side-by-side refrigerator-freezer to retrieve some butter, he made a quick survey of its contents: a recorked bottle of wine, a Chinese takeout carton, assorted flavors of yogurt, a jar of jelly, half a loaf of whole wheat bread.

A few minutes later, Diane appeared in the adjacent dining room wearing fuzzy pink slippers, blue jeans, and a royal blue fleece pullover. She'd pulled her hair into a ponytail. Much of the stress in her face and body had evaporated.

His gaze froze on her and she stopped. Seeing her in casual clothes rather than power suits or cocktail dresses made his heart lurch and aroused a deep-seated longing for their past life together. This was the woman he'd married—calm, casual, and still classy.

She closed her eyes and inhaled, then opened her eyes and grinned. Walking stiff-legged toward the kitchen with outstretched arms, zombie-like, she said, "You realize I only married you for your culinary skills, don't you?"

He recovered his composure and chuckled. "I got tired of you burning the spaghetti every week."

"Hey, I wasn't that bad."

Matt cocked his head and gave her a doubting glance, then poured two glasses of the Napa Valley sauvignon blanc he'd brought. "This'll complement the green peppers and feta." He gave her a glass and took a sip of his.

She tasted her wine. "Mmm, good." Her expression resembled that of someone sipping a cold glass of water after toiling outside for hours on a hot day. She sat on a bar stool at the kitchen island and watched him finish the omelet and butter a piece of toast.

Although her presence and the earthy aromas of mushrooms and feta recalled early days of their marriage when they'd cooked together because money was too tight to dine out, he still felt uncomfortable being alone with her now, after the divorce. To break the awkward lull, he said, "Nice place you've got."

"Thanks. I only use the bedroom anymore. The housekeeper spends more waking hours here than I do. I hired a decorator when I moved in and told her to keep it simple."

Matt plated the eggs and toast and took a seat on the bar stool next to her. "Do you want to see what I found now or after you're finished eating?"

Diane glanced at the clock. "I'll read while I eat, then we can talk."

He handed her the research he and Zach had compiled along with a summary sheet Matt had written of his father's stolen notes and documents.

"Where did you get all of this information," she asked in a voice laden with suspicion. "I know you. You're not computer savvy enough to find it on your own."

He told her the abridged version of how he enlisted Zach's help to research Saxony Partners. Then he pointed at their combined sales data and explained the link between Saxony Partners and the other *green* companies. Those initial threads of data, combined with speculation, had led him to connect Smythe and Saxony Partners with other companies buying land along Interstate 35. Matt downplayed the NAFTA-North American Super Highway angle when her eyebrows arched after he first mentioned it.

While she ate and read, he retired to the living room and clicked on her television. He found a Minnesota Wild hockey game and settled in to wait, keeping the sound low so he could hear her if she had a question.

By the time she finished her two-egg omelet and toast, she'd made her way through his folder. She set her fork down after the final bite. "Delicious. What's your secret?"

"Chervil. It's magic with this particular sauv blanc."

She yawned. "I'm fading fast. I'll make some coffee and we'll talk."

They chatted while the coffee brewed, talking about their respective condos and neighborhoods. With cups in hand, they adjourned to the living room and sat on opposite ends of the sofa.

After a sip of coffee, Diane said, "This whole thing, the scheme, the mysterious deaths, the long strip of land along the interstate, it's possible."

"Really?"

"*Possible*, but not probable. If you don't make a solid connection, no matter how much dirt you uncover, Smythe will be untouchable."

Matt's mood went from hopeful to despondent within seconds. "Why not?"

"Millionaires don't get to be millionaires playing by the rules," she said. "They bend most of them and break the ones they can get away with. Smythe wants to expand his empire. Why he's going for farmland in one long geographic strip puzzles me, but if he were buying a miles-long swath of buildings along some urban commercial district, no one would think it unusual."

"Isn't he placing a huge bet on farmland soaring in value? Most of it can't be profitably developed. If he plans to invest in local agriculture, who in their right mind wants a farm that's a mile wide and hundreds of miles long?"

She curled her feet under her and cradled the coffee cup with both hands. "The simple answer is he wants to build a North American Super Highway . . . by himself, which is ludicrous as well as impossible."

He visually absorbed her all-over beauty, letting his gaze linger on the roundness of her breasts under her fleece top and the long, slender line of her thigh. She was a natural at assuming alluring poses without seeming to notice the effect they had on men.

She took another sip of coffee. "Millionaires don't get rich by being transparent, either."

He exhaled upward through his lips. "I feel like a rat in a maze. One dead end after another."

"Remember back in the early years of our marriage when you read Sherlock Holmes all the time? There was one quote you claimed was the essence of Holmes' talent. Something about eliminating the impossible."

"Oh, right." He pointed his left index finger up. "When you've eliminated the impossible, whatever remains, however improbable, must be the truth."

"That's what you need to do with Smythe."

"I guess so. But I've overstayed my welcome. Let's drop it for tonight." He peered deep into her eyes, hoping to divine her true feelings about him. "Why did you come over and talk to me at the Dakota last weekend?"

She hesitated. Her smile was almost imperceptible. "You were right. I'm running for office. I was practicing my political skills."

"Yes!" Matt pumped his fist. "Score one for the Jazzman."

"I figured you were the last person who'd vote for me, and I saw it as a challenge to see if I could schmooze you into submission. But know this, *Jazzman*." She scowled, but her eyes twinkled with playfulness. "If you tell anyone, I'll kill you. Steven's grooming me for the next election. Nothing big, just a city council seat." She studied his expression intently. "How did I do?"

"I'll let you know after the election, Counselor."

She nodded. "Fair enough."

He tapped his fingers on the back of the sofa and glanced at the clock above the fireplace. "I should go. I've taken more of your time than I deserve." He stood. "Thanks for your input."

Diane rose too. "I need to get a ton of work done before morning. Thanks for dinner. It brought back pleasant memories."

Matt smiled. "Yeah, for me too."

He picked up his jacket and data folder as they walked to the door.

When they reached the entryway, she put his hand on his shoulder. "I have a bad feeling about Steven and Smythe." The urgency in her voice chilled him. "Be careful."

"I will."

Frozen with hesitation, Matt flashed back to one particular night two years into their marriage—a night that captured the essence of all the types of love they'd shared. The sex had always been enjoyable, sometimes wildly pleasurable, but infrequent for a young couple due to their divergent, time-consuming careers.

~

However, for Matt's twenty-fifth birthday, Diane took two days off from work to concoct an extra-special surprise for him. After relaxing and recharging herself the first day, she prepared for a night he'd never forget. His birthday was on a Friday that year, so Matt had a jazz gig and didn't get home until 1:30 in the morning. He was tired, sweaty from a too hot, too smoky nightclub, and anticipated a long, blissful night of sleep.

When he walked in the door to their apartment, he found a note written on red paper: *Go to the kitchen.* A glass of Champagne and a glass bottle of liquid sat on the counter along with another red note: *Gently warm bottle in microwave.* He removed the stopper and sniffed the bottle's contents. The aroma of spice-scented oil wafted into his nose. With both his curiosity and libido aroused, he followed the instructions. Upon opening the microwave door, he saw a third note: *Bring warm oil to bathroom.* After heating the oil, he brought it and his Champagne to the bathroom, tapped on the door, and entered.

Several lit candles gave the room a golden glow. Her trademark perfume, Beautiful, filled his nostrils and elicited instant sensory memories of passion. The romantic, mellow tones of one of Matt's trio recordings—covers of a dozen classic jazz ballads—completed the mood. The track playing when he entered was "'Round Midnight." At that moment, it instantly became his favorite song. *Their* song.

Diane sat on the edge of a bathtub full of steaming, foamy water. She was dressed in a silky white, Ancient-Greek-styled slave-girl costume trimmed with gold lace. The short dress emphasized her long legs and featured a plunging V-neck tight enough to highlight her firm, ample breasts. A golden laurel wreath adorned her hair, which had been styled by a professional salon to give her a look fit for a *Playboy* magazine photo shoot. Although she was beautiful enough without makeup, she wore more mascara and eyeshadow than usual, and her lips were glossy, dark red, and appeared fuller than usual. Diane *was* a Greek goddess. The lust in her eyes and a devilish grin confirmed her romantic intentions.

The shock and awe were so intense he nearly dropped his glass. He caught his breath in a sharp gasp. His heart raced, and his spine tingled, which ignited a spark of intense desire.

She stood and announced to him in a shy, subservient voice that belied the fiery passion in her eyes, "Master, I have been instructed by my king to serve you tonight in all ways of the flesh for as long as you shall desire this humble slave girl."

The evening took off from there to heights of passion he never imagined to be attainable. His body tingled with pleasure from the still vivid memories. The best part of that special night of passion was falling asleep in her arms and thinking he was the luckiest man on Earth. He couldn't imagine a more perfect woman gracing his life.

~

"Something wrong?" Diane's words snapped Matt back to the present.

"Huh?" He'd been staring deep into her eyes the entire time they'd been standing at her door. "Oh. Sorry, no. Just reminiscing about us back in the early days."

A perceptive leer curled across her lips. "Mmm, yeah. I have a pretty good idea of which *day* you're thinking about."

His face grew hot. He looked down with a sheepish, busted grin. "No comment."

"Uh-huh," was all she said. All that needed saying.

He fought the urge to wrap his arms around her and kiss her as he had so many times before. He started to lean forward but caught himself and extended his hand instead. She held it for several seconds and stared into his eyes. In the soft light of the hallway, he saw the brilliant blue sparkle that had electrified his emotions all those years ago. She hugged him without pressing against his body. He returned the hug, patted her on the back, and, with great reluctance, walked out.

CHAPTER 23

The following morning, before Matt could say *hello* after answering his phone, Diane said, "You've got a *big* problem."

"What's wrong?" He stood and hit the *pause* button on his portable CD player. He'd been reclined on the sofa in the farmhouse living room, studying a new piece the Minnesota Orchestra would premier the following month, and listening to a rehearsal recording as he read the sheet music for the double bass part. He was grateful for the interruption. Thoughts of corrupt businessmen, dead farmers, and conspiracies weren't helping his concentration anyway.

"I talked to Steven a minute ago," Diane said. "He told me in no uncertain terms to stay away from you, not to believe anything you say about Saxony Partners, and to tell you to never set foot in Smythe Properties again."

"No kidding?" He tried to sound flippant through clenched teeth. "I had no idea I was so important to them."

"I had no idea Steven knew him *that* well. What did you say to Smythe?"

"I *tried* to ask him about all the crap that's been going down in Straight River. He stonewalled me."

"That's why Steven was so suspicious about you last night. Oh, God . . ."

"Relax. Even if Crossley knows you were giving me advice about Smythe, you don't need to worry. Tell him it was a one-shot thing like we discussed last night."

"That was before I knew Steven and Smythe were so tight. They'll assume we're looking into this together because you're my ex-husband."

Despite his growing concern, Matt kept his voice casual. "Crossley's a pompous ass. What's he going to do, revoke my musicians' union membership?"

"If Steven gets involved, it's serious."

"He's a blowhard. All air, no substance. Typical politician."

"You don't understand what those two are capable of together. Steven's got the political contacts and the power, Smythe has the business connections and financial clout. They've each taken down politicians and businessmen simply for opposing their views. If this scheme they're working on is as big as you think, they might become more dangerous. They'll do whatever's necessary to stop you. Guilt by association. Destroy careers, hurt people financially, or physically. If the money's big enough, anything's possible."

Physically . . . Diane . . . Matt's internal alarm sounded. If her warnings about Smythe and Crossley were a legitimate assessment of their capabilities, their combination of money and influence was powerful enough to blow him away like a piece of lint. Powerful enough to hurt Diane.

"What do you suggest, Counselor?"

"Go back to teaching and making great music, Jazzman. Take care of your father's estate. Forget this ever happened. Find another way to help Betty, but for God's sake stay away from Smythe and Crossley."

Suspicion crept into his mind. "Why should I trust you? Aren't you one of them?"

A wall of invisible ice materialized over the phone line. His neck hair bristled when he imagined the frosty glare she'd give him if they were face-to-face.

"I work with Steven *occasionally*," she said. "But I'm not *one* of them."

Matt instantly regretted his insinuation. "I'm sorry. I have difficulty trusting anyone about all this. Dealing with red tape, suspicious deaths, insurance policies, and real estate deals is not in my wheelhouse of skills."

"You need to understand. This has nothing to do with my relationship with Steven. My only concern is keeping you and Betty off Smythe's shit list."

He wondered if she was sincere or if she was trying to steer him away for some other reason. Because of her personal relationship with Crossley, he couldn't rule out the possibility he'd gotten to her somehow. Blackmail? Threats? But Diane had always, always, been able to keep her work life separate from her personal life.

"Okay, you've made your point. Tell Crossley I'll back off. Nothing is more important to me than your safety. You stay out of it. Don't even mention Smythe's name again."

"Thank you." She sounded relieved but still tense. "Besides, Steven has changed over the past few months. Mainly at work is what I hear through the capitol grapevine. He seems edgier, angrier, when we're together too. I don't know why."

"That worries me more, Diane. Please be careful around him. Let me know if I can help at all."

He hung up the phone, walked to the living room window, and stared across the front yard to the fallow, rolling farmland. Fatigue weighed on him like a lead overcoat. Diane's warning was valid if Smythe and Crossley together were one of the more powerful forces in the state. Did he really believe one small-town nobody, a farmer's son, could prevail against a corporate and political machine? However, if he'd stumbled onto something serious but didn't follow through, other innocent people might end up hurt.

Betty might find a way out of this with the help of Swanny and the other farmers. After all, Matt was the outsider who wouldn't have heard about Helmer's death if he hadn't come to Straight River after his father's death. Despite what he'd learned about recent activities in Straight River, he hadn't convinced anyone else that the deaths of his father, Myrick, and Hibbert were somehow related. He rubbed his temples, trying to ease the ache he now realized had been there for days. After several minutes of fruitless contemplation staring at a gray-and-brown field of patchy snow scattered across the soil, he called Zach and told him they needed to talk in person.

CHAPTER 24

The sky darkened in the southwest, thunder rumbled, and April showers began to fall as Matt drove to the Cedar-Riverside neighborhood. The closest parking spot to Zach's apartment was a few blocks away. He trotted to Zach's and still got damp despite his hooded rain jacket.

"What's the topic, boss?" Zach said as he held the door open and Matt entered his apartment.

"I'm firing you."

Zach gaped at him. "Why?"

"I won't let you risk your health or your life for my little Don Quixote adventure."

"Risk my *life?*" Zach swallowed hard. "What the hell happened since yesterday?"

"The less you know, the better. I've got a strong sensation I'm being watched." He couldn't believe he'd uttered that sentence. *I'm in a damned spy movie.*

"Don't you want to hear what I discovered?" Zach said with urgency in his voice.

"Give me the abridged version. If I have questions, I'll call you. Otherwise, this is our last meeting. I'll find someone else, a private detective or someone in law enforcement, assuming I can convince them I'm not one of those conspiracy-theory nutcases."

"You might not be a nutcase," Zach said. "I did a tertiary search and stumbled across an organization called Millennium Four. The online info I read mentioned acquiring farms in Texas, which made me think of our long, narrow strip of farmland."

Although Diane's warning rang in his head, Matt decided to at least listen to Zach's information. "Okay, what's significant about this Millennium Four."

Zach sat in his swivel chair and slid the other chair toward Matt, who sat and gazed expectantly at his young researcher.

"I was doing a keyword search for NAFTA and the North American Super Highway," Zach said, "when I came across an article in the *Dallas Morning News* about the death of a freelance journalist. He'd written a piece about this secret group he'd infiltrated earlier this year. The details were slim, something about the group's plan to consolidate North and South America under one government to facilitate the eventual unification of the western hemisphere. He also mentioned economic war, Muslims and Chinese, and world domination."

"A major metropolitan newspaper published his piece?" Matt said with disbelief. "Sounds more like something a fringe tabloid would print."

Zach shook his head. "The *Morning News* story was about the writer's death. He shopped his investigative story to the national publications but got no takers. Then he submitted the piece to local media, who also turned him down. Eventually, an alternative weekly magazine in the Dallas area printed the article."

Matt peered at Zach and scrunched his mouth into a frown. "I don't follow you."

"A few days after the article was published, the reporter jumped out of a tenth-story window."

Matt's insides tightened. An uneasy sense of danger flowed through him. He flashed on Hibbert's apparent suicide. Betty's insistence that Helmer wouldn't have—*couldn't* have hung himself. His father's fall into the silo.

"Or he was pushed," Matt said.

"I suspected that too," Zach said. "Because—and this is the weird part—he left a suicide note that said he made up the whole story. He also apologized for violating some journalistic code of ethics because he needed the money. He thought a juiced-up article like this would be worth more in the freelance market."

Matt clapped his hand to his forehead when he processed the connection. "If Smythe belongs to Millennium Four, the scope of all the strange farm purchases now includes the southern states that I-35 runs through. The Mexican border all the way to Duluth, the largest freshwater port in the world, intersected by most of the east-west interstates. That makes I-35 the perfect choice for the first superhighway."

"But we already decided most of Smythe's purchases wouldn't benefit from a superhighway because of the limited access issue."

"That's true if he intends to *keep* the land. If we're talking multiple states, it's a national project. If he sells, it'll be to the U.S. Government. Probably at a sweetheart-deal price—for Smythe."

Zach flashed a puzzled look. "The Feds?"

"Who else?" Matt made a palms-up gesture. "According to my dad's research, these superhighways will dwarf even the twelve-lane monstrosities in the big cities. We're talking multiple high-speed train tracks segregated for passengers and freight; designated truck and passenger-car lanes; oil and natural gas pipelines; electrical substations and power lines; pipelines to move water from the Great Lakes to the dry southern and western areas; major terminals at freeway intersections to facilitate distributing traffic and cargo onto east-west routes. A mile or two wide at some points. Huge infrastructure expenditures. Buying the land might only be a small fraction of the total cost."

Zach nodded. "Smythe must think if our government gets ambitious enough to set this project in motion, they'll pay almost any price for the land."

"The Middle East wars this century have already cost well north of a trillion dollars," Matt said. "A nationwide superhighway project could cost ten times that much."

Zach's eyes bulged. "Whoa. If Millennium Four's piece of the pie is just one percent, that's ten billion dollars."

"Never hurts to follow the money," Matt said. "Smythe is probably working with a guy named Crossley in the Governor's office who can run interference, help avoid scrutiny, maybe bend some rules to allow the sales to happen fast and quiet."

"If all this is true," Zach said, "how do we know Smythe's connected to Millennium Four? He wasn't mentioned by the reporter."

"A valid question." Matt recalled the Sherlock Holmes quote as he massaged his chin. If he'd indeed eliminated all impossibilities, an interstate land grab by Millennium Four to build a superhighway was one hell of a bizarre truth. He gave Zach a bewildered look. "You got a better explanation for all the land he's bought in the last six months?"

They stared blankly at each other. Matt felt overwhelmed. The odds against him that he could achieve justice for his father and making sure Betty kept her farm had skyrocketed. After absorbing that new reality, he recalled the primary reason for his visit and reached for his wallet. "Speaking of money, how much more do I owe you?"

"Oh, right," Zach said. "Five more hours. A hundred bucks."

Matt paid him. "Thanks. Just remember, whatever I decide to do, your effort wasn't wasted."

Zach snapped his fingers. "Almost forgot." He pulled a small object from his jeans pocket and dropped it into Matt's hand. "You paid for this too."

Matt fingered the finger-sized plastic oblong. "What's this?"

"All our data."

"Everything?"

Zach nodded. "It's a USB drive. Some people call them flash drives. Plug this into any computer, and you can read or print everything we discovered. I still have a copy on my computer's hard drive in case you lose it. Redundancy in cyberspace is always smart."

"Well, how about that?" Matt said, impressed yet again by both technology and his ignorance of technology. "I've heard about these things. Never saw one in person before." He put the flash drive into his pocket and stood. "I should go."

Zach checked his phone for the time. "I've got a class in a few minutes too."

"Need a ride?"

It was still raining, so Zach accepted. "I gotta take a leak. Tell me where you're parked, and I'll catch up."

Matt gave him the location and the color of his Sienna, then left and walked toward his car. The storm front had passed, but a residual drizzle forced him to put up the hood of his jacket. He ambled up the street, surprisingly refreshed by the gray, misty ambiance.

A half block behind him, a jogger's footsteps splashed on the sidewalk puddles.

"I'm coming," said the jogger in a mock-hurried tone.

Matt turned, recognized the jogger as Zach, raised a hand in acknowledgment, and resumed walking.

As Matt crossed the street at the intersection, Zach yelled, "Watch out!"

Matt looked up the street and froze. A black SUV barreled toward him. He got a glimpse of the driver's grotesque snarl and bald head an instant before something hit him from the side as if he were a tackling dummy. As he sailed across the hood of a nearby parked car, he heard a dull thud. An instant later came the crash of shattering glass.

He tumbled to the sidewalk in an awkward, one-shouldered somersault and slammed headfirst into the corner post of a picket fence. Stunned, he lay on the sidewalk, afraid to move in case he'd injured his neck or spine. Cold rain pelted his face. He wiggled his fingers and toes, then pushed himself up to a sitting position. The world started spinning. He sank back to the ground.

Voices from the direction of the Java Joint grew louder. With great effort, Matt stood and staggered in that direction, using a parked car for support. He took enough steps for someone to notice him before he collapsed from dizziness. As his cheek slapped the cold, wet pavement, Matt's vision was reduced to the space under a parked car. On the other side of that car, Zach Perez lay sprawled in the street, face down. Then all became darkness.

CHAPTER 25

Matt spent two hours in the emergency room at University Hospital. Less than thirty minutes involved being examined, treated, and prescribed painkillers for a bruised shoulder and splitting headache. He spent the remainder of the time waiting for the doctor to decide if he'd suffered a concussion. His conclusion was that Matt's nausea and dizziness at the scene were caused by shock, not the blow to his head.

As he waited and dozed, Matt's mind whirled with memories of the driver in the black SUV. Before Zach's heroism, Matt had gotten a split-second glance at the guy. Not enough for a positive ID, but the blurry recollection of an ugly, bald, sneering brute was indelibly imprinted on his brain. Smythe's security guard?

The incident had happened so fast. An EMT at the scene had mentioned she saw a broken vodka bottle in the street and speculated a random drunk driver caused the accident. Had Matt not seen the goon in Smythe's office days earlier, he might've believed her. But he harbored no doubt that the driver, drunk or not, had intended to kill him.

Shortly after the doctor signed off, a nurse entered carrying his shirt and jacket. "You're free to leave." She smiled as she handed over his clothes. "Be a stranger."

Matt forced a polite chuckle at her ER humor. "Thanks, I'll work on it." He swallowed his dread and asked, "How's the kid?"

"Mr. Perez? He's recovering from surgery." The nurse spoke with a matter-of-fact, but still professional, tone. "He was conscious when the ambulance brought him in, so we don't think his injuries are critical."

Palpable relief raced through his veins. "Thank God. The damned fool threw himself in front of that car to save my pathetic ass."

She arched her eyebrows and nodded approvingly. "Sounds like he's a hero."

"Yeah, he is." Matt thanked her and headed to the surgery floor.

A nurse there told him the only visitors allowed to see Zach were immediate family members.

Matt jabbed a finger toward the patient rooms. "He's in there because he saved my life. All I want is a chance to thank him. I might never see him again."

"I'm sorry, but—"

"Please." He stared into her eyes and lowered his chin.

She recoiled at his pleading stare and commanding tone. Relaxing her stiff posture, she glanced down the hall in both directions, then sighed. "Third door on the left. Make it quick."

"Thank you."

When Matt entered Zach's room, he gasped at the sight of his friend. A bandage enveloped part of Zach's head. An intravenous line secured by surgical tape stuck out of the top of his hand. A hip-to-ankle cast encased his right leg. His golden-brown skin looked several shades lighter than normal. The hospital machines and monitors clicked, beeped, and buzzed.

Matt whispered, "Hey, kid."

Zach's eyelids fluttered. He squinted, turned his head, cracked a weak smile. "Hey, old man. Glad you're okay."

Matt returned the smile. "Don't suppose you memorized the license plate number," he joked.

Zach's smile waned. "I saw someone get hit by a car . . . when I was six." His voice wavered, and the words came out a few at a time. He winced each time he inhaled. "Ever since then . . . I wondered what it would feel like. Now I'm all busted up . . . still don't know. Last thing I remember . . . doing a bad imitation of Superman."

"That car would've killed me," Matt said. "I froze. When I was being attended to, I overheard someone say you pushed me out of the way. Thank you for saving my life. I owe you big-time."

Zach waved dismissively with his free hand. "Someone in the ambulance said that too. Never imagined . . . I could do anything heroic."

"Most people would've done nothing. You acted. That speaks volumes about your character."

After an awkward silence, Matt decided to let Zach rest. "I should go. I had to strong-arm the nurse at the desk to let me see you. She'll be in here any second to boot me out."

Zach gave him a sleepy nod.

"Thanks again, kid." He left, feeling lighter than he'd felt going in. Zach would be hobbled by a broken leg for the next six weeks, but at least he'd survived.

~

Following a quick cab ride back to his car, Matt returned to the farm. Depression and anger grew during the drive at the realization he and Zach had almost been killed by Smythe's goon. Zach's thread of research connecting Smythe to Millennium Four validated the theory that the stakes were high enough for violence to be utilized against anyone who got in the way.

Once he was inside the farmhouse, Matt remembered the flash drive Zach had given to him. He patted his pocket to reassure himself it was still there. The tiny object held their only documentation of a possible conspiracy. He needed to protect it in case Zach's computers self-destructed, or something worse happened to Zach and him.

He looked up the number for John Maxwell, the Lanier family's long-time attorney, and dialed. He was pleasantly surprised when Maxwell answered his own phone. Matt identified himself. After they exchanged a cordial greeting, he said, "I have a small favor to ask, Max."

"Name it," Maxwell said.

"First of all, am I officially considered a client of yours?"

"Although your father was my client, you are not until we agree upon a fee. However, I can fill out a form that summarizes this free consultation and establishes a relationship between us. Then I'll send the form to you for your signature, which will make it official."

"Let's do it."

"You sound agitated. What's the favor?"

Matt provided Maxwell with a five-minute summary of his dilemma, his escalating fear for his life, and then made his request.

The old lawyer sounded concerned yet professional as he asked questions to further his understanding of the situation. When he was satisfied with Matt's responses, he agreed to help. Maxwell reassured his new client that any information, in any form, was protected by attorney-client privilege. Matt ended the call and spent the next thirty minutes writing down what he wanted his new attorney to know about the events that had occurred since his father's death.

As he drove to the mailbox he'd chosen—one in downtown Straight River near the Law Enforcement Center—Matt kept checking his mirrors for a black SUV. If someone was following him, he didn't want to be seen entering Maxwell's office. To prevent his hands from trembling, he gripped the wheel as if his fingers were talons. Once he'd mailed the letter to Maxwell, he drove home, still checking his mirrors. No matter what happened going forward, a respected attorney now knew Matt's story and could warn any local farmers who might run afoul of Saxony Partners in the future. He savored a brief moment of satisfaction for achieving this trivial moral victory.

Safely back at the farm, Matt retrieved the key to the gun safe from its hiding place in his father's dresser and opened the tall, heavy metal cabinet stored in the front hall closet. Inside were several shotguns and rifles, a BB gun, and a variety of handguns. The rifle and shotgun he'd used as a boy were still in mint condition thanks to decades of his dad's regular care.

The stocks felt solid and familiar in his hands. The smell of burnished metal and gun oil elicited pleasant memories of family hunting trips taken years before. He checked over the rifle, shotgun, and one of the handguns, and made sure each weapon was cleaned and ready to fire. When that chore was finished, he retrieved several boxes of the appropriate ammunition from the gun safe and made the short walk to the woods on the edge of the farm. In the waning light of a cool, clear spring day, he spent about an hour shooting at cardboard targets he'd found in the gun safe. He tacked them to a dead tree and shot from various distances to reacquaint himself with the sighting, recoil, and idiosyncrasies of each weapon.

Initially, his aim was wildly off target. He hadn't handled a firearm since high school, and he repeatedly struggled with the simple act of reloading the handgun. He cursed when bullets spilled onto the ground when he reloaded a weapon, or when he missed hitting any part of his targets on more than two consecutive shots. Some gunslinger he'd be in the event of a gun battle. He'd probably end up shooting himself instead of an attacker.

By the end of his practice session, his accuracy had improved to a level almost as good as he remembered from his youth. He'd retained enough skill with the revolver to hit the human-sized cardboard target in the center third of the torso from thirty feet more times than not. With the shotgun, his accuracy was solid to about thirty yards from a standing position. He was pleased to discover he could hit center mass consistently at one hundred yards from a prone position with his hunting rifle.

Satisfied he still remembered how to shoot well enough to at least put up token resistance to an attacker, Matt walked to the garage, secured the revolver in the glove box of his minivan, and locked both the glove box and car doors. Returning to the house, he placed the rifle in the closet by the back door and hid the loaded shotgun under his bed. As he walked downstairs, the realization that he might have to shoot someone hit him like a sucker punch to the solar plexus. His knees wobbled, and nervous tremors rattled his limbs.

He poured a double shot of his father's Jim Beam Black from the pantry into a juice glass and slumped into the old recliner. Hands still trembling, he took a sip, almost spilling some on his shirt. Merely *imagining* his cardboard targets were real people made him queasy. Killing a squirrel, a goose, or a deer for food or for sport had never fazed him. The mere thought of shooting a human being, even in self-defense, grated his nerves raw and dried his mouth to the point his tongue felt like sandpaper against his palate. But if Smythe wanted him dead, he wasn't going down without a fight.

CHAPTER 26

Matt pulled into the farmhouse driveway the next night, glad to be enveloped in the peace and quiet of the country rather than the ever-present background din of downtown Minneapolis. He'd spent a hectic day arranging for temporary substitutes for his teaching load, his trio, and his double bass chair in the Minnesota Orchestra. Then he'd squeezed in a few last student lessons. As he stepped out of his Sienna and walked toward the house, he noticed Jack pacing back and forth at the bottom of the porch steps to the back door. Every other time Matt had pulled into the drive, Jack had either been zonked out on his bed inside the barn, oblivious to anything, or he'd ambled out to greet him, tail wagging, shortly after Matt closed the door to his minivan.

"What's up, old boy?" he asked as he approached the black Lab.

Jack whimpered and paced faster.

Matt knelt and beckoned the dog over with an open hand. "You hungry?"

He patted Jack's head and ruffled his fur, but the dog still shifted from paw to paw and stared at the door. As Matt stood and stepped toward the porch, Jack whimpered louder—a mournful, almost painful sound—as if he were crying "Nooo!"

A spark of concern ignited Matt's mind. He stopped and studied Jack, who ceased whimpering at once. Matt dismissed his concern as hypersensitivity and resumed his walk to the porch. But the instant Matt placed his foot on the bottom step, Jack did something Matt had never seen before. He barked.

"What is it, boy?" Matt said from the top step, now more annoyed than concerned. Still barking, Jack took a few steps away from the bottom of the porch, returned, and repeated the route several times.

Matt waved him off. But when he turned toward the door and extended his arm to insert the key into the lock, Jack doubled his barking speed and volume. Comprehension struck Matt like a lightning bolt, and he froze. The dog was warning him not to go inside.

Matt snapped his head around to look at Jack, who was still barking and backing farther away from the house. The hair on the nape of Matt's neck rose and cold sweat materialized on his skin. He peered through the door's window into the dark kitchen but couldn't see anything unusual or out of place. He heard nothing, felt no vibration from interior movement through the porch floorboards. Crouching, he inspected the door frame below the bottom hinge. Lying on the threshold was the tiny scrap of spiral-bound notebook paper he'd wedged between the door and the jamb before leaving that morning. Sometime during his absence that day, someone had opened the door.

Matt vaulted off the porch and sprinted to his Sienna. Jack stopped barking and followed him. Matt yanked open the passenger door and retrieved the revolver from the glove box. After confirming his weapon was loaded, he quietly closed the door and retreated to the barn with Jack beside him.

Inside, Matt groped for the light switch and flipped it on, then rushed to the old wall phone his father had installed decades ago. Ray had decided an extension was a clever idea so family members could communicate with each other faster than traversing the distance between house and barn. As he dialed 911, he was particularly grateful for his father's foresight.

When the dispatcher answered, Matt identified himself and said with forced calmness, "Someone broke into my house—*again*. They might still be inside. I'm in the barn west of the house."

He gave the dispatcher the address and told her he'd talked to Sgt. Gebhardt about the previous break-in. She told him a patrol car would arrive within minutes and asked him to stay away from the house until then. As instructed, Matt stayed on the line and moved to a window to monitor the house while he waited. The gun felt heavy and cold in his hand. He kept his trigger finger poised against the trigger guard but

144

aimed the barrel away from his feet and Jack in case he panicked for some reason and fired unintentionally.

As a way to release his tension, he silently hummed "The Stars and Stripes Forever" and drummed the fingers of his free hand against his leg. *Another stupid musician idiosyncrasy of mine pops up at a bizarre time.* He did an eye roll at himself but kept humming. The black-and-white arrived before he reached the iconic obligato piccolo solo, so the dispatcher had been correct. Barely two minutes had elapsed.

"The patrol car's here," Matt told the dispatcher. "Thanks."

He hung up the phone, relieved not to be alone against a possible home invader.

A single male officer stepped out, holding a flashlight in his left hand. His right hand rested on his holster. "I'm Officer Sandvik," the man said as he strode over, glancing back at the house every few steps. "Are you Mr. Lanier?"

Matt nodded and moved aside so the officer could enter the barn.

Sandvik squinted as he adjusted to the brighter light. "I understand you've got *another* intruder."

Matt thought he heard a hint of skepticism in Sandvik's voice.

"It's probably nothing," Matt said. "My dog was agitated when I got home and tried to go inside. Then I noticed that a piece of paper I'd wedged between the door and frame had fallen onto the threshold. That means someone opened the door after I closed and locked it this morning."

Sandvik jotted notes into a small black notebook. "Someone jimmy the door?"

Matt shook his head. "I didn't notice. The intruder could've easily picked the lock. Dad installed a flimsy old thing in the seventies mainly for appearances. We never locked the doors unless we went away overnight."

"Understood." Sandvik clicked on his shoulder-mounted radio and notified the dispatcher he was going to enter the house. "Stay here, Mr. Lanier. I'll check the exterior first. May I have your house key?"

Sandvik took the key and walked toward the house. He drew his service revolver and held it waist high, ready to fire. Working his way around the exterior, he stopped at each main-floor window and shone the flashlight through the glass for a few seconds until he'd checked them all.

When Sandvik had finished the exterior inspection, Matt wondered if he'd jumped to conclusions based on the behavior of a nervous dog he barely knew. Maybe Jack was simply excited to get inside and find his favorite chew toy. Matt opened the barn door and walked toward the house, intending to tell Sandvik not to bother searching the inside.

Sandvik mounted the porch steps and inserted the key into the lock. Matt refrained from yelling across the yard in case Sandvik was the jumpy type. He continued his approach as Sandvik turned the doorknob and entered the house. Sandvik's flashlight beam danced across the walls of the kitchen.

Matt was twenty feet from the door. He called Sandvik's name at the exact instant the officer flipped on the kitchen light switch.

Two seconds later, Hell erupted from inside the house.

Matt reflexively raised his hands to shield his face as he turned to dive away. Before he could take a step, the blast propelled him across the barnyard like a human cannonball. He skidded across the gravel-studded dirt and slammed chest first into a corner post of the pigsty. Disoriented for several seconds by the noise and impact, he managed to focus long enough to see a gigantic bonfire where the house once stood. Too dazed and hurt to move, Matt watched the inferno devour his boyhood home.

Because of the concussive ringing in his ears, he felt as if he were watching a disaster movie with the sound off. When he tried to sit up, a searing pain shot through his ribs. He gasped, which doubled the pain. He lay back down and concentrated on taking slow, shallow breaths.

"Sandvik!" Matt attempted to yell, but he couldn't breathe deeply enough to give the word any power. He turned his head toward the house, raising his hand to block the glare from the inferno and hoping to see Sandvik somewhere outside. Warm, wet drops pattered onto his face. He looked up. Blood covered his left hand like a crimson glove illuminated by firelight. He wiggled his fingers. Pain shot through his hand. He couldn't move some of his fingers at all. *Worry about that later. First, find Sandvik . . .*

And Jack. He'd forgotten about the old dog after Sandvik showed up. Jack had been with him in the barn. He'd followed Matt to the house. Or had he? Matt peered toward the barn door, hoping to see Jack cowering there, waiting for reassurance it was safe to come out.

"Jack!" He yelled, a bit louder this time despite the pain in his lungs.

The roar and crackle of flames swallowed his cries as if they were whispers. He steeled himself with another long, painful breath and struggled to his feet using a corner of the pigsty for support. He scanned the area and called out again for his dog and the officer. The only sign of life was vehicle tail lights disappearing down the county road. Did those lights belong to the mystery SUV? Fearing the worst but unwilling to give up, he took a wobbly step toward the barn. The world tipped sideways. The ground rushed up to meet him. Shock set in, and he retched onto the cold, hard ground.

CHAPTER 27

"Matt . . . Matt. Wake up." The muffled female voice reminded him of jazz legend Sarah Vaughan—warm, sensual tones with hints of a reedy clarinet. Was this hauntingly beautiful speaker welcoming him to heaven? A hand touched his shoulder and shook him gently.

"Mmm. Wha—" He forced his eyes open, but they balked at the bright light. Wincing, he turned away from the light and focused on the woman who leaned over him. She wore a floral nurse's uniform top. A stethoscope hung around her neck. *I guess I'm not dead—yet.*

"Where am I?" he asked.

"The Straight River Hospital," Nurse "Sarah" said.

"What time is it?"

"About eight o'clock in the morning." Her nametag read: *Julia Deason, LPN.* Taller than average with light-brown hair and sharp facial features, she projected a robust, earthy aura that suggested she'd been raised in farm country.

Memories of fire, pain, and an explosion edged into Matt's mind. He groaned. "My head's throbbing and my ears are ringing like church bells. I'm having a tough time remembering what happened."

"Your house exploded," Deason said. "You banged your head pretty hard. In addition, you've got three broken ribs, a severe laceration on your left hand, several lacerations on your back and legs, and some minor abrasions."

"Is that all? I thought it was serious."

She didn't react to his dark humor. "On a scale of one to ten, describe your pain level."

"Worst I've felt in recent memory, so I guess around four or five."

She nodded, then adjusted the drip rate on the IV bag hanging above his bed that was hooked up to his right hand. "I increased the

148

med flow, so the pain will lessen soon. We did a CT scan on your head—no fractures or brain bleeds. X-Rays showed no broken bones other than your ribs. The doc wants to keep you here for a day or two to make sure you're healing properly."

"I'm good with that," Matt said, weak and disoriented. He vaguely remembered being worked on in the emergency room. Everything since the blast seemed like a nightmare rather than reality.

He raised his left hand and studied the bandages encasing it. He wiggled his fingers with great difficulty, then wiggled his right-hand fingers in comparison. Much easier. Sickening dread hit him as he wondered if he'd recover his full range of motion enough to play his bass again. His left hand was the fingering hand. The index and middle fingers were hardest to move. They were also the fingers that did most of the fretwork.

Playing bass had been a daily part of his routine for more than twenty years. Even assuming a full recovery, he didn't know if he'd still be able to play the most technically demanding classical or jazz bass parts as fluidly as needed to keep his regular gigs. If not, could he make a living solely by teaching? In his mind, teaching paled in comparison to playing. Panic coursed through his veins. *Life without performing? Inconceivable.*

Despite his pained and confused state, frustration forced itself upward from deep inside. He wanted to lash out at something. Hate someone. But how could he lash out against a destroyed house? How could he hate an accident? All he could think of was to blame God for putting him in the wrong place at the wrong time. He suddenly recalled the suspicious events going back to his father's death. *Yes. The SUV.* He could hate the driver. And if the association he suspected was true, he could hate Leland Smythe.

"Are you okay?" Deason asked. "You look like you're about to scream."

Matt focused on her and his surroundings. "Oh, sorry, yeah. Just thinking."

He breathed deeply to calm his anger.

An aide wheeled a rolling tray topped with metal-covered dishes into the room. Deason nodded to the young man and pressed something on the side of the bedframe. The head end of Matt's mattress flexed smoothly upward, raising him to a sitting position. She pulled the tray closer to his bed. "Time for breakfast."

The aroma of food made his stomach flip but also helped burn some of the fog out of his brain. A sharp vision of the farmhouse engulfed in flames flashed through his mind. He'd called the police. The young cop, Sandvik, had responded. Had he survived? More sickening pain rattled his body.

Another memory fragment came to him as he waited for the promised pain relief to kick in. The cop had been inside the house. Turned on the kitchen light. Then, *ka-boom*. Although he wasn't sure he wanted to hear the answer, he asked, "How's Sandvik?"

Deason hesitated, then fussed with Matt's pillow before positioning the tray table across his lap. The warmth in her voice evaporated as she spoke. "The paper said he didn't make it out of the house."

Matt's muddled brain struggled to comprehend the news. He shuddered with sorrow and grief. Then he remembered Jack. Where had the dog been immediately before the blast? They'd both been walking toward the house . . .

Tears welled in his eyes. "Not Jack too."

"Who's Jack?" Deason's eyebrows shot upward and she tensed.

"My dog."

She relaxed slightly. "No one mentioned finding a dog. But I doubt the fire department has gone through all the wreckage yet."

In the few short weeks they'd been together, Matt concluded Jack owned the gentlest canine soul he'd ever encountered. On top of that, Jack's warning had saved his life. The axiom *Man's best friend* had been proven again in spades.

After an awkward silence, Deason flashed a wistful smile. "I'd better attend to my other patients."

Alone with his thoughts after she left, Matt felt as though a massive weight was compressing his body and his spirit. More than anything, he wanted to get out of the hospital. Wanted to find the people responsible for the blast. Wanted revenge for his mangled hands. With his appetite now gone, he pushed the food tray away. Minutes later, the pain meds kicked in, and he drifted off to sleep.

~

"Code Blue, room two oh seven. Repeat, Code Blue, room two oh seven." The calm, metallic voice coming from the speaker startled Matt awake. The odors of antiseptics and institutional food confused him until he remembered he was in the hospital. Hurried footsteps outside his door indicated some sort of emergency in another room.

The noises and smells and scrambling medical personnel tugged at the periphery of his memory. Something else came to him.

The hit and run. Zach had saved him from death via SUV.

Had his computer sleuth unearthed a critical piece of information that caused Smythe to escalate his attacks? Matt needed to warn him. He called Directory Assistance from the bedside phone. Moments later, he was talking to Zach at University Hospital in Minneapolis.

He inquired about his colleague's condition—improved—and related his own misadventure from the day before. "This is getting way too dangerous, kid. As soon as you're out of the hospital, get somewhere safe. Lay low for a while. If Smythe wants me dead because of what I know, you might be on his list too."

"Dude, we're getting close to breaking this mystery open," Zach said. "We can't stop now."

"There's no *we* anymore. *You* forget you ever met me. I don't want your death on my conscience too."

Matt ended the call. He felt like a sitting duck in the hospital bed. He struggled to his feet and checked the cuts on his legs. Five strips of surgical tape on each limb covered stitched-up lacerations. He assumed the wounds on his back were worse because they hurt more than his leg wounds. He knew from his high-school football days that his ribs would take months to heal fully. The bandages on his left hand restricted his dexterity, but his right-hand trigger finger still worked. Matt eased himself back down onto the mattress and stared at the ceiling, despondent. Despite the vulnerability of being stuck in the hospital, he was safer there than anywhere else. He was in bad shape, and he doubted he could defend himself against anyone stronger or smarter than a ten-year-old bully.

CHAPTER 28

When Nurse Deason woke him again, Matt didn't know if two minutes or two hours had passed. He heard other voices and forced his eyes open.

Deason smiled when they made eye contact. "You've got company."

He turned his throbbing head toward the visitors.

"Matthew," Betty Myrick said, looking as though she might cry. "I'm so relieved to see you alive."

Matt managed to croak out, "Hi, Betty." Then he noticed the looming hulk standing next to her. "Hey, Swanny."

Swanson was ashen-faced and fidgeted with the ball cap in his hands. "Jesus, Matt, you look like shit."

Betty elbowed Swanson in the ribs.

"Ow!"

"David. Mind your language, please."

"Sorry, Betty." Swanson grimaced and blushed. "How ya doing, city boy?"

"I'm alive. Glad for that." Matt reached for the water glass on his tray table to quench the gritty dryness in his mouth.

"Wish I could say the same for Sandvik," Swanson said. "A damn—uh, *darn* shame." He chanced a quick peek at Betty's withering stare. "I know his parents. He was a good kid."

"Such a tragedy," Betty said. "The blast shook my walls and almost knocked me off my chair. I thought the Apocalypse had begun. The Lord must have better plans for you if he allowed you to survive that inferno."

"Amy and me were shopping in Mankato last night," Swanson said. "Got home and saw all the flames and fire trucks. I'm a volunteer fireman, so I geared up and rushed over to help. By then there wasn't much to do in the dark. I'll go in after I leave here to spell the guys who've been on site all morning. Some of them assumed the cause of the blast was a gas leak. What do you think?"

"Makes the most sense," Matt said, "but I'm not positive." He related the events up to the explosion the best he could: Jack's nervousness, Matt suspecting a break in and calling the police, Sandvik arriving and investigating. Then, *kaboom!* Matt stared at the ceiling. More details surfaced from the minutes before the blast. "Sandvik had his Maglite," he said. "And I don't *think* he turned on the kitchen light until he'd been inside for several seconds. If there was a propane leak, he should've smelled gas immediately and left."

"Maybe the spark happened at the circuit breaker in the basement," Swanson said. "Our fire chief might figure that out. He's a sharp tack."

"Yeah. Maybe." Matt shuddered with dread. If not for Jack's warning, he would've been the one to flip on the light and be blown to pieces. "Is Jack . . .?"

His visitors exchanged uneasy glances.

"When I called nine one one last night," Betty said, "they told me to stay in my house because it was too dangerous outside, so I couldn't look for Jack. But I spoke to a fireman this morning in your driveway and told him to spread the word and look for the black Labrador who lives there."

"I'll keep an eye out for him when I go over later," Swanson said.

"Thanks, guys." Matt smiled at his friends. "I also saw tail lights of a vehicle driving away shortly after the blast," he added. "That made me think of the SUV I've seen around the place, which made me think of the SUV in the hit-and-run."

"Wait. What?" Swanson said, mouth agape. "A hit-and-run?"

"I almost got hit by an SUV the other day. A college kid who's been helping me with some research pushed me out of the way at the last second. Unfortunately, the SUV hit him and broke his leg."

Betty's hand flew to her mouth. "Dear gracious me."

"I was lucky," Matt said. "Just a few scrapes and bruises from getting shoved out of the way. But it could've been curtains for me.

The driver was supposedly drunk, but I'm not sure that's the real story."

Swanson's face filled with shock and disbelief. "Holy sh—" He cut himself off before finishing the curse.

Betty cast another reproachful glance at Swanson, then squeezed Matt's shoulder. "From now on, I'll pray doubly often for your safety."

"Thanks."

"So. How long you in for?" Swanson asked.

"Another day or so. Doc wants me to wait until my ears stop ringing and my nausea goes away. You guys visiting sure helps me heal faster."

A knock at the door caused their heads to turn. Two men wearing the dark blue uniforms of the Straight County Police Department entered.

The older one said, "Mr. Lanier, I'm Chief Flannery. This is Officer Hansen. I'd like to ask you a few questions if you're up to it."

The taller Flannery had a military bearing and closely cropped dark-brown hair. Matt guessed him to be in his forties. Hansen was a baby-faced thirty-something with a blond crew cut. His stocky frame carried mostly muscle, implying he was a regular at a weight-training facility.

Matt glanced at his friends. Swanson appeared ready to bolt. Betty studied the officers as if she was determining their fitness to talk to her favorite neighbor. After saying a quick goodbye, she ushered Swanson out the door but gave Flannery a final suspicious once-over.

Flannery gestured at Hansen to close the door. "I won't mince words, Mr. Lanier. One of my men is dead. The logical assumption, in this case, is an accidental explosion, but I don't want to overlook any other possible explanations. I'd like you to tell me everything you can about what happened yesterday up until the fire department arrived on scene."

"I'll try," Matt said. "But my brain's still pretty fuzzy."

"Whatever you can remember will help." Flannery gave him a sympathetic, reassuring smile. The chief then nodded at Hansen, who opened a notebook and readied a pen.

Matt recounted his version of the day in erratic bits and pieces as new memories returned while he spoke. He emphasized his dog had tried to warn him about some danger, which prompted him to call the police.

Flannery narrowed his eyes. "You said you'd been away all day, and when you returned, you never stepped inside the house."

Matt nodded.

"Can you prove you were where you claimed to be the entire day? Right up until the time my officer arrived on the scene?"

Unease crept into Matt's mind. "Yeah, most of it, except while I was driving from one place to another."

"Did you notice the *exact* time when you arrived at your farm?"

"No. It was dark, so I guess around 8:30 or 9:00."

"I see." Flannery frowned. "Our call records indicate you called our emergency dispatcher at 9:32 last night."

"Okay," Matt shrugged. "I guess I got home closer to 9:30 then." His unease with Flannery's interrogation increased.

"Where were you when you last remembered checking the time?"

Matt thought for a moment, sorting through his daytime activities the best he could with a throbbing head and ringing ears. "I finished a lesson at 7:00. I stopped at a hole-in-the-wall burger place on the West Bank for a bite, then drove home."

"The U of M's West Bank?"

"Yes."

"Any traffic delays on your drive to Straight River?"

"No."

Flannery gazed out the window as if he were calculating something in his head. Then he leveled a hard stare at Matt. "I know from experience that the drive time from there to here is about one hour depending on traffic and road conditions. Assuming your quick-bite dinner took thirty minutes, leaving your lesson studio at 7:00 means you could've arrived at your farm well before 9:00. That leaves at least thirty minutes unaccounted for, Mr. Lanier."

Sudden panic fueled Matt's gut and stirred a mild wave of nausea. He swallowed hard and forced it back down. Suppressing the defensiveness in his voice, he said, "What are you implying, Chief Flannery?"

Hansen glanced up from his notepad with raised eyebrows.

"Nothing yet," Flannery said. His hard stare remained, augmented by a grim set to his lips. "But I intend to conduct a thorough investigation. I owe that to my department. I owe it to Officer Sandvik's memory."

"All I can say is *my* memory is still a bit fuzzy," Matt said. "I had a long day. I might've done some paperwork in my office after seven. Or the lesson ran longer than normal since it was the last one." He turned his head to look out the window, not wanting Flannery to see the fear in his eyes. *Does he actually believe I staged the explosion? If so, why?*

Flannery pulled a slip of paper from his shirt pocket, peered at it, then focused on Matt. "Last night was the fifth time you've called the police in less than a month. Twice it was to nine eleven, plus three calls directed to Sergeant Gebhardt. On top of that, your father reported suspicious activity three times in the weeks before he died." He chuckled, but there was more annoyance than humor in the sound. "That's a hell of a lot of calls from one little farm, wouldn't you say?"

Matt remained silent. He wouldn't give Flannery additional fodder for his line of questions, wherever they were leading.

"Quite often," Flannery said, "We get numerous calls from disgruntled residents who love to complain about every little thing just to get attention. Some are borderline mentally ill and—"

Matt snapped his head around to glare at Flannery. "My father was not mentally ill."

Looking annoyed, Flannery said, "And, as I was about to say, some are troublemakers who have an agenda against anyone in power: the police, government officials, the wealthy. They'll post hate messages online, harass officials with constant phone calls, sometimes anonymously."

"Don't you believe we're the victims here?" Matt tingled with anger, wanting to stand and stare down Flannery nose to nose. "Why the hell would my father, and now me, make up bogus vandalism stories or set our shed on fire for the sole purpose of causing trouble for the police and fire departments?"

"You tell me." Flannery's eyes looked cold and hard. "I checked your juvenile record. You had your share of trouble back then too."

Matt's cheeks ran hot at the mention of what he viewed as ancient history. Yes, he'd rebelled after his mother died. But he'd only acted out against his father's abrupt use of physical beatings to deal with his grief. He broke curfew and got cited for underage drinking and smoking pot. The worst crime was breaking into an abandoned house and spray painting a wall with a crude rendition of a gang message he'd seen on a railroad car parked on tracks near the edge of town. That infraction got him arrested and dragged home to his outraged father. The beating that time was so severe Matt missed a day of school because his father didn't want anyone to see blood seeping through Matt's shirt from the cuts inflicted by his belt buckle.

That's when Matt confided in Betty. She stepped in and had a private conversation with Ray. From then on, the beatings stopped for both boys. Betty never admitted it, but Matt believed she told his father to stop the corporal punishment or she'd call the county welfare folks. If the county decided to remove both his sons from their home, Ray would be left to work his farm alone.

Betty then began to nurture Matt's talent and interest in music and urged him to apply himself in school. She knew he was bright enough to earn a scholarship to any school he wanted to attend. Matt had kissed his delinquent past goodbye and never looked back—until now.

"Yeah, I had problems when I was a kid," he said, "but I don't hate cops. I don't have any agenda of violence or harassment. Why would I harm my father's property? That's nuts."

"I find it significant that every single call to us has been about alleged crimes with no witnesses. Your sergeant buddy also tells me you want us to believe that two unwitnessed deaths—your father's and Myrick's—are not from the causes listed on their Certificates of Death. I call that suspicious behavior, if not the behavior of a mentally unbalanced individual."

Suspicious. Flannery's unspoken intention crystallized in Matt's mind. Through clenched teeth, he said, "Is the purpose of this visit to charge me with some sort of crime in Sandvik's death?"

Hansen looked up from his notes with raised eyebrows, then scrunched his lips and glanced sidelong at his boss without turning his head.

Flannery sniffed. "Oh, no," he said in a reassuring tone. "I'll wait until we finish the investigation before I charge *anyone*."

The emphasis on *anyone* was subtle, but a gnawing suspicion in Matt's mind told him that *anyone* was code for *Matt Lanier*. Staring straight through Flannery's gaze, he said, "In that case, I've got nothing more to say without a lawyer present."

CHAPTER 29

The Lanier farmstead still bustled with activity at mid-morning some thirty-six hours after the blast. The fire department had put out the fire within several hours. But a small rural county such as Straight County lacked quick, easy access to heavy machinery to remove debris. Chief Flannery had been irate that Sandvik's death investigation had been delayed for twenty-four hours until a bulldozer and wrecking crane could be transported to the scene and start the cleanup. Today, the fire chief and several firefighters focused on clearing smaller debris left in the basement, working their way to the remains of the furnace to check for a cause of the explosion.

Because a police officer had perished, Flannery ordered round-the-clock police presence at the scene until the cause of death could be determined. Every outbuilding, the driveway, and two hundred yards in both directions on the county road had been secured by yellow crime scene tape.

Clay had been alerted immediately after the emergency call came in two nights earlier. Initially, he helped with perimeter security, amazed at how many people showed up to gawk at an inferno so late at night. By sunrise, he was able to grab a few hours of sleep at home before returning around noon. The gawkers had left, so he worked several mind-numbing, four-hour shifts spelling his men until the heavy machinery arrived on the second day to deal with the debris. Thankfully, the weather was cool and sunny. Standing here for hours in freezing drizzle would've turned his duty into a mental marathon.

Staring at the devastation, Clay again shuddered with relief that fate hadn't chosen him to be lying in the morgue instead of Sandvik. And how in God's name had Lanier survived? All that remained of the house was the stone foundation and a massive pile of charred wood and demolished household items. The explosion blew out every facing window in the outbuildings. Debris from the blast had been found more than fifty yards away.

When Clay spotted Dave Swanson coming down the road toward him, he waved. Swanson waved back. Clay walked to the end of Lanier's driveway to meet him, glad to relieve the boredom by chatting with his long-time friend.

"How's it goin'?" Swanson asked.

Clay jerked his thumb toward the big machines. "Wrecking crew got here a few hours ago. At least watching them keeps me awake. I swear the guy running the material handler could pluck a two-by-four out of one of those rubble piles with that giant claw and not disturb anything else. Like playing pick-up sticks when we were kids."

"Yeah, heavy equipment operators are artists all right. Did you know Matty almost got killed in a hit-and-run the other day too?"

Clay froze, mouth agape, as that comment hit him like a shock wave. "Seriously?"

Swanson nodded vigorously. "Up in Minneapolis. He told me yesterday." Pointing at the destroyed property, he said, "Now this. What are the odds that two *accidents* happen to the same guy within a couple days?"

Clay had never contemplated the question until now. "A million to one, I guess."

"At least, if not higher. You gonna figure out the cause of the blast pretty soon?"

Clay spread his palms up and shrugged. "Hard to say. If it wasn't for Lanier's nine one one call and Sandvik's death, I'm sure Flannery would've written this off as an accident and moved on after the fire was out."

Swanson's expression tightened as he looked past Clay and nodded in that direction. "Speak of the devil."

Clay turned to see the Chief pull up in his unmarked car. He glanced over his shoulder to confirm his officers were at least acting busy, then walked to the dark-brown Ford Crown Victoria.

"What's the latest, Sergeant?" Flannery said through his lowered window.

"Still digging, sir. The fire jockeys had to hose down a few hot spots in the basement, so they're just getting to the area near the furnace. As soon as that's clear, they'll check for a leak or malfunction."

Flannery got out of his car, noticed Swanson, and scrutinized him. His upper lip curled in disdain. "You again?"

Swanson narrowed his eyes. "I'm Dave Swanson. I own the farm next door. Took a break from my chores. Came over to say hi to my friend."

"I see," Flannery said. "And a friend of Lanier's too, I presume? You visited him in the hospital yesterday."

"Our families have farmed this land for decades," Swanson said, sounding insulted that the first-year police chief didn't know the long history between the Laniers and Swansons. "Matt and I were best friends as kids. So yeah, I *know* him."

Flannery eyed Clay. "Have you questioned him about the explosion?"

"Yes, sir. He and his wife were returning from Mankato and say they didn't get home until an hour later."

"Well then, Mr. Swanson," Flannery said, "perhaps you can give me some background about your friend."

"Matt's a stand-up guy. But until he came home after his father died, we hadn't talked in almost twenty years. Based on a few conversations lately, he seems like the same person he was when we were kids."

"Hmm. Ever notice any strange behavior or activity around here since he's been in town?"

Swanson arched his eyebrows and looked at Clay in disbelief. "Hell no. He spends most of his time making repairs, going through his father's stuff, dealing with the estate. He comes and goes a lot, sometimes late at night, because he's got performances and lessons up in the Cities."

"I see." Flannery's stare elicited another glance from Swanson to Clay.

Swanson shifted his posture and wiped his palms on his thighs. "I gotta go, Clay. Let you get back to work. See ya."

When Swanson had walked out of earshot, Flannery said, "This Lanier character has caused a lot of trouble around town since he returned. Repeated calls and complaints about how we handled his father's death and his neighbor's death. Seems like a continuation of his father's claims about so-called vandalism that happened here." He gestured toward the destroyed house. "And now this? Hard to believe this explosion was a coincidence when you consider all that preceded it. I heard the local press and radio say his father was a Commie back in the day. Radical enough to incite turmoil I'll bet. Musicians these days are known to be on the radical side of the spectrum too."

"Lanier a radical? I don't think—"

Flannery flipped his hand into a *halt* motion. "Something about this explosion reeks of criminality. Some kind of insurance fraud? Or maybe Lanier went off the deep end and is capable of arson if not murder. Either way, if the cause of the blast wasn't a propane leak, I want to know immediately."

"Yes, sir." A pang of anxiety and worry dug into Clay's brain. Where the hell was Flannery headed with this speculation? He fought back his questions again, still reluctant to challenge his boss. *Don't rock the boat,* particularly *when the seas are getting stormy.*

Flannery turned to Gebhardt. "Where's Chief Stewart?"

Clay nodded toward the house's foundation. "Over there."

Flannery began a fast walk toward the still-smoldering ruin and motioned Clay to follow.

Fire Chief Bill Stewart crouched on the ground next to the charred hole filled with rubble, directing four firefighters who were carefully digging through the debris.

Over the din of diesel engines, sounds of the wrecking crew, and loud chatter of the firefighters, Flannery shouted, "Bill, how much longer before you isolate the cause of the blast?"

When Stewart looked up, his expression soured. "Oh, hi, Mike." He didn't seem pleased to see his police counterpart, but he stood and whistled for his men to stop so he and Flannery could converse. "Not sure. An hour if we got the last of the hotspots. Two or three if not."

Flannery shook his head. He appeared equally displeased to be near Stewart. "Not fast enough. I have a strong suspicion this blast wasn't an accident."

"Come again?" Stewart said. He peered at Clay, who confirmed the statement with a slight nod. All the firefighters exchanged surprised glances.

Flannery briefed the group on his interview with Lanier yesterday, stressed his growing suspicion of Lanier as the perpetrator. "As of now," he said, talking louder, slower, more emphatically, "if anything suspicious is found in the wreckage or on this property, I want to be notified immediately."

Clay forced impassivity into his expression, although his insides churned with doubts about this questionable speculation.

Stewart pointed to two of his firefighters. "They're right on top of the furnace. As soon as they clear the debris, they'll inspect the connection." He glowered at his counterpart. "I won't rush them and compromise their safety."

Flannery stiffened. "You're right. No need for anyone else to get hurt. Just find the cause ASAP." He turned to Clay. "Spread the word to your men about this."

"Yes, sir."

Flannery did an about-face and left.

"Prick," Stewart muttered when the police chief was out of earshot.

Clay suppressed a grin at Stewart's succinct assessment of his boss.

As the Straight River fire chief for twenty-five years, the no-nonsense Stewart had earned the respect of not just his men but of the entire county. The main difference between the two chiefs was the contrast in leadership styles. Flannery's ironclad discipline and insistence on blind obedience from his men contrasted sharply with Stewart's approach. The fire chief believed in letting his men think for themselves and trust their intuition rather than race blindly into a burning house based on orders or rigid protocol. He'd hinted at retirement, but most insiders doubted he'd leave unless he was forced out by age or health—or from not caring to butt heads with Flannery anymore.

"What connection?" Clay asked. "Didn't the whole house blow to kingdom come?"

"With explosions in a basement, the path of least resistance is always up. Since a furnace is too heavy to fly, and metal doesn't melt at these lower fire temps, we can check the connection between the furnace and propane tank to see if it worked itself loose or if someone unhooked it. If so, you've got yourself either a careless furnace installation or a homicide. If not, there could've been a leak somewhere else in the gas line."

"What about a furnace malfunction? Say the pilot light goes out, but the gas keeps flowing."

Stewart shook his head. "My cousin Jerry's an HVAC contractor. He showed up here this morning after hearing about the blast. Said he installed a new furnace for Ray about five years ago. The new ones have safety features that are designed to prevent malfunctions. He's worried people will blame either his product or his shoddy workmanship for the cop's death. Bad for business, you know."

Clay jotted some notes into his notebook. He was watching his men pick through debris in the yard when a shout from the basement caused a commotion among the fire crew. He hurried back to the foundation.

"What've you got?" Stewart said.

"Looks like someone disconnected the feeder line," one of the diggers said.

"Hold on, I want to see for myself." Stewart clambered down a ladder and picked his way through the rubble. He knelt to inspect the furnace, consulted with the crewmembers, then returned to the ladder. As he ascended, Stewart said through tight lips, "This was no accident."

"Son of a bitch." Clay swallowed hard. His stomach did a backflip. "Are you sure?"

Stewart wiped his sooty hands on a towel. "Ninety-nine percent. The coupling between the feeder line and the furnace is secured with a locking nut. Those suckers don't work themselves loose, even over five years. You need a pipe wrench to disconnect it."

"Any sign of what detonated the propane?"

"Most of the time it's due to a something simple but unintentional. Anything that creates a spark. Turning on a poorly wired light switch for example."

"According to Flannery," Clay said, "Lanier told him that Sandvik went inside, looked around with his flashlight for several seconds, then flipped on the kitchen light. He specifically remembered the explosion happened a few seconds *after* the light came on. If Sandvik had smelled gas in the kitchen, he would've come outside without turning on the light. But he didn't. Why?"

Stewart stated the obvious answer. "No gas aroma for him to smell."

Clay nodded. "Because propane is heavier than air?"

Stewart returned the nod. "It would've collected in the basement. Enough to destroy the house, especially if the storage tank wasn't empty. Plenty of extra to feed the fire once it got ignited."

"Could Lanier have somehow detonated the gas from outside?"

Stewart eyed him warily. "Sure, with a remote-control transmitter. But the first responders told me he was about ten feet away from being another piece of charred rubble. Either he's a moron or he severely underestimated the magnitude of the blast."

In fact, Lanier was one of the most intelligent people Clay had ever met. But book smarts didn't always correspond to street smarts or technical skill. Lack of common sense might have played a part. Or a blind desire for some sort of revenge. A sliver of doubt took root in his mind. Had Lanier played him for a sap? Did he have a secret agenda? Why would Lanier commit premeditated murder because two death investigations contradicted what he wanted to believe? Only a true psychopath would go that far.

"Terrorists use cell phones to remotely detonate bombs," Stewart said. "If they're using a visual cue to set off the bomb, they need to be at least within binocular range. A typical example is when the Taliban or some guerilla group targets a military convoy with an IED. Simply connect one cell phone to the bomb and call that number with another phone from a safe observation point. The electrical current generated by the receiving phone—the one hooked to the device—completes the circuit, which triggers the explosion. Just takes a second or two of lead time."

"Is it possible the light switching on was a visual cue for whoever detonated the bomb."

"I don't see how else a deliberate explosion could've been timed that precisely."

The men exchanged glances, both pondering other explanations. Clay furrowed his brow. "What if Lanier's lying? What if he had an accomplice and they got their signals crossed, or the bomb didn't go off right away? Lanier walks toward the house, thinking he's got to bluff Sandvik by pretending everything's okay, and *then* the bomb goes off."

Stewart tilted his head, skepticism in his eyes. "Anything's possible."

Clay ran the facts through his mind again: the police call, gas line disconnected, Sandvik dead, Lanier severely injured, no incriminating evidence found. Lanier could've lied about his innocence, but why on earth would he have been within a mile of the house if he planned to blow it up? No explanation with Lanier as the bad guy made any sense other than the man had gone off the deep end . . . or he *didn't* know about the gas leak.

Clay called Flannery at the LEC and explained the disconnected gas main and his discussion with Chief Stewart about remote detonation.

"I knew it!" Flannery exclaimed loudly enough to hurt Clay's ear. "But an unhooked gas pipe isn't enough evidence to implicate Lanier for murder. I need more, Sergeant."

"Sir, we've already searched the grounds for hours and found nothing."

"Think outside the box on this one, Sergeant. Lanier grew up on that farm. He knows every possible hiding place for anything. Tell your men to search the barn again, then the other buildings. This time have them dig deeper—literally. Check inside hay bales, behind loose boards, under piles of manure, for God's sake."

"Yes, sir." Clay snapped his phone shut after he heard the line go dead. His churning gut signified his frustration with Flannery's growing obsession to accuse Lanier of a crime.

~

An hour later, the searchers had found nothing new. Taking a water break, Clay again marveled at the deftness of the machine operator as the giant material handler grasped hundreds of pounds of debris in its steel jaws and moved it from the basement to a ground-level rubble pile. Hearing a commotion from inside the barn, Clay turned to see two of his men, Hansen and Noble, exit the barn and hurry toward him.

"Gotta see this, Sarge." Hansen said. He held a small cardboard box in his gloved hands. "Found it behind a half-rotten section of barn siding. I was kicking the boards, frustrated because we'd already searched the entire barn and had to do it again. A chunk of rot fell off, and we saw the box."

Clay donned his own pair of latex gloves and took the box from Hansen. Inside were a small spool of a fine wire filament, a length of household electrical cord, and an opened packet of alligator clips. He wasn't a bomb expert, but the conversation with Chief Stewart about cell phone bombs resonated in his brain.

His blood raced and the hair on the back of his neck prickled as he searched the grounds for Stewart. A lieutenant said Stewart had returned to the station, so Clay called and described the contents. Stewart confirmed the items could indeed be used to fashion a simple detonator but recommended consulting a bomb squad expert to be sure.

"Sweet Jesus H!" Clay blurted out when the unthinkable hit him like a sledgehammer: It was now theoretically *possible* that Matt Lanier had intentionally blown up his own house.

CHAPTER 30

A sharp knock on the door roused Matt from a doze. He turned his head toward the sound as Dave Swanson slipped into the hospital room. Grim-faced, with intense eyes, carrying a brown paper sack tucked under one arm, Swanson appeared to be as taut as piano wire.

"Time to get you out of here, Matty." His voice was low but every bit as intense as his body.

"Huh?" Matt still felt loopy from painkillers and the ringing in his ears.

Swanson tossed the sack onto the bed. A pair of jeans and a blue flannel shirt spilled out. "Put 'em on. Don't tuck the shirt in too tight. Leave it baggy so you don't look so much like your scrawny self. I'm springing your ass from this barless prison."

"What? Why? I can't leave." Matt raised his bandaged left hand. "In case you forgot, I have some serious injuries that need to heal properly."

Swanson gave him a how-stupid-do-you-think-I-am look. "You can't afford to wait until your boo-boos are all better, meathead. I came back and eavesdropped outside your room when Flannery was here yesterday. Then I was over to your place this morning talking to Clay when Flannery showed up again. Heard enough to know he's got it in for you."

A chill shot down Matt's spine. The situation was so ludicrous he still thought he might be having a surreal nightmare. "You think Flannery's serious about that crazy notion I blew up my own house?"

"As serious as a spring drought. Paper said propane leak, but I got this sick feeling the explosion was no accident. I think *you* were supposed to flip the light switch. That means someone wants you dead because you're digging around in this real estate stuff. If the hit-

and-run was the first try, this was the second. Since you survived, their next best option for shutting you down is to pin the blast on you. Damn hard to do any detective work from jail."

Matt flashed back to the aftermath of the blast when he saw the tail lights of a vehicle driving away. He groaned. "Of course. The SUV driver might've been close enough to detonate the explosion when he knew someone was inside—right after the light switched on. If Jack hadn't warned me, I'd be dead."

"That's one hell of a dog you've got."

"Tell me about it. Has anyone found him yet?"

Swanson shook his head. "We'll keep looking. Main thing is to get out of here so you ain't a sitting duck. Sign yourself out against doctor's orders. They can't legally keep you here unless you're under arrest."

Still confused, but hopeful now that he was getting help from Swanny, Matt sat up to take off his hospital gown.

Swanson pulled an adhesive bandage from his pocket and unwrapped it. "Pull your IV. I'll put this on your hand to stop the bleeding."

After Swanson applied the bandage, Matt got dressed. Putting on socks and buttoning the shirt was painful and awkward with only one good hand. His pain was lessening but still substantial. Going without pain medication might become a genuine problem. Matt put on his blood-spattered running shoes, stood, and looked at Swanson. "What's the plan?"

"Go out through the north entrance. No security cameras there. I checked earlier. I'll slip down the back stairs and drive around to meet you." Swanson pulled a Twins baseball cap and sunglasses from his back pocket and tossed them onto the bed. "Put these on after you sign out. Make sure no one gets a good look at your face. You can't outrun them in your condition. If you see any police, especially Flannery, duck into a room."

Swanson flashed a furry grin and a *thumbs up* sign, then slipped into the hallway.

Matt picked up the hat and sunglasses, gave Swanson a sufficient head start, and shambled toward the nurses' station.

Julia Deason was sitting behind the counter. Her brow crinkled and her usually cheerful countenance drooped to a maternal scowl. "Why are you out of bed and dressed?"

Through the pain he forced a smile that felt more like a grimace. "I'm much better today. I need to get to an important meeting, so I'm checking myself out."

Despite her vehement protest, Matt convinced Deason he was lucid and healthy enough to leave. He signed an Against Medical Advice discharge form, got into the elevator, and donned the cap and sunglasses when he reached the main floor. Before exiting, he peeked out and glanced from side to side, scanning for police. Despite being grateful for Swanson's unexpected assistance, he felt as if he were playing the role of some low-brow secret agent in a high school play. Breathing deeply to overcome a sudden dizzy spell, which further clouded his thoughts, he slipped out of the elevator and made a beeline for the north entrance.

As he stepped outside, Matt spied Swanson behind the wheel of a Dodge pickup idling at the curb. He hesitated because Swanson owned a Ford. Puzzled, Matt struggled into the passenger seat, gasping as pain shot through his ribs. He hadn't expected to be so weak after spending less than two days in the hospital.

"Where'd you get this truck, Swanny?"

"Borrowed it from a trusted friend. Mine's parked a few blocks away. I didn't want anyone to see my truck at the hospital because they've got security cams watching the main entrance and front parking lots. We'll switch in a minute."

Moments later, Swanson pulled into the parking lot of a deserted commercial building. They switched vehicles in seconds. While Matt fumbled for his seat belt, Swanson zipped out of the lot. He took a sharp turn too fast and drifted across the centerline before he corrected and narrowly averted a collision with an oncoming car.

Matt gasped and grabbed the door handle. "Damn, are you trying to save my ass just so you can kill me in a car accident? If I'm supposed to worry about Flannery, getting arrested for speeding won't help."

Swanson didn't slow down. "The sooner we get you out of sight of everyone, the better."

"Who's everyone?"

"Flannery, the SUV jockey, *Saxony Partners.*"

Matt stiffened. "How the hell do you know about Saxony Partners? I never mentioned that name to you."

Swanson glanced at Matt, then focused on the road. His fingers were white from the pressure he exerted on the steering wheel. "Until this afternoon, I worked for them."

CHAPTER 31

Matt recoiled as if he'd walked into an invisible door. A volcano of anger erupted from deep within. "You fucking traitor!" He wanted to assault his *former* best friend with a verbal barrage to compensate for his lack of physical ability, but he couldn't form a coherent sentence other than, "Son of a *bitch*. If I were healthy, I'd beat you senseless."

A shamefaced Swanson glanced back and forth from the road to Matt. "I am *really* sorry. But I can explain."

Matt had never felt so betrayed by anyone in his life, not even Diane when she'd filed for divorce. To calm himself, he breathed as deeply as his ribs allowed. "This had better be good."

"It sucks, but it's the God's honest truth. At first, working for Saxony seemed innocent enough. Hibbert approached me. Said his boss wanted info about the farm situation around here. Who's buying, selling, in trouble, doing okay, things like that."

Matt glared at him. "You spied on your friends and neighbors?"

"I wasn't spying. Just told him what I saw going on. Like a consultant." Swanson veered into his driveway and skidded to a stop in the wet dirt next to his house. As he got out, he said, "Leave the shades and hat on until we get inside."

With pained effort, Matt followed him inside. "Keep talking."

"A few days later, I get a letter that just says, 'Thank you,' with three hundred bucks inside. Unsigned, no return address, nothing."

"From Hibbert? Or rather, Saxony?"

"That's what I assumed. Then Hibbert calls later that day, asks about George Schultz wanting to sell some land. I confirm Schultz wants to sell. He says, 'If Saxony pays the mortgage for you, will you make the purchase for us?' I'm suspicious, of course, but he says,

'Make a deal as if you're spending your own money. I'll reimburse you and throw in a little extra for your trouble.' I figure why not?"

Swanson sat in the recliner in his living room and gestured for Matt to sit. Matt eased himself onto the sofa with a long groan. His numerous physical pains were minuscule compared to the mental pain of betrayal by the man who'd been his best friend for half of his life.

"Two days later," Swanson continued, "I get another thank you letter with seven hundred dollars inside telling me there'll be a lot more if I cooperate in the future. Then Hibbert shows up with a contract for me to sign and a check from Saxony Partners for the down payment on Schultz's land. The deal seems legit, so I deposit the check in my bank account and buy the land."

Matt gaped at Swanson. "You sold out for a thousand bucks?"

Swanson bowed his head. "Farming's tough these days. Hundreds of us farmers are still hurting from the Great Recession like all the city homeowners. The extra money came in handy. I didn't see any downside, and everything appeared to be legal."

"Unbelievable."

"After that, Hibbert told me to talk him up and put the selling bug into the old-timers around here. I worked on Helmer a bit, your dad some too."

"Aw, Jesus, you didn't." Matt slumped into the corner of the sofa and covered his face with his hands. What little energy he still possessed left his body as if someone had pulled a bathtub drain.

"I didn't want to, Matty. I *had* to." His tone was desperate, pleading. "After I signed the contract, Hibbert said if I don't cooperate, Saxony will stop payments on the Schultz mortgage. I would've been in deep shit with the bank, maybe go bankrupt, lose my farm."

Swanson pursed his lips and wrung his hands. "We're third-generation here. Eligible for a Century Farm designation if I can keep the business running for fifteen more years. Me and Amy put our hearts and souls into this place. I never imagined earning a few extra bucks would put that at risk."

Matt dropped his hands and glared at Swanson, nauseated by his betrayal. "You lowlife scum. I don't know who to hate more, you or Smythe. At least he didn't screw over his friends and neighbors."

"Who's Smythe?"

"Hibbert's boss. The head of Saxony Partners and a big real estate wheeler-dealer based in the Twin Cities."

Swanson expelled a low whistle of surprise. "So this is kind of serious?"

"Ya think? Not just for you and me either. Do you have any idea what this megalomaniac is up to?"

"Uh, yeah, he's buying up farmland in the county through Saxony Partners. Probably gonna build some big devel—"

"Not just the county. He's buying farmland all along Interstate 35 from Minneapolis to the Oklahoma border. As much as he can get his greedy hands on. A conspiracy too complicated to explain right now. I counted at least thirty purchases when I researched his deals. Now I find out he might have surrogates like you buying for him. He might control ten times as much land as I initially believed. Hundreds of farmers could get cheated out of their farms. Your land also abuts I-35, so don't think Smythe won't screw you over too. All he has to do is stop payment on Schultz's place. You'll go belly up and he'll swoop in and snatch up your land for pennies on the dollar."

Swanson's eyes bulged with shocked realization. He leaned back into his recliner. "Holy shit. I had no clue about a conspiracy. I assumed all my consulting was local small-time stuff, over in a few months."

Matt jerked his body upright, ignoring the sharp pain in his ribs. "Over? This will never be over unless you count being dead as over."

"Dead? Me?" Swanson's expression was incredulous.

"Helmer, my dad, Hibbert, all might've been killed because they got in Smythe's way, messed up his plans. Unfortunately, there are no witnesses, and we can't prove anything. I'm obviously on his hit list. So if Smythe even *thinks* you helped me, you're on that list too."

Swanson swallowed hard and his eyes unfocused.

Through the fog of pain from his injuries and the dulling effects on his brain from the pain pills he'd been taking, another suspicion broadsided Matt. If it turned out to be true, he was afraid he would try to kill Swanson on the spot. "I'll only ask you this question once, Swanny. And I want the truth." He stared deep into Swanson's eyes. "Did you have anything to do with my father's death?"

"*What?*" Swanson gaped at him, dumbfounded. "No. I could never kill *anyone*. I swear."

"But *you* were the first one on the scene."

"Matty, I—I—" Swanson's face reddened. He seemed dismayed at the possibility Ray had been murdered. Panicked too. "I swear I didn't hurt Ray in any way, ever. The police told me later he'd been dead for hours before I showed up."

Matt doubted Swanson was capable of deadly violence, but he wondered if his old friend might have unknowingly aided or abetted his father's killer. "How can I be sure you're telling me the truth when you lied to me about working for Hibbert all this time?"

"All I did against your dad was torch that old shed of yours. Saxony's—I mean *Smythe's*—orders. A warning shot. Ray hadn't used the shed in years. He'd gone into town when I did the deed. I made sure he wouldn't get hurt trying to put it out himself. I got real nervous afterward, but I figured that was the worst thing I'd have to do for them. I know it was wrong, but again, they had my balls in a vise." Swanson cradled his head in his hands, his elbows resting on his knees, looking ready to collapse in a heap on the floor. "I am *so* sorry I did even that little bit."

No one could've faked Swanson's reaction, so Matt relaxed his fist and leaned back. "Forget it. Let's focus on finding a possible killer. Have you met or talked to anyone else from Saxony Partners? A huge, bald guy in particular? He's one of Smythe's security goons and probably the guy in the SUV who tried to run me down the other day."

Swanson regained his composure, then stared at the ceiling and scratched his beard. "No. I've only talked to Hibbert. Thought he was a one-man show. He never mentioned anybody from Saxony Partners."

"If Flannery is working with Smythe," Matt said, "that would explain why he thinks I blew up my own house. If Smythe can't kill me, he can neutralize me by putting me in jail."

"A crooked police chief is a pretty serious charge."

"It happens. Mostly in big cities, but there are crooks everywhere. No reason it couldn't happen here. Now I wonder if Gebhardt's foot dragging might've been ordered by Flannery." Matt leaned back and massaged his forehead. How had a chance reunion between two boyhood friends come to this unbelievable point?

Swanson snapped his fingers. "What if we go to another police department or the FBI and tell them we suspect Flannery's working for Smythe on some scheme to—"

"With no proof and no witnesses, it's our word against theirs," Matt said. "Plus, there's no guarantee Smythe doesn't have other cops on his payroll. But we have a more immediate problem. If the cops think I blew up my own place and killed Sandvik in the process, they'll be looking for me."

Swanson's expression came alive. "Okay, first things first. Now that we know what we're up against, we gotta fight back harder and smarter. If we don't, we're screwed. We gotta assume the cops will quickly learn you left the hospital. After they check your condo, they'll talk to me and Betty, seeing as how Flannery saw us at the hospital. If I hide you here, you're safe for a while unless they come with a warrant to search my house."

"It's a start."

"If I play dumb about springing you from the hospital, I might learn something that'll help us nail their hides to the wall."

"You think you can lie to their faces about me?"

"I fooled you up to now, didn't I?"

Matt frowned. He'd always prided himself on his ability to read body language and detect voice fluctuations. "Yeah, I guess you did, you bastard. I suspected something but chalked it up to not knowing you as well as I used to. Figured you'd changed since we were kids."

"I promise to let you beat the living shit outta me when you're healthy, but right now I might be your only friend."

The *ding-ding* of a bell stopped their discussion. But instead of answering the door, Swanson hustled to a window overlooking his driveway. He came back seconds later with a grim expression on his face. "Police. Let's go."

Matt's heart leaped to his throat. "Go where? They'll see me if we leave the house."

"That wasn't the doorbell," Swanson said. "A few years ago, I installed a warning bell here in the house and a red light and buzzer in the barn to signal us whenever someone turns into the driveway. Sort of a security system for Amy's sake. Follow me. I've got about a minute to hide you."

Swanson led him down the basement stairs into a far corner of the cool, musty-smelling, cobweb-filled basement. One bare light bulb lit the way. Swanson pulled a frayed, well-worn rug back from the floor and opened an underlying wooden door.

Matt froze. A thin layer of cold sweat materialized on his back as he recognized the old root cellar they used to play in as kids. They'd pretended to be vampires or zombies who'd been buried alive and then rose from the dead to terrorize the countryside. He forced a dry swallow. "Oh, no. I'm not getting into that dirt coffin. I barely fit when I was a kid. Hide me somewhere else."

The real doorbell rang, louder and lower-pitched than the warning bell.

"Get in, you chicken shit." Swanson glared at him with an intensity as commanding as his voice. "There ain't nowhere else this safe right now. If Flannery or Gebhardt shows up with a warrant, I can't stop them from searching the place."

Sweat seeped through the bandage on Matt's left palm. *I hate it when Swanny's the voice of reason.* He climbed into the hole and crammed his body into the tight space. "Damn. Make it fast. I might go berserk and scream."

Swanson closed the door over the entry. Matt heard the rug flop onto the door. The sound of footsteps faded as Swanson raced upstairs.

Matt squeezed his eyes closed, took deep breaths, and tried to calm his racing heart and quell the panic welling up from the pit of his stomach. To distract his mind from the suffocating musty-earth smell of his tomb, he softly whistled Bobby McFerrin's "Don't Worry, Be Happy." But he did worry, and he wasn't happy.

CHAPTER 32

When Swanson opened his front door, Clay began to evaluate his demeanor, ready to catch him in a lie. "Sorry to bother you, Swanny. I need to ask you a few questions."

Swanson didn't appear apprehensive other than his eyes flicked from side to side. "What about?"

"Don't suppose you've seen Lanier? I stopped by the hospital, but they told me he'd checked himself out. Kinda strange considering he damn near died the other day. Have you seen him today?"

Swanson maintained eye contact as his expression turned to one of puzzlement. "Nope. I've been here all morning doing chores except for a few hours ago when I talked with you at his place. Betty and I visited him yesterday. He was in bad shape. I'm shocked he bugged outta there."

"Right. Has he called you?"

"No. You check his condo? That's probably where he went."

"His Sienna is still at the farm. Thought I'd check around town first."

Swanson shrugged. "Like I said, I haven't seen him."

Clay studied Swanson's face for any sign of deception. Finding none, he handed him his business card. "If you hear from him, give me a call or tell him to call me."

Swanson jammed the card into his front pocket, then stepped onto the porch as if preparing to usher Clay to his car. "Is Matt in some kind of trouble?"

Clay rubbed the back of his neck and nodded. "Yeah. Maybe worse than he knows. I, uh, need to ask him some more questions about the explosion."

Swanson turned his head in the general direction of the hospital. "Must be a misunderstanding then. Matt's not a troublemaker."

Clay followed his gaze. "Not saying he started it, just got caught up in it."

He smiled grimly before heading back to his squad car. Halfway there, he noticed a set of footprints in the damp dirt on the passenger side of Swanson's truck. He knelt to inspect them. They were fresh, large enough to be a man's, and from athletic shoes. Farmers usually wore steel-toed boots while working. He stood and checked Swanson's feet—he wore work boots. He debated whether to ask him about a recent passenger. If Swanson was hiding Lanier, confronting him might cause him to panic and do something stupid like pull a gun. Retreating for now but putting a watch on the house might be the smarter call. Clay simply shrugged and waved, acting as if what he'd been inspecting was insignificant.

Swanson gave a short nod and an abbreviated hand wave, then went inside.

Clay got into his car and called Flannery. "Lanier's not at the hospital, Chief, but his car's still at the farm. The duty nurse said he checked out against the doctor's advice because he had some meeting, so he could've taken a cab to get there. I talked with Dave Swanson. He hasn't seen Lanier since yesterday at the hospital right before you got there."

"So Lanier's running. Makes him look pretty damn guilty of something." Flannery sounded triumphant. "A God-damned cop killer. If it's the last thing I do, I'll make sure that bastard rots in prison."

"Sir," Clay said urgently, "we know it wasn't an accidental gas leak, but we can't prove Lanier set the trap."

"He's the prime suspect, which is good enough for me." Flannery's tone held a tinge of acrimony. "Put all available personnel on this. Question the hospital staff. Check their security camera footage. Ask the Minneapolis police to check his residence up there. I'll call in the BCA. I want to make sure nothing is missed. The county attorney will insist on an airtight case."

"Yes, sir." Clay's nerves fired up. Something wasn't right. So far, the evidence against Lanier was only circumstantial, yet Flannery's behavior bordered on obsession. If the Bureau of Criminal Apprehension got involved, this case could turn into a statewide manhunt. But they'd want more convincing evidence against Lanier before they spent time and money on such a shaky case.

His bigger concern was his own attitude. He worried that his friendship with Lanier had clouded his judgment. However, his cop instincts leaned toward believing Lanier over his own boss. During his nearly twenty-year career in law enforcement, he never imagined he'd have a reason to doubt any police officer's integrity—until now.

CHAPTER 33

After what seemed to Matt like hours of mental torture, Swanson opened the root cellar door. Matt struggled to quell his shaking. His breath came in short gasps, on the verge of hyperventilating. Sweat trickled from his face despite the fifty-five-degree temperature. He struggled out of the hole with Swanson's help and shuddered. "When I die, don't bother with a coffin. Toss my body onto a huge bonfire."

Swanson shot him an exaggerated eye roll. "Get over it, ya big baby. That was Gebhardt. He knows you're missing, but I'm not sure he's on your side. He might've been trying to trick me into telling him I sprung you."

"I have to trust him, for now." Despite their history, Matt still wasn't sure if he could trust Gebhardt, especially given his reluctance to help so far. The smart play would be to call him, feel him out, then convince him to keep digging and find the real killer. He inhaled slow and deep to help clear his head and winced when his ribs protested.

"How's your pain?" Swanson asked.

"Bad and getting worse. Haven't taken a pain pill since breakfast."

"Amy might have something strong. I'll check the medicine chest. And speaking of food, c'mon up and have some chow. Never hurts to fill your belly in case you have to hide again." Swanson led the way up the rickety wooden stairs to the kitchen. "Check the fridge. Should be some leftover roast beef from last night."

Matt opened the refrigerator and found the meat along with some potato salad and green bean casserole. Moments later Swanson returned holding a prescription bottle.

"Tylenol 3." He handed the bottle to Matt. "A little past the expiration date, but they oughta do the trick."

Matt opened the bottle and counted a dozen or so pills. "Thanks." He popped one into his mouth and washed it down with a glass of water.

The men set about plating, then devouring, their food at the kitchen table.

Swanson stared out the kitchen window. Intense concentration showed on his face. "Can't use your car. Can't go to your condo. Flannery will ask the Minneapolis police for a stakeout five minutes after he discovers you're not in the hospital. I can hide you here for a while, but that ain't a long-term solution."

Matt shuddered at the mere mention of his temporary coffin. "Once in that crypt was enough. But while I was in there, I remembered I saw a Mercedes SUV parked outside Smythe Properties. I got a strange feeling about it, like a premonition, so I wrote down the license plate number. Clay could look up the owner, then check with the Minneapolis police to see if anyone got the plate number of the hit-and-run SUV and compare the two. Getting the driver on a hit-and-run charge might lead to answers about everything else."

"Yeah, sure," Swanson said with faux confidence as he regarded Matt with a squint and a smirk. "Easy peasy, nice 'n' easy." He paused. "Assuming Clay's on your side."

"Got a better suggestion?"

"Nope." Swanson burped and pushed away from his empty plate, then stood and grabbed his dishes.

"Let me help clean up," Matt said and started to rise.

"Sit," Swanson commanded. "You're *my* patient now. Rest and finish eating."

Matt complied, grateful that Amy's leftovers tasted so much better than hospital food. While Swanson worked, Matt mulled possible next steps that might keep him alive and out of jail.

"So, where you gonna hide?" Swanson said after he'd loaded the dishwasher.

"You've already risked your ass getting me this far. The less you know from here on, the better."

"I get that, but how you gonna nail Smythe or Flannery if you're in hiding?"

"I need some time to heal before I can fight back at all. I'll work out the rest of the plan while I'm recuperating."

"Let me do *something* for you. Anything. I feel responsible."

Swanson's palpable remorse triggered a twinge of sympathy in Matt, which in turn triggered another piece of his nascent plan. He visualized a supply list: innocuous but sturdy transportation, warm clothes, foul weather gear, a handgun, a rifle, ammunition, a week's worth of food, tent, sleeping bag, and related camping equipment. With intentional vagueness, he said, "Food, clothes, wheels, a weapon."

Swanson waggled a forefinger and bit his lower lip. "Orvie O'Connor, over to the junkyard, owns some pretty decent wrecks. I've been in the market for an old pickup to haul wood and gravel. He has several that are good for a few thousand miles. I can get one for a couple hundred bucks. We'll call it a rental, so no title transfer."

"Sounds perfect. Just make sure it's not so wrecked as to be conspicuous."

"Right. Let's go to the Salvation Army thrift store for some clothes. No security cameras there. On the way back, we'll stop at the bus depot. If you still think calling Gebhardt's a good idea, you can use the old payphone there. Less chance of a trace."

"What about weapons?"

Grinning, Swanson jerked his thumb toward the back door. "Follow me."

He led Matt outside to a steel utility shed, unlocked the door, and opened it with a dramatic sweep of his arm. "Shall we step into my armory?"

The shed smelled of gun oil and bluing and featured a workbench laden with a variety of tools and bullet-making equipment. Swanson flipped on a fluorescent light fixture suspended from the ceiling. To the right of the bench was another padlocked door. Swanson unlocked and opened the door to reveal the biggest gun safe Matt had ever seen.

Matt exhaled an impressed whistle. Swanson owned at least twenty weapons ranging from pistols, revolvers, and BB guns to rifles, shotguns, and a semiautomatic assault rifle. In addition to the firepower suspended on the wall of the safe, the floor was stacked with at least a dozen boxes of several types and sizes of ammunition.

"I think we can find something to arm any self-respecting fugitive," Swanson said in an earnest used-car-salesman voice.

~

After loading Swanson's truck with food, weapons, and ammunition, the two men drove to the thrift store and bought clothing for Matt. Next, they headed for O'Connor's salvage yard. Matt wore his Twins hat and sunglasses and stayed in the truck while Swanson negotiated with O'Connor for a gray Dodge Ram pickup whose exterior showed plenty of scratches and dents but not much rust. The high-mileage, late-model crew cab had been used long and hard for the past three years by an itinerant construction worker who lived in a fifth-wheel he hauled around the western mountain states driving from job to job. During his free time, he would then go off-roading to fish, hunt, and camp. Even though all the electronics and safety features worked well, the price was right because O'Connor couldn't guarantee the transmission or suspension much past the Straight County line. Matt slid into the driver's seat of his new truck and followed Swanson to the bus depot—a small storefront in the much larger, but now-unused passenger railroad depot. After parking, he sat immobile, still unsure about calling Gebhardt.

Swanson exited his truck and walked to Matt's window. Through the glass, he mimed holding a phone. "You gonna make the call?"

Matt lowered the window. "I feel like I'm signing my death warrant."

"Seriously?" Swanson looked and sounded incredulous as he handed Matt some coins. "Your death warrant got signed the minute you figured out Smythe was stealing land from good, honest farmers. The hit-and-run and the explosion prove that."

Matt stepped out of the truck and walked toward the pay phone outside the depot—an old-fashioned, aluminum-and-plexiglass booth with a bifold door. Swanson stood watch nearby, trying to look inconspicuous but failing. Matt inserted the coins and punched in the phone number. Claustrophobia enveloped him again—not as much as when he'd been in the root-cellar coffin, but enough to prickle his skin with cold sweat.

Gebhardt answered after two rings.

"Clay, it's Matt."

"Where in the God-damned *hell* are you? Why did you leave the hospital?"

"Why do you think?" Matt said, instantly steamed by Gebhardt's reaction. "*I* think your boss wants to throw me in jail for a murder I didn't commit. I'm not giving him that chance."

"You need to come in if you're innocent. Running will only make things worse."

"Why should I surrender when I can't trust you? From my standpoint, the SCPD has dragged its collective asses on this from day one. How many more people need to die before you guys decide to do your job? Protect and serve? I haven't seen much of either in our neighborhood." Matt fought the urge to yell. "My father and the Myricks deserve justice. Dad may not have been a saint, but I'd at least like to know how he died. Now your chief wants to pin a ludicrous murder charge on me."

"Take a breath, Matt." Gebhardt spoke in a soft, calming tone. "I'm on your side. I can't control what Flannery does, but I'll do everything I can to help you."

Matt glanced around through the scratched windows, suddenly paranoid that hidden eyes and ears were spying and eavesdropping on the conversation. He also doubted Gebhardt's claim of allegiance after Swanson's duplicity, but he still needed outside help. "I appreciate that, but I didn't call to plead for mercy. I want you to check out a license plate. The owner of that SUV I've seen around the farm may be Smythe's muscle, a bald monster who—"

"Hold on," Clay interjected. "Who's Smythe?"

"Oh, sorry. Leland Smythe owns Saxony Partners and dozens of other shell corporations from Minnesota to Missouri, maybe all the way to Texas. I think he's the mastermind of this farm conspiracy my father was compiling research on. Smythe's got a giant thug working for him who drives the SUV that tried to run me over in Minneapolis.

If we can find this guy and get him to confess he committed crimes under Smythe's orders, we can stop this insanity."

"You give me a random license plate number and expect me to bust up a conspiracy with statewide, maybe nationwide, implications?" Gebhardt's tone had returned to irate. "Get real."

"I'm not asking you to bust up the conspiracy. Just track down the owner of the SUV. If he works for Smythe, he knew Hibbert, which means he might have some information about what happened to Myrick and my father."

"It's not that simple, Matt. I—"

"It's *never* that simple, Clay. Time to choose. If you believe I murdered Sandvik, find me and arrest me. If you believe I'm innocent, track down the SUV driver. Either way, get off the damn fence and take a stand."

Matt slumped against the wall in the tight booth and fought the urge to put his foot through the plexiglass. Why the hell was Gebhardt so reluctant to investigate now that he had something tangible to check out? Did he fear reprisals from Flannery if he continued his investigation into the three recent deaths?

"*Please.*"

Gebhardt exhaled loudly, creating a *whooshing* sound over the phone line. "Gimme the plate number."

Matt recited the letters and numbers from memory. *Bass clef and baseball. Unforgettable.* "Thank you, Clay."

"Don't get your hopes up," Gebhardt said. "On the surface, your theory sounds crazy and paranoid. I'm only doing this because you're a friend."

After hanging up, Matt took a huge breath and stepped out of the phone booth, wincing from the stinging pain. Swanson looked at him expectantly. Matt shook his head and shrugged.

Swanson frowned and checked his watch. "You'd better shove off. No sense hanging around and getting spotted by the cops." He pulled a fistful of cash from his jacket pocket and thrust it into Matt's hand. "Don't be an idiot and use any plastic."

Matt counted the wad of bills. One thousand dollars. "Swanny, I can't—"

"Don't even think of saying *no*," Swanson said as he held up his hand. "This is Smythe's money. Use it to keep yourself alive. If you need more, contact me."

Matt shoved the money into a pocket of his newly acquired cargo pants and zipped it closed. "Thanks."

Then Swanson handed him a small, oval-shaped object. "This is my old flip phone. I keep it for a spare in case the smartphones Amy and I bought a few months ago turn out to be duds. It'll make and receive calls and texts but not much else. My number's in the directory."

Matt examined the phone. It looked familiar. "This is the type of cell phone I tried once, years ago. Didn't like the flimsy little antenna or using a telephone keypad to write text messages."

"It'll do in an emergency," Swanson said. He showed Matt the basics: *on* and *off*, accessing the directory, how to place a call, and how to send a text message.

"I'll stick to phone calls but thanks." Matt said and slid the phone into another pocket, afraid he'd somehow break the damn thing if he tried to use it for anything more complicated. As he reached for the driver's door to his truck, Swanson thrust out his hand to block it.

Scarlet-faced, with his head lowered, he spoke softly. "I know I betrayed my best friend, and I don't expect you to forgive me." His gaze lifted and locked onto Matt's eyes as he raised his right thumb. "But I swear on my grandmother's Bible I'm on your side now."

A lump formed in Matt's throat. He recalled the solemnity only young boys could bring to the ritual of becoming blood brothers. Some thirty years ago, the two of them had pricked their thumbs, pressed them together to mingle drops of blood, and vowed that whenever one of them said, "I swear on my grandmother's Bible," whatever followed was the equivalent of testifying in front of God himself.

Matt studied Swanson's face, looking for the honesty, the sincerity, the loyalty that had been there in the past. Swanson's eyebrows arched with hope. The start of a smile showed at one corner of his mouth. Age lines, a weather-beaten complexion, and a few extra pounds hadn't eroded his gregarious nature, positive outlook, and cheery disposition. Other than being masterfully deceived and used by Smythe, Swanny had remained Swanny. Matt raised his right hand, extended his thumb, and pressed it against Swanson's stubby digit.

"I swear on my grandmother's Bible I believe you." Matt wondered if Swanson was in so deep that even a blood oath between two former best friends was just another lie. He hoped not.

They shook hands. Swanson clapped him on the shoulder. "Get the hell outta here, city boy. Call me if you need anything else."

Matt climbed into the Dodge and rumbled out of the depot parking lot, heading toward I-35. When he reached cruising speed on the interstate, he repeatedly checked his rearview mirrors for police, sheriff, or state patrol cars. After ten miles, he relaxed his tense grip on the wheel enough to allow blood to flow to his fingers again. He considered several possible hiding places for the next forty miles of rolling farmland and suburbia until he reached the southern edge of St. Paul. There he tuned the radio to Minnesota Public Radio's news station. Moments later, he heard a news bulletin that sent a chill through his body.

"Straight County Police Chief Michael Flannery announced that Matthew Raymond Lanier of Minneapolis is the prime suspect in the murder of Officer Steven Sandvik. Sandvik died in a suspicious house explosion on the Lanier farm in rural Straight River. Lanier should be considered armed and dangerous. He's white, approximately six feet tall—"

Matt clicked off the radio and sagged into the seat, feeling weak and overwhelmed. The last forty-eight hours had just gone from absurd to surreal. As he approached the I-94/I-35E junction, a powerful urge hit him. He veered onto the Kellogg Street exit and headed for downtown St. Paul.

CHAPTER 34

Diane stood in the hallway outside her condo, still wearing work attire. She'd removed the coat of her black pantsuit, which revealed a white short-sleeved mock turtleneck top. Matt had hoped for a pleasant greeting after he'd called her from the lobby and she'd buzzed him up, but her frown and crossed arms dashed that hope.

"What are you doing out of the hospital? I heard the news report and was worried sick that you might've died. Now you're up and about two days later?" Her features softened as she examined his visible injuries.

He held his hands up in surrender. "I can explain."

She touched a bandage on his cheek, then led him inside and closed the door. "This had better be good, mister."

"I need to sit. I hurt less in that position." He moaned as he sank into the plush leather sofa, then sighed once he got comfortable. Jasmine hints of her perfume drifted into his nostrils. "First, I apologize for not believing you about risking my life."

"When did *that* revelation get through your thick skull?"

"Right after I went flying through the air from the explosion. I can't prove it, but the blast was no accident."

"I told you so, you big, dumb . . ." She balled her fists and shook them. "Arghhh."

"Swanny snuck me out of the hospital. Then he confessed he'd been working for Smythe."

Her eyes widened in shock. "What?"

"Smythe set him up as a shadow farmland owner. Dozens of people up and down I-35 might be secretly holding properties for Smythe." He filled her in on what else had happened in the past few days.

"Are you positive Swanny's on your side? What if this is another setup?" She'd asked a valid question. Swanson had proven he was a good enough actor to pull off the double agent shtick. The hospital breakout might've been another devious step in Smythe's master plan to send Matt on the run, then bring in the cops as allies.

He wiggled his right thumb. "Not this time. He and I are square. He got me out of Straight River too."

"Why did you come here?"

"I heard a radio bulletin as I was driving north. The Straight County Police Chief suspects me of murdering the cop who died when the house exploded." He formed air quotes around *suspects.*

Her hand shot to her mouth as if it were the business end of a spring-loaded trap his words had triggered. "Oh, my God."

"I'm innocent. I wanted to tell you in person, so you'll see the truth in my eyes. Smythe wanted me killed in the blast. No witnesses. An apparent accident. He goes on his merry way." Matt looked at the floor but forced his gaze back to hers. The pain centered in his chest dug much deeper than the wounds caused by the explosion. He was desperate to tell her how much he still loved her, but couldn't form the words, didn't dare risk rejection right now.

"Matt, I . . ." She grasped his hand and squeezed. "There's got to be something we can do to prove your innocence."

"I convinced Gebhardt to check out the license plate of the SUV that's been lurking around the farm. I'll bet it was the one that tried to run me down."

"Do you think it will lead to anything?"

"It's all I have right now. If there's no connection, I'm screwed." He wiped sweat from his forehead but noticed his extremities felt numb with cold.

"You look ill. Can I get you something?"

"Some water, please. I need to take a pain pill."

She went to the kitchen and returned with a full glass of water. Handing it over, she sat beside him on the couch. He swallowed a pill and washed it down with large gulps, draining the glass. He sensed her body heat and noticed their shoulders and hips were touching. His pulse quickened as he suppressed an urge to wrap his arms around her.

"Where will you go until then? Every police officer in the state will be searching for you."

She was in enough trouble already because of her association with him. He couldn't risk telling her anything more, so he lied. "I haven't figured it out yet. My priority is to heal. Then I can better defend myself from whatever Smythe throws at me."

Diane pivoted sideways and locked gazes with him. Her eyes revealed deep pain.

"What's wrong?" he asked.

"I broke up with Steven."

A small swell of hope beat through his heart, but he maintained a somber expression. "I'm so sorry, Diane. You're way too good for him. He didn't deserve you."

"The political campaign's history too, but I haven't told him yet. My heart was never in it. I'm more of a policy wonk. Roll up my sleeves and solve problems, not spout platitudes and suck up to donors and voters."

He hoped to see relief or pleasure in her expression assuming she was glad to have made that decision. Instead he saw despair. "You should be relieved to be out of politics if that's what you want."

She bit her lip and blinked rapidly several times before releasing a long sigh. "It's not the politics, it's my entire life. Everything I've ever done has been to please someone else. Debutante, college, career, politics, Steven. The only thing I did on my own was marry you." She focused on her hands knitted together in her lap. "Then I destroyed us because I let my father control me instead of listening to my heart."

Matt was always at a loss when she was upset. He reached over and touched her knee.

She flinched and made eye contact. "When I broke up with Steven, he got violent. Nothing serious. He slapped me and called me a bitch."

Rage surged upward from Matt's core, infusing him with a jolt of violent energy. The darkest side of his psyche shocked him with an image of how remorselessly he could slice off Crossley's genitals, stuff them down his throat, and choke the slimy bastard to death. He shook off that visual and managed to speak with a gentle, caring tone. "Diane, I am *so* sorry."

She leaned toward him, and he opened his arms to her. His anger was tempered by the joy of once again holding the love of his life. He stroked her hair and her back, feeding on her warmth, unable to hold her tight enough. His physical pain subsided as he inhaled the floral-shampoo scent of her hair and perfume, like rudimentary aromatherapy. He ran his fingertips across her bare forearm, marveling at the softness of her skin.

Finally breaking their embrace, Diane sat up and blinked away tears. "I didn't mean to unload on you."

As she reached across him to the end table for a tissue and returned to her position, her breasts brushed against his arm. Despite all his injuries and the lingering effects of getting his brain rattled twice in the same week, hot waves of desire flowed through him.

"I understand" he said. "Things build up."

Her moist eyes sparkled as she leaned in and kissed him tenderly on the lips, lingering for an extra second. She sighed and relaxed her body. Stunned but aroused, he leaned into the kiss. She didn't pull back. Was this a pity kiss? Was she on the rebound from Crossley? Was she saying goodbye forever? Whatever the reason, he didn't care.

He pulled her closer, reacquainting his mouth with hers. Diane moaned and parted her lips, inviting his tongue to explore further. Matt tasted her, teased her tongue with his, wanted to pull her into him so completely that they fused together. She slid her hands behind his neck, pulling his lips tighter to hers. Their kisses were hungry, eager, desperate. She pressed her breasts into his body as she ran her fingers through his hair. The tingling in his groin grew to a throb. This was real passion, long dormant, now rekindled like a smoldering wildfire fanned by a gust of wind.

And then her phone rang. *Perfect timing.* Matt opened his eyes and saw his frustration at being interrupted mirrored in her eyes. Another ring. He released his grip and pulled back.

Sighing, she grabbed her cell phone from the coffee table, studied the screen, then showed it to him.

Crossley. That bastard.

Diane stiffened and put the phone to her ear. "What do you want, Steven?"

Matt sagged back into the sofa and tried to adjust his body to minimize the pain until the Tylenol 3 kicked in.

"What about him?" Diane said to Crossley. . . . "Impossible. He'd never kill anyone." Her voice was icy and confident. "There must be some mistake. I'm sure he's innocent." . . . "I—" . . . "Of course not." She winced. "Why would he come here?"

Matt sensed she'd hesitated long enough for Crossley to suspect she was lying.

"He's not here." She scowled and rolled her eyes upward while Crossley spoke. "I *know* the law, Steven."

Matt suppressed his fight-or-flee instincts as he wondered if Crossley was stalling until one of Smythe's goons arrived.

"Call *you* instead of the police?" She'd recovered and was the strong, confident lawyer again. "Why would I do that if my life might be in danger?"

Crossley must be swearing a blue streak to himself for committing such a gaffe.

"Careful, Steven," Diane said, glancing at Matt with fiery eyes. "That sounds like a threat to me. Maybe I *will* call the police." . . . "Too late. You've already hurt me." . . . "And you can find yourself another puppet politician too."

Impressive, Matt thought. She'd meant what she'd said earlier. Triumph shone in her eyes.

"I'm perfectly calm." . . . "Oh, and one more thing, Steven. Don't *ever* call me at home again." She turned off her phone with a flourish.

Matt nodded appreciatively at her performance. "Nice work, but he still suspects you've talked to me. Someone's probably on their way over already."

"I'll tell security no visitors."

"Doesn't matter. He'll come with police, or fake police, or have one of Smythe's thugs break in. I need to leave now."

She patted his thigh. "At least tell me where you're going?"

He shook his head. "You're safer if you don't know."

"I understand, but I had to ask. I'll try to help from my end." She gazed at him with hunger still in her eyes. "We'll sort us out if—*when*—you get back."

"There *is* one thing you can look into."

"Anything."

"Millennium Four. Ever heard of it?"

She pondered for a moment and shook her head.

"Zach found out about them a few days ago."

Matt summarized Millennium Four's activities and ultimate goals: a network of superhighways across the continent and consolidated political power in North America, all for unknown reasons other than obscene profits for insiders like Smythe and Crossley. He finished with the mention of the freelance reporter who'd infiltrated the group, published an article exposing some of the key players, then promptly died of an apparent suicide.

"If the Federal government is involved," he said, "this whole plan may have global significance. Zach put all his research on one of those flash drives. It's in a safe place for now. After I return, you and I can look at it together and figure out what we're dealing with. Right now, all I care about are my father and the Myricks."

"I've overheard Steven use the term *M4* once or twice on phone calls," she said. "I assumed he was discussing economics, money supply, that sort of thing."

"*M4* is enough of a coincidence for you to dig deeper."

"I'll do what I can."

"Thanks. I'd better go now." He stood, and she did the same.

Diane brushed a wayward lock of hair from her forehead. Her eyes were pools of deep azure. If she'd taken one step toward the bedroom, he would've followed her like an alpha male wolf during mating season. He flashed back again to the wild, sexy birthday present she'd given him early in their marriage. This time, the need to get moving interrupted his memories. They kissed again, this time with complete familiarity. It took all the willpower he could muster to pull away.

"Stay safe." She kissed him again while caressing his cheek.

Matt searched Diane's eyes once more for a hint of her true feelings. Had the break up with Crossley clouded her judgment? *No.* He knew her too well.

"I'll come back." He caressed her cheek. "Or I'll die trying."

CHAPTER 35

The clock on the wall above Clay's cubicle in the LEC indicated he'd searched the National Crime Information Center's database for more than an hour. He'd gone through every file in the United States containing the surnames Wit, Witt, and Witte. Now, he'd reached a dead end. Struggling to keep his eyes open, he yawned and wiped his face with both hands. Over the past seventy-two hours, which included the Lanier farm explosion, he'd work at least forty of those hours.

God, I need some sleep, but I'll regret it forever if Lanier dies because I can't track down a lousy thug. Finding the name of the owner of the mystery SUV based on the license plate number Lanier had given him had been easy. Charles Arthur Witt's driver's license photo certainly looked sinister—bald, ugly, scowling. Unfortunately, Witt's resemblance to a man who might've tried to kill Matt with an SUV didn't mean he was a criminal. And this Witt character had a strangely clean and abbreviated past. Other online searches revealed only a few years of credit and employment history. Even Witt's job history had abruptly ended more than a year ago and showed no connection to Smythe Properties or any other company owned by Smythe.

As he sipped a cold cup of coffee pot dregs, one last possibility came to mind. He typed in *W-h-i-t-t*. Two minutes later, as he read the third file in the list, he leaned forward in his chair, instantly wide awake.

Charles Alan Whitt. Convicted six years ago: Assault and Battery. Convicted four years ago: Involuntary Manslaughter plea bargained down from Voluntary Manslaughter. Served eighteen months of a four-year sentence. Domestic assault: Dismissed when the woman,

Whitt's live-in girlfriend at the time, never showed up for the trial. Dishonorable discharge from the Marines for assaulting an officer.

Clay let out a low whistle. *Bingo.* The clincher was, Charles Alan Whitt's job and credit history stopped shortly before Charles Arthur Witt's had begun. Whitt had become *Witt*, and he was definitely a suspect capable of violence. Not only capable of attempting a hit-and-run, but also capable of killing Hibbert, Ray Lanier, and possibly Helmer Myrick.

Vibrating with renewed energy, Clay made a call to the Pennington County sheriff's office in Rapid City, South Dakota. The clerk who answered connected him with the ranking officer on duty, a Lieutenant Zajac. Clay introduced himself.

"Straight River, eh?" Zajac paused. "Is this about the Wayne Hibbert case?"

"Um, not exactly."

"Not *exactly*? You understand we've got written instructions from your Chief explicitly stating he's the only authority we may deal with concerning the Hibbert case."

"I know, Lieutenant." Clay put as much conviction as he could into his lie. "I've got a highly speculative lead on another case that might, just *might*, be related to Hibbert. Call it a cop's intuition. If my lead pays off, I have a way to tell Flannery without him thinking I went against orders."

"Alright, what do you want from us?"

"Were there any violent crimes reported in or around Rapid City between March twenty-eighth and thirty-first?"

"Let me check," Zajac said and put him on *hold*.

Clay rapped a pencil fast and hard against the desktop, releasing the nervous tension generated by his guilty conscience for subverting direct orders and chain of command.

Minutes later, Zajac came back on the line and ran down a short list of reported incidents.

Clay said, "Any of the victims mention a huge bald guy as the perpetrator or maybe an accomplice?"

"Pardon me for asking," Zajac said, sounding impatient now, "but what're you digging for?"

"Between you and me? A miracle."

"A miracle?"

Clay tossed the pencil across his desk. "I've got a high-profile case here with a lot of circumstance and speculation and a friend who's been accused of killing a police officer."

"Sheesh. I thought we had bad days around here. Let me check."

Papers rustled for a handful of seconds before Zajac spoke again. "A hooker who was beaten by her john described a large bald guy."

Clay sat bolt upright. His heart rate kicked into high gear. "If I send you a photo, can you show it to her and see if she can give us a positive ID?"

"I'm sorry, Sergeant, but the hooker didn't press charges, and we're understaffed. We can't devote any personnel to help you with a hunch."

"If I come out there, can I investigate on my own? Strictly as a private citizen, of course."

"It's your gas money. I *can* give you her name and a general area to search. Most prostitutes around here work a certain neighborhood."

"I'll consider it," Clay said. "Thanks for your help, Lieutenant."

Demoralized after his earlier excitement, he hung up and stared at the wall. Lanier was in hiding, foolishly believing he could fly solo against a corrupt, powerful organization. If this tenuous out-of-state lead produced a positive ID of Witt and placed him in South Dakota around the time of Hibbert's death, Clay could at least bring Witt in for questioning. Waiting for either another lead or the South Dakota authorities to work with him wasn't an option. Odds were, Lanier would be dead before either of those things happened. After checking the time, Clay heaved himself up out of his chair and went home to pack an overnight bag.

CHAPTER 36

Not far from the Excel Energy Center arena in downtown St. Paul, East Seventh Street was home to several bars that catered to Minnesota Wild hockey fans in season and locals the rest of the year. Matt walked about six blocks through a chilly drizzle from Diane's condo to a nondescript place on Seventh called Shea's Irish Pub. Once inside, he removed his jacket and shook off the moisture, then scanned the room.

The wood was mahogany. The lights were low but had a warm hue. A small stage filled one corner, but no band was performing. The sound system played Irish folk music—The Chieftains' version of "Hard Times Come Again No More." Matt chuckled. *I wish*. The Wild had the night off, so only a handful of patrons were present. They gave him a cursory scrutinization before turning back to their conversations or the early-season Twins game on the wide-screen behind the bar.

Matt ordered a Guinness on tap, then sat at the booth farthest from the door with his back to the wall so he could see the entire room. He felt conspicuous because of his injuries. If the police description of him had mentioned his bandaged hand and cuts, an attentive citizen might notice and report him. Thankfully, no one at the bar paid him any attention after his entrance.

The bartender brought the pint along with a cardboard tray of peanuts in the shell and a friendly, "Here you go, buddy. Should I start a tab?"

"Not tonight." Matt tossed him a ten-dollar bill. "Keep it."

"Thanks." The bartender scooped up the bill, gave him a world-weary smile, and returned to the bar.

As Matt sipped the rich, creamy stout, his plan for the next few days came into focus. He would go on the offensive, initiate a confrontation where he controlled most of the circumstances of any battle that might take place: the site, the access and escape routes, tactical advantages such as terrain and cover. He could only stack the odds slightly in his favor because he'd be fighting alone. Ideally, he'd capture his attacker or attackers and force them to confess the truth about Smythe and Millennium Four. But how?

The key was not to raise Smythe's suspicions that Matt was laying a trap. He needed to find a balance. Leave enough clues about where to find him and still have Smythe believe his hired guns would easily ambush Matt at his hiding spot. All Matt needed to do was continue playing the hapless musician running for his life.

His biggest challenge would come if and when whoever Smythe and Crossley sent to kill him this time found him and attacked. If they believed he'd panicked and ran to his planned hideaway without thinking, they'd be overconfident and not waste excess manpower on eliminating a minor annoyance. Matt stood half a chance against two or three attackers. Any more than that and he was a dead man. Ideally, the bald SUV driver would show up alone, eager to prove Matt couldn't get the better of him a third time.

A secondary worry was being hunted simultaneously by the law. Secondary because if the cops tracked him down, they wouldn't kill him unless he fought back. However, assuming that Flannery worked for Smythe only guaranteed Matt wouldn't be immediately executed. They'd stage a fatal accident, or his suicide, or recruit another prisoner to kill him in jail.

And what if his trap failed and his last chance for survival was to shoot his attackers? Could he pull the trigger on another human? With shaky hands and closed eyes, he downed the last swig of Guinness and visualized taking aim at the big, bald SUV driver and pulling the trigger. Easy, right?

After walking back to his truck, Matt drove north out of St. Paul onto I-35. He took the North Branch exit, stopped at a gas station to fill up, then found a small motel nearby. He paid for the gas with his credit card. If Smythe or Flannery had access to a credit card tracking service, those charges would show up, and the chase would be on.

Matt paid cash for the room to lessen his risk that Smythe would discover his exact location and surprise him with a late-night raid. He fell asleep with his mind whirling like a spring tornado, enumerating all the ways his plan could fail. Once asleep, he alternated between dozing and jerking awake from nightmares of explosions, car crashes, and showdowns on dusty western streets featuring him and the bald guy wearing cowboy hats, dueling at high noon.

~

Up at dawn and minimally refreshed, Matt dressed, grabbed a quick fast-food breakfast, and headed north on I-35. He took the Cloquet exit to Highway 33 north, then drove to US 53 and headed for the Iron Range. He made sure to stop for gas again and use his credit card. After passing through Eveleth and Virginia, he took the exit to US 169 and began the final leg of his drive. Arriving in Ely well before noon, he stopped at the biggest canoe outfitter in town and rented a canoe, paddles, a portage pack, a personal flotation device, a sleeping bag and pad, a tent, an aluminum cook kit with four nesting pots, and some other essential wilderness camping gear. He also bought a five-hundred-yard spool of clear monofilament fishing line for an idea he'd developed while driving. Even if Ferdie Olson was open for business this early in the season, because of their personal history, Matt refused to rent his gear from Ferdie for fear of connecting another innocent friend to his disastrously snowballing quest.

As he paid for the rentals, Matt casually mentioned his plan for some preseason paddling from Snowfall Lake. He wanted to leave enough clues for Smythe or his underlings to find him, but not so many that they'd suspect a trap. The upside was, if no one tracked him down in the next several days, he'd at least bought some time to heal his injuries and clear his head. That was his preferred outcome because the increasing dryness in his mouth and agitation in his stomach indicated his growing lack of confidence in his battle plan. *Who knows, maybe a few days alone to clear my mind will allow me to devise a plan that makes a ton more sense than the beginner-level improv I've come up with so far.*

CHAPTER 37

Dragging into the LEC after a thirty-six-hour whirlwind trip which included twenty hours of driving to and from Rapid City sandwiched around a day-long street search and a short nap, Clay felt surprisingly alert and eager to share what he'd found as he strode to Flannery's office. The Chief couldn't possibly ignore this new twist in Hibbert's case. Flannery's office was empty, so Clay went to the squad room where he found Hansen typing at his computer terminal.

"Where's the chief, Hans?"

Hansen paused and looked up from his task. "Flew out of here about an hour ago, Sarge."

"Where to?"

"Didn't say, but he was plenty pissed."

Clay grunted, then lumbered back to his cubicle. Protocol dictated he clear his intentions with Flannery before going after Witt for questioning. However, he rationalized he could forego permission because he also intended to arrest the violent Witt on behalf of the Rapid City police for beating up the hooker. Act first in the interest of public safety. Worry about the job consequences later. Especially if Flannery was indeed one of the bad guys.

Lanier might also recognize Witt based on his mention of seeing a bald hulk more than once, so Clay decided to ask Swanson if he'd seen or heard from Lanier in the past few days. The Straight River Hospital security camera footage he'd checked before going to South Dakota showed Swanson walking into and out of the hospital the day Lanier went missing. No camera had recorded Lanier leaving the building. Follow-up questions to the security staff revealed that one service entrance lacked surveillance cameras. Although Lanier had left the hospital soon after Swanson's departure, Clay had no proof that Swanson had helped Lanier in any way. Now, with the distinct possibility that *Witt* had triggered the explosion with the intention of killing Lanier, Swanson might face an equal amount of danger. He might also be willing to lead Clay to Lanier.

No one answered either Swanson's landline or cell phone, so Clay grabbed his hat and jacket and exited the LEC with an urgent, energized stride. Minutes later, he pulled his squad car into the driveway of the Swanson farm. Clay parked behind Swanson's empty truck and knocked on the farmhouse door.

No one answered.

He walked to the center of the cluster of outbuildings and stopped. Hearing no sounds from any of them, he tensed. Something felt wrong, and Clay was through ignoring his instincts. He reached for his sidearm, then checked the garage and the chicken coop.

No Dave. No Amy.

He walked to their cavernous barn, opened the door, and peered into the darkness as he groped for a light switch. Putting as much command and confidence into his tone as his apprehension allowed, he called out, "Police. Anyone here?"

"Help." A woman's voice. More of a groan than a word.

"Amy?" Clay flipped on the light. His heart leaped into his throat when he spied Dave and Amy Swanson tied to barn posts ten feet apart but out of sight of each other. Dave's chin sagged to his chest, and Amy was nude. Her clothes sat in a heap next to her.

"Good God!" Clay ran to Amy, tore at the knots in the rope, and freed her from the restraints. He grabbed a nearby horse blanket to cover her. After easing her down to the ground, she collapsed, half conscious.

He turned to Dave, whose face was caked with blood. One eye was swollen to twice its normal size. Blood and some other liquid that smelled like vomit had soaked into the dirt floor at his feet. The added smell of manure made Clay want to retch, but he held it in and moved into triage mode. He untied Dave and struggled to ease the large man to the floor.

"Swanny! Wake up. It's Gebhardt. Who did this to you?"

As soon as he asked the question, the answer came to him. *Witt.* His insides did a backflip. The urge to retch was immediately replaced by the desire to beat Witt into a bloody, unidentifiable mass of flesh.

Dave was incoherent, so Clay turned back to Amy. "Talk to me, Amy. How did this happen?"

"He must've snuck in here on foot," she said. A bruise covered one cheek. Dried blood trickled from her nose to her upper lip. She was shivering. "I've never seen him before. He wore a ski mask, so we didn't see his face. He's huge. Bigger than Dave. Rotten teeth. Sour breath. He kept groping me and . . ." She trailed off, then flung her hand to her mouth. Her eyes widened. "Is Dave okay? Is he—"

"Easy there." Clay held Amy down with a gentle hand as she tried to stand. "He's badly injured. You rest while I call an ambulance."

The EMTs arrived within minutes and proceeded to administer first aid to the couple. A whiff of smelling salts revived Dave.

"I'm sure I know who's responsible," Clay said. "But why was he here? Why'd he beat you and Amy?"

"They sent that oversized troglodyte to grill me about where Matt's hiding." Mumbling through swollen lips, Dave sounded dazed and distant.

"Who's *they*?"

"Flannery and the Saxony Partners fella, Smythe."

Clay recoiled at the mention of his boss, although this connection to Witt and Smythe brought Flannery's recent behavior into focus. "When did you figure Flannery for a crook?"

"Me and Betty were visiting Matt at the hospital when Flannery showed up. His attitude made me suspicious, so I left Matt's room but eavesdropped through the door. He sounded ready to arrest Matt for murder right there. There's no way the Matt we know would do something that stupid *or* that evil. Then you and me were talking at Lanier's farm and Flannery copped the same bullshit attitude. That's when I figured he had something to do with Saxony Partners. I worked for them too, and Hibbert forced me to do some, uh, questionable stuff."

"Chief's always been a prick-in-the-mud," Clay said. "But I kept giving him the benefit of the doubt since he's relatively new. Were you hiding Lanier?"

Dave nodded. "I wasn't sure you were on his side either, so I played dumb. My gut told me to hide him before you arrested him."

"I *am* on his side, but you gotta tell me where he is so I can help."

Dave glanced at his wife, who stared blankly at the floor. He stifled a gasp and winced as an EMT dabbed at his bloody eyebrow with antiseptic. "I wouldn't talk because I honestly don't know where he went. But when he groped Amy, I thought sure he was going to . . . to . . ."

He pursed his lips tight, fighting to hold his emotions in check.

Amy looked at her husband with eyes that flared with intensity. "He didn't rape me, David. He just wanted you to believe that so you'd tell him what he wanted to know."

Dave rubbed a tear from his cheek with a balled fist. "He still groped you, hit you. I saw him raise his hand. I heard the slaps." His voice quavered, but he breathed deeply and said in a tone of ill-contained rage, "Nobody touches my wife that way and gets away with it. Ever!"

Clay shuddered to imagine what they'd endured. He desperately wanted to rewind the clock to before Witt showed up in the barn. If he'd acted on Lanier's suspicions about the deaths of the two old men sooner, he might've stopped Witt before any of this had happened.

"What's his name, Clay?" Dave asked. "I'm gonna hurt him bad."

"Without you giving me a positive ID, I can't be sure, but I think his name's Witt."

"Well then, Witt's a dead man."

Dave seemed ready to either break down or go berserk, so Clay brought his focus back to Lanier. "What did you tell Witt about Matt?"

"Witt said he knew Matt was somewhere up in the Boundary Waters, but he didn't know the exact location. When he asked for specifics, I blurted out the first place that came to my mind, Snowfall Lake."

"Why there? Doesn't make sense for a man who should still be in the hospital."

"We reminisced about our canoe trips up there during dinner last week," Dave said. "Makes sense for Matt, injured or not. He knows the area. No motors or planes allowed. He'll have some warning if anyone's coming for him." His expression turned fearful. "Witt said if I wasn't right, he'd come back and kill us."

"That son of a bitch." Clay furrowed his brow, trying to develop a plan on the fly. "I don't have the luxury of waiting for Witt to return. If I did, Flannery would put the kibosh on a stakeout in a hot minute. I've gotta go up and find Lanier before Witt does. You think any outfitters are open for business?"

"Not sure," Dave said. "Ice might not even be off the lakes yet."

Clay massaged the back of his neck. "Why the hell would he go up there if he can't paddle a canoe?"

"Call Olson's Outfitters," Dave said. "Olson will know if it's canoeable up there. Tell him it's a police emergency and Matt's in danger. When Matt worked up there, old Ferdie treated him like a son. He'll bust his ass to help."

Clay had little confidence in his ability to pull off a wilderness rescue against an unknown opponent. A better option would be to call in experts like local county search and rescue personnel. However, giving them a location that was the equivalent of a dart thrown at a map of the million-plus acres of the Boundary Waters Canoe Area Wilderness—more commonly referred to as the BWCAW, the BWCA, or the Boundary Waters—would get him laughed off the phone.

"Damnation, Swanny, I know you're traumatized, and you probably had your bell rung by Witt, but I need to be closer to one-hundred-percent sure about this."

Dave raised himself off the ground with his elbow, brushing aside the EMT's doctoring efforts. He looked at Clay with surprisingly clear, focused eyes. "If Witt thinks Matt's up north, there's a reason. So yeah, Matt's up there. Maybe he left a trail for them to find. Maybe he's setting up an ambush of his own."

Clay rubbed his hand across his jaw as he digested the possibility that a farm-boy-turned-musician possessed the balls and the wherewithal to take on a violent career thug. Was Lanier so desperate that he saw a firefight as the best response?

"This all seems so crazy." Clay checked his watch. "I'm going home, explain it to Margaret, and get a few hours of sleep. It'll be dark soon. I doubt they'll go after him until morning. I'll head up tonight, arrive at daybreak, start paddling ASAP."

"I'm going with you," Dave said. He struggled to sit up, but his expression became woozy and he collapsed onto the wood floor.

Amy perked up instantly. "David Swanson, you almost died today! The only place you're going is the hospital."

Clay emphasized Amy's words with a gentle stiff-arm to Dave's shoulder. "Amy's right, Dave. Let me deal with Witt."

Dave protested with a feeble groan as the EMT's lifted him onto a stretcher and carried him out.

~

Before lying down for some shuteye an hour later, Clay called Olson's Outfitters and left a message saying he'd be up there on police business tomorrow morning. He then called another outfitter in Ely—the town nearest to Snowfall Lake—and reserved a canoe and the necessary gear. He hoped to talk a park ranger into helping him paddle if the outfitter couldn't find a guide for him. The outfitter also said ice-out had occurred a few days earlier on the small and medium lakes such as Snowfall, which improved the odds that Lanier might indeed be in the Boundary Waters.

As Clay packed personal gear into his car around midnight, a pickup truck cornered hard onto his street and skidded to a stop in his driveway, blocking his car. "Jesus H. Christ," he muttered. "What the hell is this?"

Dave Swanson stepped from the truck wearing camouflage hunting clothes under a dark-colored down vest, a camo bill cap, and sturdy boots. He gripped the fender for balance as he walked gingerly toward Clay. His facial cuts were bandaged, but his eyes and one cheek were still badly swollen.

"I'm going with you." Swanson's voice was clear and strong.

Clay groaned. *Damned civilians wanting to play cops and robbers.* "Swanny—"

"I can't face Amy until I stand up for her honor," He hung his head. "I gotta do this."

Bringing a civilian on police business broke more rules than Clay could count. Then again, he was fighting against expert rulebreakers in Smythe, Witt, and his own damn boss. On the plus side, Swanson knew the Snowfall Lake area and could paddle a canoe. Despite his injuries, he was still as strong as two ordinary men. Most importantly, his motivation could never be matched by a guide or park ranger.

Swanson glanced up through downcast eyes. "Doesn't matter what you say. I'm going. If I have to, I'll follow you. I want Witt."

Clay stared long and hard at the bruised and bloodied bear of a man who stood before him. "You strong enough to paddle?"

"Hell yeah." He was stone-faced, with a piercing stare.

"Amy okay with this?"

"Don't matter if she is or not."

Clay exhaled through puffed cheeks and flipped his arms up a foot in exasperation. "Let's go."

Swanson pulled a duffle bag and a small arsenal of firearms and ammunition from the bed of his pickup truck and tossed them into Clay's trunk.

As Clay slid into the driver's seat, he shook his head and muttered, "God help us."

CHAPTER 38

Matt woke up shivering, with numb toes, a stiff back from sleeping on the ground, and throbbing pain from his wounds. He peeked out the tent flap at the predawn glow of the eastern sky. The weather had cleared as he'd expected and dropped the temperature below freezing. His exhaled breath formed a vapor cloud that hung together for several seconds.

He was camped on Big Island in Crystal Lake, two short portages out of Olson's Outfitters on Snowfall Lake and a popular first-night stop for canoeists who only had a few hours before dark to get into the Boundary Waters. The nearest civilization, other than a few outfitters on the lakes near the access road, was the town of Ely some twenty miles to the west. Secluded enough for most situations. Except this was not most situations. Dealing with hungry bears, isolation, and harsh weather were child's play compared to fighting for his life against humans who intended to kill him.

Big Island was oblong—a half-mile long east to west and a third-mile wide north to south—and dominated the western third of the lake. A small bay with a sand-and-gravel beach fronted Matt's campsite on the southeastern section of the island. Red pine needles, or duff, carpeted the otherwise bare, rocky soil composed primarily of Precambrian granite, basalt, and greenstone that had been scoured for centuries by glaciers. Grass was a rarity in this cold, rocky terrain since topsoil was scarce. The site's two amenities, common to all Boundary Waters campsites, were a steel fire grate and a latrine far enough back in the woods for privacy. Two other campsites, both unoccupied, were situated on the southeast and northeast shores of Crystal Lake. Each site was at least a mile from the other two.

From the campsite, the land rose gently for about half its width, then steepened into a bluff some thirty feet above the lake. The bluff was nearly devoid of trees because its height attracted lightning strikes and straight-line wind gusts. Those accumulated natural events left their marks on a dozen or so trees that now either stood bare and burned or had toppled and begun to decompose. This left a rough oval about twenty yards in diameter resembling the head of a man who was bald on top but had a healthy mop of hair on all sides. The trees below the summit included a smattering of birch and aspen scattered amongst the old growth pine—white, red, and spruce. The trees were tightly spaced over much of the terrain. A few narrow footpaths allowed campers to reach the latrine, access the blueberry patch near the summit, or circle the perimeter of the island.

Already wearing polypropylene long underwear, two pairs of socks, camouflaged cargo pants, a flannel shirt, and a wool sweater, Matt donned his down jacket, boots, and insulated gloves and climbed out of his tent. He lit a small campfire, gulped a few pain pills with a cup of water straight from the lake, and prepared a breakfast of instant oatmeal and instant coffee.

After he'd eaten and cleaned up, Matt made his way to the top of the hill to inspect the fortifications he'd cobbled together since arriving. Situated on the western third of the island, the summit afforded a partially obstructed 180-degree view toward the south. He'd spent many first nights here during trips he'd guided for Olson when he was in high school and college. Because of its topography, this island was as good a place to defend himself as any he'd ever seen in the Boundary Waters.

He'd constructed his fort in the center of the rocky bluff's "bald spot." The fort's salient features were two massive white pines that had fallen almost parallel to each other and formed a shallow, unbalanced V with a huge boulder. One tree rested mostly on top of the other, creating a breastwork about three feet high. Matt used branches and rocks to fill the larger cracks. When completed, he had more than fifteen feet of partial protection from the downed trees plus a six-foot-wide by four-foot-high wall of solid protection behind the boulder. Natural firing slits at each end of the wooden barricade allowed him to shoot in relative safety. He'd even stockpiled a dozen or so fist-sized rocks to throw in case he ran out of ammunition.

As Matt made his final defensive preparations, he was painfully aware of his strategy's one significant flaw: He was alone against an unknown force. He hoped two attackers at most would show. He doubted an army would show up, and he didn't expect an air attack. Motorized traffic in the BWCAW—boats, snowmobiles, ATVs, and low-flying planes and helicopters—was illegal except for emergency rescues by authorities. The Forest Service and other agencies constantly monitored the wilderness for infractions. Matt's worst-case dread was that a small squad of armed mercenaries in canoes would attack the island on multiple fronts.

Because of that, a subconscious pall of foreboding had gnawed at his nerves and disturbed his sleep with nightmares of blood, pain, and death. He simultaneously wanted to be found and not found. He'd pinned his survival hopes on Witt underestimating him by assuming the wimpy musician would be an easy target.

"Am I crazy or what?" he said to the sky.

He wedged a few more rocks and branches into some noticeable gaps in his tree wall, then returned to the shore and patrolled the perimeter of the island along a narrow footpath. Shortly after returning to his campsite, a distant crash from the south broke the dead silence and echoed across the still water. Startled, Matt jerked his head toward the noise. From his guide days at Olson's Outfitters, he recognized the familiar sound of a canoe banging hard against rocks. Someone had probably slipped and fallen while portaging.

~

"God damn it, Flannery, I *told* you to be careful," Witt said in a raspy whisper. He picked himself up off the snow-covered portage trail, pissed at his clumsy accomplice.

"Sorry," Flannery muttered as he rolled to his hands and knees. He stood up carefully and rebalanced the heavy portage pack on his back. He'd lost his footing and slipped forward, knocking Witt off balance and the canoe from Witt's shoulders. The crash and scrape of Kevlar on granite as the canoe slid downhill toward the lake was magnified by the early morning quiet.

"If Lanier's on this lake, he heard us for sure. Don't fuck up again. Go slow. Crawl if you have to."

Up until then, Witt had been in a good mood since arriving in the Boundary Waters. It started the previous day after Smythe learned that Lanier's credit card had recently been used at an Ely canoe outfitter. A few hours later, after some of Witt's tried and true *gentle* persuasion, Swanson had spilled his guts about where he thought Lanier would run to—Snowfall Lake. Smythe immediately dispatched Witt and Flannery to track Lanier down and remove what Smythe had referred to as "the annoying thorn in my side."

When Witt found a pickup truck parked at a deserted Olson's Outfitters, his hunting instincts clicked into overdrive. Lanier was somewhere out in the woods cowering like a frightened deer trapped in a box canyon. Thinking about the shooting gallery he would soon be treated to, Witt nearly got a hard-on. *I wonder if Ely's big enough to have hookers.*

After finishing the rest of the portage, the men loaded their gear into the canoe. "Get those fishing rods out," Witt said. "Make sure the landing net is visible too."

"Right." Flannery complied, and they pushed off onto Crystal Lake.

Witt thought it best to conceal their identities as much as possible in case Lanier was watching for any paddlers coming his way. The less time Lanier had to run, hide, or prepare to fight, the better. Although Witt couldn't disguise his bulk, ball caps pulled low on their foreheads concealed the men's faces, and they wore clothing typical of what anglers would wear in early April. The presence of fishing gear completed the charade, even though the fishing opener was more than a month away.

When they rounded a peninsula that formed a small bay on the south end of the lake, the island they expected to see that hosted a campsite appeared to the north, a mile away. Witt adjusted their course toward the bluff that crowned the island and the men increased their paddling speed.

~

Mild panic propelled Matt into a sprint up to the bluff. He trained his binoculars on the southern shore more than a mile away. The dim morning light made it difficult to see any movement on the water. There was a chance some legitimate paddlers were getting a jump on the official canoeing season, but his churning stomach told him assassins were on his trail.

He scrambled down to camp and checked his weapons. The Remington deer rifle borrowed from Swanson was the best defense from his hilltop fort, but he tucked the loaded Glock 17 pistol into his belt as a backup. He had fifty rounds of ammunition for each. He hoped that would be enough.

Estimating he had about fifteen minutes before two paddlers in a canoe reached his island—several minutes longer for a solo paddler— Matt prepared for war. He doused the fire, collapsed his tent, crammed the kitchen gear into his portage pack, and dragged everything inland to where he'd stored his canoe, out of view from anyone who might paddle past his campsite. The less evidence of his presence on this island an enemy got, the better. He stashed the equipment under the overturned canoe and laid a few large pine boughs over the hull for camouflage.

By the time everything was secured, he was panting hard. His pulse thundered in his ears as his mind whirled. His throat tightened as he swallowed what little saliva remained in his mouth. He'd never felt this nervous and panicky in his life, and he did not enjoy the feeling.

For the third time since he'd arrived on the island, Matt pulled a small tape recorder from the pocket of his down vest and checked the battery. He then replayed what he'd previously recorded: his name, location, reason for being there, a description of his weaponry and ammunition, and his goal of returning to civilization alive and with his attackers either captured or killed. Recording his account of what might happen today was a feeble insurance policy, but it was the best method he could devise to document the truth: he was *not* a cop killer and only intended to shoot in self-defense.

Matt found a spot on a fallen tree that hid him from view but allowed him to see anyone paddling from the south. He sat and focused his binoculars on the canoe, now less than a quarter-mile away. Seconds later, his stomach began to spasm.

The paddlers were Flannery and the big, ugly bald man.

~

Witt and Flannery paddled to Big Island, then rounded a rocky point. A campsite came into view in a small bay. Witt guided the canoe toward the gravelly beach landing and they eased the craft into shore, parallel to land. While Flannery braced the canoe with his paddle, Witt stepped out and walked to the fire grate. He touched the iron— still warmer than the ambient air. The ashes were wet from a recent dousing. Footprints showed in the damp earth and in the dusting of snow protected by the tree canopy. He crouched and did a quick scan of the woods beyond the campsite. Pulling his Colt 1911 from its holster, Witt turned to Flannery and nodded. That familiar tingle of heightened anticipation shot into his fingers. Every instinct told him the man on this island was now his prey. The hunt was on.

Flannery stepped onto land and drew his pistol. Both men took cover behind two large, adjacent trees in the campsite as they scanned the area.

Witt whispered, "Fresh prints on the ground. Recent fire. Unless he stayed here and moved on, he's hiding in the woods."

Flannery pointed to a narrow path winding through the woods behind the campsite clearing. "Let's check the trail."

They crept forward, weapons at the ready. After going about twenty yards, Witt spotted a well-concealed canoe hidden by several pine boughs. From the lake, the hidden gear would've been invisible. The discovery confirmed that Lanier was on the island and probably hiding.

"I'll call Smythe first. He wants to know when we've found Lanier. Stay here and stand watch. I'll bring our rifles for this hunt."

Flannery nodded, gripped and regripped his pistol, and took cover behind a large pine.

Witt returned to their canoe, removed a satellite phone from his Duluth pack and tapped in Smythe's number. When Smythe answered, Witt said, "I found him, sir. Cornered him on an island a few portages in from where you thought he'd run to."

"Will you have any problem finishing the job?" Smythe asked.

"No, sir. Shouldn't take more than a few minutes."

"I won't tolerate another screw up. Call me when you're finished."

"Yes, sir." He hung up and stowed the phone in the pack. For the first time in his relationship with Smythe, Witt felt a twinge of fear that he might fail, mainly because he'd never had trouble staging accidents before. But today, he reassured himself that Lanier's luck would end on this God-forsaken island.

~

With minutes to go before a probable showdown, Big Island now seemed like a death trap to Matt. The seclusion worked both ways. If those men killed him and dumped his body deep in the woods, no one would ever learn the truth. Unless Matt killed or incapacitated his attackers, Smythe's men would either starve him out or overtake him if he was foolish enough to attempt an escape by canoe.

There was no doubt now that he would soon fight for his life, and the thought of taking a fatal bullet put his stomach over the edge. Worse yet, he was flooded with paralyzing doubts about his ability to shoot at all, even in self-defense.

He leaned over and vomited his breakfast into the brush. With shaking hands, he took a swig of water from his canteen and rinsed the foul taste from his mouth. Clearing his stomach helped cleanse his body of fright and doubt, and he sensed a small surge of resolve, knowing that his fight was morally honorable. Matt's heart clung to the slight hope that Smythe's men would paddle past his campsite and portage into the next lake, thinking he'd paddled as far from civilization as possible to decrease the odds they'd find him. But his head knew they would check every campsite along this route before moving on.

Matt sat back on the tree stump, cradled the Remington tightly in his lap, and resumed his watch. In the absolute stillness of the wilderness, his musical memory cued up the final passages of Mozart's Requiem Mass in D minor. The music was simultaneously powerful and uplifting yet foreboding and depressing in its finality.

He recalled how Mozart was reputed to have said, "I fear I am writing a requiem for myself."

Dry-mouthed, his nerve ends tingling, Matt drummed the fingers of his right hand against his thigh. Was this desperately concocted trap he'd set for his pursuers merely the orchestration of his own requiem? He stood and chambered a shell. *I guess it's time to find out.*

~

After rejoining Flannery, Witt turned his attention up the path. Each man had switched to rifles because firing through the trees would require more accurate aim than pistols could offer. They walked a few yards to where the path forked. Witt motioned for Flannery to go right. Witt went left, peering through the trees on each side of the trail as he walked. While scanning the hilltop, a swift movement caught his attention. He tightened his grip on his Colt AR-15 semi-automatic rifle. Might've been a bird or a squirrel—or a man. He crept forward ten paces, alert for more movement or sound. His energy built in anticipation of the battle to come. He stopped, did a quick check all around, then moved up another five paces. A flash of dark material above some fallen trees caught his attention. He fired into the downed trees where he'd seen the movement, emptying his magazine.

"We got him, Flannery! Top of the hill behind those downed trees." Stoked on adrenaline, Witt ducked behind a boulder and reloaded.

"I see him," Flannery yelled from some thirty yards to Witt's right. He then fired half a dozen rounds at their target.

"Double-flanking maneuver," Witt yelled. "Stay wide."

"Roger that."

No one could shoot in two directions simultaneously, so when Witt and Flannery reached the summit, one of them was guaranteed a kill shot. Witt started uphill along the narrowing, overgrown path. After a few steps, his foot caught on something invisible, and he fell forward. A metallic *clank* and rattle broke the silence as he almost face-planted into a downed tree. His hands, still clutching the AR-15, scraped against a large rock. Stifling a yelp of pain, he scrambled for cover behind a tree. An instant later, he heard another *clank* followed by a rifle shot from the summit. Witt flinched and braced for a bullet's impact.

Flannery emitted an agonized groan. "I'm hit! I need help, Witt!"

His words echoed across the wilderness, seemingly as loud as the gunfire.

"Ahhh shit," Witt muttered. Neither lucky shots by Lanier nor confirmation that Flannery had been shot were in the battle plan.

Looking for the cause of his stumble, Witt noticed a tangle of fishing line around his ankle. One end of the line trailed into the underbrush, leading his gaze to a metal cooking pot, lid ajar, with a handful of rocks spilling out. *God damn that wimp-assed musician.* Crouching low, he hurried back to the fork in the trail, then crept up the right fork until he found Flannery laying behind a large pine tree, ashen-faced, and breathing hard through bared teeth. His hand covered a bloody wound on his right shoulder.

"How bad?" Witt asked.

Flannery grimaced as he held his hand gingerly over the wound. "Bone's hit. Damn, that hurts. Can't move my arm. I tripped on something halfway up the hill. Heard some loud metallic rattle right after that. Fell on my face in plain sight. Couldn't take cover in time."

"Fucking scumbag Lanier fooled us." Witt said as he examined the wound. Anger electrified him down to his toes. He'd expected the firefight to be over by now with Lanier's body already beginning to rot deep in the woods. Now he'd have to waste five more minutes dealing with that putz, then babysit Flannery all the way home.

Witt unsheathed his hunting knife and sliced off a strip of Flannery's trousers. He tied a crude tourniquet over the wound, then reached for the pistol Flannery had dropped after he'd been wounded.

Crack! Thud! A shot from Lanier's position hit the tree protecting Flannery. Witt grabbed the gun and dove back to safety. *Maybe that damn musician is smarter than I thought.*

"Can you shoot left-handed?" Witt said to Flannery.

"Well enough at close range. Long range is gonna be tough."

He helped Flannery into a sitting position against a tree, shielded but able to see uphill toward Lanier's position by peeking around the tree. "If anything moves that isn't *me*, shoot it. If he's dug in up there, I'll need to get in close to take him out."

Flannery nodded as he settled his pistol unsteadily into his blood-covered left hand.

Witt swore under his breath. His partner was done fighting. He'd seen it before. Guys who talked tough and acted tough, but as soon as they got an owie in a firefight, wanted to crawl home to Mommy. *Fuck him. I'll take out Lanier myself and let Flannery save his own ass.*

He crept to the canoe, pocketed an extra magazine for both his pistol and AR-15, and checked to make sure the rifle had a round chambered. Defeating an opponent who held the fortified high ground would be challenging. But Witt was confident Lanier would make a rookie mistake or panic. He settled in behind a large boulder that gave him a clear view of the wooden part of Lanier's fort and took aim through his scope, waiting for Lanier to make one of those rookie mistakes.

CHAPTER 39

Thirty minutes after Smythe's men had landed, and five minutes after the last exchange of gunfire, Matt spotted two more paddlers rapidly approaching in a second canoe. The vessel was halfway between the peninsula and Big Island. Matt trained his binoculars on the occupants. When the canoe appeared in a wide gap between the trees, he got a clear and focused view. The paddlers were Swanson and Gebhardt.

What the hell? Matt's surprise turned to disbelief, then devastation, then hopelessness. Were they friends or foes? His lone consolation was that he now knew the last name of the ugly bald guy who would probably end his life. Thanks to the stillness of the morning, he'd heard Flannery cry out "Witt" after the initial exchange of gunfire.

Suppressing a primal scream of rage, Matt lowered the binoculars and picked up his Remington. Gebhardt the cop would *never* allow a civilian into this situation. Swanson's presence only made sense if Gebhardt also worked for Smythe. Matt's head throbbed from the confusion piled on top of all the stress and physical trauma he'd been through lately. Aiding and abetting a cop killer was a serious enough charge to convince anyone to tell the truth. *Or,* Swanson had deduced Matt was on Big Island solely from their casual dinner conversation last week. Either way, those two had played him like a Stradivarius. Matt's mental energy dropped to a new low.

Protected from gunshots by his prone position behind the log barricade, Matt had a view of the lake that gave him sporadic glimpses of the approaching canoe from gaps in the thick stand of trees. As the canoe reached the spot on the lake where it was again fully exposed, Matt nestled his cheek against the rifle stock and took aim. His hands shook so badly he knew he'd never come close to hitting the canoe, let alone either man. Nausea welled up again. *I barely managed to shoot at armed enemies who shot at me. How can I shoot at two of my oldest friends without being positive they intend to kill me?*

Then he thought of his father, the Myricks, and all the farmers who might have their lives and livelihoods ruined by Millennium Four. If he died because he wouldn't fight for his life while he held a small advantage, no one would be able to stop the conspiracy's land grab. A blanket of calm overtook him, almost spiritual in nature, as if someone or something was assuring him he was right to fight back. The nausea subsided, and his hands steadied. After waiting until both men were clearly visible, Matt focused the crosshairs on Gebhardt's chest, took a slow, deep breath, and moved his finger to the trigger.

A gunshot crackled the air from the bottom of the hill an instant before he could fire.

Matt flinched and ducked but heard no ricochet of a bullet off the rocks or splintering wood near his fort. He peered over his barricade and refocused on the canoe. The men were paddling furiously toward the west end of the island. Another shot rang out from what he presumed was Witt's location. Gebhardt pulled his pistol and returned fire. Swanson paddled toward safety like a man possessing superhuman strength. *What the hell again?*

Matt's friends *were* his allies. He regained his composure and unleashed a volley in Witt's direction. Unable to see Witt, Matt aimed for large boulders and trees near him, hoping to get lucky with a ricochet. At minimum, he wanted to prevent Witt from freely shooting at the canoe. His allies were four or five paddle strokes away from rounding the point of the island and escaping Witt's fire. Between Matt's and Gebhardt's covering fire and Swanson's furious paddling, the canoe made it to safety with Witt having only gotten off a few shots. Moments later, he heard another short exchange of gunfire.

The odds were now three against two in Matt's favor. And if he'd actually wounded Flannery, the odds were effectively three to one. Flannery had been silent since his yelp of pain and hadn't fired since the initial salvo. If that was a ruse to focus Matt's concentration on Witt, then Flannery might be crawling up the hill on the neglected flank like a snake preparing to strike. Matt crept to that flank and scanned down the eastern slope. He saw no movement other than a gray jay swooping from tree to tree.

The question now was how to unite with his new allies. The pathetic little fort of granite and white pine, his Alamo, would protect them only if Swanson and Gebhardt scaled the steep, rocky northern slope behind him. But first they'd have to figure out a way to get from canoe to shore; there were no safe or easy places to beach the craft on the north and west sides of the island.

Matt yelled, "Swanny, Clay, I've got the high ground!"

A burst of shots rang out from Witt's location. Matt ducked, then did a quick scan down each side of his summit perimeter. He saw no sign of activity on the eastern slope. Not having heard shots from any other direction, he assumed Witt was firing. Matt kept glancing in Witt's direction, watching to see if he had snuck along the west shore to ambush his friends.

Seeing no movement from Witt, Matt crawled to the east end of his barricade again to check if Flannery was mobile and trying to reach the summit. That side of the hill was still quiet, so he returned to the west side of his fort to keep a lookout for Witt.

Seconds later, the crunch of a branch broke the silence. Matt whirled and pointed his rifle toward the noise.

Swanson's head poked up above the crest of the hill. He froze, mouth agape as he stared at the rifle barrel. An instant later, a sheepish grin materialized on his face. "Cavalry's here."

Matt lowered his weapon and exhaled a huge sigh of relief. He'd almost shot an ally *again*. All this indecision roiled his stomach and planted serious doubt in his mind. Would he be so indecisive if Witt or Flannery popped their heads above the breastworks?

Swanson clambered up the final few feet and took cover behind the boulder. He sported a black eye, swollen lips, a bandaged nose, and several small cuts and bruises.

"Swanny, what the hell happened to you?"

"Nothing."

"That's *nothing*?" Matt exclaimed.

A shot from below ricocheted off the granite. Swanson peered over the boulder, rifle poised, ready to fire back at the shooter.

"How'd you get ashore?"

"We jumped from the canoe onto a three-foot-high rock ledge. Let the canoe float free. Gebhardt's down below but protected from Witt. He got nicked in the leg before he could take cover."

"How bad?"

"He said just a scratch."

"How did Witt find me so fast? I was leading him into a trap, but he and Flannery showed up sooner than I expected. I couldn't finish setting up all my defensive measures."

"I had to tell him. But I had a good reason."

Matt did a double take. "A good reason? You swore—"

"I said I had a good reason." Swanson's expression changed to fierce intensity. "Leave it at that. Where's Witt? I got a score to settle."

Matt pointed toward Witt's location. "He *was* behind a clump of trees and a large boulder near the south shore. Not sure if he's moved."

"What about Flannery?"

"Down the east slope. He cursed and groaned, so I think I hit him."

"Let's assume he's not hit. If he's stalking you, Witt might be providing a diversion."

Swanson peered over the rock wall and was greeted with half a dozen shots from Witt. He ducked, then popped back up when the firing stopped and ripped off a volley of his own before returning to safety.

"You got a plan?" Matt asked.

"Clay said he can't climb up here with a bullet wound, so we should go down to him and talk it over. Strategy depends on if he can walk at all."

"Makes sense."

Swanson turned and glared at him, an expression made more ominous and foreboding because of the blood, swelling, and bandages. "I pretended to agree, but I'm goin' after Baldy." He turned away. "You two do whatever you want to with Flannery."

"No," Matt said. "We stick together. Now that we have a firepower advantage, we don't need to kill anyone. I need someone to roll on Smythe so I can get my life back."

Swanson's face turned crimson. "Fuck Smythe! This is war. They ain't gonna surrender because it's three against two. They won't stop until we're dead. All you need to do is take out Flannery. I'll handle Witt. I want to hurt him first. Then I want him to beg me for mercy."

Matt grabbed him by the collar with his right hand. "Damn it, Swanny, you sound crazy. This isn't playing war as kids. I need you to stay rational and in control. Otherwise, all that comes of this is Amy buries your reckless ass."

Swanson clamped his hand over Matt's and pried it off his collar. "I'm in control. Leave me the fuck alone."

Matt grimaced as pain shot through his fingers.

"Hey, Witt," Swanson called out. "It's your worst nightmare come for revenge."

"I thought I told you to stay in your barn, Farmer Dave!" Witt said, then unleashed a short burst of shots at their fort.

"You should've killed me when you had the chance, you spineless coward, 'cause you ain't leavin' this island!"

"Oh, my God." Matt's gut twisted in agony. Witt had gone after Swanny. He hoped Amy was okay but didn't have time to ask before Swanson started shouting again.

"I'm gonna do to you what you did to Amy, you fat rat bastard, except I'll use my rifle! And there ain't gonna be a happy ending because I'm gonna blast a couple of hollow points up your ass!"

Matt cringed. His best friend had transformed into a raving, bloodthirsty animal.

"If you think Flannery's gonna help you, *Witt-less*, think again. I sliced his throat before he knew what happened. Just like slaughtering a hog on my farm."

Matt raised his eyebrows in disbelief and whipped his head around to face his friend.

Swanson made a *shushing* motion with his forefinger across his lips to acknowledge his subterfuge.

"Bring it on, Farmer Dave," Witt said. "I want to finish what I started!"

"What the hell happened back home?" Matt demanded.

Swanson stared up at the sky, bit his lower lip, seeming to struggle to control his emotions. "He got the jump on us when we were doing chores in the barn. Tied us up. He couldn't break me after he did this." He pointed at his face. "So he started in on Amy. She said he didn't rape her, but I don't believe it. I couldn't see. Witt beat her for sure and at least pretended to rape her. I freaked out. Panicked and made a wild-ass guess. Thought if I gave him a location, any location, he'd stop. Told him you were here because we talked about it last week."

Matt slumped against the boulder, struggling to comprehend this latest bout of brutality against his friends and family. He looked away, ashamed to make eye contact. The depths of his despair dug deeper than ever into his psyche.

"I am so, so sorry, Swanny."

Swanson backhanded Matt to get his attention. "I'm gonna get that cocky asshole. Cover me. I'll work my way down the hill and—"

"No." Matt grabbed Swanson's arm when he attempted to stand. "You'll be dead within seconds. Witt wants you to do something stupid like charge after him. We need to work as a team, or we're all dead. If we don't stop him here, imagine what he'll do to Amy."

A switch seemed to click on in Swanson's expression. The scowl disappeared. His eyes took on a pained, faraway look. Then he refocused on Matt. "You're right. I'm with you."

"That's more like it. Let's check with Clay."

They each fired a few shots toward Witt to cover their departure, then clambered down the hill to the rocky shore. After checking the narrow trail in both directions for signs of the enemy, Matt stopped cold. With time to digest what had happened in the last hour, he realized Swanson and Gebhardt had paddled a long way across Crystal Lake before Witt shot at them. Then when Witt *did* shoot, he missed. Even if Matt had provided cover for the paddlers, an ex-

Marine should've hit one of them in the handful of shots he got off. Swanson *said* Gebhardt had been nicked while climbing ashore, but what if he was lying? And while Swanny's story about him and Amy and Witt in the barn *sounded* plausible . . .

Matt tightened his grip on his rifle. His head throbbed from the stress, the trauma, the pain from his injuries, the pressure to make the right decisions, the encroaching paranoia. Confused and agitated, he wanted to scream all the stress out of his body and expel it into the stratosphere.

"Why's *Gebhardt* up here with you? You're the one who didn't trust him when he came looking for me at your house."

Swanson looked at him, clearly annoyed. "He drove to South Dakota to get a positive ID of Witt from a hooker Witt beat up. Clay talked her into filing charges. That gave him a reason to bring Witt in for questioning about Hibbert. Clay played a cop's hunch, and it paid off."

"You sure he's on our side? Especially if Flannery's a crook too?"

Swanson thrust his right thumb forward. "Never doubt him again, Matty. He told me the details of his search in Rapid City during the drive up here. He stood up to an entire gang. Once he found out the hooker was the gang leader's sister he wouldn't leave. Got slapped around a little, he *said*. Ask me, if a white cop stands up to any gang, odds are he gets hurt bad—or dies."

Matt stood in stunned silence, staring at Swanson's thumb, rubbing his own right thumb with his forefinger, racked with guilt that he'd failed to completely trust two of his oldest friends as adults. He'd assumed the worst with both men, believed they wouldn't remain loyal to him after he'd deserted his hometown. His big-city attitude made him forget that small-town loyalty ran deep and didn't diminish with time. He released his death grip on the Remington. "Okay," he said, fully chastened. "I'm sorry."

They walked back toward Gebhardt as far as possible without being spotted, then crawled to within whispering distance, protected from Witt's view by large boulders. Swanson trained his rifle on Witt's location and acted as a lookout.

Gebhardt's skin was pallid. His trouser leg was stained with blood.

"You all right?" Matt said in a muffled voice.

"Just a scratch. Hit me as I climbed ashore." Gebhardt nodded in Witt's direction. "He must've moved closer after we paddled to safety. Luckily, I was still able to cover Swanny. What's the situation?"

Matt took off his jacket, pulled out his knife, and cut a long strip of sleeve from his flannel shirt. He bandaged Gebhardt's leg as he filled him in on the events that had transpired. When he'd finished describing the initial encounter, Matt said, "I owe you an apology. Swanny told me what you did in South Dakota. Thank you."

"Just doing my job." Gebhardt's tone contained no trace of resentment, and his enigmatic expression unsettled Matt.

Swanson glanced back at the other two long enough to ask, "What's the plan, Clay?"

"Won't be easy to capture either of them," Gebhardt said. "Witt's a pro. Ex-Marine. Killed a man a few years ago. Probably killed Hibbert. Make a mistake against him, and it'll be your last. Not sure about Flannery. He was in the ROTC in college for a couple years. Bailed for some unknown reason—grades, maybe. But ROTC's more about leadership skills than combat skills."

"Tell us what to do," Matt said, assuming Gebhardt would take command.

Gebhardt gestured at his wounded leg. "Not sure I can walk much. All I'm good for is covering fire. Besides, you know this island better than anyone."

As soon as Matt took the hint that Gebhardt wanted him to take charge, a plan crystallized in his mind. "Okay, we need about five minutes. Swanny and I will take out Flannery. A path circles the island, so we should be able to get close to Flannery without him hearing us. You stay here and distract Witt. Negotiate. Tell him if he cooperates, he'll get a lighter sentence, anything to keep him away from Flannery. Exchange gunfire if necessary. If he moves from where he is now, yell to warn us."

"Roger that." Gebhardt struggled onto his good knee to peer over his protective boulder and cover the other two while they reloaded. "Witt! This is the police. You're under arrest for the assaults of Amy and Dave Swanson."

"So what?" Witt said, his voice full of contempt. "Fuck 'em. Fuck all of you. You ain't leaving this island alive."

CHAPTER 40

When he and Swanson were halfway to the east end of the island, Matt stopped and held up his hand. He crouched and pointed down the trail to the right. Some twenty yards ahead, wisps of vapor billowed from behind a tree.

He turned to Swanson and mouthed, "Flannery."

Swanson nodded and crouched beside him.

Matt whispered, "You go left toward the shore, far enough that you can see him and cover me. I'll go right and get as close as I can. When I give you a hand signal, toss a rock or snap a twig so he'll turn toward you. I'll jump him from behind and disarm him. Got it?"

"Got it." Swanson crept ahead off the path and toward the lake.

When Swanson reached his hiding spot behind a large white cedar, Matt crept to a point a few yards behind and to the right of Flannery. Despite the chilly temperature, clammy sweat coated his palms. An invisible force constricted his chest.

Flannery sat slumped against the downhill side of a large red pine, glancing back and forth with a pained, panicked expression.

Swanson picked up a small dried branch and bent it slightly, then nodded at Matt.

Matt made a short chopping motion with his hand.

Swanson snapped the branch and ducked behind his tree.

Flannery flinched toward the sound and fired two shots wildly into the trees.

As Matt sprang forward, Flannery spun toward him and raised his weapon to shoot. Matt slammed Flannery's head with the butt of his rifle, which dropped him like a bag of rocks. Swanson sprinted to Matt's side. Flannery's right sleeve was soaked with blood despite a crude bandage wrapped around his shoulder.

"I'll search him," Matt said then pocketed Flannery's handgun and tossed Flannery's rifle deep into the woods. "Cover me."

"You bet." Swanson went into a defensive crouch between Matt and the campsite and checked to make sure a shell was chambered.

Matt rolled Flannery onto his side and patted him down, front and back, confiscating only a small hunting knife from his belt. When he glanced up, Swanson was gone. He caught a glimpse of his friend disappearing through the trees toward the campsite.

"Swanny, no," Matt said in a stage whisper, not wanting to alert Witt that someone was headed his way. He grabbed his rifle and tore after Swanson, desperate to catch him before he got to Witt . . . or Witt got to him.

Seconds later, a burst of gunfire from the direction of the campsite echoed across the island. Matt ducked for cover behind a tree. An invisible grip, as if from a giant hand, clutched at his throat. His heartbeat pounded in his ears like a thundering bass drum.

When he heard groans behind a large boulder on the edge of the clearing, Matt crept toward the campsite. With his finger poised on the trigger and his gut knotted with dread, he rounded the boulder. Ten yards away, Swanson was lying on his side, one arm raised as a shield against a blow. Blood covered him from shoulders to knees. His face was contorted in a grimace of pain and rage.

Witt loomed over his victim, gripping his rifle barrel like a club. Blood ran from his leg and lower abdomen, and he wobbled where he stood. "Guess I'll have your wife all to myself now, Farmer Dave."

Matt stopped short, vaguely aware that he was fully exposed.

Witt raised the weapon above his head and prepared to crush Swanson's skull.

"No!" Matt screamed, but he couldn't unfreeze his hands to fire at Witt.

Startled, Witt turned toward the sound. His eyes blazed with pure evil. He lowered his rifle, flipped it around, and aimed it at Matt.

From behind a tree across the campsite, Gebhardt yelled, "Drop it, Witt!"

Witt pivoted and fired a shot at Gebhardt as he dove for cover.

Gebhardt fired back and missed.

Witt lay huddled behind a downed tree, struggling to pull his rifle from under his body. He'd escaped Gebhardt's line of fire but not Matt's.

Matt raised his Remington and settled the stock against his shoulder and cheek. The cold wood and colder steel chilled his hands and face. He aimed as Witt pulled a pistol from his shoulder holster. His scope focused on Witt's face, which showed a mixture of contempt and bravado as if to say *You don't have the guts to pull the trigger.*

Gebhardt called out, "Give up, Witt. You're under arrest."

Matt and Witt both fired.

Witt's bullet zipped past Matt's ear with a sharp *crack* that sent a shockwave through him. Matt's bullet tore a hole in the center of Witt's torso. Blood spurted from the wound.

All of Matt's accumulated pain, frustration, and rage poured into his trigger finger. He aimed and fired again.

And again.

And again.

"Matt! Enough!" Gebhardt yelled as he hobbled toward him.

Matt pumped his rifle for another shot, but Gebhardt grabbed the barrel and forced it downward. Witt's face was a mass of reddish-pink pulp. Blood oozed from his neck and chest. The acrid smell of gunpowder stung Matt's nostrils.

"Don't waste the lead," Gebhardt said somberly.

Matt dropped his weapon. It clattered to the rocky ground.

A moan from Swanson got their attention. Gebhardt limped to him, but Matt couldn't move. Couldn't think. Couldn't breathe. Couldn't look away from Witt's bloody corpse.

"Matt, get over here."

The command snapped Matt out of his daze, and he rushed to his friends. A visual check of Swanson's wounds dropped his stomach like an anchor.

Gebhardt knelt and did a quick triage while Matt sprinted into the woods to fetch the first-aid kit from the pack stuffed under his canoe.

When Matt returned, Gebhardt opened the first-aid kit and pulled out bandages, gauze, and antiseptic. "Three of these wounds are superficial—in his arm, the side of his torso, and his right thigh. This one punctured a lung."

Swanson's labored breathing—more of a wheeze—confirmed the diagnosis.

Gebhardt pointed to Swanson's midsection. "This one's bleeding the worst. Might've hit his aorta."

He examined the available bandages, then pulled a handkerchief from his pocket and stuffed it into the bullet hole after applying antiseptic to the wound.

Swanson spasmed and groaned.

"Easy, Dave. I know it hurts, but we gotta stop the bleeding." Gebhardt spoke calmly, cheerfully. But his expression was cheerless.

Tears trickled down Matt's face. He took Swanson's bloody hand in his and squeezed it gently. "Come on, ya big moolyak, hang in there. We'll get you back to Ely and . . ."

"Did I get him?" Swanson said in a weak voice.

Hesitating, Matt choked back a sob, then glanced at Gebhardt, who gave him the smallest of nods. Matt swallowed hard and took a deep breath. He locked eyes with his blood brother and held out his right thumb. "Yeah . . . you got him."

Swanson appeared to fight harder for his next breath. Then he raised his bloody right thumb and pressed it against Matt's. "Good. It was way too quick, but he won't bother Amy . . . or you . . . again."

"This is all my fault, Swanny."

Swanson closed his eyes, then opened them and gazed unseeing at Matt. "Nah. My fault. Got greedy . . . had my head turned by that damn Smythe." Each word came softer, more pained and labored than the last. Blood trickled from the corner of his mouth. He drew a slow, gurgling breath, squeezed his eyes shut, grimaced. "Tell Amy . . . I'm sorry . . . and I love—"

The silence of the wilderness overwhelmed the scene. Even the early arriving birds fell quiet. Matt sat back on the cold, muddy ground. Numbness spread across his entire body. He cried until no tears remained.

Gebhardt hoisted himself up to sit on a large flat rock, then appeared to float in a daze for a minute. Shakily, and with some effort, he stood and stared out at the lake.

Eventually, Matt stood and joined his friend. "Although it doesn't matter now, thanks for tracking down Witt and connecting him to Smythe."

"Dead or alive, it mattered to me," Gebhardt said. "Thank you for the, um, gentle nudge to get off my ass."

When Matt comprehended the comment, he patted Gebhardt on the back. Inhaling a lungful of frigid air, Matt gazed around the island and across the lake.

The sun peeked through a hole in the clouds. The air smelled pure, with a hint of pine, a hint of spring. Patches of snow dotted the shadier areas of the forest. The sunshine created shimmering patterns of light on the rippling water. In the distance a large bird soared high above the lake—an eagle or a turkey vulture.

How ironic that such a pristine, peaceful place had been the scene of the bloodiest, most traumatic day of Matt's life. How much death had this isolated combination of rocks, trees, water, and sky witnessed since the glaciers formed the land thousands of years before? Predators had routinely killed prey for food, of course. Maybe there had been a rare fatality during the Voyageur Era. But never had there been this much senseless human suffering in such a brief time. Matt stared at his blood-stained hands.

All because of me.

No. All because of Smythe.

He faced Gebhardt. "Let's have a little chat with our prisoner."

CHAPTER 41

Flannery was awake but still lying on the ground when Matt and Clay arrived. Once they convinced him that if he didn't cooperate, he'd be left to die on Big Island, he agreed to talk. Gebhardt carefully peeled the blood-soaked, makeshift tourniquet from Flannery's shoulder and began to administer first aid. Matt pulled out his tape recorder and waggled it. Gebhardt gave him a couldn't-hurt shrug. Matt sat next to Flannery and pressed *record*.

Flannery confirmed what Matt had suspected but couldn't prove: Smythe and Crossley were the masterminds behind Millennium Four, a real estate scheme to buy up farms along Interstate 35 in Minnesota, Iowa, and Missouri, if not farther south. "M4," as the principals usually referred to it, was stealing the farms for a fraction of their value wherever possible. Then, when the time was right, the organization would quietly sell the land to the federal government for an exorbitant profit.

Smythe and Crossley had approached a small group of young, ambitious Senators and Congressmen whom they thought might be interested in their concept of developing a nationwide superhighway system as a first step toward facilitating the consolidation and expansion of the country's dominance in the world. The pols were intrigued but wanted to see if the prototype, Millennium Four, worked at all before they committed to organizing other clandestine groups to acquire land corridors along the rest of the interstate highway system.

They bought the theory that the federal government would get the land faster and cheaper through M4 than if they were forced to negotiate with individual farmers. Once the Feds acquired the land, they'd begin construction on a massive superhighway system that would jump-start the economic and political unification of the U.S.,

Canada, Mexico, and eventually Central and South America. Their ultimate goal? Create the most dominant empire in history—the United States of *the Americas*.

According to Flannery, Smythe was strangely apolitical. His solitary goal was profit and the massive ego trip he would enjoy if he pulled off the real estate scheme of the century. To him, it was a modern version of the 19th Century railroad tycoons who acquired all the preferred real estate on which to build the nation's railroad system. Because he was the majority stakeholder in M4, Smythe expected to turn his millions into a billion or more. He'd only used the lure of rebuilding America's dominance to obtain buy-in from politicians. They would prove useful in helping with coverups and doing some political arm-twisting to resolve any problems that might arise.

That's where Crossley came into the picture. His goal was to use M4 as a springboard to the upper echelon of political power. If the prototype was successful, being on a first name basis with many of the nation's future leaders would guarantee his ascendance to the Washington elite. Together, Smythe and Crossley made a formidable combination of Midwestern money and power.

Matt was dumbstruck. Had his father foreseen all this? Or had he only been concerned about protecting Straight River farmers from getting cheated out of their farms by the unscrupulous Hibbert?

He peered at Flannery. "All this death and destruction for a ludicrous grand scheme devised by a bunch of seriously deluded egomaniacs that has almost no chance of success?"

Flannery shrugged. "As you may have noticed by now, Smythe doesn't take *no* for an answer." He grimaced as Gebhardt dabbed his bloody wound with an antiseptic wipe, then huffed out a short, bitter laugh. "And it's not *my* ludicrous grand scheme. I'm only in it for career advancement."

"You're a small-town police chief," Gebhardt said. "Why the hell would Smythe tell you all these secret details?"

"I didn't know until a few days ago. Once Smythe decided Witt needed my help to kill you," Flannery nodded at Matt, "I demanded a damn good reason to put not only my career but also my life on the line."

"You're willing to obstruct justice and commit murder all for a better job?"

"Not just a job, a significant law enforcement position. Chief of police in Minneapolis. Chicago after that."

Sick of the big picture lunacy, Matt focused on questions more important to him and the local farmers. "Did Witt kill my father?"

Flannery looked away from his captors. "Yes."

"How?" Matt swallowed hard, not sure he wanted to know the details.

"Witt opened the silo hatch late one night, then waited in the woods until Ray noticed it early the next morning. He knew no one else was around at that time and figured Ray would climb up himself to close the hatch. Once Ray started climbing, Witt came out, forced him to the top at gunpoint, and pushed him in. The corn did the rest."

"Did Hibbert kill Myrick and make it look like a suicide?"

"Hell no." Flannery coughed, then grimaced as Gebhardt tightened the bandage on his arm. "Myrick had a heart attack."

"Why did the autopsy confirm suicide?"

"Witt was at the Eagles Club that night keeping an eye on Hibbert. Myrick collapsed and died in the parking lot. Witt called Smythe for instructions. Smythe knew about the bank loan and their insurance policy. When Betty went bankrupt, Smythe planned to take her farm for pennies on the dollar. Smythe told Witt and Hibbert to drive Myrick's body back to his farm and string him up. He told me to blackmail Dr. Vincent and force her to falsify the autopsy results."

Matt shook his head, disgusted. *Smythe is one conniving, heartless bastard.* "What happened to Hibbert?"

"I didn't ask, but Witt left town for a few days. I'm pretty sure he tossed Hibbert off that cliff in the Black Hills."

"Sounds like Hibbert had no clue what he was getting into with Smythe," Gebhardt said as he wrapped Flannery's arm to his body with an elastic bandage to help immobilize the shoulder for the journey back to Ely.

"The understatement of the year," Flannery said wryly.

Matt stopped the recorder. He noticed Gebhardt's shaking hands and the sweat on his brow. "We gotta get going, Clay. You two need to get to the hospital."

Gebhardt nodded, a look of relief on his pale face.

The sky was clearing. The sun was a few degrees past vertical. Matt said, "We can reach Olson's before sunset if we paddle fast."

Gebhardt glanced skyward. "Let's take only what we need. Flannery can carry a few things. We'll handle the canoe and the rest of the gear."

They helped Flannery to his feet and escorted him to the boat landing. After retrieving Gebhardt's larger canoe from the lake, Matt packed his essential gear and laid it in the bottom of the boat for Flannery to recline on. Then he turned to Gebhardt and nodded toward the bodies. "What about them?"

"Not much we can do," Gebhardt said. "When we get back to Ely, we'll call the sheriff's office. They can arrange to get the bodies out by helicopter or seaplane." He walked to Witt's body and knelt.

Matt scoffed. "You're wasting prayers on that piece of shit?"

"Nope." Gebhardt searched all of Witt's pockets. He removed the man's car keys and examined his wallet but found nothing else of significance. He stood and tossed the keys to Matt. Clay's face showed strain from the simple act of kneeling and standing. "His wheels might contain some evidence we can use."

Once Flannery was settled into the canoe and centered, they shoved off. They set a respectable pace during the initial paddle and portage, but as the trio walked the final portage to Snowfall Lake, Gebhardt's limp was more pronounced.

Matt said, "You sure you're okay, Clay?"

Gebhardt, who was leading the way as they two-man-carried the canoe, waved off his concern. "Yeah, the bullet got a little more muscle than I thought."

At the portage landing, Matt got a good look at Gebhardt's leg. Fresh blood glistened on his trousers. "You sprung a leak."

Gebhardt groaned and sat on a nearby boulder. Sweat trickled down his temples despite the near-freezing temperature. "I guess all this walking doesn't help."

Matt removed the last large bandage and the adhesive tape from the first-aid kit. He wrapped the bandage around Gebhardt's thigh and taped it as tightly as he dared without cutting off circulation. "Better?"

Gebhardt nodded. They reloaded the canoe and began the final leg to Olson's. Matt paddled as hard as his tired, pained body allowed. Gebhardt struggled to maintain a consistent paddling stroke.

To keep Gebhardt's mind off his pain, Matt said, "When you arrest Flannery, he'll have to spill it all, won't he? We can shut down Millennium Four."

"I doubt he'll cooperate. He's in way too deep to do a plea bargain. The tape won't be admissible in court. Flannery will claim we stuck a gun in his face and forced him to confess all the M4 bullshit. The best I can do is press charges against him for this fiasco. That should earn him a long stint in the state prison."

"But we've got so much more now. Dead bodies at a crime scene. Witnesses and corroboration. The research Zach and I did on Saxony Partners. *Plus* my taped account of what's gone down on this island along with Flannery's confession. That's a start. Diane Blake will help us too. She's got plenty of connections in the Attorney General's office who'd love to get a crack at Smythe."

Gebhardt shook his head. "Matt, you have a college degree, and you're a freaking musical genius, but this is real world cops-and-robbers. It requires more street smarts than book smarts. Smythe won't allow two speedbumps like us to slow him down, let alone stop him. An army of lawyers will run interference for him and disavow any knowledge of anyone's actions—particularly Flannery and Witt. We can try to overcome that, but it might be smarter to cut our losses now and get home ASAP. Can't do much about your dad's murder because Witt already paid with his life, but we can resolve Betty's situation."

"You're probably right," Matt said. Gebhardt's plan made better sense. They'd stop Millennium Four later, he hoped.

Gebhardt stopped paddling and glanced back at his soon-to-be-former boss. "What the hell did you say to Anne Vincent to keep her quiet about the suicide call on Myrick's autopsy?"

Flannery, shivering on the bottom of the canoe, stared up at the sky. "Smythe found out she had an affair with a DA years ago and told me to threaten to leak the fact if she didn't cooperate."

Gebhardt shook his head. "You are one sorry-ass excuse for a lawman." His voice dripped with contempt. "I'm ashamed to say, up until a few days ago, I actually respected you."

Matt stopped paddling and ran one hand over his face. "I've got to say I'm a little overwhelmed by today's, um, activities. How do cops handle all this stress?"

"Ain't easy." Gebhardt faced forward and cradled his head in his hands. He appeared to be totally exhausted, as if he might fall overboard. "Sometimes we don't. PTSD isn't just for soldiers."

With the sun gradually receding, they resumed paddling. An hour later, as the faint pink-orange sky backlit the tallest pines on the western horizon, they reached Olson's Outfitters.

"We're back, Flannery," Matt said as they coasted the final few yards to the dock. "Sit up so we can haul you out."

Flannery lay motionless in the bottom of the canoe. Matt nudged him with his paddle—once, twice. No response came other than a small groan. Fresh blood seeped through the bandage Gebhardt had applied at the last portage landing.

"Shit," Matt said. "He's out cold."

"Wonderful." Gebhardt's voice dripped with sarcasm. "He's probably in shock."

Matt steered alongside the small dock and held the canoe as steady as his injured body would allow. "You get out here," he said, "then I'll run the canoe ashore so we can lift him out easier."

Gebhardt dragged himself up and out of the craft onto the dock. Matt backed off and paddled full speed onto the adjacent sandy beach, trying to get as much of the canoe onto shore as possible. He stepped into the shallow, ice-cold water, wincing in anticipation that his thrift-store hiking boots would leak. To his surprise, they didn't. He hauled the canoe ashore, and the two men slid Flannery onto the beach. It took several minutes for them to get him to the main lodge building because Gebhardt's leg and Matt's left hand were virtually useless.

Gebhardt was panting hard and sweating when they set Flannery down on the three-step-high porch in front of the main door. Matt's ribs and hand throbbed from his exertion. After taking a pain-clearing breath, he retrieved a key from the same spot the key had always been hidden when he worked for Olson—hung from a small nail tacked to the back of the bird feeder mounted on a porch post. Matt thanked God that Ferdie was a man of rigid habits and not prone to making changes in his life or routines without a good reason.

Matt unlocked the door and switched on the overhead light. They dragged Flannery inside. Gebhardt collapsed onto the nearest chair with a huge groan. Matt tried to revive Flannery with several gentle slaps on the cheek and loud commands to wake up, but the man remained unconscious.

"This is a problem," Matt said. "We can't take the chance he dies before we get him to Ely. We have to call an ambulance."

Gebhardt nodded. "I'm pretty wasted myself. Not sure I can help you with him anymore." In the incandescent light, his complexion looked more pallid than it had in daylight. "So let's at least fix one thing before we call for help in case a deputy sheriff beats the ambulance here."

"Fix what?"

"Give me Flannery's cell phone."

Matt gave him a puzzled look but removed Flannery's phone from the small pack he'd carried up from the canoe. "No cell towers anywhere near here that I know of. Your call won't go through."

Gebhardt smiled slyly. "Not calling anyone. I'll text Dr. Vincent, the county coroner, and get Myrick's autopsy corrected."

Matt started to protest, then quickly understood that Vincent would assume Flannery had sent the text. He handed the phone to Gebhardt. "Is it legal for you to pretend you're him? Doesn't he have to give the order?"

"Technically, yes." Gebhardt turned on the phone and began to type with his thumbs, squinting to see, grunting when he mistyped and had to make corrections. When he'd finished, he held the phone out for Matt to see.

Matt read the message. "Looks like what a police chief would say."

"All you gotta do is swear that Flannery sent this text *before* he passed out."

Matt raised his right hand as if taking an oath. "I'll take our secret to my grave."

"Depending on the cell coverage, Vincent might not see this right away, so take the phone with you when we go to the hospital. As soon as you're close enough to a cell tower, the text will be sent. You'll see a little icon that says *delivered* after that happens."

"Okay," Matt said.

Gebhardt pressed the *send* key and slumped back against the chair. His eyes widened, and a pained, dizzy look came to his face. "Uh-oh," he said, then promptly passed out.

"Clay?" Matt reached for his shoulder and shook gently. "Clay!" He heard a faint moan in response. He did the same cheek-patting routine he'd done with Flannery to no avail. Remembering his basic first-aid training, Matt eased Gebhardt from the chair and laid him down on the floor, then covered him with a space blanket from his pack.

"Great," Matt muttered as he contemplated the two unconscious men. He hustled to Olson's office phone and dialed 911. Flannery being out cold was good because he couldn't pull rank and talk the Ely authorities into believing him over his sergeant and a man wanted on suspicion of killing a cop. Gebhardt being out cold negated that advantage and then some because Matt had no one to back up his version of today's events on Big Island. Even if the Ely sheriff believed him, Matt feared Smythe would get wind of what had happened and dispatch a new hitman to take him out, police protection or not.

When the emergency dispatcher answered, Matt had a sudden inspiration of what he hoped would be improvisational genius. "This is Sergeant Clayton Gebhardt of the Straight County Police Department," he said. "I need an ambulance at Olson's Outfitters off Fernberg Road." Matt groaned and made his voice sound shaky and weak. "I and my chief, Michael Flannery, sustained gunshot wounds.

We've both lost a lot of blood. Flannery is in shock and unconscious, and I'm . . . close . . ."

"I'll send someone immediately, Sergeant," said the female dispatcher, then paused. "A deputy is about twenty minutes from you, and the ambulance will arrive in less than thirty. Stay on the line with—"

Matt hung up. Now that he knew who to expect, and when, he could set the rest of his plan in motion. He found a flashlight from Olson's equipment room and hustled out to Witt's SUV. He searched for anything that might be useful but only found Witt's cell phone. Then he hustled to his canoe and removed the personal gear he'd brought so only the cops' gear would be found at the scene. He took his gear to his truck, pulled the keys from his pocket, and drove out of Olson's toward Fernberg Road. He turned into the first side road he reached, which he knew led to several private lake cabins whose owners weren't likely to be there this early in the season. Sprinting back to Olson's, he checked on Gebhardt's condition—steady breathing but no sign of waking. Flannery was the same except his breathing was more erratic. He took Flannery's phone as well, then glanced at the clock. Ten minutes had elapsed since he'd called for the ambulance.

He made a final check of the room to make sure he hadn't forgotten any of his gear or personal belongings, then stepped outside and walked toward his parked truck. When a siren wailing in the distance and then quickly coming closer indicated the deputy's car had turned onto Olson's access road, Matt stepped into the thick pine forest and crouched behind a large spruce until the sheriff's department cruiser sped past. As it disappeared around a bend, he resumed his walk to the truck, got in, and drove out onto Fernberg Road headed for Ely. Several minutes later, the ambulance zoomed past, lights flashing and siren blaring. Matt pulled over and let it pass. He'd solved one problem—getting medical help for two wounded men. But now he had a bigger problem—how to continue until Gebhardt regained consciousness and could corroborate his story.

CHAPTER 42

After calling Witt's satellite phone for the third time in the past two hours and getting no answer, Leland Smythe paced the floor of his home office, clenching and unclenching his fists. Even if the sat phone had malfunctioned, Witt should've been able to return to civilization and call from either his cell phone or a landline with an update by now. Based on Witt's confidence level that morning, eliminating Lanier should have been done hours earlier. He grudgingly admitted the pesky musician may have put up a stiffer fight than either he or Witt had anticipated.

Smythe stopped pacing and called Crossley. "We have a problem."

"Oh?" Crossley sounded unconcerned.

"Our field representative hasn't reported in since he called this morning. Too much time has elapsed for the job to have been successfully completed."

"I see. What's our course of action?" Concern was now evident in Crossley's tone.

"We assume a negative outcome. Do we have a contract man in Duluth?"

"Yes, one of our more reliable local operatives."

"Send him to Ely. Have him check the hospital. There may have been some sort of accident. If so, instruct him in the usual procedures for dealing with medical issues based on what he discovers. Our opponent may have had reinforcements, which would explain the delay. If there's nothing amiss at the hospital, instruct our agent to check that outfitter's place for any indication of what may have happened. If he needs help, you take the corporate jet up there at once."

"Consider it done," Crossley said. "I'd love to get my hands on that damn musician. He cost me my prized puppet for state political office, not to mention one hell of a good lay."

Smythe rolled his gaze upward and sharpened his tone. "Your personal life does *not* interest me. We don't know the situation right now, and I'm unaccustomed to not knowing. However, if the musician is as lovesick over his ex-wife as you claim, I'm sure he'll try to contact her."

"I knew they were up to something. I should've gone to that bitch's place and caught them together. I would've done the gorilla's job myself for free."

"Calm down. You can do what you want with her once she's served our purpose. You did install wiretaps on her phones, didn't you?"

"Yes. After our opponent left the hospital, I called her and got the distinct impression she'd talked to him recently. I put the tap in the next day when she was at work. I'll check right away. He may be spilling his guts to her as we speak."

"If you're not needed in Ely, be ready to surprise them at her condo in case our musician friend shows up." Smythe walked to the window and gazed out onto his estate. The full moon lit the immaculate landscape with a vibrant blue-white glow. "Did you identify the man who saved our opponent near that coffee shop?"

"Yes, we got his name and address. He's a college student, computer major, lives in that neighborhood. If he wasn't a random Good Samaritan, our best guess is he might also be a student of the musician. But we haven't seen him carry an instrument. Might be because of the cast on his leg."

Smythe believed in neither coincidences nor heroism. Until proven otherwise, he would assume Lanier had recruited a soldier for his little army. This brought a smile to his lips. It mattered little how many hapless, naive civilians Lanier recruited for his foolish attempt to meddle with Millennium Four. Its network of informants, muscle, money, and political connections was virtually indestructible.

"Good," Smythe said. "Keep eyes on him. If things have gone badly and he meets with the musician in the next few days, we can deal with both at the same time. Less risk. If they don't connect, the student will make enticing bait to lure our target into the open."

"Right. Anything else?"

"Yes. Be prepared for anything. I am through being subtle. If necessary, we'll mobilize a small army to stop this troublemaker."

CHAPTER 43

Unsure of what the next twenty-four hours would bring, and not having eaten anything other than a few handfuls of trail mix since breakfast, Matt decided to get his injuries and bandages examined, then find some food. He would have about a thirty-minute window of opportunity with a doctor or nurse before Gebhardt and Flannery arrived via ambulance. Because of the time lag, he hoped the ER staff wouldn't connect him to the two men.

At the Ely hospital, Matt entered the emergency room. He figured it was his sole option for immediate treatment in a small town after hours. The waiting area was empty, so he quickly got in to see the on-call physician, a sincere-looking man about Matt's age named Anders.

After studying Matt from head to toe, Dr. Anders gestured toward the bandages on his hands—dirty, torn, and stained with blood. "What happened to you?"

Matt had been able to ignore his own pains until now, but the question triggered his senses, and he became acutely aware of his agony. Hoping Anders wouldn't press him for details, he said, "Industrial mishap."

The doctor raised his eyebrows above his glasses and pursed his lips. "Industrial mishap?"

Matt pleaded with his eyes at Anders for a hint of understanding and discretion. "I'm more worried about the stitches in my back."

Anders narrowed his eyes, hesitated, then glanced around the ER. "Sure. There's no one else here who's in worse shape. However, we just got word an ambulance is coming in with two gunshot wounds."

"Is that so?" Matt said, feigning surprise.

Anders led Matt back to a cubicle where he examined his back wounds. "Let me guess. Flying glass from your industrial mishap?"

"Yeah. Broken ribs and a rattled head too." He winced as Anders peeled the blood-crusted bandages from his back.

"A few of these lacerations are a little weepy. Might be infected since the bandages haven't been changed and . . ." He exaggerated a sniff. ". . . you haven't showered in several days."

"Guilty on both counts."

Anders spent a few minutes cleaning the wounds. "They aren't as bad as I thought. I'll apply a topical antibiotic now and write you a prescription for penicillin. Anything else hurt?"

"Three broken ribs."

"Not much I can do for them except prescribe pain meds. Let me see your hand." Anders cut the dressing and peeled it off. As he cleaned the wounds and plied the fingers every which way, Matt winced and inhaled sharply.

"You understand you've sustained tendon damage in your left hand, don't you?"

"Yes, but the doctor said if I stayed patient and kept my hand immobilized, I should regain full use of my fingers."

"Judging by the blood on your bandages, it appears that wasn't possible."

"Couldn't be helped."

"There appears to be some tissue damage since your initial treatment. If, and I emphasize if, you haven't stressed the injury too much, the damage will be minimal. You'll be typing almost as fast as you used to."

If? Minimal? Almost? Matt's stomach did a nosedive. This was a second opinion that confirmed his left hand might never fully regain its dexterity and strength. *Damn Smythe to hell yet again.*

Anders finished cleaning up Matt's wounds, then stepped out to write the penicillin prescription. As Matt dressed, the stress of the past few weeks boiled over. A tsunami of fatigue and devastation flooded his body. The walls of the treatment room converged, threatening to crush him with claustrophobia. His entire body vibrated. *Swanny's root cellar times one hundred.* His panicky mind yelled at his body to get out now before he cracked up.

"I gotta leave," Matt said when Anders returned.

Anders' eyebrows popped upward. "Now? You need that penicillin prescription before you go. It'll only take a few minutes."

"I'll pick it up later." Matt stood and walked decisively down the hallway toward the hospital exit, ignoring Dr. Anders' fading protestations. His growing sense of impending doom would not yield to Ander's calm logic. He tried to appear confident of his decision, tried to appear in control, tried not to run to his truck as he held back another primal scream of rage.

Inside the relative safety of his truck, Matt regained some composure and drove off in search of food. Because it was the off-season, few restaurants in Ely were open late on an early-April evening except the local chain sandwich shop. After purchasing a foot-long steak-and-cheese sub loaded with several veggie garnishes on hearty Italian bread, along with chips, a cookie, and a large black coffee, he sat in his truck and devoured the food.

As he ate, Matt noticed how useless his left hand was for gripping anything, even a sandwich. Playing bass again seemed like an impossibility. He forced down his simmering rage and frustration with several gulps of tepid but strong coffee. But he needed to survive and stay out of jail before he could worry about anything else.

He finished his meal, started his truck, and headed down Sheridan Street, the main drag. Finding a space on the curb, he parked near a bar with several other cars parked in front. A few people were on the sidewalks in the vicinity, but no one took notice of him. He pulled the cell phone Swanson had given him from his jacket pocket. He made a quick call to Directory Assistance, asked for Ferdie Olson's phone number, and dialed.

Ferdie answered with a gruff, "Hullo?"

"Ferdie, this is Matt Lanier. I worked for you back in the—"

"Matt Lanier! What a surprise. Or maybe not. Any chance you're calling about a phone message I got on my off-season line from a sergeant in someplace called Straight River? Or is it about the call I just got from the sheriff saying that same sergeant called for an ambulance from my business earlier tonight?"

"How did—" Matt started to ask how Olson made the connection until he remembered who he was talking to. Ferdie Olson looked, sounded, and acted like a coarse, common Iron Ranger, but Matt had never met anyone with keener powers of observation. Not big on book learning, Olson possessed a Ph.D. in street smarts, logical thinking, and common sense. "I mean, yes. The sergeant's a good friend of mine."

"You need answers? Help? Or both?" Olson said in his usual get-to-the-point manner.

"Answers first. Help or advice if the answer's not good. I don't want you to take any risk, so let's keep it on the phone, okay? If the wrong people find out you even talked to me tonight, you might get into trouble."

"I ain't worried. If I die tomorrow, I won't have no regrets. What're the questions?"

"Who's the most trustworthy person in the sheriff's department?" Matt hoped Olson's network of friends and acquaintances in the Ely area was still extensive.

Olson took less than a second before speaking. "Hank Rodde. Good man. Known him forty years."

"Any chance he'd ever take a bribe or look the other way for someone?"

"Old Hank sees law enforcement as the highest calling there is. Wouldn't be tempted to do anything the slightest bit shady, let alone illegal. Everyone around here wants him to be sheriff, but he don't like the politics. Royal pain in the ass, he says."

Matt sighed with relief. If Olson had said all the law enforcers in Ely were more crooked than a deer trail through the woods, Matt would've needed to rethink his plan. "I need you to call Rodde tomorrow morning. Give him a heads up that I'm bringing in some more evidence and a witness to verify my story. When I'm ready, my friends and I want to talk to him in person."

"Sure thing. I'm guessin' this is serious."

"Life and death. Please don't tell anyone but Rodde."

"I won't. Anything else?"

"Does the sheriff's department have secure computer connections, servers, all that internet stuff?"

"State-of-the-art's what I heard," Olson said. "I'm no computer *goo-roo,* but the new sheriff is a young fella who promised to modernize the department. It was big news about all the fancy technology he bought since he took office."

"That's all I need to know for now. Thanks, Ferdie. I owe you again."

"Ain't nothin'. When you get this trouble resolved, let's get together for a snort. Maybe dip a line in Snowfall."

"I'd like that." Matt wondered if the day would ever come when he could relax with an old friend and mentor and fish for walleyes on a pristine lake as he sipped a beer. He glanced around outside his truck, suddenly aware he'd let his guard down. "I'd better go. Gotta keep moving."

"Just keep your eyes and ears open and watch your back, son."

"I will." Matt rang off and called Zach Perez.

"Dude, I've been worried sick." Zach said after Matt identified himself. "I figured Smythe's guys killed you and tossed your bloody corpse into a dumpster. What's up?"

"The situation is bad, but I still believe I can stop Smythe. Is there a way for you to securely send our research to a sheriff's office?"

"I can encrypt our information here, and if I send it to a secure website or email address, it'll be virtually untouchable."

"Good. Be ready to send it tomorrow morning. I've got evidence that isn't viable in court on its own. So our data will solidify our case when I go to the police."

"Call me when you're ready to proceed. You'll receive the data within seconds."

"Thanks." Matt ended the call and tapped in another number.

"Hello?"

The sound of Diane's voice gave Matt a powerful endorphin rush. Tension and pain flowed from his body like water down a bathtub drain.

"It's me," he said.

A half gasp, half cry came over the phone. "Matt, you're alive! Where are you?"

"First, tell me you're okay."

"I'm fine. Steven was traveling around the state with the governor earlier this week, so I haven't seen him. How are you?"

A burst of energy replaced Matt's waning tension once he heard Crossley hadn't harmed her. "I'm all right, but the situation is bad."

He gave her a quick synopsis of the day's events but couldn't bring himself to tell her who put the final bullets into Witt's body. She reacted appropriately and sounded quite distressed by the news of Swanson's death.

"Why haven't you gone to the police?" she said with panic in her voice. "Men are dead and injured. The hospital is legally required to report all gunshot wounds. The police will find out. Flannery will give your name to the authorities."

"I can't trust *any* law enforcement yet because I'm still suspected of killing a cop. And I can't prove my innocence until Gebhardt can verify my side of the story." He spoke louder and with more irritation than he'd intended. Lacking total control of his emotions as well as his body added to his accumulated anger. Slamming his good fist through a wall would feel *so* cathartic. "But I *will* get this mess straightened out tomorrow with help from you and Zach."

"Why me?"

Matt was about to explain his plan for tomorrow until he realized reuniting with her was far from a done deal. If he told her now but was captured or killed before they could go to the sheriff together, she'd be more vulnerable against Smythe and Crossley. She stood a better chance of surviving by honestly pleading ignorance when questioned by anyone from M4 or the authorities. "I'll tell you everything when we meet. It's too dangerous right now."

"Then come here. I've got connections in the DA's office. You'll be safe."

"No. It'll take too long. Gebhardt can't travel, and he's the only one who can corroborate my story. If things go right tomorrow morning, then you can bring in additional legal power."

"I still wish you'd come here but, okay. I'll come right away." Diane now sounded eager with anticipation. "Where are you?"

"I'll meet you part way. I don't want you to know where I am in case Smythe or Crossley finds out you talked to me. Do you remember the Thompson Hill Rest Area?"

"In Duluth, just off I-35?"

"Yes." Matt checked the time. "Pack a bag and meet me there at midnight. I'll get there before you, so when you arrive, I'll signal you somehow. What are you driving these days?"

"A tan Lexus."

"One more thing. Do you have a weapon?"

She paused. "A twenty-five-caliber Beretta. I got my carry permit a few years ago after a serial rapist terrorized my neighborhood."

"Bring it with you, ready to use. Just in case." He had no idea what *just in case* meant other than Smythe had been one step ahead of him from the beginning.

"I will, but are you one hundred percent sure that bringing me along is a good idea?"

"You're worth the risk. If we're together, they can't kidnap you and use you as bait to draw me out of hiding. Plus, if someone tries to hurt you, they'll have to kill me first."

"Now that you mentioned I should bring a gun, I'm having second thoughts. I'm no good in a shootout. Fighting Millennium Four by yourself is a battle you can't win. Going to the police *now* is the safest, sanest option. Please reconsider and return to the hospital and talk to the police. The ER doctor has probably called them already."

He remained silent long enough to give her the impression he was reconsidering. "No. If I turn myself in, I lose any control I still have. I'll fight Millennium Four on my own terms. Win or lose, at least I'll know I gave myself the best chance to succeed."

She fell silent, so Matt peered through the window of the bar. A young couple was giggling, feeding each other nachos slathered in gooey yellow cheese, sipping pints of beer. A normal couple. Happy. In love. *Will I ever again have that with Diane?*

Growling something that sounded like *Arghhh*, Diane finally said, "Okay, you stubborn fool. You win. I'll see you at midnight."

CHAPTER 44

Tingling with anticipation of his reunion with Diane, Matt sat in his truck, which was backed into a parking space at the Thompson Hill Rest Area. Ten minutes earlier, he'd parked at a nearby convenience store and hiked to the woods on the edge of the rest area's parking lot to surveille the grounds for signs of an ambush. Satisfied that no trap had been set, Matt retrieved his truck and drove to the northeast end of the lot where he had a clear view of the entire rest area. A catnap before leaving Ely had helped restore his energy, but he still felt like he was at ten percent of his usual mental and physical strength.

Situated off Interstate 35 at the crest of a ridge that rises hundreds of feet above Lake Superior, Thompson Hill serves as the tourists' gateway to the inland seaport of Duluth, Minnesota, and doubles as a rest area for weary travelers. Two passenger vehicles had pulled in during the thirty minutes Matt had been observing. Both parked in front of the visitor's center, well away from his truck, and left after the drivers had used the facilities. Other than that, three semitrailers were parked in the truck parking area on the southwest side of the facility, their cabs facing away from him.

When a car turned into the lot but didn't park next to the building, Matt's senses shifted to high alert. The car idled at the opposite end of the lot with its headlights shining at him. When the headlights went out, Matt trained his binoculars on the car's windshield, hoping to recognize the driver. The eerie yellow glow of the sodium-vapor street lamps illuminated the swooshed *L* on the grille indicating a Lexus. The driver's face was hidden by the glare.

The dashboard clock read 12:05. *It must be her*. Matt flashed his headlights *on-off* in acknowledgment but got no response.

Was she afraid to drive closer or step out of the car for fear of being seen? He couldn't blame her. Now certain the driver was Diane, he stepped out and waved.

As he did, the Lexus' headlights blinked *on-off-on* in response, and the car moved toward him. Trembling with excitement, Matt opened the rear driver-side door of the pickup, preparing to transfer his gear into her car.

He placed his backpack on the ground, then glanced up at the Lexus, now less than fifty feet away. Over the next second, Matt observed and analyzed three pieces of data: First, the silhouette of a passenger. Was it a man or a woman? Second, the driver's silhouette was a man's. Third, something other than a hand or an arm protruded from the open driver's window. That bit of sight reading triggered an involuntary flight reaction that propelled him into the back seat of his truck an instant before two gunshots rang out and two bullets slammed into the rear fender with a dull *ping*.

Matt drew his Glock 17 and aimed through the half-open back door of the truck, ready to shoot if a man appeared. He was sprawled across the back seat with his feet almost hanging out the open door. He remained flat, so he'd present a smaller target, hoping his dark clothing helped camouflage him against the dark-gray back seat.

When the shooter or any part of the Lexus failed to appear in the gap after several seconds, Matt reanalyzed the situation for the strategies the shooter might employ. His best option, his one chance for survival, was to improvise: Do the unexpected and catch the killer off guard.

He clenched his teeth, feeling like he could grind them to dust, as a surge of adrenaline kicked him into high gear. He depressed the red panic button on the key fob, and his truck came alive with flashing lights and rhythmic honking. Three quick shots rang out. None hit him. He heard no sounds of impact on the truck. Reaching back with his free hand, he gripped the handle to the right-rear door, kicked the half-open left rear door all the way open, and jerked himself toward the passenger side.

Crack-Crack-Crack! The left-rear window shattered, and a hole appeared in the seatback above where his legs had been an instant earlier. His gun still trained on the gap, Matt moved his feet until he found some traction on the floor. More shots plowed into the driver's side of the back seat. Matt opened the right rear door and propelled himself out and onto the concrete. He scrambled to all-fours and crept to the front fender as another shot thunked into the truck's cab. He peeked above the hood and spotted a lone shooter still focused on the rear seats.

Crossley!

Barely in control of his rage, Matt brought the Glock up over the hood and let loose two rounds. In his haste, they flew high and wide. Fortunately, his volley had caught Crossley by surprise. Instead of returning fire, Crossley dove into what he believed to be the safety of the Lexus's driver seat, unaware that Matt had moved to a point where he had a clear shot.

Matt fired three more rounds. The front passenger window shattered. Metal pinged. At least one of his shots struck home because he heard a yelp of pain. He ducked below the fender as Crossley fired two erratic shots that sailed high overhead. A second later, Crossley fired another shot. No metal *ping*. No shattering glass.

Still crouched behind the truck but wanting to hear if Crossley was moving to counterattack, Matt clicked off the key fob's panic button. Silence descended on the area. Above the ringing in his ears, he heard the soft murmur of the idling diesel engines of the trucks at the far end of the rest area. A long, tense minute passed. Rising slowly, he peered over the fender toward the Lexus, ready to fire again if Crossley stirred. Matt hadn't noticed the other passenger moving at all, but the second individual might be creeping up behind him for a kill shot. He checked his rear and his flanks, but neither saw nor heard anything moving. For a few seconds, he thought past fight or flight. Circling around his truck toward the Lexus, Glock trained on Crossley, questions raced through his mind. Why had the *driver* also been the *shooter?* Why hadn't the passenger run for cover or picked up Crossley's weapon and returned fire?

The man's left eye, cheek, and shoulder were covered in blood. A bullet hole disfigured his forehead. His right eye was open and unseeing. Mere hours ago, Matt had seen the same vacant stare in

Swanson's eyes. He relaxed his grip on his Glock as he reached the driver's door, but he froze when he got a clear view of the passenger. He dropped his gun hand, numb with shock.

"Diane!"

She lay slumped against the window frame. Blood covered her head and neck and flowed down under her coat collar. Shards of glass in her lap glistened in the light of the parking lot's overhead lamps.

Matt raced to the passenger door and ripped it open. Glass crunched underfoot. The headrest was streaked with blood and brain matter. Her right temple had a gaping hole in it. He felt her carotid artery. No pulse. "OhGodohGodohGod no!"

Why was she in the car? He couldn't believe she'd willingly accompanied Crossley. If she had, she would've also been shooting at him. *But if she was on my side, why didn't she warn me? Why didn't she get out and run once the car had stopped? Why not at least duck?* His mind whirled with confusion. *Maybe Crossley knocked her out before the gunfight. Again, why? Does it matter?* Diane was dead. Nothing could change that fact. But it *did* matter because she died from *his* bullet. A bullet meant for Crossley.

As he fumbled for his cell phone with his free hand, Matt blinked back tears. After he'd reflexively tapped 911, he focused on Crossley again through the shattered window—mouth agape, eyes frozen open, staring into nothingness, half his head a bloody mess. The urge to blow the rest of his head off overwhelmed Matt, and he stifled a paroxysm of fury.

The dispatcher came on the line. "Nine one one. What's your emergency?" The voice was calm, professional, reassuring—nothing remotely resembling Matt's state of mind.

Through a haze of sudden exhaustion, he comprehended the brutal facts. He'd killed two more people. Nothing good would come from calling the authorities. With Smythe's power and resources, Matt had zero chance of avoiding murder charges. The truth wouldn't be enough to counteract the narrative Smythe would create for the press piranhas to devour and disseminate. He envisioned a banner-sized headline in the local newspaper:

Jilted Ex-Husband Slays Former Wife and Her Lover.

Even if Matt cooperated with police and they believed his version of the story, once Smythe could track his movements again he'd be a dead man. He scanned the area. No cars approached. Nothing moved. The rest area was quiet except for the muffled traffic of the nearby freeway and the idling diesels at the far end of the lot.

"Nine one one. What's your emergency?" The repeated request sounded like a looped recording of the previous time the dispatcher spoke, but it crystallized Matt's thoughts.

He hung up and pocketed his phone. Unlatching Diane's seat belt, he cradled her in his arms and stroked her blonde hair, so soft, so thick. A subtle citrus-and-herbal shampoo aroma mixed with a hint of her Beautiful perfume clashed with the metallic smell of blood. He hugged her tight, willed her to respond to his touch, knowing she wouldn't. He wanted to somehow restart her heart, heal the bullet wound, and bring her back to life. Hell, trade his life for hers. He was the one who should've died. Once again, his good intentions had resulted in disaster. He tilted her body back and memorized her face one last time, struggling to ignore the blood. Her expression looked peaceful, serene actually, considering she'd died such a violent death. He hoped she hadn't suffered too much in her last minutes.

"This is all my fault," he whispered. "I never should've asked you for help." He blinked back tears unsuccessfully, and they streamed down his cheeks. He leaned down and kissed her lips. Still warm. Still sweet. He pulled away. A tear dropped onto her cheek. He tucked a loose strand of golden hair behind her ear.

After settling her body back into the seat, Matt stood and turned toward Lake Superior in the distance. Its dark mass was outlined by the lights of the buildings along the shore. The lift bridge in Canal Park was in the raised position. The silhouette of a lake freighter glided through the canal, outlined by its deck lights, headed for the dark void of the inland sea, en route to somewhere east.

He envisioned the dark void of life without Diane. Life without the possibility of Diane. Life without a reason to live anymore. During their years apart, he'd never given up hope that someday, somehow, they would reconcile. Her death had destroyed his last shred of hope. Matt's body and mind went numb.

The distant wail of a siren jarred him back to the present. Had the truckers been roused from their sleep by the shots and shattering windows and called the police? If so, they'd remained in their cabs and hadn't dared to emerge and gawk at the crime scene.

His instincts told him that waiting for the police to arrive was his worst option. He could always surrender later when he was ready to talk and knew what to say and how to say it. If only Gebhardt hadn't been critically wounded and they'd been able to stick together . . .

The siren grew louder, then moved northward, which meant the squad car had taken the Boundary Avenue freeway exit and was heading for the rest area. For the last time, Matt gazed at his beautiful Diane. Then he ran to the truck and drove out the northeast side of the lot seconds before the police car entered from the southwest. He wasn't ready to surrender—*or* to die.

CHAPTER 45

Matt spent the rest of the night in a campsite at nearby Jay Cooke State Park, reclined in the driver seat of the truck, sleeping in fits and starts. The shattered back windows allowed cold April air inside, which chilled the sweat he broke into every time he dreamed of Diane, bloody and lifeless in his arms. He woke when sunlight filtered through the trees and onto his face.

Despite a meager night's rest, he was able to think more clearly about why she'd been with Crossley the night before. Now intimately familiar with the tactics of Millennium Four personnel, he concluded the best explanation for her behavior was that Crossley had forced her to accompany him as a hostage in case Matt somehow sensed a trap and had been ready for an attack. If true, then the most plausible explanation for why she was Crossley's passenger was to pull off the jilted-lover, murder-suicide scenario. She might've been drugged, unable to resist Crossley or to help Matt. Crossley's fatal mistake was overconfidence—believing he could kill them both with no help. He almost succeeded, but he'd been a beat too slow. Or, more accurately, Matt had been a beat too fast.

No matter the reason why last night had gone down the way it did, he needed to focus on his next move. Fight today or run for now and regroup? The last compelling reason for him to keep battling was that Clay and Zach needed him.

Matt showered and shaved at the campground bathhouse, then changed into his last clean outfit. He threw his bloodstained clothes in the campground dumpster. Next, he made the short drive west and north to Cloquet and stopped at a local discount store on Highway 33. There he bought a down vest to replace his bloodied jacket and some heavy-duty transparent plastic sheeting and duct tape to repair the broken windows of the truck. Once he'd covered the windows with plastic, he drove downtown, found a mom-and-pop diner that he doubted would utilize security cameras, and devoured a bacon-and-eggs breakfast complete with orange juice, a gooey caramel-nut roll, and lots of coffee.

As he ate, Matt considered picking up Zach in Minneapolis and bringing him to deputy Rodde in Ely to further corroborate their accumulated evidence. After the previous night's carnage, he also feared for Zach's safety. He'd feel better if the kid was with him. Strength in numbers. However, Flannery's recorded confession along with Gebhardt's version of Witt's attack on the Swanson's and the shootout on Big Island were the most damning pieces of evidence against Smythe. The sooner he presented those facts to the authorities, the better. Then he'd have Zach send their data via email as planned.

On the road again and revitalized to a small degree, Matt headed north toward Ely, barely aware he was driving. The fact he had killed Diane still consumed his thoughts. What had he missed when her car drove up? Who could blame him for returning Crossley's fire? If he'd hesitated an instant longer, he'd be dead. If that had happened, she would've been at Crossley's mercy. Since he'd already used violence against her once, Crossley's idea of mercy might've been sexual abuse, slow torture, or . . . Matt shook his head vigorously to force those gruesome thoughts from his mind.

Halfway to Ely, he turned on the radio, hoping to distract himself with music or talk. Minutes later, a local newscast began. He didn't pay much attention until he heard the words *Ely Hospital*. He lunged for the volume button and turned it up as the announcer droned:

"To repeat, we have an unverified report that an unknown assailant snuck into the Ely-Bloomenson Hospital early this morning and killed two men who had been admitted last evening with gunshot wounds. A hospital spokesperson stated the men had been stabilized soon after arriving and were in no danger of dying from their wounds. The killer escaped and should be considered armed and dangerous. The victims' names are being withheld pending . . ."

Smythe had struck again.

Matt swerved to the shoulder and slammed on the brakes, which elicited a long horn blast from a semitrailer driver who'd been tailgating him for the previous few miles. Gebhardt had been Matt's last chance to corroborate what had happened in the Boundary Waters. His last chance to nail the bastard and expose him as a ruthless criminal. His last chance to make sense of all the killing, especially Diane's death.

Flannery's death powered a brutal fact to the forefront of Matt's brain: during all his efforts to right the wrongs perpetrated by M4 operatives, he'd forgotten to force Flannery to admit he'd framed Matt for Sandvik's murder and to rescind the warrant for his arrest. *I am still a suspected cop killer.*

He slumped forward until his forehead smacked the steering wheel. Anguish and futility ignited the urge to vomit. He choked down the bile rising in his throat. A wave of fatigue flooded his body, leaving him numb. Constant high-stakes pressure over the past few weeks had crushed his will to live. He might as well go to Smythe, spread his arms in a sacrificial pose, and say, "Put me out of my misery."

Nevertheless, Arlene Lanier had not raised either of her sons to give up when things got difficult. To quit now would render those unintended, unforeseen deaths senseless as well. His energy to fight was depleted, yet he couldn't stop if the smallest chance remained that he could prevent others from dying. He made a U-turn and headed down Highway 53 toward Straight River.

CHAPTER 46

Six hours later, Matt arrived at John Maxwell's office to finalize the documents he'd asked Max to prepare. He'd stopped for gas at a convenience store in a small town north of Duluth and called his attorney from there. He then placed a call to the Forest Service ranger station in Ely and left an anonymous message that two men were dead on Big Island in Crystal Lake. He hoped scavengers wouldn't do too much damage to Swanson's body before it could be recovered and given a proper burial.

"You sure you want to do this?" Maxwell asked after he'd greeted Matt and presented the small pile of documents for him to sign. He was a fit-looking grandfatherly type with a thick mane of silver hair who projected small-town innocence. Matt's father had hired him for his no-nonsense approach and his ability to avoid baffling his clients with legalese.

"It's the best way I can think of," Matt said. "Not that my brain is working at one hundred percent right now. I don't want anyone else to die because of me."

Maxwell shook his head. "As your attorney, I strongly advise you to reconsider and go to the authorities. All running will do is further convince them of your guilt."

"No, Max. If I surrender to the cops, I might as well cut out the middleman and surrender to Smythe. Unless you get me out on bail within a few hours, Smythe will pay off some lowlife jailbird to kill me in prison."

Maxwell exhaled through puffed-out cheeks. "If you insist." He gestured at the documents on his desk. "You're all set. I just need to talk to your young friend."

Matt pulled out his phone and called Zach.

"Dude, you okay?" Zach said.

"I'm safe for now, but the situation is deteriorating fast."

"How fast?"

"Life-or-death-critical. *Your* life." He didn't divulge any details, worried the kid would freak out if he learned so many people had died in the past few days.

"Tell me about it," Zach said. "I'm really nervous about this M4 business. Feels like someone is watching me."

Matt sat upright and stiffened. He'd worked hard to keep Zach as anonymous and uninvolved as possible since the hit-and-run that broke the kid's leg. Now, the risk for this final meeting had doubled. He needed his computer genius to stay mentally focused for the next twenty-four hours. That would be much tougher if Zach turned paranoid and did something irrational.

"Anyone in particular?"

"I've noticed some tall guy in dark clothes and a baseball cap a few times when I walk to and from the bus stop. I made eye contact once. He just nodded and smiled and walked on by. Didn't seem like spy behavior, but there was something about him that worries me."

"He might be getting you comfortable with his presence in the neighborhood. We'll assume he works for Smythe, which is why we need to act fast. I have a plan that might guarantee your safety and protection. You interested?"

"Hell yeah."

Matt explained his plan as succinctly as he could. Zach asked a few clarifying questions, then readily consented. Both agreed it was risky and flawed but better than nothing. The weakest link in the plan was the presumption that Smythe would keep his end of the bargain, which was based on the hope that he would agree to the terms.

"Ready to talk to my lawyer?" Matt asked.

"Ready," Zach sounded resolute.

Matt handed the phone to Maxwell and sat back in his chair. Some of the weight of the past weeks slid away as the burden of monitoring Zach for the foreseeable future shifted to someone else. Exactly how long would depend on Smythe. Tense and nervous, Matt stood and paced the office, drummed his fingers against his thigh, unsure he could pull off this Hail Mary play.

While waiting for Maxwell to conclude his conversation with Zach, Matt went into the outer office and used the desk phone to called Betty Myrick.

After identifying himself, Matt said, "Did anyone talk to you about Helmer's cause of death?"

Betty explained that Dr. Vincent had called to confirm Helmer had suffered a fatal heart attack and both the autopsy report and official cause of death had been corrected.

"I'm so relieved and happy for you." Matt barely held back a flood of emotions. He'd at least achieved one positive outcome for his efforts.

"How can I ever thank you for saving my farm?" she said.

"No need for thanks. You're like family to me, and family helps family any way we can."

Maxwell appeared in the doorway and gestured to Matt that Zach was ready to speak with him. After saying a quick good-bye to Betty, Matt entered the office and took the phone from his lawyer.

"I was going to come up tonight, kid, but if you're being watched, I'll come up tomorrow morning. We'll be safer with more people around. It'll also be easier for me to see if anyone's watching your apartment. Be ready to go at nine."

"I'll be ready," Zach said.

Maxwell slid a new document across the desk as Matt turned off his phone. "One last signature."

This document confirmed he'd set up the plan and all its contingencies for the sole purpose of protecting one Zachary Felipe Perez. The document contained Zach's Social Security Number, birth date, current address, family members, and other pertinent information. Maxwell had said he'd attach a photo of Zach to the document after he printed a copy of the selfie Zach sent over the phone.

Matt signed and slid the document back to Maxwell, then tossed the pen onto the desk and stood. "He's a good kid, Max. Brains, talent, potential. He just needs to forget the last few weeks with me and get his life back to normal. Take care of him."

"I'll do the best I can with the powers and responsibilities you've given me."

"Thanks."

They shook hands and Matt left. He glanced from side to side as he walked down Main Street to his truck, feeling more vulnerable in Straight River than he had up North. To remedy that problem, he headed straight for O'Connor's salvage yard.

CHAPTER 47

Before Matt could proceed with relative safety from discovery, he asked O'Connor to consider a trade—the shot-up Dodge Ram for another old but reliable pickup truck. Because of the Dodge's new battle scars, the best O'Connor could do in terms of an equal-value trade was a ten-year-old Ford F150 with twice the mileage and rust as the Dodge. Matt was relieved he no longer needed to drive a bullet-riddled truck, although if he were ever stopped by the police, he'd have to do some fancy talking to explain why he had no registration papers.

As if on autopilot, Matt drove from O'Connor's junkyard to the county road that led to his boyhood home. He parked on a rise where he could stand and see the three farms that had been integral to the first half of his life: his parents', Swanson's, Myrick's. Early spring in southern Minnesota farm country was often bleak. Vast expanses of fallow fields on the gently rolling terrain were brown and gray, speckled with patches of dirty snow and blotches of mud in low spots. At this point in the season, the land looked barren and lifeless, incapable of any growth or regeneration—precisely the way he felt right then. Yet, miraculously, every year this land invariably proved to be some of the most fertile, productive farmland in the world.

The yellow police tape had been removed. Most of the rubble had been cleared away, leaving just the stone foundation encircling a giant hole in the ground. The site had a bizarre look. All the outbuildings were intact, yet they lacked a farmhouse to anchor them, give them purpose. That was Matt's situation in a nutshell—anchorless, dependent on outside forces to propel him one way or another.

Smythe had gotten a twofer by destroying Matt's past—his boyhood home—as well as his future. Music had been Matt's stone foundation, his anchor until a few days ago. But how could he play bass or make any sort of a living through music with a mangled hand? The debris of his current life included the inability to go out in public without the fear of feeling the sharp pain of a bullet through his skull followed by instant darkness. How could he rebuild a normal life if every law enforcement official in the state was on the lookout for him? Worst of all, how could he find the strength to go on living with no chance of a life with Diane?

He inhaled the spring air—clean and crisp but not yet redolent of the wildflowers that would soon blossom along the country roads. With his eyes closed, Matt reminisced back to when he was ten and bubbling with energy, riding his bike from his house to Swanny's on a glorious Saturday morning, eager to set out on a new adventure with his best friend.

In the distance, the sound of an approaching car refocused his attention to the present. He started the truck and headed for the Swanson farm, staying in the vehicle until the car passed on its way toward town. An hour remained before darkness set in. He grew more nervous and apprehensive that a Smythe operative might spot him so close to ground zero, his father's farm.

Matt parked, got out, and knocked on the front door.

Amy appeared at the window a moment later and peeked through the lace curtain. As soon as she recognized him, her eyes widened with apprehension, and she jerked the door open. "What is it, Matt? Where's Dave?"

Matt's heart sank to his shoes. *She doesn't know yet.* "Can I come in?"

"Sure." She beckoned him inside, searching his eyes for a clue as they walked.

He'd just sat on her sofa when he comprehended her bruised face. The image imprinted on his brain so sharply he wanted to scream. Witt had used her for a punching bag merely because Swanny had helped Matt's escape from the hospital.

Lacking time to tread softly with her feelings, he spoke bluntly. "It's bad, Amy. Dave is dead."

She inhaled a ragged half-gasp and drew back, but her expression indicated she wasn't entirely surprised by the news. "I knew things would end in disaster. He left here so crazy." She blinked back tears. "I was furious at him for leaving but also for getting hooked by Smythe's money."

"You knew all along?"

She shook her head. "I forced him to explain everything after we almost got killed in our barn by that monster Witt."

"Dave didn't have a choice after Smythe got him into the Schultz deal."

She forced her gaze upward to meet his. "It's my fault he's dead. I should've known he'd go berserk. He was so protective of me."

Matt grasped her shoulders and squeezed lightly. "No. Don't ever think that. It's Witt's fault. All Dave wanted to do was make things right with you. We thought Clay could arrest Witt and get him to confess what he'd done for Smythe. Unfortunately, Dave wanted justice right there on the island. He was crazy with anger. I'm not sure he believed you when you said Witt didn't rape you." Matt lifted his eyebrows and tilted his chin down. "Did he?"

"No, but I knew he would if he came back. Then he would've killed us both. He didn't say it, but I felt it. I saw it in his eyes." They exchanged knowing glances at the horror of what could have been.

Matt inhaled and exhaled slowly, trying to keep his voice from showing how shaky he felt inside. "If it's any consolation, that monster won't bother you or anyone else again. Ever."

She nodded. Stared at the floor. "How did Dave die?"

"He wanted to avenge your honor. I tried to settle him down. Thought I had for a minute, but I turned my back, and he charged off after Witt. I couldn't get to him in time to help. There was a shootout. They died within minutes of each other."

"I didn't get to say goodbye." Her voice was flat, toneless, devoid of emotion. "He just left without a word."

Matt forced back his remorse as he stood face to face with another living victim of Smythe's ruthless greed. "I notified the authorities earlier, so they'll retrieve his body. But for my safety, please don't tell them I reported the deaths. I still need to fix my situation before I can deal with the police."

After taking a moment to process the information, she nodded, then gazed past him to the mounting darkness outside. Deep sadness showed in her eyes. Tears streamed down her face. "He loved you like a brother even after you left for Minneapolis. Always talked about the great times with Matt Lanier."

Matt caressed his right thumb with his forefinger as his memories took him back to that brief, solemn ceremony between two young boys thirty years ago. He then squeezed his eyes closed, a futile attempt to force the horrors of Big Island from his mind.

"I didn't know it until yesterday, but Swanny was the truest friend I'll ever have."

Amy heaved a huge sigh and dabbed her eyes with a tissue. "What about you?" she asked. "The police still believe you killed Officer Sandvik. I don't, of course, but is it wise to be here with the authorities searching for you?"

"I'm not sure." Matt shrugged. "I took the risk because you deserved to hear from me what happened to Dave. I owe my life to him and Clay. If they hadn't shown up, *I'd* be dead. Guaranteed."

"I appreciate that." She nodded, looking pensive.

"I'm innocent, but I can't trust the police to protect me from the man who framed me. He's also responsible for everything bad that's happened to you, Betty, and many other good people."

Matt glanced at the clock. He was apprehensive about staying too long in one place. "I'd better leave. Still not a hundred percent sure Smythe or the police aren't watching this place."

Amy nodded. "Before you go, there's someone I'd like you to see."

She led him by the hand to her kitchen—a spacious, country-style room—and pointed to the floor next to the wood-burning stove in one corner.

A black animal lay curled up on a dog bed but lifted its head when it heard approaching footsteps.

"Jack, old boy, you survived!"

A powerful surge of love and relief hit Matt so hard that tears welled up in his eyes. He rushed to the black Lab and knelt beside him. "I thought you were either fried to a crisp or blown to pieces."

Jack stood with considerable effort, but his tail wagged with gusto. His eyes were bright and alert as he took a tentative step toward his master. Matt hugged him tight but eased off when Jack whimpered and squirmed. He stroked Jack's fur and scratched him behind his ears and under his chin.

"The poor creature was in bad shape when he showed up," Amy said. "Covered with cuts and bruises, burrs in his coat, blood caked all over. So I rushed him to the vet."

Jack busied himself licking Matt's hands and face and nuzzling him as much as his old achy body would allow.

"I'll be happy to take care of Jack until you get matters sorted out," she said. "Betty wants to watch him part of the time too. He can't replace our husbands, but he's a good dog, and he gives us someone to talk to now that we're alone."

"Thank you." Matt's heart fluttered with gratitude that the two women would have each other and Jack while they adjusted to widowhood.

She waved dismissively. "One tiny bright spot in this dark time."

Matt checked his watch and glanced toward the large front window. "I'd better go. I've dodged too many bullets, real and figurative, to expect my luck to continue."

They hugged. Amy held him tight for a long time. Although she didn't seem to blame him, he regretted that a chasm would always exist between them once she had time to reflect on the past month's events.

After saying goodbye, Matt stepped outside and headed for his truck, inhaling the faint essence of fertile loam that wafted past on the southerly breeze. He'd loved that harbinger of planting season for as long as he could remember. It represented rejuvenation, renewal, the beautiful seasonality of Minnesota farm country. Sighing wistfully, he got into his truck and headed for Interstate 35.

CHAPTER 48

At 8:30 the next morning, Matt arrived at the Java Joint and ordered coffee with an added shot of espresso, desperate for energy from any available source. He'd parked his new pickup truck a block away on a side street and walked to the coffee shop from the opposite direction in case any spies near Zach's apartment were watching for him.

Despite a few hours of decent sleep in a warm, quiet motel room, he felt more exhausted than he'd felt after Thompson Hill. Maybe it was exhaustion no amount of sleep would cure. Maybe it was the weight of doubt that he could keep Zach alive after losing so many others. Like being pummeled by a pile driver, that doubt threatened to force him down through the seat, through the floor, and bury him deep in the earth.

Because of Zach's unease about being watched, Matt remained hyperalert. He found a small, empty table in the corner of the room where an inner wall intersected an exterior window that faced Riverside Avenue. Partially shielded by a three-foot section of solid wall below the glass, he could monitor the foot and car traffic along Riverside and the cross street in relative safety. Smythe's men could be lurking in the shadows or in any of the buildings with a view of Zach's apartment. They'd probably be armed. After scouting for thirty minutes, he called Zach.

"I'm coming up now. Be at the door, just in case."

"I'm ready," Zach said.

Matt hung up and headed outside, donning his Twins cap and sunglasses as he walked to the exit. He scanned the faces in the room for customers who didn't fit in with the general vibe of the crowd. No one gave him more than a quick glance.

Outside, he stopped, pulled out his phone, and pretended to check messages. Cars of all shapes and sizes filled the street parking spaces he could see. Away from Riverside, a young couple walked toward him holding hands. Behind them, a young man with a backpack slung over his shoulder ambled along, his eyes locked on his smartphone. The other direction—the intersection of Riverside and the cross street—was tougher to assess. A dozen or so pedestrians were crossing the street or waiting for the light to change at all four corners. No one seemed to focus on him.

Matt pocketed his phone and strode toward Zach's building. As he turned onto the walkway to the entrance, he heard two car doors slam in quick succession. Immediately tensing, he stopped in the doorway of the foyer and pretended to fumble for his keys like a tenant might. He glanced backward. Two large men in dark clothing hustled toward him from across the street. Each man had a hand in his jacket pocket. Each glowered at him.

Damn it. How did I not notice them earlier? Matt pulled the foyer door shut and groped for a lock even as he doubted that a low-rent building like this would be equipped with outside security measures. The men were now at the junction of the street and the walkway to the building.

Taking the stairs two at a time, Matt ascended to Zach's place as the foyer door opened. Zach stood in the open doorway with crutches under his arms.

From the foyer doorway, one of the men said, "Hold it, Lanier!"

"They've got guns!" Zach shouted.

Matt glanced down the stairway. Each man held a pistol raised and ready to shoot. Matt dove at Zach like a linebacker going after a running back.

Zach—frozen in place, mouth agape—staggered backward from the impact and fell into his office chair. His crutches clattered to the floor.

Matt caught his balance, veered left behind the door, and slammed it closed as four shots thudded into the steel door. The sound of the impact of bullets on steel was louder than the report from the weapons. *They'd used suppressors.*

"Holy shit, they shot at us!" Zach said, panic-stricken and wild-eyed.

Matt engaged both locks an instant before the men reached the door. A fist pounded on steel and rattled the doorknob. Then one of the men either kicked the door or threw a shoulder into it. The door shuddered but held fast.

"Get away from the door in case they succeed," Matt said. "Out of the line of fire." He backed to one side of the doorway, Glock 17 at the ready, aimed at the entry side of the door.

Zach moved to the corner behind the door, next to a window. When two more shoulder slams shook the door, Zach's good knee gave out, and he collapsed onto his bed.

"Give up, Lanier. You're trapped," said one of the men. "Come with us, and the kid won't get hurt." His voice sounded low and menacing with a hint of a Northeast accent.

"Not gonna happen." Matt braced for another assault on the door. "If I surrender, you'll return and pick off the kid anytime you want."

"Boss said to tell you he don't care about the kid."

"Bullshit." If Matt had learned anything, it was that Smythe was meticulous, always calculating. He covered every contingency, planned for any outcome. The two of them were loose ends who needed to be eliminated.

"Check the street, far side," Matt said to Zach in a whisper. "These two have the dark-blue sedan about fifty feet right of this building."

Zach gave him a nervous nod and peered through the dirty-white sheer curtain down to the street. "No one out there."

"Keep an eye out for backup. Tell me if anyone who's not a tenant approaches this building."

"Okay."

"Come on, Lanier." The other attacker was speaking. "It's over, and you know it." His voice was higher, with a Midwestern accent. He tapped on the door with what sounded like the butt of his weapon.

Matt turned to Zach. "Any of the tenants at home right now?"

"I doubt it. Most either work days or go to school."

A muffled voice on the other side of the door caught Matt's attention. He guessed one of the thugs had called Smythe. Seconds later, the man said, "Will do."

Moments later, Zach said, "They're outside." Then, "They're getting into the car. Looks like they're going to sit there."

"Good. We bought a little time. Is there a back door to this building?"

"First floor, opposite corner from me."

"We'll assume it's being watched too. But we need to call Smythe immediately."

"Right. Everything's ready to go."

After they'd double-checked their data and hardware so the next few minutes would go as smoothly as possible, Matt took out Flannery's phone and weighed it in his hand. He scrutinized Zach, alert for any sign of doubt or hesitation. "You ready with your laptop info?"

Zach nodded as he licked his lips and pushed his glasses up the bridge of his nose with a finger.

Matt shook all the *what-ifs* of the past weeks since his father's death from his thoughts. The gun battle on Big Island notwithstanding, he felt like a rookie soldier thrust into battle with no training: scared, unsure, mind racing, body in panic mode, with no idea of the negative impact stress imparted on sound decision making. If this ploy didn't work, he and Zach would certainly die. But he could think of nothing else other than surrendering, which would also mean death.

He clapped Zach on the back. Forcing confidence into his voice, he said, "Once I call Smythe, we've got to see this through. If we catch him off guard with this plan, we can get out of here, and you can resume a normal life. You still with me?"

Zach nodded so vigorously he almost flung his glasses off his face. The gunshots had obviously driven home Matt's warning of a life-or-death situation.

"Okay, here we go."

CHAPTER 49

Matt tapped the call button on Flannery's phone. While he waited through two rings, he took a long, slow, meditative breath, much like he did prior to stepping onstage for a musical performance. One final clearing of the mind for the imminent period of intense concentration and mental gymnastics.

Smythe picked up. "Mr. Lanier, I presume."

"You presume correctly, Leland. Or should I call you Lee?"

"Oh, an informal chat? Shall I call you Matt?"

Smythe spoke with the condescension he'd used in their previous conversation. If nothing else came of Matt's battle against Millennium Four, wiping that arrogance out of the prick's voice at least once would be a small moral victory. Also, bringing Smythe down a notch might antagonize him enough to give Matt a tactical advantage. Keep the man off balance, and he might make a mistake.

"You've tried to kill me four times now and failed each time," Matt said. "Today's lame attempt with the two goons was the worst, but I guess you're running low on front-line manpower. Because I've also suffered some casualties, I'm calling our battle a stalemate."

"I have no idea what you're talking about," Smythe said. "Attempts on your life? Goons? You must be either drunk, high, or seriously delusional."

"I'm sober, sane, and dead serious."

"Alright. For my own amusement, I'll play your little hypothetical chess game. Based on what you claim has happened, I hardly think this is a stalemate. You clearly—"

"I'm not done talking, you conniving bastard."

Zach recoiled from Matt's outburst. Matt ignored him.

"Think of me like a cat with nine lives," Matt said. "Chances keep increasing that one of your next five hit attempts on me will be witnessed by someone and result in you getting connected to the crime. Now that I understand the scope of M4, I know you value your supposed invincibility more than anything except the money you expect to make. You can't kill me without gambling that my death will be witnessed, traced back to you, and fuck up your plans.

"I can't get you arrested because you've stayed above the fray like a mad-genius puppet master, and no sane person will believe my story without witnesses and corroboration. Neither of us wants the cops involved right now because I've got a witness against you, and my going to jail will only keep me alive for so long. Ergo, according to the rules of chess, neither of us can checkmate each other. Our only option is to give up the game. Stalemate."

"Hypothetically again," Smythe said, "I happen to think this is merely a complicated endgame. If you choose to give up now, whether to the police or to me, you will most certainly lose."

Matt sensed a tiny crack in the veneer of Smythe's condescension. He chuckled, trying to sound condescending himself. "So naïve for a sophisticated millionaire. I'm not talking about surrendering to you or the police, you arrogant prick. I'm proposing a trade. A deal, to use real-estate-tycoon lingo."

"I'm listening." Smythe sounded more annoyed than interested.

"A life for my silence."

"I don't understand."

"If my friend and associate, Zach Perez, stays alive, I won't go public with the data we have on Millennium Four, Saxony Partners, the North American Super Highway, the bribes and blackmail you've used to obtain silence or cooperation from key players, and every bit of anecdotal evidence regarding the thefts of the farms along I-35 and those you've had killed who stood in your way."

Smythe's chuckle had a nervous edge. "You've written quite the fairy tale, Mr. Lanier." The condescension returned. "You have *absolutely no proof* of my involvement in anything you've mentioned other than the fact that Saxony Partners is one of my companies. *That* begs the question, 'Why are we having this conversation?'"

"You *need* to make this deal because you overlooked one small detail."

"Which is?"

"Virality."

Smythe's silence was validation that he had, in fact, overlooked that small but vital detail. "Virality?" he asked, obviously puzzled.

"I didn't know what it meant either until recently. But Zach says if the right person posts a video on YouTube for example and sends it to a small group of other *right persons*, that video will be seen by more than a million people in less than twenty-four hours. Some posts receive tens of millions of hits. The same applies to the other major social media sites. Zach is a computer genius. He assures me he can connect with dozens of *right persons* and broadcast our story to the world faster than it takes you to purchase a latte at Starbucks."

"What's your point?" Smythe finally raised his voice. His irritation was a positive development.

"We've prepared an email with all our data compiled into a concise story augmented by meticulous annotation and supporting documents. The clincher is a fascinating recording that will elevate the rather dry details of M4's activities to a global phenomenon that every news outlet in the world will pounce on and play with for days and days, perhaps weeks or months. For security, Zach has encrypted everything and surrounded the files with a firewall and a bunch of other protective measures I can't begin to comprehend. In addition, he'll periodically transfer his files to random locations in that cyberspace cloud thing he told me about."

Matt gave Smythe time to digest this news, resisting the urge to pound away at him.

After a tense few seconds, Smythe said, "Again, assuming I am in anyway connected to your bizarre fabrication, why don't you send out all this information now?"

"Because then your primary goal in life will be to kill us simply for revenge and because you detest loose ends."

"You mentioned a recording. That's impossible, which renders your entire story specious." Smythe's voice dripped with indignation. "To help prevent corporate espionage, every single phone in all my businesses, as well as those of each of my employees, have been set up to detect and prevent unauthorized recordings. If any sensitive conversation had been secretly recorded, I would know."

Matt *tsked* like an annoyed parent to a clueless child. "I didn't record a *phone* conversation. I recorded an in-person confession by Flannery that was witnessed by Sergeant Gebhardt. Flannery gave you up one hundred percent, hoping we'd spare his worthless life. How ironic. I *did* spare his life; you didn't."

"You're bluffing, Lanier."

Matt had assumed Smythe would dismiss his claim as a desperate threat. But he also noticed Smythe had dropped the *Mister* shtick. The crack in his veneer had widened.

He held the phone near Zach's computer and gestured for Zach to play the Big Island recording. The computer virtuoso had digitized the analog tape after Matt's call the previous day. That was a crucial part of the plan—make sure Flannery's confession couldn't easily be erased or destroyed. The sound was loud and clear, much better than the sound quality of Matt's pocket recorder. Other than the background wind noise wafting in from Crystal Lake onto Big Island, Matt might've been listening to a professionally-recorded audiobook.

Three minutes into the more than ten-minute-long confession, Smythe said, "Enough."

Zach glanced at Matt for direction. Matt nodded and returned the phone to his ear. Zach stopped the recording.

"Convinced yet?" Matt asked, barely able to control his nerves at this critical juncture in the discussion.

"People will say anything when someone sticks a gun in their ear," Smythe said. "Unless a lawyer was present, and the recording was verified by an impartial third party, that confession will never stand up in court."

"The only downside is you not going to jail," Matt said. "But I can live with that. The bottom line is, once all the farmers in the Upper Midwest hear about your grand plan, no one will sell to you or anyone else for an artificially low price. Better still, government watchdogs will make damn sure no government entities dare get into bed with you because of the political and fiscal backlash. The feds will double-

and triple-vet every company that wants to get involved to make sure you aren't connected. If a North American Super Highway is ever built, you'll never make a dime off it."

"What makes you think you two won't end up dead anyway?"

"I'll take my chances, but Zach gets an insurance policy—a lawyer beyond your reach. If Zach doesn't contact him before a certain specified time each week, my lawyer will press what we call the nuclear button, which will release all the M4 data and Flannery's soliloquy to the scandal-hungry media. Not as devastating as the nuclear button in the White House, but it'll sure as hell blow your empire to smithereens."

As Matt paused for a breath, he noticed Zach staring at him with an expression of hope and admiration. "My lawyer has engaged a backup lawyer to take his place if he dies or is otherwise incapacitated. And that lawyer will engage a surrogate, *ad infinitum*. Each will be carefully chosen to ensure you can't bribe or blackmail them. Each will be paid a modest but still-generous sum from a trust funded by my father's estate proceeds. The unbreakable chain of lawyers will last for the rest of your miserable life. It will be disbanded once Millennium Four and your name are dusty footnotes in history books."

Sweat cooled Matt's brow. He'd survived everything Smythe had thrown at him to this point. How dare he naively presume he could end things on his terms, cease running, prevent further deaths?

"What if Mr. Perez's death is from a disease or an accident of his own causing?" Smythe said. "People contract cancer. They step off street corners and get killed by buses. Why should I suffer for a death with which I had nothing to do?"

"That's the fun part, *Lee*. I gave my lawyer discretion over when to press the nuclear button. If he finds out Zach died in any marginally suspicious way, he might take you down to console himself for the premature loss of another brilliant young mind. But he'll be ultra-scrupulous because we are both men of integrity. For what it's worth, I give you my word we'll play fair."

Matt glanced out the window to check the dark sedan, content to give Smythe plenty of time to consider the deal. More than a minute passed. Was Smythe stalling? Setting up an ambush?

"Very well, *Mister* Lanier. I accept your terms."

Immediately after hearing those words, Matt was buffeted by a wild array of emotions. Triumph came first, then flipped over to doubt and mistrust, then settled on resignation. He had no choice but to assume Smythe would act in good faith. He kept a hint of skepticism tucked away in his thoughts.

"All things considered," Matt said, "A wise decision. To show me you're negotiating in good faith, tell your two men outside to drive away. If I see either them or their car when we go outside, the deal is off. Is that clear?"

"Crystal. I'll call them immediately."

Matt clicked off and gave Zach a *thumbs up*.

Zach returned the gesture and slumped forward in obvious relief.

The sound of an engine turning over filtered through the window. Matt looked out to see the dark sedan pull away from the curb. He angled his view to see the car approach Riverside Avenue, stop at the red light, and make a right turn.

"Okay, the car left," Matt said. He turned to Zach. "Do you have a friend you can stay with for at least a few days?"

"Yeah, I think so," Zach said.

"Call him. Since Smythe knows you live here, it's safer for you to lie low for a while in case he goes back on his word."

"Good idea," Zach said, then made a quick call.

Zach's friend agreed to help, so Zach and Matt packed enough of Zach's essential belongings to see him through the next several days. Zach shouldered his backpack and grabbed two plastic bags in both hands that he could hold onto despite needing to grip his crutches.

After one final check of the room and a glance out to the street for a sign of Smythe's men, Matt picked up Zach's suitcase and tucked his Glock into his waistband, hidden from view under his jacket but easily accessible if needed. Forcing a reassuring smile, he said, "Let's get out of here."

CHAPTER 50

As they started down the steps, Matt scanned the foyer from side to side. Halfway down, a faint noise caught his ear. He tapped Zach's shoulder. When Zach stopped and looked back, Matt put his finger to his lips, motioning for silence. The noise had sounded like wood creaking under a shifting weight, but it had come from somewhere below them.

The stairwell blocked about half their view of the lobby. Matt remembered there was also a small alcove on the side of the staircase. He pulled the Glock from his waistband, then nudged Zach forward. Descending the remaining stairs, Matt's peripheral view widened as they neared the front door to where he could see the entire lobby but not the alcove. Zach had begun to push on the door when Matt heard another noise, a soft metallic *click*. He leaped to the door and put the pistol barrel to the shocked young man's temple.

"Drop your weapons, or I kill the kid!" Matt said, spinning to face the alcove. He dropped the suitcase and grabbed Zach's arm to keep him from bolting.

Zach jerked and shied away from the cold steel. "What are you doing?" he said, panic in his voice. "You gone loco for real?"

Two men stepped from the alcove, holding pistols tipped with suppressors pointed at Matt and Zach. One said, "No, *you* drop it."

The voice was *not* that of either of the first two assailants. *Son of a bitch. That lying bastard Smythe set up a second ambush.*

"Not happening," Matt said. "Call your boss."

The gunmen eyed each other without lowering their pistols.

"I just made a deal," Matt said. "This isn't a God-damned bluff!"

Smythe had played him for a naïve fool once again. Shaking with rage, Matt was concerned that if one of the men shot at him, he might flinch and accidentally shoot Zach. He focused on the one who'd spoken, the shorter man. "I am *not* fucking kidding. If you haven't communicated with Smythe in the past five minutes, you don't know what's going on."

"What're you doing, Matt?" Zach sounded near tears.

Matt thrust the gun barrel harder against Zach's head, felt him trembling. "Smythe wants me dead, but he doesn't want a public bloodbath and witnesses. Go on, call him. Now!"

The shorter man turned his head slightly toward the taller man. "This wasn't the plan. Better call the boss."

Tall Guy nodded and eased his phone from his jacket pocket. He made the call with his gun still in his hand but not pointing at anyone.

Zach expelled a sigh of relief that they'd gained a momentary reprieve. But Matt kept the barrel of his Glock jammed against Zach's head. This was no time to accept anything without verification. He pulled Flannery's phone from his pocket and handed it to Zach. "Can this phone do that video thing you mentioned?"

"What?" The panic had not left Zach's voice. "You mean Facetime?"

"Right. Does this phone have it?"

"Yeah, it's an iPhone."

Matt gestured at Tall Guy. "That an iPhone too?"

Tall Guy nodded.

"Get ready to call Smythe, Zach. If we need him to see us so he knows I'm not bluffing, tell him to switch to Facetime."

"Okay, but can you get the gun out of my ear please?"

"Sorry, can't do that yet."

"*Madre de Dios.* I don't wanna die!"

When Tall Guy had connected with Smythe, he said, "Lanier's got a gun on the kid. Says he'll waste him before he surrenders. Says you don't want that to happen. But they're trapped in the lobby. We can kill them both if you want."

After hesitating, Tall Guy hit a button on his phone and held it toward Matt. "Mr. Lanier," Smythe said over the speakerphone, "I apologize for the oversight by my operatives. I hadn't foreseen our recent negotiations."

"Bullshit!" Matt said. "You just switched to Plan C after we made our deal. Your men could have popped out from their hiding spot and shot us when we stepped into the hall, but they didn't. Why? Because they were going to disarm me and kidnap us. Why again? Because you were going to force me to undo the lawyer watchdog plan. How, I don't know. My guess is you'd threaten to torture or kill Zach if I didn't call off the deal, but you'd let him go if I cooperated. Then you'd make us give you the Flannery recording and all our M4 data. *Then* you'd renege on yet another promise to me and arrange one of your tragic accidents to silence both of us forever. Am I right?"

Everyone in the lobby exchanged nervous, distrustful glances. Three trigger fingers fidgeted on three trigger guards for a silent minute that seemed like an hour.

"Mr. Heisler," Smythe said in a tone that throbbed with anger, "You and Mr. O'Hara will do as Lanier says. Do *not* follow through on the instructions I gave you a few minutes ago."

"Yes, sir."

"Lanier," Smythe said, "I'll say this only once, so listen carefully. *You* are a dead man. No matter where you go, no matter how well you hide, no matter how long it takes, I will not stop until I've hunted you down and killed you. And this time, *I'll* pull the trigger."

Chilled to his core by the finality of knowing he'd never be free as long as Smythe remained alive, Matt refused to show any fear. "Bring it on if you're man enough. I'd love to settle this one-on-one."

A soft click indicated Smythe had ended the call. Heisler slid his phone into his pocket. The hired guns looked at Matt for instructions.

"Drop the weapons and your car keys," Matt commanded. "Then get against the wall."

They complied and stepped back to the alcove wall.

"Pick them up, Zach." Matt swung his Glock around to cover the men. "Put one pistol in my pocket. Hand me the other. Keep the keys."

Zach limped forward, stuffed the car keys into his pocket, then picked up the pistols and returned to Matt's side.

Matt swapped his Glock for a suppressed Beretta. He looked at the tall guy, Heisler. "Call the morons in the blue sedan and tell them to pull up in front of the building and park. Have everyone in the car come inside with their hands up. Remind them what Smythe said. Emphasize what I'll do if anyone so much as looks like they're going to pull a gun."

Heisler gave him a bewildered stare but made the calls.

Thirty seconds later, the blue sedan pulled up and parked in front of Zach's building. The two men who'd shot at them earlier got out and walked toward the building with half-raised hands. Matt felt minimal relief but didn't discount the possibility that a third or fourth set of hands were holding locked and loaded weapons in that car or another vehicle.

When the men entered the lobby, Matt said, "Remove your weapons slowly, with two fingers, and give them to the kid."

They did so with sullen expressions. Zach stuffed the weapons into one of his bags.

"Now, give me your phones and car keys and join your friends over there." He nodded toward the alcove.

The men exchanged puzzled glances, then handed over keys and phones and slowly went to the alcove.

"Everybody lie face down."

More puzzled glances were followed by compliance.

"Stay there for five minutes unless you have a death wish," Matt said. "Let's go, Zach."

Zach picked up his bags and crutches and elbowed the door open. Once they were both outside, Matt pressed the silenced Beretta into Zach's back.

Zach stiffened but kept walking. "What the—"

"Just for show in case someone else is waiting to ambush us." Matt repeatedly glanced up and down the street looking for any sign of yet another trap. There was a decent chance Smythe had foreseen more trouble from Matt and would activate Plan D at any moment.

When they reached the blue sedan, Matt knelt and fired a suppressed round into each of the front tires. The rubber exploded with a *poof.*

"In case they have extra keys," he said. Rising quickly, he scanned the street in both directions.

A woman halfway down the block had turned toward the unusual sound. Seeing nothing other than two males standing quietly next to a parked car, she pivoted and resumed her walk.

"I'm parked down the block to the right and around the corner," Matt said and nudged Zach in that direction. Matt walked far enough behind Zach and to his left to look natural and hide the fact he was holding a pistol. He checked over his shoulder every few seconds but didn't see the goons emerge from Zach's building until he and Zach had neared the corner.

The two-hundred-yards to the relative safety of the Ford pickup seemed endless because Zach still struggled with his crutches. After an interminable three-minute walk that Matt would have sprinted in less than thirty seconds, the pair reached the truck. While Zach unloaded his things and clambered into the passenger seat, Matt scanned up and down the street for armed attackers, police cruisers, or any unusual activity for a quiet, big-city residential street on a weekday morning.

When Zach was belted in, Matt slid behind the wheel and fired up the engine. Within moments, he turned onto Riverside and headed for the nearest entrance ramp to Interstate 94. As he merged onto the freeway, a small seed of hope sprouted in his heart. Realizing he'd barely breathed since the armed showdown, he heaved a huge sigh and tried to exhale the tension that constricted his torso. He glanced over at Zach, who peered intently out the back window, on high alert for any vehicle that might be tailing them. They'd not spoken since starting their walk.

"You can breathe again," he said, giving Zach a reassuring look.

Zach glanced sidelong at him, apparently unwilling to remove his focus from a possible tail. "*Madre de Dios!* What the hell was that all about?" He lapsed into a short rant in Spanish, then returned to English. "I can't believe you were willing to kill me."

"Sorry, kid. I improvised when the situation changed. That's what I do best. I wouldn't have killed you—couldn't have—but they didn't know that."

"Do you understand how close I came to shitting my pants? I've never been so freakin' scared in my life." Zach was still trembling. "And how did you know Smythe was going to try to kidnap us?"

"Smythe sounded too agreeable to the deal we made upstairs. I wasn't sure, but when I heard those noises in the stairwell, I knew something was up. When they didn't shoot at us again, I figured the next logical plan would be to kidnap us. I took a risk. We got lucky."

"So it's over then?"

"For you, yeah. As soon as I drop you off at your friend's place, I hope this'll be the last time we see each other. Stay inside as much as you can for a while. Take a friend with you when you go out. Maybe change your name for extra protection. And for God's sake don't forget to contact John Maxwell every week. If he thinks you're dead and presses the nuclear button to take the M4 stuff viral, all bets are off."

"Don't worry. I might even move in next door to the guy so he can see me come and go every day."

"Nah, stay in the Cities. Much better educational and vocational options here."

Zach managed a weak smile. "I guess you're right. I don't like the smell of manure, either."

Ten minutes later, Matt pulled onto the street Zach had directed him to and stopped in front of a three-story apartment building that contained some fifteen to twenty units. He noticed a tenant punching numbers into a keypad by the front door. *Good. An added layer of security.* The neighborhood seemed quietly normal. A few pedestrians, the occasional car, nothing unusual.

They got out. Matt unloaded Zach's suitcase, backpack, and the two plastic bags, repeatedly checking in all directions for attackers. He gestured at Zach's belongings. "Need help getting inside?"

"No thanks. I'd rather have you split right away. Wouldn't want your death on my conscience if Smythe found us in the next minute and shot you on the street. I'll call my friend from here."

Matt chuckled, his first genuine laugh in weeks. "Yeah, a conscience can be rough on a guy."

Zach gave him a wry smile. "I'd say thanks, but I haven't quite figured out what to be thankful for yet."

Matt contemplated that statement. Yes, they were still alive. Hopefully, Zach would resume a normal life. But he'd carry mental scars for a long time, maybe forever. Having to check in with a lawyer every week might increasingly weigh on him as the months passed. The possibility still existed that Smythe would abandon his Millennium Four quest and focus his massive resources on killing them both just to get revenge, the last laugh, his own perverted checkmate.

"You're right," Matt said. "*Thanks* doesn't work here. Let's leave it at good luck. Be a stranger."

"You too." They shook hands.

As Matt opened the door of his truck, Zach said, "Hey, old man?"

"Yeah?"

"If this Millennium Four stuff ever gets shut down and we're still alive, let's get together for coffee at the Java Joint. I'll buy."

Matt threw him a casual, unmilitary salute. "You got it, kid."

As he drove away, Matt contemplated his immediate future. He'd made so many mistakes. Tried so hard to do the right thing. Compounded matters for the worse thanks to physical injuries piled atop mental and emotional stress. He'd foolishly kept pursuing his goals despite not having any investigative skills, police training, or combat experience. His strongest urge was to fight on and avenge the deaths he'd precipitated. His primary hope was to give a modicum of worth and reason to those unintended consequences of his decisions and actions. Too many friends had made the ultimate sacrifice for his small victories—saving Betty's farm and keeping Zach alive.

What he would not do—*could* not do—was resume his place in "normal" civilization. He had violently taken human lives, and he could never erase those nightmarish memories and feelings. He felt a great need for some sort of penance, deprivation, hardship. Maybe that would help put the past month's events into perspective. Maybe he'd emerge a stronger human than he was today. Maybe such a life would help him devise a way to defeat Smythe.

As if on cue, a song popped into his head. A song he hadn't performed since the last high school dance his short-lived rock band had played at Straight River High. The melody came to him first, then the lyric. The Allman Brothers' classic, "Midnight Rider," had been popular with farm kids back in the day and was one of the band's go-to songs. As the lyrics ran through his memory, Matt decided he'd run now with the hope that someday he wouldn't have to hide. *I'm sure as hell not gonna let Smythe or the police catch* this *midnight rider.*

Without thinking, he'd driven onto eastbound I-94 toward downtown St. Paul. Light snow was falling. Large flakes splattered against the windshield. A late-season Alberta Clipper, not unusual for mid-April, had dropped the temperature twenty degrees and changed a beautiful sunny day into an early March, in-like-a-lion type of day. Mesmerized by the hypnotic effect of flapping wipers and swirling snow, Matt drove on in a robotic state.

He needed to fight on as a different person with a new life. Not a fresh start. More like a transformation based on the hard lessons he'd learned. One lesson was that nobility, which he'd always considered to be a virtue, was sometimes seen as a weakness in the real world. Nobility had gotten him a mangled hand. Nobility had cost innocent lives. Nobility had almost gotten him killed. The other hard lesson was that integrity had its limits. Doing the right thing, whether or not anyone witnessed it, didn't guarantee the morally right outcome.

Matt would figure out his future alone, away from all people and outside communication, like a guru atop a mountain searching for the secret of life. He'd find a place where no one would be hot on his trail closing in for the kill. Someplace to be alone with his pain, with no responsibilities except to get mentally and physically stronger. Someplace to prepare for his inevitable rematch against Millennium Four, which up to now had been an unbeatable foe.

To his left, the state capitol building glided past, looking like a snow globe through the swirling flakes. Perched atop the main entrance and backed by the massive dome, the gilded *Progress of the State* quadriga—four horses pulling a chariot guided by two women and a man—glowed like a beacon of hope.

The freeway split loomed ahead. I-35E headed north. I-94 headed east. Time to decide. Doubting his sanity but trusting his heart, Matt flicked his turn signal on, checked the traffic over his shoulder, and changed lanes.

"Life number five, here I come."

AUTHOR'S NOTE

Thank you for reading *Straight River*. If you enjoyed it, please tell your friends and family who love to read. Also, consider writing a *brief* online review of the book at your favorite book website. Word-of-mouth advertising and online reviews are the keys to success for most authors. We don't have the advantage of national advertising campaigns, book tours, and other publicity that big publishers provide to their bestselling authors. Here are some popular online review websites for you to consider:

www.amazon.com
www.goodreads.com (my personal favorite)
www.barnesandnoble.com
www.librarything.com

Simply go to your preferred website, type "Straight River" into the search box, and follow the prompts to write your review. Some websites may require you to sign up before posting reviews. Please follow me at **www.chrisnorbury.com** for news about upcoming events and future projects.

Sincerely,
Chris Norbury

Please turn the page for a preview to the award-winning sequel to *Straight River*,

CASTLE DANGER

CHAPTER 1

Matt Lanier stood on the middle of Snowfall Lake, gasping for air, wobbling on his snowshoes. His leg muscles quivered on the verge of collapse. His pulse pounded like double-time timpani beats in his chest and temples. Each icy inhale rasped his throat. Gusts of wind threatened to knock him off balance. If he fell, he doubted he could stand again, let alone walk. Microdiamonds of snow whirled across the open expanse of white and crackled against the hood of his parka. He'd hit "the wall" many marathon runners experience after about twenty miles, except his wall was made of ice.

The last ominous measures of Bach's *Toccata and Fugue* echoed in his brain. His choices were unequivocal: keep walking or die.

If he'd ignored the emergency flare he'd seen and heard yesterday, he certainly wouldn't be risking his life for the stranger lying at his feet. Instead, he'd wrestled with his conscience a hundred times today about whether he should've feigned ignorance.

If he jettisoned the bleeding, unconscious trapper here in the middle of this large, oval-shaped lake in the heart of the Arrowhead region of northeast Minnesota, he would easily reach safety by himself. If wolves didn't feast on the remains, or a Forest Service plane didn't discover the body before ice out, it would sink to the bottom. No one else would ever know what had happened out here.

He looked back at the mummy-shaped load on the makeshift sled tethered to his waist. Wisps of breath vapor rose slowly through a frosted patch of the black scarf covering the mummy's face. Incredulous, Matt snorted and shook his head. "I'll be damned," he said to his cargo. "Looks like we keep walking." Even his voice sounded iced over.

The temperature felt like minus twenty Fahrenheit. The wind-chill? Too cold to compute. At his last rest stop two hours ago, he'd burned his remaining fuel. Building a fire and shelter to warm up would take time he didn't possess. His high-tech clothing couldn't protect him indefinitely from the lethal cold, and the deer hide cloaking his shoulders and torso would only buy him a few extra minutes of warmth.

Since leaving his campsite in the pre-dawn light, he'd covered approximately eight of the ten miles he needed to travel in order to reach safety. Sunlight reflecting off the crystalline snowpack stung his eyes as he gauged the angle of the impotent January sun. Mid-afternoon. He'd badly miscalculated his travel time. *Good plan, genius.* Two hours of light. Two miles to safety. Too much to ask of his body?

After dropping his ski poles, he pulled off the Gore-Tex outer mitt and the insulated inner glove from his right hand. He fumbled in the outer pocket of his parka with stiff fingers for the last of his venison jerky. The few bites of dried deer meat comprised his only energy source for this final push. Crusted ice cracked off his ski mask when he opened his mouth. Chewing the jerky was easy once it broke into small, icy meat chips. After eating the last salty but otherwise tasteless bite, he donned his glove and mitt. A handful of snow helped him swallow the food but numbed his mouth and his throat and did little to ease his thirst.

He glanced at the head of his human cargo. "You damn well better stay alive," he said, angry at the man for intruding on his life, "because I'll get royally pissed if I do all this work for nothing."

His unconscious passenger replied with breathy vapors. Matt had wrapped him in all the warm layers of clothing and materials he could spare. Every piece of exposed skin was covered, but he made sure the face coverings were loose enough to allow air to reach the man.

To make the sled, Matt had cobbled together his cross-country skis, a nylon tarp, driftwood, rope, bungee cords, and straps cut from a spare Duluth pack. He pulled the sled with a rope looped around his torso. To brake the sled on down slopes, he'd fastened his ski poles to the tips of his skis with duct tape on the basket ends. He pushed backwards on the poles when he needed to stop the sled from crashing into his heels. The rig was heavy and clumsy but worked well enough.

His passenger tended to slide off the sled when Matt dragged it across slanted terrain such as portage trails or snowdrifts. Repositioning the man several times per hour had been the main time waster and a major pain in the ass. Alone and with no gear to carry, he could've traversed anywhere in the Boundary Waters at about three miles per hour. Dragging two hundred fifty pounds of dead weight through snow-drifted lakes and across rugged, rocky portages, he traveled little more than one mile per hour.

He picked up his ski poles, checked his towrope, and found his guide point, a long narrow peninsula jutting out from the southeast shore a mile away. Once he reached the point, he'd turn southward and travel downwind to Olson's Wilderness Canoe Outfitters.

Matt tried to take a step, but the motion electrified his nerves with pained fatigue. "Damn. Don't give out now, body." A jolt of adrenaline, called up from a hidden reserve of survival instincts, steadied Matt's rubbery muscles. He breathed deeper, slower, willing oxygen to saturate his blood.

He forced his body back into work mode and groaned from the exertion. He was almost ready to give up when the sled grudgingly moved from the deep powder. He took a step, then another, and he was under way. A feeling of triumph surged through him.

He set his concentration on ignoring the fatigue, ignoring the searing pain in his muscles, ignoring their pleas to give up. To help maintain his energy and pace, he began to hum Ella Fitzgerald's smoking hot version of *How High the Moon* with Count Basie's band. With every step, he dreamed of warmth, rest, food, and gulping quarts of water instead of chewing handfuls of snow. He plodded on, fighting for balance as the raging northwest wind tried to topple him.

The wind had scoured most of the loose snow from the surface of certain spots on Snowfall Lake. Matt rejoiced when he hit those spots, because he maintained a faster, steadier pace—almost two miles per hour. The sled skimmed across the hard-packed snow and he could almost run in his clumsy snowshoes. Then he'd hit a patch of deep powder, and his spirits sank as his pace slowed.

He cleared the peninsula as the sun touched the tops of the tallest trees in the southwest sky. Shadows stretched across the snow-covered lake and deepened the green of the pines and the brown of the aspens and tamaracks, which in turn highlighted the white birches. Angling to the south, he finally got the damned wind out of his face. Although it was a huge psychological boost, the tail wind added nothing to his speed.

Matt intuitively set his course for the boat dock, still unseen through the whorls of loose, powdery snow. He'd worked several summers for Ferdie Olson in high school and college, guided dozens of canoe trips, and knew his way back to this place as well as he knew the way back to anywhere he'd ever lived. Sweating now, he dug deep for extra energy and quickened his pace. The finish line of his marathon was in sight. A quick glance back at the injured trapper revealed he was still breathing.

Despite the sweat dampening his body, Matt couldn't remember the last time he hadn't been shivering. Rigid with numbness, his face felt like an ice mask. The wind continued to swirl microscopic snow particles into his eyes, blurring his vision. Above all, his stomach growled non-stop. He hadn't eaten a full meal since an early breakfast of walleye garnished with dried morel mushrooms he'd harvested in the fall. Since then, he'd burned thousands of calories.

Matt slogged on toward Olson's Outfitters, head down to maintain forward momentum. He estimated his remaining distance every few minutes. One thousand yards. One yard equals two steps. Two thousand steps left. He hummed Tchaikovsky's *Marche Slave* in an attempt to maintain a steady pace and because the title seemed appropriate for the situation.

A faint outline of the main building, the lodge, appeared. *Ignore the deadly cold.* He hummed louder. *Ignore the pain.* Five hundred yards left. *Rise above the agony. Balance. Breathe.*

He glanced back at his passenger. "Dying ain't allowed today, pal."

Unless what awaited Matt at Olson's was a cop with a nervous trigger finger.

AWARDS & PRAISE FOR
CASTLE DANGER

- **2017 B.R.A.G. MEDALLION**
- **2018 FINALIST—MN WRITES, MN READS SELF-PUBLISHED AUTHOR CONTEST**
- **2017 HONORABLE MENTION for GENRE FICTION—WRITERS' DIGEST SELF-PUBLISHED BOOK AWARDS**

"This was a very well-done book. You have a strong opening that attracts the reader. You have incredible pacing. The events keep building throughout the book, relentlessly. I was most impressed with the setting. So often the setting is just a throwaway to the thriller, but you made the setting be a character in the novel, which is what the best genre authors do. I'm thinking of Chandler and LA and Connelly and LA (as well.) I was reminded of the works of William Kent Krueger, and that's a compliment indeed."

—Judge, 25th Annual Writer's Digest Self-Published Book Awards.

To purchase *Castle Danger*, visit your nearest independent bookseller or check www.indiebound.com. *Castle Danger* is also available at Book Locker, Amazon.com, Barnes and Noble.com, Apple's ibookstore.com. Or, click on https://books2read.com/u/bro1Mw for other options.

CPSIA information can be obtained
at www.ICGtesting.com
Printed in the USA
LVHW032013280722
724651LV00002B/157